For Dad, who, despite telling me to 'get my head out of the clouds' at the dinner table so many years ago, still told me I 'was the best'.

For Mike, who continues to give me the support I need to do this writing thing.
I love you both so much.
Your faith keeps me going.

Contents

Chapter One: Slave Market	5
Chapter Two: Aboard La Estrella del Mar	20
Chapter Three: In Qadis	32
Chapter Four: Aboard the Phoenix	37
Chapter Five: An Impasse	47
Chapter Six: Waiting	53
Chapter Seven: The Wickedness of Vrouwen	59
Chapter Eight: An Unpleasant Party	72
Chapter Nine: Boyle	83
Chapter Ten: Knots	102
Chapter Eleven: On La Serina del Sol	110
Chapter Twelve: Bad Dreams	123
Chapter Thirteen: Keelhauled	138
Chapter Fourteen: Dream Warfare	145
Chapter Fifteen: The Beating	163
Chapter Sixteen: Battle Stations	172
Chapter Seventeen: The Trap is Set	183
Chapter Eighteen: Broadsides	194
Chapter Nineteen: The Boyle is Lanced	205
Chapter Twenty: Cat's Tail	211
Chapter Twenty-One: Tanya Bird	215
Chapter Twenty-Two: Little Bruja	220
Chapter Twenty-Three: Bad News	230
Chapter Twenty-Four: The Bargain	235
Chapter Twenty-Five: Gale	258
Chapter Twenty-Six: Jager's Revenge	263
Chapter Twenty-Seven: Rescues of a Different Sort	267
Chapter Twenty-Eight: Off Course	276
Chapter Twenty-Nine: Trial by Snake	280
Chapter Thirty: Ekua	292
Chapter Thirty-One: Fond Farewells	301
Chapter Thirty-Two: Ambush	306
Chapter Thirty-Three: Escape	314
Chapter Thirty-Four: Wrongs Made Right	324
Chapter Thirty-Five: In the Wrong Place at the Wrong Time	335
Chapter Thirty-Six: Zombi	345
Chapter Thirty-Seven: One Body, Two Minds	359
Chapter Thirty-Eight: A Second Reunion	367
Chapter Thirty-Nine: The Burden of Mortality	379
Chapter Forty: Love Never Forsakes	388
Chapter Forty-One: The Colour of Eternity	393
Chapter Forty-Two: The Last Word	397
About the Author	404

Chapter One: Slave Market

AFTER FOUR DAYS of enduring the dank and cramped quarters in the lowest deck of a three-masted *nao*, Miriam Medina thought the port of Santa Sul in Tenerifa could not come soon enough. A stiff breeze threatened to pry her from where she stood at the *Phoenix's* rail. Her head veil whipped about her face, making the muslin abrade her cheeks. Above her, sail billowed and yards groaned. Ships of all descriptions littered the bay, their masts cutting the sky into shards. One ship in particular held her interest—a wide-bellied carrack with the stars of Sul emblazoned on its sails. *La Estrella del Mar* was docked at the port's stone mole. Anxiety assailed Miriam, as much as the wind.

Are they still in the hold? she asked.

Standing beside her, Alonso de Santangél glimmered faintly, unseen by anyone save those with the Sight. He was both a handsome seraph and the rat inhabiting her pocket. At the moment, the rat was twisting about, trying to make itself more comfortable. Alonso looked as if he wanted to do the same. *They haven't unloaded them yet. Don Lope is haggling with a port official. You're cold. We should go below.*

She said nothing but gripped the ship's rail tightly, causing the stump of her little finger to bleed.

Now look what you've done! Standing here isn't going to hurry things, Miriam. There's no point in waiting for someone who—

I'm not leaving until I see him.

She felt Alonso's prick of annoyance, and then it was gone. He wasn't happy with her dismissing his suggestion, even less so with her wanting to catch a glimpse of Joachin de Rivera, her husband and patriarch of the Tribe. La Estrella del Mar was Don Lope's slave ship. Joachin had stolen Don Lope's gold, and later, had humiliated him by knocking him out and dressing him in a *puta's* gown. The night before the Tribe was to set sail, Don Lope had captured Joachin, his cousin Iago Gonzales, and friend Barto of Andor. It was almost certain Don Lope would sell them at the slave market in Tenerifa.

She tamped down her impatience. She shouldn't have been so short with Alonso, but she suspected he had been about to denigrate Joachin as a lowlife and a thief, something he did fairly often. *Just a little longer—please.*

His expression remained pained. After a few minutes, he nodded at the ship. *You're about to get your wish. They're bringing them up from below.*

She tensed with worry and anticipation. The last time she had seen Joachin, he had been in bad shape—barely conscious after receiving a flogging at the Grand Inquisitor's hands. She had rescued him, only to have him apprehended by Don Lope. A crowd was swelling onto *La Estrella's* waist. Most of the slaves were black-skinned, but a few were white. It was hard to make out features; she couldn't tell if Joachin was among them. Suddenly, streams of water flew into the air, tossed by the crew. As it struck the slaves, they ducked and shied. Salt water was painful on open wounds.

They're cleaning them up for market, Alonso said unnecessarily.

Knowing that didn't make her feel any better. With the dousing done, she watched as the slaves were forced back below. She wanted to row a cockboat across the bay and attempt a rescue. *I couldn't see them*, she said, striving for calm. Better to say 'them' than 'him' for Alonso's sake. *Were they in the group being washed on the waist?*

I would've had to leave the rat to tell for sure. Alonso needed a physical host so they might communicate. *All I know is, they're still on the ship.*

He wasn't about to give away any details. Over the past few days, he had barred her from his thoughts, but she still managed to catch a few glimpses of what he had seen. In segregated sections, men, women and children lay on pallets on *La Estrella del Mar*. The men were shackled at the hands and feet. The women and children were left unbound, but they still had no recourse when they fouled themselves. There had been a dozen deaths already, all of them children. The crew had thrown the bodies overboard.

She dug her nails into the wood. Somewhere below the spar deck, Joachin lay chained in his own filth, his wounds turning septic. She couldn't reach him fast enough.

A voice hailed her. She turned to see Zara, Luci, Casi, and Maia approaching them at the rail. Alonso disappeared as Zara blundered into his space. He disliked sharing the same spot with the living, saying possessing the rat was hard enough. For a moment she worried the rat might bite her, but she felt its breathing slow. Alonso had lulled it to sleep.

"Is that it?" Zara pointed at *La Estrella del Mar*, unaware Miriam had banished Alonso.

Miriam nodded. She hadn't shared what she had learned of the slave ship, but she suspected the women knew. They had seen such ships before, although it was more likely they were familiar with the oared galleys rowing between Gibralt and the land of the Turques.

"I asked Ximen where the slave pens are, but he's no help," Zara said. As the Tribe's Rememberer, Ximen recalled anything a Tribe member, living or deceased, had experienced. His talent was so developed, he sensed memories deriving from events occurring only moments before. "None of us has ever been here, so he has no idea."

"Fra Francis says once we get through the gate, we pass through the *souk*, then head for the main square," Luci said.

"That one!" Zara made a face. "How do we know he won't take us to the slave block and sell us, himself?"

Over the last four days, Zara's suspicion of Francis had become wearing, especially in the closed quarters they had had to endure. Miriam strove for patience. "He wouldn't do that, Zara."

"Why not? He has no morals. He's a priest and a spy."

"He hopes to convince us to go to Inglais. He thinks we can help secure the Inglaisi Crown." She dropped her voice, hoping Zara would do the same.

Zara didn't. "As if we'd help a queen with more blood on her hands than the Grand Inquisitor! Any involvement of our part would be seen as sedi...seda—" She gave up finding the word. "We Diaphani must stick to ourselves," she added, looking to Luci and Maia for support.

The peal of a watch bell interrupted them. Suddenly, there were twice as many crew swarming the deck. Luci squeezed against the rail as two men ran past her. One glowered, having to manoeuvre his way around Zara, a sizeable detour. Miriam cast a parting glance at *La Estrella del Mar*.

"'Hoi! You *vrouwen*!" Jager de Groot, the *Phoenix*'s bosun, lumbered toward them with that rolling gait all the crew had. He was a big man, blonde, with fists the size of dead eyes—those wooden blocks used to secure the ship's rigging. His shirt flapped about him like a dirty sail. "We need to top th' water. Get below!"

When he wasn't bawling orders, he eyed them suspiciously, his lips pursing as if he sucked vinegar. Over the past few days, Luci had heard him complain to his mates—*Why do these vrouwen travel alone? I tell ye, somethin' ain't right.*

Zara confronted him. "I am *not* going back down there! I've been cooped up for four days, and I am sick and tired of it!"

"Fine! Get knocked over th' head, old cow."

Her mouth fell open. "How dare you speak to me in such a way! I'm a paying passenger!"

Miriam steered her to the companionway, about as easy as maneuvering a cart with one wheel. "Don't give him more reasons to hate us, Zara."

"Why? He doesn't scare me!"

She pulled her along. "Luci overheard the crew talking last night. They wonder why we aren't travelling with our men. The bosun thinks we've either run away or rid ourselves of them. Apparently, Ximen doesn't count, being old and blind. Nor Francis, because he's a priest."

"Women can't travel on their own?"

They had told Captain Vrooman that Joachin and the others had been detained and would be joining them, but the crew remained superstitious. "If we cause too much trouble, the bosun will convince the crew we're bad luck. He might even say we've cursed the ship."

"I *should* curse him. He's a bully and a brute."

"For heaven's sake, keep your voice down." Good gods, dealing with Zara was like teaching a chicken to swim. "Our foremost duty is to find Joachin, Iago, and Barto. Once they're on board, all suspicions should cease."

"There you are!" a pleasant, male voice called.

Miriam sagged in relief as Francis met them at the top of the companionway. He always seemed to know what was happening, even when he wasn't around. If the crew muttered about curses, she hoped his presence quelled suspicions. He smiled ingratiatingly at the bosun. "Allow me to accompany you below decks, ladies. Let's not get in Mister de Groot's way."

"Where have *you* been?" Zara glared at him as if he had wandered off against her wishes.

"Speaking with the captain." Another brief smile touched his lips. Over the past few days, Francis had convinced Captain Vrooman he had taken the Tribe under his wing to build a new temple in Xaymaca—all to the glory of Father Church.

"*That* one." Captain Vrooman was another with whom Zara wasn't much impressed. He had been in the habit of inviting Francis and Ximen to share his table, but he hadn't extended the same courtesy to her or Miriam. *And we're the ones in charge!* she had complained the night before. "What about?" she demanded.

Francis glanced at Jager de Groot. The bosun was busy with the water casks, but Miriam suspected he bent an ear. "About the procurement of certain goods."

Meaning Joachin, Barto, and Iago, of course.

"And?" Zara pressed.

"And I know where we might find them." He regarded Miriam with concern. "Your hand looks as if it's bothering you, Miriam." Fresh blood had seeped through her bandage.

Miriam glanced down at her hand. It was a strange glamoury Rana Isadore had set upon her. Perhaps the only real thing about her *was* the finger stump, although the *hymenoptera* welts were still painful beneath her veil.

"Here, now!" Zara clucked. "We can't have that. Come down, Matriarch, and I'll replace that dressing. As for *you*–" she eyed Francis sourly, "see if you can't find some ointment while you're procuring our *goods*."

Francis bowed. "That was foremost in my mind." With only a few words, he had misdirected Zara and she hadn't even suspected. Francis was an expert manipulator, a great advantage for a spy. *Let's hope his talent is enough to secure Joachin, Iago, and Barto*, Miriam thought.

An hour later, she, Francis, Luci, and Maia squeezed their way through the crowd on the mole. They stopped briefly at an herbalist's tent where Francis procured a balm of comfrey for her hand. As they left, they were bombarded by merchants hoping for sales. Turbaned men shouted at them in dialects they didn't understand. Their wives shook copper pots or bolts of cotton in their faces. Urchins plucked at their sleeves. Francis intervened, but often, he had to push their pursuers away. After each attempt, Miriam's respect for him deepened. There were few languages he didn't know. By the time they had forced their way beneath an ancient gate leading to the *medina* proper, her talent as a *sentidora* had spun out of control. The bombardment of so many people left her dizzy and sick.

"How much farther?" she gasped. Now that they had passed beneath the gate, the crowds were less thick, although both sides of the street were lined with shops.

Francis pointed. "After we go down this alley, we come to the main square. We cross it, then come to another street that leads to the stocks. The slave pens are on the far side."

"What time is the auction?" Luci clutched at her side.

"Noon." He squinted at the screens overhead, shading the street. Above them, the sun was a crosshatched ball. "We should make it."

Maia nodded. She had left little Grim in Zara's care. Miriam suspected she was afraid someone would outbid her for Barto. Of the three men, he was the largest, so he would fetch the highest price.

"I'm surprised the slave pens are inside the city's walls," Lucy said. "Wouldn't it make more sense if they were along the quay?"

"They are," Francis replied. "The slave ships dock further down the wharf. We're on a promontory, so we're angling towards the other side. We'll soon pass beneath the north gate. This way, we don't have to fight bigger crowds."

Thank heavens for that foresight, Miriam thought.

As promised, they passed beneath another keyhole gate before stepping onto a sunny esplanade. This side of the port was broader, making room for cargo. Camels brayed from where they were picketed. Horses milled and stamped in makeshift corrals. Poultry roosted despondently in cages, looking as if they might expire from the heat. The air stank of tar and dung. From somewhere beyond the quay, a bell tolled noon.

"We need to hurry. This way." Francis led them past the paddocks.

They came to a place where a small crowd had gathered before a low platform. Dilapidated shacks stood behind it, looking as if a strong wind might knock them over. A portly man in a worn leather doublet, dull pantaloons, and ankle-high boots, climbed onto the stage.

"M' lords and ladies!" he bellowed, snagging everyone's attention. "I bring you quality goods, the pick from Afrik. Step up and examine 'em. They've only been on board a few weeks, so still pretty fresh." He signalled a burly assistant to bring forth the slaves. From the nearest shack, a line of six black men appeared, chained at the ankles and wrists. As they shuffled, their skin shone greasily—an old trick, Francis had said, to hide welts. They ranged in age and size, but they shared one thing in common. They gazed out on the world as if they were no longer a part of it. They seemed the epitome of hopelessness.

A number of customers approached them, demanding they open their mouths so they could check for rot. The auctioneer forced the slaves to comply. Then they were made to bend their arms and legs to prove they were able. Miriam's stomach turned at the sight of it. *Joachin is depending on me*, she told herself, sickened by her own unwillingness to interfere. She couldn't create a scene. After the first group were dealt with, they were taken away. She caught her breath as a group of children replaced them. The eldest looked to be no more than eight. The little ones clung to each other and eyed the crowd, as if too terrified to cry.

"And here we have the young'uns, suitable for pages or maids. Or gentlemen's companions." The auctioneer winked. A few buyers guffawed. Miriam spun about, wanting to pick them out.

"Easy, now." Francis nudged her elbow. "If it makes you feel any better, they'll all go to that woman over there." He pointed to a well-appointed noblewoman dressed entirely in white. She stood a ways from the crowd as if choosing to keep her distance. A servant shaded her with an umbrella while she cooled herself with a fan. A chamberlain stood to her right.

Miriam released her jaw. She had been grinding her teeth.

"Just watch. They're about to begin."

As the auction progressed, Francis proved right. The woman's chamberlain outbid everyone who challenged her. When the bidding ended, he shepherded the children away. "It isn't a great outcome," Francis said, watching them go, "but she won't abuse them."

"How do you know?" One little boy had started to cry. Miriam's heart went out to him.

"Consider what she's wearing. White is her trademark."

She frowned and then understood. The woman wanted black children so she might flatter herself in her social circles. Dressed in silks and satin, they would surround her like black pearls around a diamond. They were jewellery, embellishment. When she tired of them, she would discard them for something else.

Mariam was so angry she found it hard to breathe. "That's terrible! They're children, not things!"

"The world is a terrible place," Francis agreed. "Speaking of which—look who's here." On the opposite side of the crowd, Don Lope appeared. Her fury dissipated as she shrank behind Francis. "Don't worry," he whispered. "He won't know you. You look like Rana Isadore. I just thought it wise not to draw attention to ourselves."

She drew in a breath to steady herself. He was right. The callousness of the noblewoman had been a breaking point. She needed to concentrate on the matter at hand—they were here to buy Joachin, Iago, and Barto. Don Lope wouldn't know who she was. She never thought she would be grateful for Rana's glamoury, but she was now.

A new group of slaves was ushered onto the platform. According to the auctioneer, they were ne'er-do-wells from various jails or other penurious circumstances. Joachín, Barto, and Iago weren't among them. "They aren't there," Luci said, crestfallen. She wasn't the only one who was disappointed.

"Perhaps in the next group," Francis murmured.

As the afternoon wore on, eight more groups were displayed and sold. At the end of the auction, Don Lope headed for his ship while his men organized their human cargo. Miriam wanted to chase after him, to demand he release Joachín, but she knew better than to try. She turned to Francis, frantic to salvage whatever scrap of hope he might offer. "Is there another auction, later?"

He stared after Don Lope, his expression troubled. "I don't think so."

"Why weren't they here?" Luci asked anxiously.

"I don't know. I'll learn what I can." He headed for the auctioneer. They exchanged a few words. When he returned, the news wasn't good. "There are no more slaves in the pens. All I can surmise is, they're still on *La Estrella*."

"But, why?" Luci pressed.

"I don't know. Maybe Don Lope didn't want to sell them. Maybe he intends to keep them onboard until *La Estrella* docks in the New World."

"If Joachín's welts are festering, the poison will travel to his heart." Miriam felt her own constrict as she said it. "We have to do something, Francis. Surely, you can come up with some kind of a ruse to have them released." It was disturbing to realize how much she had come to rely on him in so a short time.

"If we had more time, possibly, but under the circumstances, I don't think we do."

Her heart sank.

He eyed her dubiously. "There *is* one thing that might work. I don't suppose you have coin."

She flushed with new hope. "Not coin, but this." She handed him the pouch Joachín had taken from Don Lope in Qadis. He eyed it curiously and then opened it. His eyes widened at the sight of the nuggets. "Where did you get these?"

"From Don Lope. Joachin stole them from him. The first time was when we were in Marabel, the second, when we were in Qadis. Hopefully, the nuggets look like any other."

"He stole them *twice*? That's a story I'll have to hear when I get back." He tied the pouch to his belt and strode in the direction of *La Estrella del Mar*.

"What do we do while you're on the ship?" Luci shouted after him. "Wait for you, here?"

"No." He turned and waved. "The sun is about to set. Go back to the *Phoenix*. It isn't a safe for you ladies to be out on the streets after dark."

"When will you return?" Miriam called.

"If I'm not back with the men by midnight, tell the captain we'll be there by dawn."

She nodded. She would have Ximen advise Captain Vrooman. He would listen to another man. "Gods' speed," she shouted. If anyone could release Joachin and the others, it was Francis. "We should hurry," she told Maia and Luci.

They headed back the way they had come. Dusk drenched the town in ambers and indigo. Men smoked openly at the tables now, their hookahs coiling before them like serpents, the smell of hashish and *qahwa*, a bitter drink from Ethiope, thick upon the air. Common houses were open for business, offering everything from beer to girls. As they passed, they were eyed with speculation. Francis was right. It was a mistake to loiter. They hurried for the jolly boat, glad to see the *Phoenix's* sailors waiting to escort them back to the ship.

Little Grim was fussing. Under the dim light of their alcove's lantern, the baby's face was turning red. *It won't be long before he's screaming*, Casi thought.

"I can't do a thing with this baby." Zara unwrapped his swaddling. "I need to sponge him off and give him fresh water. We're nearly out. Be a good girl and go fill that pail." She nodded at their water bucket standing in a dark corner. "And don't dawdle."

"I won't." Casi grabbed the pail and skipped out the door. It was good to have an excuse to leave their nook. Babies had a tendency to smell. Other than Zara and fussy Grim, everyone was napping. It was nearing the end of *siesta*, of what had been a hot and boring afternoon. Maré, Miriam, and Maia had gone to the slave market to fetch Iago, Joachin, and Barto. Maré had said it was too dangerous for her to go, so being asked to leave their cramped space on the orlop deck was a relief. She felt like a canary, freed from its cage. *And if I'm lucky, I'll catch sight of Maré coming back with Iago*, she thought.

She hoped Iago was okay. As much as he annoyed her at times, he was still her brother and she had worried about him. She had tried to hear his thoughts, but her talent didn't seem to work over water. Everyone else on board the *Phoenix* was another matter.

On the second deck, none of the crew loitered or snoozed in their hammocks. It seemed today, they preferred to spend their free time in the open air. She sighed in relief. She didn't like their conversations or their thoughts. The discussion she had heard last night still disturbed her:

Where are th' men? I tell yer, it don't make sense.

It ain't like they's sailin' alone. There's th' priest an' th' old man.

Any priest who listens to women, ain't a proper priest. Good Book says, 'Let no woman usurp 'thority over man. For Adam was first formed, then Eve'. Not th' other way 'round.

Never realized you was such a hand at scripture, Jager.

Nothin' wrong with it. You should try it, Ignaas.

Cap'n says we ain't s'pposed to talk religion.

I ain't talkin' religion. I'm talkin' about trouble on board. Ship's no place for women. That fat, old one—she's got th' evil eye. I seen her lookin' at me crossways. An' th' one with th' veil—

Oh, come on, now! Ye sayin they's witches? They ain't nothin' but simple women!

Aye? Well, we'll see when their men show up. I'm guessin' they won't.

After that, their conversation had turned to the journey and the weather. It had been a relief when they were called to their watch. She didn't like the starboard crew or the bosun, Jager de Groot. She had drifted off to sleep after that. *I hope he's sleeping, now*, she thought. Hopefully, she wouldn't run into Jager while fetching water.

She glanced about quickly as she climbed onto the waist. Some of the crew were scrubbing the deck with holey stones. She ignored them and made her way to the cook who was plucking chickens for the captain's supper. He had wounded his leg, somehow. Maybe all sailors weren't mean. Beside him, a boy of about fourteen sat on a low stool.

She cleared her throat, hoping she wouldn't sound fearful. "I need some water." She held out the pail for them to see.

"Aye?" The cook squinted at her. Feathers had settled onto his grey hair and his grizzled face. The boy watched her with a closed expression, saying nothing. "Seems a bit soon to be takin' your ration, ain' it?"

"It isn't for me. It's for the baby. He's sick."

He frowned. She had said the wrong thing. Anyone sick on board was a risk. Luckily, she could tell from his thoughts he wasn't unsympathetic. "Is he, now?" He pursed his lips.

"Or maybe he's just hot. Auntie wants me to bring him some water so she can cool him down." Technically, Zara wasn't her aunt. She was a great third cousin, but she had known her all her life.

"Well, we can't have that, can we, Kip?" The cook glanced at his assistant. The boy looked uncomfortable. She wasn't sure why. Was it the baby, or because she was a girl? "Tell yer auntie to bring 'im up here, so he can get some fresh air. I'll have broth for 'im later, if there's anything left o' th' captain's soup."

"Oh, he isn't eating real food. He's still...." She turned a bright red. It was embarrassing to speak of such things before an old man and a teenaged boy.

"Well, tell his *moeder* she can have th' broth if she wants," the cook replied implacably. "If th' babe's still on th' breast, she'll need it."

Casi blushed even harder. The cook eyed her. "You, too. Yer a skinny one. Y' need some meat on them bones. Come see me in th' galley later, and I'll give y' some soup." The boy smirked.

She shrank with embarrassment. She *was* skinny, but after days of beans and hard biscuit, the chicken broth was appealing. Not knowing what to say, she turned to go.

"Wait! Ain't y' forgettin' somethin'?" the boy pointed out. "Th' water for th' babe?"

She swallowed and offered him the pail. He took it and ladled a small portion of water into it. "Thank you," she muttered after he was done.

"Mind, y' don't spill," he said, in that superior way all boys had. "Water's precious on a ship."

The cook smiled.

"I won't." She made her way carefully to the companionway, sensing they watched her all the while. The boy's interest in her felt particularly acute. Did he think she was incapable of carrying a bucket? *I'll show him*, she thought. Stepping carefully, she descended the companionway without mishap. As she turned to take the second, someone grabbed her by the arm. She let out a small cry.

"What are y' doin' with that?" Jager de Groot towered over her, a blond, sweaty giant. His hand was calloused and thick. Other than the two of them, they were alone. His thoughts were a mix of malice and suspicion. His grip hurt her arm.

"It's water," she stammered. "For the baby."

"Why?"

She wasn't about to make the same mistake she had with the cook and the boy. "He's hot and fussing. Auntie sent me."

"How long did you spend at the water?"

"A few minutes." Why was that important?

He shook her arm. Fear raced through her. The water slopped over the side of her pail. "Did the cook give y' all that? What did you say t' him?"

"Nothing! I just asked for water!"

"What else?"

"I didn't do anything!" *Let me go!* Why was he being like this? Why was he attacking her?

I know what yer about! You mean to hex our water! If any o' us sicken, I'll drown ya with m' own hands!

He was the ogre from the fairy tales her brother used to tell. In another second, he would smash the life from her with those big hands. "I...I wouldn't!" She couldn't stop her teeth from chattering. Her heart was pounding so hard she was seeing spots. "I don't know how to hex water!"

"YAH!" He released her as if burnt. "HOW DID Y' KNOW I WAS THINKIN' THAT?" He grabbed her again by the back of the neck.

"Let me go! You're hurting me!" The pail's handle slid through her hands. Water slopped everywhere.

"What's going on here?" Zara appeared half way up the lower ladder, with Little Grim in her arms.

Thank heavens for auntie! Never in her life had she been so glad to see her.

Jager released her and his cheeks shook. He pointed at her, his fingers forming a starburst of Sul. "FOR SHE WHO DIVINES MUST BE CAST OUT, AS VERMIN FROM GARMENTS!" Then, before she could react, he backhanded Casi so viciously, it sent her reeling. Her temple struck a bulkhead. The world blackened and there were sparks. Then pain chased the dark. She hurt so much she felt sick.

"Casi!" Zara cried out in horror. There was a curse, some creaks and scrabbling. Someone fled up the ladder. Jager.

"That's right! You'd best run from me!" Zara shouted after him.

Little Grim was set beside her, a squirming mass. Warm hands clasped her by the shoulders.

"Casi, can you speak? Let me see your head...." Fingers prodded her temple, making her moan. "All right, I won't touch it. We'll put a compress on you, instead. Can you sit up? Maybe stand, so we can go below?"

She started to cry, ragged, harsh hiccoughs that came from her stomach as they forced their way up. Everything hurt.

"Oh, here now! You rest here a minute! We don't have to go just yet."

No one had ever struck her like that. Why had she let it slip, that she had known what he was thinking? *Because he scared me, that's why. I should have been stronger, more careful.* How could he think I would poison *the water?* What had he said about vermin and wickedness? None of it made any sense.

She sucked in a shuddering breath and rubbed her head. "I'm sorry, Auntie."

"What happened?" Zara helped her to sit.

She stared at her miserably. How could she admit what she had done? Her weakness had put them into danger. Maybe Jager would think he had imagined it, but she doubted he would.

Zara pursed her lips. "Well, don't worry about it." She surveyed the companionway to their deck below. "It's going to be difficult maneuvering the ladder with Little Grim. I can take him first, then come back for you. Or...can you manage on your own?"

She nodded and regretted it. It hurt to move her head. Auntie was eyeing her like an eagle its eaglet. "I think so."

"Good." Zara cast a baleful glance up the companionway. "If it's rations he's on about, I can do without." She turned to her. "I'm sorry, Casi. I should've gone for the water myself. That brute won't dare cross me. If he does, he'll suffer the consequences. Come along now, but watch yourself." She descended to the lower deck.

Auntie was furious, she could tell from her thoughts. She said nothing more about Jager de Groot, but she, *Maré*, and Miriam would discuss him later, at length. Maybe they would even tell the captain what he had done.

She called after Zara from the top of the stair. "Maybe we shouldn't say anything, Auntie! I don't want more trouble."

Zara's voice floated up to her from below. "Don't you worry, *niña*. That bosun's the one who should worry, *not* you."

She followed her down the ladder, too sick to reply.

Chapter Two: Aboard La Estrella del Mar

FRANCIS SET HIS fists on his hips and waited at the bottom of *La Estrella del Mar's* gangplank, hoping he looked as officious as possible. The crew eyed him suspiciously. "I would speak to the Master of this vessel, the Vizconde de Qadis," he announced in a superior tone. "I'm told he's on board." It was hard to look down one's nose when one was trying to intimidate those who stood at a higher level.

A grizzled bosun leaned from the ship's rail. "Who asks for 'im?"

"Fra Francisco, Papal Nuncio, representative of His Holiness' interests in Esbaña, Tenerifa, and beyond. I must speak with the vizconde on a matter of great urgency."

"Aye? An' what might that be?" Clearly, the crew felt they were in safe waters here, beyond the Temple's reach.

"That's not your business, you ignorant lout! Fetch me the vizconde at once, so I might be escorted onto this vessel!"

He waited impatiently as the third mate motioned to one of the ship's cabin boys to pass along his request. The lad soon returned and whispered into the bosun's ear. "Very well," the bosun said. "His lordship'll see you. Come aboard."

Francis lifted his skirts and stepped cautiously, taking care to look as dignified as possible as he ascended the gangplank. He glared at the crew as he stepped onto the waist, hoping to impress upon them that it was only a matter of time before the Solarium uncovered their multiple sins. Many of them found his scrutiny too hard to bear.

The boy led him past an open hatch which exposed the cargo below. In the dim light, men lay on their backs, their legs and wrists manacled to their neighbour. It was impossible to tell if Joachin de Rivera and his companions were down there.

He was escorted across the waist to an ornate door set beneath the quarterdeck. At the boy's rap, it was opened by a steward in red and black livery. The boy took his leave and the steward led him past officers' berths to a small day cabin. At an oak table, Don Lope sat at leisure with his officers, nephews or more distant relations foisted onto him into service. Such was the way of things in Esbaña. Behind them, another door led to what he assumed was the captain's cabin. Ships of this size and layout were similar everywhere.

He acknowledged the party with a brief nod. Don Lope recognized him in turn. "I'm given to understand," he said lazily, "you seek audience with me regarding some matter of interest to the Temple? How can I be of service to you, Fra Francisco?" For all his running of a slave ship, he was immaculately dressed. He looked as if he had just come from a function at court.

"I'm seeking three reprobates, whom I'm told are from your dungeons in Qadis. I believe you're transporting them to the New World."

Don Lope turned an inquiring eye to his officers. "We've no reprobates on board, only slaves and cargo. If I might ask, who is it exactly you seek?"

"I'm looking for one Joachin de Rivera, Iago Montoya Gonzales, and Barto of Andor. The first two are Diaphani, the latter is not."

"And your interest in them would be?"

"They're wanted on charges of theft and defacement of a holy relic. They stole a small statuette from the *Cappella de l'Angelus* in the Holy

City, then attempted to melt it down for its gold. I've been sent by His Holiness to bring them to justice."

Don Lope looked surprised. "I see. As it happens, they are on board. But you must understand, Luminance, I too, have my quarrels with them. Especially with Joachin de Rivera. For me to release him to you, I require two things. First, written proof from his Holiness that you do indeed seek him for these transgressions, and secondly, recompense to me for what he's done. He stole my goods. Furthermore, he's tarnished my reputation beyond repair."

Francis linked his fingers. "Nothing is beyond the Temple's influence, Don Lope. Not even one's good name."

Don Lope's face soured. "So, you've heard of my embarrassment. I don't know whether to be relieved or discomfited by it."

"You were victimized, Don Lope. A terrible joke to be sure, finding oneself trussed up in a *puta's* gown. The Holy Office can resolve that."

"How, if I might ask?"

"One word from me as to your difficulty, and his Holiness could name you a holy martyr."

Don Lope's mouth fell open. "A holy martyr? But, doesn't one have to die to become a martyr first?"

"Not necessarily. In the year 533, Saint Persimmion was dealt with in a similar fashion, after working with the Sisters of Mercy in Venicia. He discovered they weren't nuns per se, but sisters of a different sort. In your case, the manner in which you were wronged would count." As far as he knew, there was no Saint Persimmion, nor any community of female religious known for their lusty ministrations, but Venicia *was* notorious for catering to all manner of sexual tastes. "Of course, you might also be required to purchase an indulgence or two," he added.

Don Lope considered it. "Then, I'd be claimed...a living saint!"

"Well, I wouldn't go so far as to promise beatification, but you might be hailed a living martyr."

"Which means I could build my own chapel in Xaymaca and demand tribute. Indulgences for indulgences." He pursed his lips and nodded. "Yes. The idea has merit."

Gods, the audacity of the man. Trussed up in a whore's dress, and he thinks he's the Pope. "Or perhaps another kind of honour might be feasible."

Don Lope smiled. "Why not discuss it over dinner, Fra Francisco? We were about to dine. We'd be delighted if you would join us."

"I would be honoured," Francis replied smoothly.

Dinner consisted of three courses: a tasteless ox-tail soup, followed by overdone lamb, and finally, oranges steeped in honey and cinnamon—better offerings than what they would see once the ship set sail. Don Lope dismissed his officers so he and Francis might talk further about his beatification.

Francis dabbed his lips as the steward removed his plate. "That was delicious." The lie was more satisfying than the meal he had just eaten. It was always best to flatter one's host, especially when one wanted something.

Don Lope waved the compliment aside as the steward poured them small cups of *qahwa*. "Not as good as what I might have offered you at my palace in Qadis, but we're on tight rations, here." He took a small sip. "You understand, of course."

"Of course." The brew was bitter, but it teased the nose. Francis liked it. "This is very good."

"Yes. It's become a habit of mine. I restock it whenever I'm in port."

"From Afrik, isn't it? I wonder how it might do in the New World."

"If I were a farmer I'd try growing it, but I am not." Don Lope dismissed it with a lift of his hand. "Let's get down to business, Fra Francisco. I'm much swayed by your offer of sainthood. However, I'd still require a letter of conduct from His Holiness if I'm to release Joachín de Rivera and the others to you. Also, confirmation that my reputation would be restored."

"You do realize these things take time."

"The beatification can wait. More immediately, I'd need eighty-eight thousand *soltars* to cover my losses."

Francis choked on his *qahwa*. "Eighty-eight thousand?"

"Yes. Joachín de Rivera stole a purse from me containing six nuggets of New World gold. That is their estimated value."

Could the gold be that pure? The purse contained only five nuggets. Why six? Why not ten? "I don't travel with that kind of largess." He dabbed at his lips with his napkin. "But I could have it transferred to you. As for proofs, His Holiness will require verification as to the value of the gold before he depletes his coffers."

"I've no such thing. Only my educated opinion."

They took each other's measure over their cups.

"I'd feel much better if you could show me a letter of conduct from Roma," Don Lope said. "Surely, you have one."

He didn't, but given time, one was easily forged. "In most places, my ring is proof enough." He flashed it for Don Lope's benefit.

Don Lope smiled mockingly. "Tenerifa *isn't* most places, Luminance. There are many things, including that lovely bauble on your finger that can be bought here."

Francis frowned. "Are you suggesting the stone isn't genuine?"

"I'm certain it is."

"Then I fail to follow your line of thought."

"It's a matter of trust—"

"Am I to understand you *don't* trust His Holiness?" He was on familiar boards, now. Gods, it felt good to commit oneself wholly to a part. His next few words might suggest the Don's attitude was disturbing, even heretical.

Don Lope paled. "Certainly not! But you must see the difficult position in which you place me! My ship sails at dawn, Fra Francisco. If I were to release de Rivera to you now, I'd have nothing to show for him!"

"You'd have the gratitude of the Holy Office and its blessing! That should be more than enough for you, Don Lope!" He took a deep breath as if to calm himself and sat back down. It was never wise to overplay one's role. "Surely, you know the good works you do today are given back to you tenfold in heaven."

"Be that as it may, you must have some funds. His Holiness wouldn't have sent you on this mission without them." He glanced at the pouch dangling at Francis' side.

Mierda! He had been so close to getting de Rivera released, but the vizconde was a cagey one. "This?" He patted it. "Travelling funds, mostly." It had been a mistake to take it from Miriam. "I have more at my disposal, of course, but I'd need to make arrangements. If it eases your concern, I can make you a partial payment." There was a money changer in the *souk*. He could trade one of the nuggets for coin. Hopefully, it would be enough.

"How much of a partial payment?" Don Lope quirked an eyebrow.

"Fifteen thousand *soltars*?" One nugget had to be worth that much.

A brief smile touched Don Lope's lips. "I suppose I can accept that, especially if sainthood and the remaining *soltars* lie in my future. Let's drink to seal the bargain. Come to my private chamber, and I'll pour you a glass from my personal stock."

"Excellent." Francis congratulated himself. With luck, he would have Joachin de Rivera and his compatriots in hand by moonrise.

Don Lope shouted for the steward. It was dark outside the cabin. The man appeared with an oil lantern to light their way. Francis followed Don Lope into his quarters.

The great cabin was much larger than the room they had left. Horn windows glimmered halfway up the back wall, their sheen catching the illumination from nearby ships. A small, snug bunk lay to one side, with a narrow bureau and wash basin. A sturdy oak table lay opposite, littered with astrolabe, quadrant, and maps. The steward cleared a space and set the lantern there. Two well-upholstered chairs sat in the centre of the room. As Francis stepped into the suite, the reek of urine and rot struck him with such intensity, he had to force himself from clapping a sleeve to his face. Don Lope's nostrils flared briefly, but other than that, he gave no sign the stench bothered him. He invited Francis to sit and poured them two glasses of sherry. The steward closed the door behind them, his face bland. Francis wished he had left the door open to clear the air.

Don Lope settled into one of the chairs and sipped his glass. Francis tossed the sherry back, hoping it would deaden his sense of smell. He was about to comment when a low moan emanated from behind them.

He turned about to see what had caused the sound. Behind them, a half naked man lay on the floor, his neck encircled with an iron manacle that chained him to the boards. He could move no further than a foot in any direction. His back was a criss-cross of oozing welts. He lay in a pool of his own shit and blood.

My god. Francis stood and pointed. "Is that...?"

"Joachín de Rivera? Indeed it is. Not much of a man, is he? I like him better as a rug."

Gorge rose to Francis' throat. He set down his glass. He had to get Joachín out of there. If he remained, he would soon be dead. "I protest this...this inhuman treatment of a prisoner! I demand you release him immediately!"

"Oh, he'll be released. Once he's paid for."

"He's half dead! I expected him to be whole!"

"Why do you care?" Don Lope swirled his sherry. "After what he did to me, he deserves what he gets."

"You're in grave danger of risking your immortal soul, Don Lope!" Threats of eternal damnation usually worked on Esbañiards. "Only the Evil One treats sinners so poorly!"

Don Lope blinked at him. "I find your reaction odd, considering you want to take him to Roma to burn."

"That is not for you to judge! His Holiness will deal with him as he sees fit! Give me the keys. I'll release him, myself!"

"There's still the matter of my payment."

"There's an even great matter of your excommunication! His Holiness wants him returned whole and in good condition so he may repent of his sins!"

Don Lope shook his head. "I'll never understand you priests. What does it matter how he dies?" He lifted a hand in surrender. "Fine. If it means recovering what I've lost, I'll treat his wounds." He yelled for the steward. The man appeared immediately. "Get the surgeon," he ordered. "Tell him that piece of *mierda* needs fixing. Then I want this room cleaned. It's revolting." He regarded Francis as the steward left. "You may as well go, too, Luminance. I want my money."

"I'm not going anywhere until you treat him."

He shrugged. "Suit yourself."

They waited in silence. The steward arrived with the surgeon who was out of breath. Don Lope kept a careful distance between himself and the doctor who held a glowing poker in his gloved hands. Francis knelt beside Joachín to cup his head. Joachín cracked his eyes to stare at him blearily. Francis wasn't sure he knew what was happening. Cauterizing his wounds was the only way to save him.

"You might want to give him this." The surgeon handed him a biting stick. Francis set it between Joachin's lips. As he glanced down at him, he noticed the man bore a tattoo. It was poorly done—against his will, perhaps? He thought only Diaphani women wore tattoos. More riddles needing answers. As for the burning, it might very well kill him. *Don't take him yet, Goddess*, he sent. *He's more valuable to me alive.*

As the poker struck him, Joachin arched his back and screamed. The stick fell from his mouth. The surgeon was experienced in such matters and accounted for them. Joachin shrieked a second time before passing out. The doctor continued his grisly task until he was done. Burnt skin and hair overwhelmed the reek of feces and urine. Francis stared at the broken mass that was Joachin de Rivera. *Don't die*, he thought. *If you do, Miriam will never support my efforts to set Ilysabeth on the throne.*

"Get him out of here," Don Lope said.

Francis confronted him. "What of the other two?" There were still Iago Gonzales and Barto of Andor to consider.

"They're below."

"In a similar state?"

"No. My dispute was with de Rivera. Their only mistake was to associate with him. Other than a few cuts and bruises, they're fine."

"I can trust your word on that?"

"As much as I trust you'll be back shortly with my money. My officers will see you off the ship." Don Lope settled into his chair and sipped his sherry. A cabin boy scrubbed at the mess behind him.

The money changer was still open for business. Francis untied the pouch from his belt and fingered the nuggets inside. The largest was bent in the middle like a fat, crooked worm. He selected one of the smaller pieces. "I want to convert this into *soltars*," he said.

The merchant eyed it dubiously.

"Go ahead. Test it."

The man bit it for softness. "Where did you get this?"

"The Holy Land. Taken as a tribute by the Knights Templar, then donated to the Solarium in Roma. Can you convert it?"

"Of course. I must weigh it first, Luminance."

He waited while the man set the nugget onto a small scale, and then squinted to calculate the weight.

His eyebrows rose. "Nine troy ounces. Assuming the gold is pure."

"Why don't we assume it is?"

The merchant smiled faintly and set his palms on either side of the scale. "I could determine the purity with acid. If you're in a hurry, we can forego it. I can offer you the going rate for eighteen karat." He had sensed his need for haste.

"And that would be?"

"Ten thousand, eight hundred *soltars*."

The gold was a deep yellow. He suspected the purity was closer to twenty-two. Even if it were that high, he was still short a third of his goal. He fished another nugget from the pouch. "What'll you give me for the two?"

The merchant weighed them together. "Fourteen and a half ounces. Seventeen thousand, four hundred *soltars*."

Francis did a quick calculation. "Seventeen thousand four hundred and ten, point eight seven-five *soltars*."

"Yes, less fifteen percent to cover tariffs and my service. The best I can offer you is fourteen thousand, nine hundred *soltars*."

From the smug look on his face, there was no moving him. He didn't have to haggle like the other merchants in the *souk*. Obviously, the Temple was less feared here in Tenerifa, but the money was close enough. He didn't have to sell the other three nuggets. Don Lope would accept that amount.

"Done."

He waited as the merchant disappeared into the back of his shop and then returned with a small chest holding his coin.

"A thousand blessings on you and yours." The exchanger made him a salaam.

Francis was enough of a religious snob to ignore him.

Upon returning to *La Estrella del Mar*, he was immediately conducted aboard. Darkness had swallowed the port, but the ship's lanterns cast dull circles on the water. The first mate escorted him to the captain's quarters while the rest of the crew looked on. He was ushered past the officers' berths and into Don Lope's chamber.

The cabin stank less now. The floor had been scrubbed clean. As for Joachin himself, there was no sign. One of the cabin's great windows had been opened, allowing the night breeze to freshen the air. Don Lope lounged in his chair. "I take it you were successful getting my money?"

Francis nodded. "Yes. I have it."

Don Lope steepled his fingers as if contemplating his next move in a game of chess. "You made an interesting exchange with the money changer, I'm told."

Francis stiffened. They had had him followed. Did Don Lope know about the nuggets? He must. "Are you in the habit of having members of the Solarium shadowed, Vizconde? I told you I needed to make arrangements."

"My first mate also claims he saw you at the slave auction today, standing with three Diaphani women. When does a priest associate with such riffraff?"

"He associates with them when they are *conversos*. They're part of my entourage heading to the New World. His Holiness is anxious to establish a Temple there."

"Or he associates with them because he isn't really whom he claims."

A cold worm of fear crawled up his spine. He was too much of a professional to show it. "What are you suggesting?"

"I suggest you're no priest. You're a thief or a spy. Perhaps both."

The best defence was always offence. "Have you taken leave of your senses? I am Fra Francisco, Papal Nuncio to His Holiness in Roma!" He thrust a forefinger at him. "Don't test Father Church, Don Lope. Push too far, and you'll live to regret it. I have a much greater reach than even your fantastically inclined mind can imagine in this Sul-forsaken outpost. Neither distance nor position will protect you from the wrath of our Holy Father if he learns you've questioned me!" He drew himself to his full height. "How dare you?"

Don Lope glanced away as if bored. "You priests are a windy lot, if that's what you really are. I think you knocked the real Fra Francisco over the head and took his goods. Just like you've stolen mine." Two of his officers appeared at the door. "Seize him."

Gods, this wasn't happening! They grabbed him by the arms. "Release me this instant!" he demanded.

Don Lope motioned to an open-mouthed cabin boy who stood in the doorway. "Julio, bring me that pouch he wears at his belt."

The boy looked terrified. Francis didn't have to read his mind to know he thought it a mortal sin to steal from a priest. But the boy feared Don Lope more. He untied the purse from his belt.

Don Lope spilled the nuggets onto the table. "You see," he said softly, "I'd be a fool if I didn't recognize my own property. This purse..." he held it up, "looks very much like the one taken from me by Joachin de Rivera. Of course, I could be wrong..." he plucked the worm-shaped nugget and admired it, "but I'm not. Throw him below with the others," he told the officers.

"I will call Sul's wrath down upon this ship!" Francis cried. It was a lame threat. The officers' expressions tightened, but so did their grips. He was taken from Don Lope's presence, marched across the waist, and forced down a companionway to the slave deck. Men lay at his feet, chained and prone. He was strong-armed through them to a bulkhead near the bow. With one final attempt, he fought Don Lope's thugs, only to earn multiple blows to the head and gut. He was thrown roughly onto a pallet, then chained at the ankle and wrist to his neighbour. His head throbbed. He breathed through the pain and forced his eyes to focus.

Not far from him, Joachin de Rivera lay in a stupor. He was bound to a giant who eyed him balefully. Barto of Andor, Francis guessed. The man reminded him of a glowering, caged bear.

"Do you remember me?" he asked. He wished his head didn't hurt so much. "We met briefly, on board the *Phoenix*."

"I remember you." Barto said it as if he wished he didn't.

"How is he?" He glanced at Joachin.

"Alive. Just."

"I was hoping to get you all out."

"You failed."

The place smelled like a latrine. Their situation was terrible, but perhaps salvageable. The slave deck was only half full. If *La Estrella* docked at one of Afrikan ports to take on more men, they had a chance. He didn't think Don Lope would waste any opportunity for profit.

"You're that priest."

He rolled over as far as he could to see who accused him. Iago Gonzales lay at his back. "In a manner of speaking," he replied.

"I heard the crew talking, above." Iago's voice floated out of the dark. "They say you're the one who insisted they treat Joachin's wounds."

"I did that. Yes."

"If you hadn't, he would have died. You saved his life."

"Let's hope."

"We need to get out of here."

"That's the plan." They were five days out from Cabo Verdes, the next port of call. They would need a diversion to escape. Pray to Lys Joachin de Rivera was recovered by then, and that the winds of fate blew with them.

Chapter Three: In Qadis

UMBERTO SHIFTED FROM foot to foot. His back and legs pained him. Over the past three days he had hardly slept while Tomás, the Grand Inquisitor, moaned in his sleep. As well as drowsing fitfully, Tomás had soiled his bed linens several times with no more control than a babe. Umberto had had to supervise the monks as they washed Tomás' befouled body, explain away his tattoo, 'it was inflicted upon him by a powerful witch, but he overcame her, so it is his badge of courage!' and apply cold compresses to Tomás' head. The monks had been about to change Tomás' sheets, when Tomás awoke.

"Where is she?" he asked groggily. He groaned and closed his eyes to shut out the candle light.

Umberto dismissed the monks with a wave. If Tomás realized others had attended him as he lay in such a state, it would only add to his outrage. "Go!" he whispered, shooing them. Thank Sul, Tomás hadn't befouled himself since they had bathed him an hour earlier.

As the monks departed, he drew close to Tomás' side. "Whom do you ask for, Radiance?" He wasn't happy divulging what he suspected Tomás wanted to know.

The question only agitated Tomás further. "Who do you think? Is she in custody?" He set a shaking hand to the bandage about his head.

Umberto felt the tension drain from his shoulders. He wanted to know about Miriam Medina, of course. "Yes, Radiance. She's safely under guard."

"And de Rivera?"

The dreaded question, how to explain that de Rivera and Rana Isadore had escaped after they had left him for dead? At first, it seemed they had vanished into thin air, but it soon became evident that wasn't the case. Rana Isadore's demon had created a portal that led from the apse to the outside world, or perhaps to a precinct in hell–who could say? He wasn't knowledgeable in such matters, but one thing was certain, Tomás wouldn't be pleased with the news. "I don't know how to tell you this, Master, but they got away. The demon Belial...."

Tomás clutched at his sheets and uttered a noise so alien Umberto could only describe it as a snarl. It terrified him. His hands shook. "By the time we reached you, the demon had vanished...and so had they! We had to see to you, take care of your injuries!"

"I'll flay you alive!"

"Master, even *you* didn't think she had that kind of ability! To raise a demon so diabolical–"

"There was no demon!"

"But there had to be! She told you, herself. Those scars on her body came from an evil fiend, a...an *hymenoptera*!" There! He remembered the name!

Tomás looked as if he were about to combust. "You've bungled things again, you moron! That wasn't Rana Isadore! The woman who attacked me in the chapel was Miriam Medina!"

"That isn't possible. Miriam Medina is currently in your suite under strict guard–"

"THAT ISN'T MIRIAM MEDINA!" He struggled to rise, his fingers forming claws as he strained to reach Umberto. He fell back onto his pillows and breathed hard, his yellow eyes as bright as agates. Other than the scar that ran like a bolt of lightning from his forehead to his chin, his face was as pasty as the bandage about his head. Had he the strength, he would've throttled Umberto, then and there. *Thank Sul he doesn't*, Umberto thought. "You mustn't strain yourself, Master!"

Tomás glared at him as if he might kill him by intent alone. It wasn't fair. Of all of Tomás' servants, he was the most loyal. "How was I to know?" he muttered peevishly. "I don't have your insight. I've done nothing but spend the last few days watching over you, praying for your deliverance!"

"I doubt that very much." Tomás eyed him like a snake choosing whether or not to strike.

Umberto pursed his lips.

"Oh, stop pouting. You're too ugly for it. The woman in custody may look like Miriam Medina, but she is, in fact, Rana Isadore. At least you had the sense to keep her under lock and key. That *is* the case, isn't it?"

"It is." Umberto kept his face carefully bland. With a master like Tomás, it was best to reveal the facts in small bits, especially when the truth was unpleasant. He cleared his throat to change the subject. "But, Master, I still don't understand. Wasn't there a demon?"

"No demon. Just Miriam Medina and her flea-bitten lover, Joachín de Rivera. As for Rana, she cast a glamoury on Miriam and herself. I'm not sure how she did it, but I'll find out. I suspect her unrequited love for Angél Ferrara has something to do with it. How long have I lain here, unconscious?"

"Three days, Radiance."

"Maybe I should have you flogged for three days to make up for it. Well, she's gone by now, probably on a ship heading for the New World."

Here was a chance to redeem himself. Umberto cleared his throat. "While you were incapacitated, I made some inquiries." Pray to Sul he had enough information to spare his backside. "The woman I thought was your sorceress—" Tomás cast him a dark look, "but who is, in fact, Miriam Medina," he added hurriedly, "may have boarded a *nao* bound for Nueva Esbaña. The ship's register mentioned a group of unspecified passengers, mostly women and children. They set sail before I could detain them."

Tomás' nostrils flared. "That's them. Where were they bound?"

"Santo Domingo. From there, to Xaymaca, so it could be either place."

"And de Rivera? Did he board with her?"

"I don't know. The manifest didn't mention any injured male coming on board."

"Then he didn't. They may have turned him away, because he's too sick to sail. Sailors are a cautious lot. Either he's dead, or in Qadis recovering. I need to know. Bring Rana Isadore to me, plus several birds-doves or chickens, whatever you find. We need to determine exactly where they are. I'll have her scry."

"Are we going after them, Master?"

"We are."

"How in your condition, if I might ask?"

"My debility only slows me momentarily, Umberto. They mustn't think they've escaped me. Before you fetch Rana, bring me knives, ink, and the book. There'll be something in it to enhance my healing."

Umberto bowed. He would go to his own chambers first, to retrieve the grimoire. Tomás had insisted he keep the book private. If any sanctimonious Solarium officials found the thing, then it would be he, Umberto, who would be charged with heresy and witchcraft. Tomás would disavow any knowledge of it. Worse, he would lead in the questioning.

And if *he* were to accuse Tomás of witchcraft, under torture? No one would believe him. Perhaps he should consider his own protective tattoo.

He paused at the door. His back ached terribly. "Are you going to punish me, Master? For allowing Miriam Medina and Joachín de Rivera to escape?"

The question floated on stale air.

"That depends on how successful you are over the next few hours. Bring me the book, then Rana. See what you can learn of de Rivera's whereabouts without bungling anything else. I'm tired. Get out of my sight."

Umberto fled. He didn't think it prudent to mention that while he had left her alone, the girl he thought was Miriam Medina had tried to hang herself.

Chapter Four: Aboard the Phoenix

"WHERE ARE THEY?" Miriam stood at the rail, peering at the dock on the far shore. It was pinpricked with light from countless lanterns. Above the town, the torch of a great lighthouse shone, a beacon to ships further out to sea. Zara had doctored her hand with the comfrey. It hurt less, but that was because she was distracted by worry. It had been two hours since they had parted ways with Francis. He should have been back by now with Joachín and the men. Luci and Zara had waited with her. Maia had gone below decks to tend to Little Grim. Casi huddled beneath Luci's arm, a lone chick wanting the comfort of her hen.

"Something's wrong. I know it." Luci glanced down at Casi. "Mi corazon, I know your head hurts, but are you certain you can't hear anything?"

Casi shook her head.

Luci met Miriam's gaze. "I don't think her talent works over water. I wish we knew what was happening."

"The negotiations might have been tricky. Francis will have taken pains to avoid suspicion."

"Perhaps, you could talk to...Alonso?"

That old Diaphani superstition. Luci always mentioned Alonso reluctantly, as if naming a ghost brought ill luck. "I haven't been able to find him since we returned." Had Alonso been avoiding her? Surely not.

Zara slapped the rail. "Well, I can't stand around here doing nothing. I'll ask Ximen."

"He might not tell you. He's been close-mouthed, so far."

"He's being protective, as usual. Don't worry. I'll force it out of him." She bustled off, a ship sailing for a distant port.

Luci grabbed Miriam by the arm and pointed. "Is that them?" A small craft, not much more than a dark smear on the water, had set off from the dock, its rowers hard at work. After a few minutes, the coxswain's voice carried over the waves, a bawdy shanty setting the beat. Luci stiffened, but Casi wasn't paying attention. As they watched, the jolly boat headed for a galleon.

"I thought as much, when they sang that song." Luci glanced down at Casi a second time.

Usually Casi was full of questions, but tonight she was quiet. Jager had struck her, probably the only time in her young life it had occurred, Miriam thought. The women had discussed it. Jager had shouted something at Casi about *diviners*, which meant he suspected them of witchcraft. Zara vowed he would answer for it, but they had to consider the ramifications. Joachin, Iago, and Barto needed to return with Francis before they sought justice with the captain.

The insistent peals of the watch bell cut through the air, announcing the change in crew. "We should go below," Miriam suggested. The starboard watch headed to their posts with Jager de Groot leading the way. Luci gave him a hard stare, then glanced away, as if having second thoughts. Better not to antagonize him. Once everyone had squeezed into their small space on the orlop deck, Miriam left them to find Alonso. *He won't want to leave, but I'll insist. I need to know when Francis will appear with the men.*

It took her another half hour before she spotted his rat creeping out from behind a barrel. She knew it was him from the bald patch on one haunch. The spot was bigger; perhaps his possession made the animal age faster. She held out her hand. The rat bared its teeth, then clambered onto her palm.

Alonso flowered into being beside her, his back against the barrel, one leg crooked and the other flat. *Sorry about that. Sometimes, it's hard to control their nature.*

Where have you been? I've been worried sick!

His glow dimmed a little.

Forgive me. It's been a stressful day. I've needed to talk to you.

He made a face, the sour expression at odds with his saint-like glow.

Joachin and the men weren't at the slave auction. Francis has gone to free them—

I know. I just came back from La Estrella del Mar.

And?

And...they're still discussing it.

There was something he wasn't telling her, she was sure of it. Both he and Ximen had been tight-lipped.

Alonso, please. Other than the one time she had pleaded with him not to leave her, she had never begged him for anything. *I need to know how Joachin is. All you've told me is, 'he's alive'. I'm frantic with worry.* She squeezed him and felt a slight buzz.

He eyed her steadily, his blue eyes reminiscent of a cool mountain lake. *There are some things you're better not knowing.*

How can you say that? It's better if I do.

I was happier when I didn't.

He meant her relationship with Joachin, of course. After the *hymenoptera* had attacked her, she and Alonso had had one night of loving—a spiritual and sexual experience. When he had died for what she thought was the last time, Joachin had filled his void.

Did he think she would give Joachin up for lost? That the four days they had spent at sea would diminish her longing? She had been so caught up in her fear for Joachin, that she had neglected Alonso. *I know how hard this is,* she said.

I don't think you do. His look was anything but forgiving. *Since you want to know so badly, I'll tell you. Your husband has been much abused. Don Lope has been using him for a carpet. The wounds on his back have* turned septic because the vizconde grinds his heels into him every night. He lies in his own feces, my love, unaware of where he is or how he got there.

She uttered a small cry.

Feel better now?

His contempt cut her to shreds. The floor lurched. The world turned grey. She slumped against a cask, feeling faint. Alonso vanished as she lost hold of the rat.

"Miriam?" Luci appeared from around the barrel. "Are you all right?"

She shook her head, unable to speak.

"What is it?" Zara was beside her in an instant. "Tell us."

She found her breath because the choice was to never breathe again. The vision Alonso had painted was too terrible to bear alone. "We have to do something...Joachin is dying." She clutched at Zara. "He is dying!"

Luci turned white. The rest of the Tribe came up behind them.

"Did Alonso tell you this?" Zara was bent on extracting facts.

"No, but that's what will happen if we don't rescue him in time! A tattoo! Surely, we can save him with a tattoo! Like the ward we used to keep Rana at bay!"

Zara took a deep breath. "If it's tattoos he needs, then he hasn't entered the Summerland yet. I can ask Ximen, but I don't think any such exists unless it's placed on him directly. Hopefully, your spy can free him, and then Iago and Barto will bring him here. Only then, we might—" She looked to Luci for support.

"We should pray," Luci said.

"Pray? Why is that always your last resort?" Anger filled her now, which was preferable to feeling hopeless. She glared at Luci and swiped at the tears on her cheeks. "If Francis can't free Joachin, the last thing I'll do is to trust a goddess who, at best, expects us to help ourselves, and at worst, does nothing!" She shoved Zara aside.

"Matriarch, stop!" Zara clutched at her. "Where are you going?"

"I'm going to find Joachin and save him! I'll fight the entire crew of *La Estrella del Mar* if I have to!"

"Dear Lys, she's lost her mind!" Zara cried. "Luci, Maia, help me!"

The rat leapt onto Miriam's ankle and clung there. Alonso appeared in a flash. *Stop it! I'll go!*

She sucked in a breath and stopped struggling.

"Thank Lys," Zara muttered, still hanging on.

You're hysterical. Alonso looked as grim as a knight about to head into battle. *You're not in your right mind. I shouldn't have been so blunt, but I lost my temper. I'm sorry. You can't blame me for not liking him, all things considered.*

Relief flooded her. *You'll go to him, Alonso? Give him strength like we did for Casi when she was bitten by that viper?*

I don't know what I can do. I'll see.

All about her, the women watched as they continued in silent conversation. She was barely aware of them. *Alonso, I love you! You know I do! But if you'd do this…!*

His glance speared her. *I love you, too, more than what is good. I'll do it, but remember, if our places were reversed, he wouldn't do this for me.*

He was right. Joachin would never aid an enemy, especially if he held the advantage. Alonso was the better man, morally and ethically.

He was gone before she could tell him so.

"I guess *he's* talked some sense into you." As Zara released her, she felt the Tribe's tension ebb.

Joachin de Rivera wasn't where Alonso had last seen him. He took note of Don Lope and his officers in the great cabin, of the steward and cabin boy cleaning the suite, of the crew at their posts on each deck. But of Iago, Barto, and Francis Walington, also known as Fra Francisco, there was no sign.

Did Don Lope free them? he wondered. *Did I miss seeing them return to the Phoenix?* It was more likely the Inglaisi spy had been found out by Don Lope. They had to be on board. Alonso rematerialized on the slave deck.

The place shimmered with dark emanations, waves of misery and despair so palpable, he felt the pain like a physical force. The stench of the place was unbearable. Of late, he had become more sensitive to such things. Perhaps it had to do with the length of time he spent in limbo, or his attunement to animal senses. All about him, men moaned and suffered. Some failed to move. He sorted through the hurt and followed one throbbing thread in particular.

Joachin de Rivera lay like a dead man on a pallet. He was chained at the ankle to Barto of Andor. Across from them, Francis dozed fitfully next to Iago.

Alonso tried to remain as objective as possible. The abuse Joachin had endured over the past few days had proven to be too much. The man no longer inhabited his body. His silver thread, that umbilical cord connecting body to spirit, spiralled off into the ether. He didn't have to guess where it led. Joachin approached death's borders.

I could let him go, he considered. *If he's already too far gone, he can't come back.*

It was a tempting thought. With Joachin out of the way, there would be no competing for Miriam's love. But would she believe it if he told her Joachin was beyond saving? It was getting harder to keep his thoughts to himself. With something like this—

No. The three of them were too entangled for her to miss the lie. There was nothing for it, but to go after de Rivera. If Joachin wanted to sever ties with his mortality, then he, Alonso, would break the truth as gently as he could to the woman they loved.

He focused on Joachin's shining tether and travelled its length, expecting to arrive at that place where Sul's light shone everywhere and nowhere at once. After many twistings and turnings, and one alarming bout of vertigo that spun him end over end, he found himself floating down a long, dark road-the last place he expected to be. Boulders dotted the way. Far ahead, a figure staggered, dragging a gleaming rope behind him. With each faltering step, Joachin stirred clouds of dust that might have lain there for centuries. He seemed intent on reaching a distant sunrise beyond a far hill. What lay there? Was it the place the Diaphani called the Summerland? Would his mortal life be done, his silver cord snap, once he arrived?

Maybe it was better if it didn't.

He turned the thought over in his mind. Sul had said his own fate was to die, over and over, until he took his final journey into the Light. So far, he had been reduced to possessing rats, a squirrel, and a dog-all for Miriam's sake. If Joachin went to the Summerland, he would no longer need a body. It would be free for the taking. He, Alonso, could return to Miriam in Joachin's form.

The problem was, he couldn't possess a corpse. Sul had said there needed to be a spark of life. Which meant he would have to wrest control from de Rivera. Hardly difficult, considering the man's state.

At that thought, all the boulders lining the road trembled into life. Rocks stretched into lumpy bodies with cone-shaped heads. Eyes, as shiny as obsidian, watched him over razor-sharp beaks. A bolt of alarm ran through him as they spread their inky wings. He didn't dare move. *Vultures*, he realized, but a far cry from their earthly counterparts. These were huge, fantastically shaped. As they settled to preen, the desire for meat bombarded him from all sides.

He drew in a cautious breath. They had come into being the very instant he had contemplated overpowering Joachin. Vultures were carrion-eaters. When they weren't feeding on the dead, they contributed to it, pecking and gorging to speed death along. *Which was what I was about to do*, he thought. *Speed Joachin's death along.*

Shame engulfed him. He shrank into himself, feeling small, contemptible. How could he have considered such a thing? Like any man, he was susceptible to temptation–even a lifetime as a priest hadn't spared him from that. But this, he could not do.

As one, the vultures stretched their foul wings and flew away into the dark. He breathed in relief when they disappeared. The air felt cleaner. *I feel freer*, he thought. Which was what one generally felt when one did the right thing. What would have happened if he had chosen otherwise? Would he have become one of them? Thankfully, that was something he would never know. Ahead, Joachin continued to struggle. It was time to do something about that.

He floated up behind him, the light from the sun filling his eyes. *De Rivera!* he shouted. *Turn around!*

Joachin kept marching.

He materialized in front of him, barring his way. *Wake up! If you go on, it will be forever!*

Joachin still didn't see him.

Oh, for Sul's sake. He grabbed him and shook him hard by the shoulders. As he expected, they were more solid in this place, they had a mass.

The sudden contact roused Joachin. He sucked in a deep breath, then glared at him as if he had disturbed him from a deep sleep. *Let go of me! Who the hell are you?*

Alonso removed his hands. *I think you know who I am.*

He watched as Joachin's eyes widened in recognition. *You're him. Her priest.*

From the way he said *him*, he didn't mean Fra Francisco. His dislike bombarded him in red waves. Joachin hadn't expected him to appear as he was, blonde, attractive, and strong. That pleased him somewhat.

What are you doing here? Have you come to bedevil me? Joachin demanded.

Don't be insulting. I have better things to do. Do you even know where you are?

Joachin considered their surroundings and blanched. *What is this place? Am I dead—like you?*

How annoying to be reminded. *No. You aren't dead like me. But if you keep following this road, you will be.*

He studied the ruddy horizon. *I was thirsty. I thought if I rounded that hill, I could drink—*

You can still go there. Gods forbid I should stop you.

That earned him a glare. *I'm not ready to die, yet. Why are you here? Have you finally had enough?*

No. I'm here on Miriam's behalf.

Joachin glanced away. *So what now?*

Behind them, the long, dark road ended in nothingness. Before them lay mystery and light. *Now, we go back. Unless you really do want to carry on.*

He shook his head.

Very well. I can take you, but you'll have to let me lead. How amazing to have those words come from his mouth. He hated helping him, but there was no other way.

You'd do that? For me?

Let's get one thing clear. I'm not doing it for you. I'm doing it for Miriam.

Joachin regarded him without saying anything. Alonso sensed his thoughts: here was a man who accepted a burden despite his own disadvantage. And he did it to make the woman they loved happy, even if it cost him his peace. Was Alonso a saint or a fool? Joachin wasn't sure. *If our fortunes were reversed, I wouldn't do this for you*, he said. *Even if she begged me.*

I know it. He had the impression Joachin had never run into another quite like him.

I can see why she loves you, he said abruptly. *You're the better man. I know what this costs you.*

If the concession was supposed to make him feel better, it didn't.

You think of me as your enemy, Alonso de Santangél, but I tell you this. From now on, we're no longer rivals, at least not on my part. From here on, I'll respect your feelings. I'll be mindful of the time I spend with Miriam and not begrudge you your time with her. If you help me return, you deserve my consideration and respect. It isn't much to give, but it's all I have.

You're right. It isn't much. What did he expect? That they'd be the best of friends?

Joachin grimaced and regarded the distant sunrise. *I don't think I'll ever fear death, again. I suppose I'll be in a lot of pain once I return to my body?*

Most likely.

Very well, I'll deal with it. Thanks for coming to my rescue. I would have gone on, if not for–

Save your breath. I don't need your gratitude. Alonso grabbed him by the arm and the dark road disappeared.

Suddenly, they were engulfed in flames. The abrupt shift was too much for Joachin. He gasped as the cauterizations across his back burst into fresh agony. Alonso felt the burn too, reliving the flames from which Miriam had pulled him when she resurrected him so long ago. As Joachin screamed, he sought relief in the only way he knew how. He reached for what he had once been–replenishing, rejuvenating rain.

Slowly, Joachin's pain ebbed to a dull throb, something Alonso knew he could handle on his own. When they were sufficiently recovered, he dropped from his body, a dead leaf falling from a tree. He had nearly spent himself restoring his rival, but thanks to him, Joachin would live.

Still, it didn't make him feel any better knowing he had done the right thing. When he returned to the *Phoenix*, he wouldn't have the strength to possess the rat. Miriam would have to wait until morning to learn how things went, assuming the dawn replenished him.

Alonso wasn't sure it would.

Chapter Five: An Impasse

HAD UMBERTO BEEN absent another ten minutes, Rana would have succeeded. She had torn the sheets, secured them to a chandelier, and wrapped them about her throat. Umberto had found her kicking feebly, the chair toppled at her feet.

She hurt all over, her neck especially, but dull lethargy outweighed the physical pain. Before she had attempted her death, she had beseeched the goddess: *please, let me die.* She had had a shred of hope then, believing she might actually accomplish it, but she had failed. Perhaps the goddess was punishing her.

Love makes one mad, Rana thought. She had sinned for it, murdered for it. In spite of that, Angél would never be hers. Especially now, trapped as she was. The disaster she should have foreseen, the catastrophe that ruined her chances with Angél as surely as if she had taken her life, had occurred.

She was pregnant with Tomás' child.

She sat limply in a chair of velvet brocade, wondering if she could find death in simple things, like forcing her heart to stop. From across the room, her jailer, a Luster monk with a disapproving expression, watched as if suspecting she might succeed. After hanging herself, she had stopped eating but Umberto had finally seen through the attempt. They had forced food into her this morning.

No matter what happened, Tomás could never learn of her pregnancy. He would use the child for his own purposes. Even though she loathed the fetus, the babe was also a part of her. Better it die along with its mother, than to be used as a tool or worse. Perhaps if she enraged Tomás to a point of losing control, he would kill her before realizing he murdered both mother and child.

The door to her prison opened. The frowning monk glanced up to see who had arrived. Umberto ignored him as he hobbled toward her. His facial lines were more deeply etched than usual. He looked as if he had aged a decade since she had seen him last.

"You're to attend the Grand Inquisitor," he told her without preamble.

"I'm not well."

"Starve yourself and sicken. You brought this on yourself."

"I'm weak. I don't think I can walk."

"Then you'll be carted like baggage. Or dragged by your hair." He smiled as if enjoying the prospect.

She shrugged. "Do what you will."

If it were possible for him to scowl more deeply, he did. "Find a *litera* for her," he ordered the monk. "I also want six doves delivered to the Grand Inquisitor, along with a knife and bowl of water."

"Holy water, Brother?"

"Not required."

The monk hid his hands inside his brown sleeves and bowed. As the heavy doors closed behind him, Umberto sneered at her. "So, Rana Isadore—" he paused as if expecting her to react to him knowing who she was, "no matter what pretty disguise you wear, you learn escape is impossible. We'll always find you in the end."

She closed her eyes to shut him out. Other than her pregnancy, it didn't matter what he said.

A claw caught her by the chin. Her eyes flew open. Umberto was no longer sneering. "I don't know what prompted you to try to kill yourself, but if you try again, you'll fail. You're the Grand Inquisitor's property. It's not up to you to decide whether you live or die."

She stared past him as if he weren't there. It irritated him further. He leaned into her face. He stank of rotting teeth.

"There are things worse than death, you know. I've seen some of the things the Grand Inquisitor has done to those who cross him. You wouldn't like his *toys*." He drew back to see if his threat carried weight.

"Let him use them, then."

With a curse, he released her and stood back, his expression one of disbelief. "That glamoury has done something to you! Why are you so different? Why do you wish to die?"

She regarded him with empty eyes. The litter had arrived.

They hoisted her into the half-seat as if she were no more than a wooden doll. Two Luster monks carried her down a long hallway while Umberto followed, shouting at them to slow down so he might keep up. After many turnings, they came to a dusty aisle in a little-used part of the temple. Judging from the torches set into the walls and the number of monks going to and fro, this was where they had sequestered Tomás. She had learned from her jailer he had been injured. She didn't care how.

As they entered a smaller and simpler room than his suite, she saw he bore a bandage about his head. A thick dressing also covered the right side of his lean, scarred face. A faint stirring of satisfaction infused her, but it was short-lived.

"What's this?" Tomás noticed her in the chair. He straightened against his pillows and then looked as if he regretted moving too quickly. He rounded on Umberto. "Why has she been treated to a litter?"

"She refused to walk, Radiance."

"Did she?" Tomás pursed his lips. "We can remedy that. Come down from that throne at once."

She remained where she was.

"Drop her."

The monks did. The chair landed with a crash and splintered. The impact threw her against one of the sides. She bit her lip to keep from crying out. Her ribs would bear a new bruise tomorrow—if she survived that long.

"What's the matter with her? Has she been drugged?" Tomás glared at Umberto as if he were to blame.

"No, Radiance!"

"Then what have you done?"

"Nothing! She...I meant to tell you this before. She isn't herself."

"Explain."

"The thing she did. It affected her."

Tomás flushed hotly. "Get OUT!" He waved his hands, then grabbed his head and groaned. Umberto and the monks hurried for the door. Rana lay where she was. "Not *you*, Umberto! Stay with the girl! Everyone else leaves!"

The monks fled. Umberto hobbled to Rana and set a hand upon her arm. "You!" he sputtered. "I've had just about enough of you!"

"What's going on? And how dare you refer to anything that goes on behind my doors!" Tomás glared at him.

"Forgive me, Radiance, but I didn't think what I said reflected—"

"What's wrong with her? Is she hurt?"

Rana laughed feebly. Tomás, asking after her welfare. How out of character.

"She isn't in her right mind. She tried to kill herself."

Silence fell. Her thoughts spun...was Tomás shocked? A sick cunning wrapped her in its embrace. If she provoked him enough....

"Why?" He threw the question at her. The word struck like a nail biting into coffin wood.

She remained mute. Uncomfortable with the silence, Umberto broke it. "I already asked her that, Radiance. She won't say."

"Then make her."

A smile touched Rana's lips.

"You see? She finds entertainment in threats!"

"I never threaten. Bring her here."

Umberto hauled her unresisting from the remains of the chair. What if she found the strength to attack Tomás, to provoke him? She was weak, dizzy. Who had attacked him in the first place? Whoever it was had been stronger than she.

Umberto forced her to stand at his side.

"I don't care why you tried to kill yourself," Tomás said tightly. "Your reasons don't matter in the least. What matters is you'll continue to serve me as long as I wish. You're going to scry for me, now. I want to know the whereabouts of Miriam Medina and Joachín de Rivera. Umberto, give her the birds."

Rana stared at him. Was it possible? That Miriam and Joachín had done this to him? Umberto presented her with two struggling doves. She kept her hands at her sides.

Tomás frowned and pressed his lips together tightly. "Do it for her," he ordered.

Umberto's admission of her attempted suicide appeared to have made an impression on him. Perhaps he had decided to treat her less harshly, despite the threats. Umberto gasped in vexation, and then twisted the birds' necks in quick succession. He pressed a long blade into her hand so she might carve their breasts and drip their blood into the waiting bowl. Her fingers curled around the knife. The steel felt cool, an old friend about to give her what she wanted. Unfortunately, Umberto wasn't entirely stupid. He kept his hand locked over hers.

She might have had the strength to stab herself, but she couldn't fight him. Success might still be found in opposing Tomás. "I won't." She met his gaze and waited for what seemed an eternity.

"Let her go, Umberto," Tomás said finally.

"Radiance, I dare not! If I do, she'll gut herself or strike you!"

She couldn't read Tomás' expression. There was a question in his glance, as if he were considering and discarding her reasons. Perhaps he had tortured enough victims to know when they had reached their limit.

"Take the knife from her, and remove those." He indicated the doves. "Have her escorted to her room. If she won't scry willingly, then we'll find something to make her." He smiled coldly. "See she's watched, as before. I think by this evening, our sorceress will discover there are some things she values even more than death."

Umberto called for the monks. As they drew Rana from the room, she tried not to care. There was nothing with which Tomás could threaten her that would make her change her mind. She stumbled amid her escort, but the calm assurance with which he uttered those words bothered her.

There was nothing she valued more than dying, was there?

Chapter Six: Waiting

MIRIAM COULDN'T SLEEP. She tossed and turned all night, waiting for Alonso to bring her news. When she could stand it no longer, she roused herself and found the rat in its corner by the vinegar. Its stiffened limbs confirmed it was dead.

"No!" She clutched it and then set it down abruptly, knowing it wasn't Alonso. For him, death was an imposition, a temporary obstruction. He would find another host, but how long would it take? Had he been able to help Joachin as he said he would?

There was nothing for it but to go above and wait. Surely Francis would appear with the men. She sent a prayer of intercession to the goddess, feeling guilty she only sought her when things were dire.

Luci and Casi were at the rail as she stepped onto the waist. The sky was a soft pewter, the water a dull, uneven steel. The sun was yet to rise. The offshore breeze felt cool.

"Any sign of them?" She scanned the grey water. On the distant quay, a few early risers moved. The great beacon that was the lighthouse still shone.

Luci shook her head. "No. Any word from...?" She dropped her voice and looked away as one of the crew walked by.

Miriam waited until the man was out of hearing. "No. Unfortunately, the rat died. I'm not sure whether it was its time, or if something happened to Alonso." She filled Luci in on the details but kept them to a minimum so as not to upset Casi further. The girl was soft-hearted about animals.

"I don't like that Fra Francisco hasn't returned with them yet." Luci always referred to Francis by his clerical name whenever the crew was in hearing distance.

"Nor I. Have you seen Ximen this morning?"

"He was talking to the cook earlier. They seem to get along."

"Two old men. Things in common."

"Yes." Luci smiled. "He's also avoiding Zara."

Miriam knew why. Zara pestered Ximen unmercifully, never giving him a moment's rest about Joachín, Iago, and Barto. "He's been too close-mouthed," she said. "Trying to protect us from the worst." She cast a lingering glance at the dock, hoping to see four men disembark from *La Estrella del Mar*. When they didn't, she strode off in search of their Rememberer.

"All I can tell you, is they're still alive. I don't know about Barto or the priest." Ximen couldn't advise her directly about Francis or Barto. They weren't of the blood.

She had finally found him near the bowsprit. Unlike the women who relieved themselves in a chamber pot between the water tuns on the lower deck, he visited the heads. "You needn't protect me, Ximen." She cast him a warning look. "Alonso's told me everything about Don Lope's mistreatment of Joachín. We've had this conversation before. You mustn't keep things from me."

"Some things aren't fit for a woman to hear."

"No? Or is it a matter of keeping me from storming that boat and demanding Joachín's release?"

His look was one of tested patience. "It isn't a *boat*. It's a ship."

"That isn't the point."

"Joachín's in better shape now than he was. They've moved him below. Iago is with him. I think I saw Francis briefly through Iago's eyes, but I can't be sure. It was the middle of the night."

She drew in a quick breath. "Can you see Francis, now?"

"No. Iago's sleeping."

She released her hands from where she had been clenching the rail. *I need to stop doing that,* she thought. Maybe Francis was arranging the men's release as they spoke. Maybe protocol dictated that prisoners were released at sunrise. Maybe they'd arrive soon. Maybe, maybe, maybe! She hated *maybes*. One thing was sure, she would have to prevent the *Phoenix* from sailing at dawn. She glanced at the quarterdeck where Captain Vrooman and his officers were gathering. Below, Jager de Groot and the crew mingled, awaiting the master's morning address. The sun broke on the eastern horizon, turning both sky and water a glorious red.

Or perhaps it wasn't so glorious. What was that old saying? Something about *red skies come morning, mariners take warning?*

She shivered. For the first time ever, she didn't welcome the day.

"I expect a well-run ship, with strict attention to detail. No shirking of duty, no drunkenness or debauchery of any kind." Captain Vrooman cast a glance at Miriam and the women where they stood in a tight group on the larboard side of the *Phoenix*. Most of the crew stood opposite. "We're sailing late in the year, so not as likely to run into trouble, but an *orkaan* is always a possibility." He shifted his weight from foot to foot.

"*Orkaan?*" Zara lifted an eyebrow at Miriam.

"Hurricane."

Zara hugged herself.

"In the case of a storm, all passengers will stay safely below. I need all hands alert and clear-headed at all times. If any man breaks the rules, he'll be dealt with severely."

"Where's anywhere on this floating tub that's safe?" Zara looked around.

"That is all." Captain Vrooman turned to his first mate. "Mister Landseer, lay aloft and loose all sail."

The first mate stepped forward and repeated, "Starboard Watch, lay aloft! Loose all sail!"

Miriam's stomach tightened. She reached out to the captain. "No! You can't! You mustn't!"

"Carry on." Either Captain Vrooman hadn't heard her or he chose to ignore her. "I'll be in my quarters if you need me," he told the first mate. He descended the companionway leading to the waist. Jager de Groot and the starboard crew scrambled up the ratlines to balance on the yards, loosen gaskets, and roll down sail.

"Captain Vrooman!" She intercepted him on the deck. "We can't leave! Fra Francisco and the rest of our company haven't yet arrived. My husband and two others will be accompanying him! Surely, we can wait a little longer!"

He frowned. "Fra Francisco assured me he would arrive before dawn, Madam. Either he has broken his word or he's made other arrangements. It's now a half hour past sunrise. I'm expected to leave on schedule this morning. The weather is changing. The sooner we sail, the better."

"An hour, only! I beg you! An hour can't make such a difference!"

"Very well. You have one *half* of an hour. If they aren't here by then, I have no choice but to cast off. Stand by, Mister Landseer!" he shouted up at his first mate.

"Stand by, Captain?" Mister Landseer glanced down at him from the quarterdeck.

"We'll wait another half hour for the missing passengers. If they fail to arrive by then, set sail."

"Aye, sir."

Captain Vrooman nodded at Miriam as made his way to his cabin.

For the next thirty minutes, Miriam and the women watched the waters of the bay, refusing to give up hope. As time passed, the wind grew brisker and the dock busier. Numerous jolly boats slid over the water, their crews hard at the oars, but none of them approached the *Phoenix*. When three bells announced the hour, Mister Landseer shouted for the crew to stand by.

In despair, she listened as he gave the command to set the main sail, foresail, and mizzen. First the higher sails were raised, then the lower. Francis and the men still failed to appear.

"Where are they?" she moaned. "Casi," she said desperately, seeing her with Luci. "Find Ximen. Surely, he'll know what's happening."

Casi hesitated.

"It's all right. I wasn't thinking." Casi had been too frightened to go anywhere herself, ever since Jager de Groot had attacked her.

"It doesn't matter. He's here." Zara nodded at Ximen who approached them from the main deck. His expression was tense.

"I've seen them," he said quietly, reaching them. "Francis has been caught. He's down in the slave deck, in chains."

"No!" Maia clutched at Little Grim. The baby began to squall.

"What went wrong?" Miriam asked. If only the rat hadn't died. She had to talk to Alonso.

"Francis was exposed. The nuggets...Don Lope recognized them. In any event, before he was uncovered, Francis talked Don Lope into cauterizing Joachin's wounds. He and Iago are hoping they might escape once the ship docks in Dakra."

"Where is that?"

"It's a port on the Afrikan coast. Francis thinks Don Lope will stop there to take on more slaves."

She wished her hands would stop trembling. "That means we may not find them until both ships dock in Nueva Esbaña."

"Is Barto all right?" There was something in Maia's tone that made Miriam think she had given up hope of ever reuniting with him. Little Grim quieted too, as if needing to hear.

"He's fine. Angry." Ximen looked as if he were about to say more but decided against it.

Maia drew in a deep breath. "If he's angry, he'll survive."

"But what if Don Lope sells them in Dakra?" Luci asked. "We'll never know where they might end up!"

"We must see what transpires." Ximen's pale eyes gleamed. "It isn't as if we're completely blind. I'll know through Iago, and the Matriarch, through Alonso." Miriam had failed to mention that Alonso, too, was beyond reach at the moment. "As for Joachin, it's the goddess' mercy he is where he is. It may not seem so, but this way, he's likely to survive. I have hope now, where before, I had none."

"And let us not forget our Inglaisi spy," he added. "Francis Walington can talk the barnacles off a barque. I wouldn't put it past him to already have an escape plan in place."

Zara folded her arms. "Much good he's done us, so far. I say we're better off without him."

Chapter Seven: The Wickedness of Vrouwen

AS THE PHOENIX headed for open sea, Miriam finally left the spar deck when she could no longer see Tenerifa. The sails bellied and cracked above her, the deck shifted and rolled, growing unsteady underfoot. Other than a few neighbouring ships etching the horizon like scrimshaw, the world was a composition of sea and sky, one part grey and the other part blue. She felt small and inconsequential, as if she were of no account.

Keep him safe, Lys. Bring us back together again. Don't let him die.

If the goddess heard, she gave no indication. Miriam stifled her impatience and suffered another stab of guilt. Why should the goddess listen when she paid her no heed unless she wanted something? It wasn't fair to turn to someone only when it was convenient to do so, whether it involved a goddess or not. Over the past few days, she had also given little thought to Alonso, unless it was to have him reassure her Joachin was still alive. He deserved better.

She hugged herself against the breeze. *I love them, both,* she thought miserably. *I can't help it.*

Joachín had been the cause of her father's demise; he had instigated the deaths of many of the Tribe's men, although, in truth, that sin fell at Tomás' feet. She had despised her attraction to Joachín, even though she had eventually succumbed to it. He had never been the perfect man; his morals left much to be desired–his thieving, primarily. But he never stole out of greed. Only to survive, and later, to ensure their survival.

As for Alonso, he had always been the honourable one. He had sacrificed himself in an ultimate act of love. And then, after she thought he was gone forever, he returned. *By then, I was married to Joachín. Our plan was to sail to the New World, to escape Tomás once and for all. Who knew I could love two very different men at the same time, and in the way I do? A year ago, I would have said, 'impossible'.*

A year ago, the world was a much smaller place.

How had everything become so entangled? She should have stayed in Granad and married the mayor's son.

But that would have been impossible, too. Tomás would have made it so, or perhaps a goddess with her own plans.

She sighed and gave one last look at the sea before heading for the companionway. The men on deck eyed her as she steadied herself. Mister Landseer stood at attention on the poop and touched the brim of his hat as she passed. She managed to reach the stair without mishap. It was time to find Alonso. Hopefully, he had found a new host.

The starboard watch was off duty as she descended into the dusky confines of the main deck. One man had been playing a fiddle. He stopped mid-strain as she appeared. Jager de Groot had his back turned to her, but he swung about. The men had been dicing. She was fairly certain the captain forbade that. All talk stopped.

She ignored their stares and descended the ladder to the lower deck. The animals were kept in pens there, those that would meet their fate as food for the captain's table or were being shipped to the New World. She wanted to check on Fidel, Joachín's horse. The stallion was too strong-willed for Alonso to possess, but she wanted to make sure he was all right, as circumstances allowed. Fidel would be miserable, cooped up as he was.

The crew had yet to muck the stable. Her eyes watered; the place stank of urine and manure. As she passed a jumble of stacked chicken's cages, she was thankful for the lanterns and their light. A cluster of sheep eyed her blearily and shifted uneasily in their pen. She considered them briefly and wondered if Alonso might choose one for a host. The poor things were matted and filthy. She didn't want to touch them to find out.

He would make his presence known to her, one way or another. She edged past the sheep. Beyond them, Fidel drooped his head over his stall.

"Here, boy." She reached out with her good hand to rub him on the neck. He snorted and pulled his head up, his eyes narrowing and his mouth pinched. She drew back immediately, afraid he might bite her. "I don't blame you," she muttered. "I'd be upset if I were stuck down here, too."

The fire went out of him as he recognized her. He sidled from hoof to hoof before settling, and then extended his nose to snuffle her face. She didn't understand how he knew her. She looked and smelled like Rana Isadore. She rubbed his shoulder. "I know it seems like forever to you, but in a few weeks, we'll make landfall. You'll be free again, able to run in a new land. I'll check up on you often, I promise. Make sure the captain keeps you as healthy as possible." He nickered softly. A lump formed in her throat. Horses had a hard time making the crossing. Only half of them reached the New World. She would have to make sure Fidel did, both for his sake and for Joachin's. His water bucket was only a quarter full. A rat huddled beside it. Fidel saw it and drew back.

Without thinking, she reached down to grab it. The rat was a darker grey than the last. Alonso sprang into existence.

"There you are!" she exclaimed.

I came as soon as I could. He was out of breath.

It was a relief to touch him again. *Are you all right? I found your old host this morning—*

I didn't have the strength to sustain it. By the time I finished with Joachin... let's just say, it took some doing. It was the first time she had ever heard him mention Joachin without anger or bitterness.

What happened?

He was on death's borders. Heading for the Summerland, I think. If he'd have gone any further, I don't think I would have been able to bring him back.

"Thank you, Alonso!" She nuzzled the rat against her cheek. In her mind, she held him close. There was a brief tingling as her arms swept about him. The rat squirmed. *Oh! Sorry! I didn't think!* She had invaded his space.

It's all right. I'll endure it. For you.

I wish you didn't have to. Why is this happening? When you were Blanca the dog, we could touch...sort of.

I don't know. Maybe it has something to do with the number of times I've died. Or the number of hosts. I wish.... He looked at her wistfully.

She knew what he was thinking. More than anything he wished they might make love, as they once had.

Perhaps we'll find a way in the New World. That seemed as likely as north turning into south, but she said it to offer him comfort.

Perhaps.

It was best to change the subject. *Did you see Francis?* They settled onto the hay outside Fidel's stall, the rat nestling in her lap.

From what I can tell, he made the mistake of going to a money changer. Don Lope had him followed. He recognized his own purse and gold.

She frowned. *I never should have given him that pouch.*

It wasn't your fault. Francis should've been more careful, making sure no one was trailing him.

Do you think they'll dock in Dakra? Ximen thinks they might.

Perhaps. With both of us watching, we'll soon know.

She sighed. *Six weeks, Alonso. And then the New World.*

From beyond the pens, there came the scrape of a boot against wood.

Alonso stared past her. *Gods, Miriam! Get up!*

She sprang to her feet, not knowing to where the rat had scampered. Jager de Groot lumbered towards her from out of the murk. He paused when a short distance lay between them.

"What's yer bus'ness down here?" Behind her, Fidel tossed his head. Jager came no closer. She wondered if something had happened between him and the horse to keep him at bay.

"This is my husband's horse, Fidel. I was checking up on him." She pointed at the bucket. "He needs more water."

"Ya? Well, good water's in short supply. Y' were talkin' down here."

"I was talking to the horse. It soothes him."

"No, y' were talkin' t' someone else. Who's Alonso?"

"Alonso isn't anyone. You're imagining things."

They locked eyes. Fear curdled her gut. If Jager feared witches, he would see her handling a rat as proof. Witches kept animal familiars, demons who did their bidding. Usually, they were cats, but they could be anything-rats, goats, even a horse like Fidel. She released her breath slowly. If he had seen Alonso's rat, he would have accused her of witchcraft.

"Knew an' ol' woman once, who talked in th' dark like you do."

She said nothing.

"She claimed it were nothin', too. Then bad things started t' happen. Goods went missin'. People got sick. Turns out, she'd made a pact with th' devil."

Someone had to come. She wished they would.

"They burned 'er for it. What's wrong with yer hand?"

The change in subject was so immediate, it unsettled her more than his insinuations did. "How is that your business?"

"Everythin' on this ship's my business. What did you do to it?"

"I injured it."

"Y' injure yer face, too?" He stepped closer, peering. "Why hide it?"

His fingers twitched. He intended to rip her veil away. If he saw her skin, he would shout plague or accuse her of some evil. "Step any closer and I'll scream! My women are right below! They'll come running! Who will Captain Vrooman believe when I tell him you tried to rape me?"

"Rape you?" That stopped him cold. His eyes widened and his jaw fell. "You *stomme hoer*! Y' think I'd taint m'self with th' likes o' you?"

"Leave me alone or I'll scream this ship to timbers!" Behind her, Fidel snorted.

Jager shifted from foot to foot. He was making up his mind to move.

"Leave me alone!" There was no getting past him. She held her hands up to prevent him from tearing away her veil.

He stepped closer. "I had a *vrouw* once. Pretty face, but she was th' devil on th' inside. Like th' Good Book says, 'Give me any plague, but a plague o' th' heart! Any wickedness, but the wickedness o' *vrouwen*!"

She drew in a lungful to scream.

"What's going on down here?" Ignaas the cook, appeared with a cleaver in his hand. She suspected he had come to retrieve a hen for the captain's supper. Kip, his assistant, stood wide-eyed behind him. She leaned against Fidel's stall.

"Yah! I caught 'er down here!" Jager was still red in the face, but Ignaas' arrival had snuffed some of his fire.

"That's *her* horse." Ignaas pointed at Fidel with the cleaver. "If she wants t' come down here an' check up on him, there's nothin' wrong in that."

"She was *talkin'* to somethin'!"

"Ye been at yer beer already, Jager? Y' ain't makin' sense."

"Lazy idler! What do y' know?"

"I'd say I know when a lady's bein' cornered, and when she's not. Starboard's done. Yer wanted above."

"Ain't for you t' tell me, ol' man!"

"Mebbe not. Any more than it's right fer you t' badger her." He stuck out his grizzled chin.

Her heart still pounded, but her fear was subsiding. Thank heaven, Ignaas had come when he had. Not every hand on this ship was a brute.

Jager pointed a meaty finger at her. "Of *vrouw* came sin! An' through her, we DIE!"

"Y' missed yer callin', Jager. Shoulda found yerself a pulpit, like all them other Temple thumpers," Ignaas said.

Jager swore and pushed past him, knocking him against a chicken crate. Ignaas fell, causing the wood to crack. As the hens flapped, Kip helped him right himself. "Thanks, lad," Ignaas told him. He cocked a grizzled eyebrow at Miriam. "Y' all right, Missus?"

Miriam nodded. "Yes, thanks to you."

He nodded after Jager. "Don't know what his story is, exactly. Fer some reason, he talks like he's holier than Sul, with all them Good

Book quotes. Ye keep clear o' him, all right? Now that I seen what he's about, I'll watch out for ye."

"I'm grateful."

"Don't mention it." He cocked an eye at her. "It's none o' my business, but yer face...." He hesitated. "Caught a glimpse of it, th' other day." He looked apologetic.

She froze.

"Had a daughter, once. Had arms an' legs like yers, fire burned." He raised his palms as if to stave off her protests. "Now, I don' know that's what happened exactly, but between yer skin an' hand, I figure y' got pain. I've a salve that might help. I put it on m' leg, whenever it acts up. I don' mind sharin' it with ye."

"That's kind of you." She wasn't about to dissuade him of his belief about being burned. "I'm doing what I can. I know a bit about healing. My father was a physician."

"Was he? Then you'll know more 'bout it than me." He indicated the caged chickens with his knife. "I'm about t' take care o' th' captain's dinner. You might want t' go t' below. Most ladies don't like th' sight o' blood, though mebbe ye've seen yer share."

"I'll do that. Thank you, Ignaas."

He pulled his grey forelock. "Don't mention it. An' you ladies feel free t' wander atop. It ain't healthy for yer t' be down here all th' time. It's hot, smelly, an' bug ridden. Bad enough we have t' pen th' beasts." He paused, then turned back to her. "That girl, th' one 'round Kip's age...." He gave a sly but amused glance at his assistant, "she's like a young bird. She'll get sick if she's cooped up too long. I been showin' Kip 'is knots. I can teach 'er, too, if she likes."

"You mean Casi?"

"Aye, that's 'er. She came t' get water yesterday, for th' babe. I think young Kip here, would like some comp'ny 'is own age."

"I never said!" Kip reddened.

"'S all right, boy. No harm done." Ignaas patted his arm.

Miriam smiled. Was Ignaas matchmaking? Even if he were, he was also being kind. Young people liked to associate with those of their own age. "I'll pass along your invitation."

"Do that. An' come visit, too. I got lots o' stories 'bout th' sea an' far off lands that'll amaze ye." He reddened, as if embarrassed by his boasting. "Well, it's a way to pass th' time."

"I will." It was good to know not all the crew were against them. As she headed for the orlop deck, she felt more settled than she had in weeks despite the unpleasantness with Jager de Groot. She and Joachin might be parted, but at least he was alive and would survive. Francis was with him aboard *La Estrella del Mar*. Iago and Barto, too.

As bleak as things looked, there was hope.

We just might survive this crossing after all, she thought.

"It *is* a problem we need to attend to, Old Man. What do you know of it?" Zara had cornered Ximen. The Tribe was sitting in their dark alcove, whispering among themselves. Miriam had told them of her run-in with Jager de Groot and the crew's suspicions they were witches.

"I've already wracked my memory, Zara." Ximen looked ruffled. "Don't you think I'd have advised the Matriarch by now, if I had a ready answer? No one in my reckoning has ever been stung by an *hymenoptera*, and then had her body stolen by that same witch who attacked her."

"Perhaps we need to tackle this problem in parts," Luci suggested. "Other than Ignaas, the crew have never seen Miriam's face. If we remove the glamoury Rana set upon her—"

"We should have nothing to do with *that* one." Zara crossed her arms. "We find a way to lift the glamoury from the Matriarch, then let Rana deal with her own disaster. Problem is, she's still in possession of Miriam's finger. To break the glamoury, we need it back. There's no way the captain will turn this boat around and take us back to Esbaña—"

"It's not a boat. It's a *ship*." Ximen looked pained.

"The only other way is if the goddess intervenes," Luci continued. "Only Lys has the power to transcend dark magic. We must pray for a miracle."

Miriam had little faith in miracles, but Luci had the right sense of it; to break Rana's curse, they needed bigger magic. Any attempt aboard the ship would be perilous. It was better to wait until they reached land. "Whatever we do, we mustn't give the crew any reason to fear us. Ignaas suggested we feel free to wander about the waist. We should do that so we become more familiar to them, ordinary."

"Perhaps if we ingratiated ourselves in some way?" Luci looked thoughtful. "The crew is less likely to resent us if we're helpful."

"If it's cooking that's needed, I can help with that." Zara set a forefinger to her lips. "Most men appreciate a good meal." She glanced sidelong at Ximen. "An' bless that Ignaas for taking the Matriarch's part, even if he isn't the most flavourful of cooks."

"Whatever we do, we must remain above suspicion," Miriam reminded her. "If Casi's run-in with Jager is any indication, he won't like us helping with the food or being near the water. We need to take pains to make sure no one becomes ill."

Zara looked affronted.

"Which isn't to say the cooking *won't* be improved by you, Zara. We'll all be better for it."

"Perhaps there's spare sail that needs mending? Other repairs?" Luci glanced about the group.

"Ignaas thought Casi might like to learn knots," Miriam said. "He's teaching Kip, his assistant."

Casi perked up at this, but her enthusiasm quickly faded. "Will you be on deck at the same time, Maré?" she asked. Luci nodded. "Then I'd like that."

"Good. Let's start today." Miriam stood. "Excuse me, but I must find Alonso. He's yet to appear this morning."

"I found his old host." Ximen wrinkled his nose. "I disposed of it."

"Nasty pests," Zara sniffed. "Never thought I'd see the day when a dead priest animates a rat."

"Keep your voice down, woman! The crew might hear you!" Ximen chided.

His rebuke startled her. Zara glanced apologetically at Miriam. "Sorry, Matriarch."

Luci leaned beyond their snug corner to take a quick glance. None of the crew was in the vicinity. "It's all right. It must be change of watch. I don't think anyone was close enough to hear."

"A good thing," Miriam whispered. "It also gives me a chance to collect Alonso."

She found him crouched between two casks near the companionway. As she set him into her pocket, he flowered into being, holding her hand. At that same moment, Piet Spoor, one of Jager's crew, clattered down the steps on some errand. As he passed her, she said nothing to him nor he to her, but she felt his stare as he retreated to the opposite end of the deck. She ducked behind some barrels of molasses to shield herself from view.

As she squeezed into the small space, she realized she hadn't left enough room for Alonso. He still gleamed, but ever so faintly, like an after-image one sees after turning away from the sun. He squatted beside her, part of his body obscured by a barrel. She shifted to accommodate him. They sat cross-legged, like two children sharing secrets. Her back lay to the opening, but it was unlikely Piet would see her once he returned. She squeezed Alonso's hands and felt a warm buzz.

Is this all right? I thought the displacement might—

No. It's fine. I've enough room. The other way was a bit disconcerting.

They could be this close, at least. I'm happy you're here. He brightened a little at that. She drank in his blue eyes, the blonde hair that gleamed softly about his shining face. He still wore the robes of a monk, but they fell about his form in a perfect chiaroscuro. The only thing keeping him from looking every inch the seraph was his lack of wings.

Her throat grew thick. He *was* her angel, her knight in spiritual armour. All this time, she had been treating him as far less than he was. Who else had been so constant, had loved her so much that he refused to be parted from her, even in death? Joachin loved her, but according to Alonso, he had been trying to reach the Summerland. His pain had made him think of how he might relieve it and nothing more. She couldn't blame him. But Alonso had also suffered, and here he still was.

When was the last time she had said she loved him? It wasn't recent enough.

The light in his eyes intensified. He leaned in to kiss her.

As their lips met, an explosion of light sent her reeling. Desire made his spirit merge with hers, but the radiance was too much, she couldn't contain him, it left her gasping. Then, like a sunset fading on a perfect day, all the more bittersweet because it was done, the intensity subsided. Her vision returned; she could breathe. Alonso sat before her once again, shimmering like ethereal quick-silver.

I love you so much, she told him. She meant every word.

I know. Heaven lay in his eyes. *I love you, too. More than you'll ever know.*

He had overwhelmed her; they both knew it. He also knew she still loved Joachin, but that was all right. She loved Alonso, too—maybe more. She didn't want to return to the Tribe just yet. It was hard to be distracted by their concerns or their talk of finding a way to return her to her former self. Alonso didn't care what she looked like. Rana wasn't who he saw. She realized she was tired. She needed privacy, sleep.

Sleep here.

She met his gaze. It was dangerous to be away from the others for too long.

I'll keep watch. I don't sleep, anyway.

The idea appealed. With the Tribe, there was never enough room to accommodate him. Everyone was squeezed so tightly together. But here, in this nook....

She curled onto her side, making a pillow of her arm. He settled behind her, tingling all the way down her back and legs. It took a bit of getting used to, but it was tolerable, like a warm, energizing blanket. He didn't put his arm about her; they both knew that would be too much. If only there was a way for them to be together in a normal way. The thought suffused her with guilt. That wish betrayed Joachin. And that remorse betrayed Alonso.

I'm sorry. She had spoiled the moment.

Don't be.

Then why do I feel as if I've wronged you both?

He sighed, sending a tingle down her spine. *You needn't tell me how impossible things are, Miriam. Love is its own strange land. But if it's anything, it's adaptable.*

He was speaking about himself. She wasn't ready to be convinced. *It's madness.*

Would you rather live without it?

No.

There you are, then. I've been a priest, with no one but the Temple to devote myself to. I'd rather have you, with all your complications.

They were quiet for a moment. After a time, he spoke again. *What else can love be, but a kind of insanity? It's too big, too encompassing for us mere mortals. We seek to limit it, to keep it for ourselves, but that's the whole point. Love isn't about confining. It's about accepting. Sul taught me that.*

She thought of Lys. *The gods are a paradox. I'm glad we're here, Alonso.*

I'm glad, too. Sleep now. I'll keep watch.

She did.

Just before the crew changed, Zara and Ximen found her. "Ximen said I'd find you here!" Sara accused. "What are you doing? We were so worried!"

Miriam rose with Alonso. "I didn't mean to upset you. It's all right. Alonso's been with me, keeping watch. I needed some time to think."

"You weren't thinking, you were napping! Next time you run off for a snooze, let us know! We were afraid someone abducted you! I don't trust these sailors!"

"You're right. I'll say something next time." For there *would* be a next time. It had been wonderful spending time alone with Alonso. The Tribe would have to get used to her being away. Alonso met her glance and smiled.

The watch bell clanged. Piet Spoor came running towards them from the opposite side of the deck. Seeing them, he stopped abruptly, swallowed, and then bolted past. With a nervous backward glance, he clattered up the companionway.

Zara watched him open-mouthed. "Where'd he come from? I didn't realize he was still at large down here!"

"Mister Landseer assigned him to sherry duty," Ximen said. "He's been watching the stores at the other end of the deck."

"He acts like he's seen a ghost!"

Miriam stiffened, hoping there was no substance to Zara's words. It was rare among the *gachós*, but the Diaphani weren't the only ones to exercise the Sight. Had Piet seen her with Alonso? Was that why he looked so pale? "Let's hope he hasn't," she whispered.

Chapter Eight: An Unpleasant Party

IT WAS SHORTLY after Vespers when, once again, Umberto came for Rana. She had refused to eat the meal the monks had provided. Even had she wanted to, her nausea prevented it. Her plate lay untouched. Umberto scowled at it, but said nothing. He had brought her a new set of clothes and said Tomás had ordered she wear them. The grey silk gown and matching mantle were better than anything she had ever owned. The slippers were of the softest leather. Once again, she was escorted from her suite. She said nothing to Umberto as the monks navigated her litter to Tomás' sick room. Blood might still course through her veins, but it was only a matter of time before everything stopped.

She wasn't prepared for the sight that met her eyes as she entered Tomás' bedroom.

A small group of men, save for Tomás who remained bed-bound, stood as she was carried into the chamber. They had been seated about his bed. Among them was a nobleman in a leather cuirass covering him from shoulder to hip. Although his hair and beard were silvering, he was in trim form and looked to be a fighting man. Beside him stood a tall Negro in blue and gold livery. And on the far side of Tomás' bed was Angél Ferrara.

She caught her breath as she locked gazes with Angél. His dark eyes bore into hers as if he couldn't get enough of her. His face flushed and his breathing deepened. Without knowing how she knew, Tomás had told him she would be joining them at their meeting. Angél had been waiting for her.

Or rather, he had been waiting for Miriam Medina.

A sharp pain of longing speared her through. In spite of everything that had occurred–Angél's rejection of her, his desire for Miriam, even his surrendering her to Tomás to spare himself, she still loved him.

She was a fool. Angél was her only weakness. Tomás knew it.

"Ah, here she is! *Mi doña*, I'm so pleased you could join us!" Tomás smiled expansively. He was so ebullient she hardly recognized him. "I was telling these men you've been unwell, that you might have to wait to learn their good news, but I knew you'd want to hear it for yourself."

He waved at the monks to set her down. They did so carefully. She flushed under Angél's gaze. What kind of charade was this?

Tomás glanced at the nobleman and his black servant. "My dear sister is as anxious to travel to the New World as I." The label made her stare at him in surprise, and then quickly, to Angél. His expression gave nothing away; he knew better than to challenge it. Tomás appeared the picture of civility. "*Hermana*, allow me to introduce to you Capitán Diego de Carazo, *Gobernador* of Puerto Pío. *Ser* Ferrara, you're already acquainted with."

She nodded, swallowed.

"I think you remember *Ser* Ferrara telling us a short time ago he had a charter to carry cannon to Nueva Esbaña? As it turns out, Capitán de Carazo is the captain of that ship, *La Serina del Sol*. A happy coincidence, is it not?" He turned to Capitán de Carazo. "We seek a wealthy husband for her in the New World. She's had several offers. I know the families, but in our position, we must be careful. For my sister, I require only the most stable and respectable of men."

Capitán de Carazo smiled graciously. "I understand completely, Fra Tomás. If I weren't already married, I'd seek your lovely sister's hand, myself."

Tomás smiled warmly and turned to her. "You see, *mi bonita*, you've nothing to fear. It's all been arranged. *Él Capitán* will see to our needs, provide for us as befits our station. In spite of my health, we shall endure."

He expected her to participate in this sham, but she didn't have the strength for it. She remained mute while Capitán de Carazo filled the awkward silence. "If I may be so bold to ask, how did you come by your injuries, Grand Inquisitor?"

She could tell from the glint in Tomás' eye he wasn't happy with her. He turned to Capitán de Carazo. "It was a shocking and evil circumstance. I was attacked by a Diaphani witch and her lover in this very Solarium. Even though my sister seeks a marriage, I'm still a servant of Father Church. We mustn't linger here. My assailants have fled to the New World, where I will track them down."

Capitán de Carazo and his manservant exchanged a glance. Rana wasn't sure whether de Carazo believed Tomás, or whether the interchange meant something else. The captain bowed slightly. "We shall do everything in our power to help you in that regard, Fra Tomás. But I must warn you, it may be difficult. There are many islands, and many places for renegades to hide."

"The reach of Father Church is long. His justice must be meted. We have ways of learning the truth." Tomás glanced at Angél and then allowed his regard to fall upon her. His message was clear: *if you fail to scry or do whatever I ask, I'll destroy the one thing you cherish more than your miserable life. I'll kill Angél Ferrara. I'll also tell him it was in your power to prevent it.*

He had guessed correctly and found her one weakness. She let out a low moan and sagged in her seat. As much as she detested herself, she would do whatever he asked to save Angél.

"Great Sul! Miriam, my dear, forgive us!" She heard the triumph in his voice. "We've tired you unnecessarily, or perhaps it's the excitement of the coming journey." He waved in Umberto's direction. "Take her to her rooms and see she gets something to eat. If we're to sail tomorrow, she must build up her strength."

"As you wish, Master," Umberto replied gruffly. He snagged her by the forearm and then thought better of it considering their company. He released her and called for the monks.

As they hoisted her chair, she looked one last time at Angél. His expression was one of misery and yearning, and, Lys, could it be true–remorse? Did he regret turning her over to Tomás? A tiny flush of hope infused her. He wanted to be with her, to save her! Then the delusion cut her on the truth. It wasn't she he longed for. He wanted Miriam Medina. He still believed she was.

For the first time in months, she wanted to cry. She fought to keep her face from crumpling. Her hand strayed to her belly, where it froze there. Tomás' get lay in her womb, a worm, leeching her of life. Her hand dropped limply to her side.

As the monks manhandled her chair for the door, her gaze fell dully upon Capitán de Carazo's major-domo. She hadn't seen many dark men in her travels, but of those she had, none were as finely dressed as he.

His brows lifted in surprise. Then his face split into a grin. His teeth had been filed into points, making him look lion-like. There was also a strange energy about him that made her skin crawl.

She shivered and glanced away. He had been overbold, the mark of a man with nothing to fear. Capitán de Carazo was the master and he the servant, but she wondered if that were so. Whatever their relationship, she knew a dangerous man when she saw one. If it was possible to avoid him within the close confines of the ship, she would.

Tomás found her several hours later. For Angél's sake, she had eaten a thin soup with bread, but hadn't managed to keep it down. Fortunately, Umberto hadn't seen her vomit into her chamber pot. In spite of the suicide watch Tomás insisted they maintain, the old man had allowed her the privacy to relieve herself. She had covered the bowl with a small cloth so the monks might dispose of the contents, with no one the wiser. As she returned to the table, she felt shaky and weak. The Luster monk who had been assigned as one of her minders regarded her with disfavour.

"So, I assume I now have your cooperation," Tomás announced as he walked into her suite. He limped slightly. It was strange to see him upright and moving; only a short while ago, he had been confined to his bed. He had also removed his bandages. He turned to dismiss the monk and close the door. The back of his skull bore a large bump and a purple bruise, but the gash was healing. A new scar cut across the left side of his jaw, but the seams were even and covered in scab. She ignored him and glanced away.

"Well, I suppose that's better than the impertinence I suffered last time. I'll take that as a *yes.*" He noticed her half-finished bowl of soup. "Umberto tells me you've had some broth. It pleases me to know you're eating."

Why was he being so accommodating? He was almost conciliatory. Surely, he didn't suspect her pregnancy. If anything, it would infuriate him. This wasn't Roma with its lax moral standards. This was still Esbaña. Priests were expected to remain celibate.

"Umberto is bringing some birds. He'll arrive shortly." He settled opposite her and flicked a few bread crumbs aside that the monks had missed. He clasped his hands. "I expect you're surprised to see me up and moving around."

She shrugged.

"Still the sparkling conversationalist. Shall I tell you why?"

It was too dangerous to ignore him for long, especially with Angél in custody. "You will, whether I want to hear it or not."

"I've a new tattoo. I wonder if you can recognize it." He didn't wait for her to answer, but removed one of his boots. With a grunt, he exposed his bare foot and lifted it so she might see the instep. A new mark had been carved there, a heptagram. The skin was still an angry red beneath the ink, but she knew it–*La Estrella del Este*, the Star of the East, a potent sigil for healing. When she had been her ugly, corrupted self, she had tried it to remove the *hymenoptera* bites. The tattoo had failed.

"How can you...?" She was stunned to see it there. Judging from Tomás' newfound health, it seemed to be working.

"So you *do* recognize it. I found it in the grimoire."

"It's one of Lys' marks. But why is it working? Did you dedicate yourself to her?"

"Don't be ridiculous. And I'll remind you to keep your mouth shut about such things. You're lucky we're alone. If any of the servants had heard you...." It would have meant her death. Why hadn't she thought of that before? Now, it was too late. Besides, things had changed. Angél was his insurance she would cooperate.

"You did this yourself?" she asked.

"Of course. I'm not such a fool to trust anyone else."

Even a bread knife had been absent when the monks had brought her soup. She suspected Tomás had ordered them to prevent any sharp objects from coming into her presence. For the first time in weeks, she looked at him carefully. Four hours ago, he had been bedridden and wincing in pain. Now, other than a limp caused by the new tattoo, he was nearly recovered. It had to be the new glyph. Why was it working for him when it hadn't for her? Lys was a cruel goddess. It wasn't fair.

"As you can see, I took the book's advice. Place these things where they're hidden. Seemed sensible. If it keeps working the way I hope, I shouldn't be at all surprised if I'm completely cured by tomorrow. It's a miracle, really."

"How will you explain it to Capitán de Carazo?" She couldn't help shudder at the thought of his manservant. "He's seen you with a head bandage."

"I hadn't thought of that. Perhaps I'll have to wear it for a time to alleviate suspicion." Even for the short while they had been speaking, she could see the cut across his jaw was lessening. The original scar remained as it was. Tomás shifted his weight as if the chair were too confining.

Her nostrils twitched. Ever since she had been stung by the *hymenoptera*, her sense of smell had grown acute. The air tasted of him, of sweat, of lust.

He lifted an eyebrow. "I know we've not been on the best of terms. At times, I've been impatient with you, but I do value talent, intelligence...and beauty." He cleared his throat.

What is this, she wondered? *He knows who I am beneath the glamoury, but he's reacting to me as if I'm Miriam Medina.*

"It may be your wish to suicide has awakened pity in me, or perhaps it's something else." His expression softened. "I'd have you work with me, willingly. I can make it worth your while."

"You have a strange way of suing for my cooperation. You hold Angél as ransom."

He pursed his lips with impatience. "I don't understand why you still want him. He's beneath you."

She was tempted to retort, *and you aren't?* But she held her tongue.

He leaned on an elbow. "Tell me. How did you enact the glamoury? We haven't had a chance to discuss, yet."

They had, but he had chosen to rape her while believing she was Miriam Medina. How much to tell? Would it make any difference if she told him she had murdered Tanya to break the Tribe's ward? She regretted doing that, now. Probably best not to.

"I made a blood sacrifice. It was strong enough to draw...." As of old, she was tempted to refer to Miriam as *that Medina bitch,* but those fires no longer burned as hot. Perhaps wearing Miriam's guise had changed her feelings about her and herself, "...to draw Miriam to me. To complete the glamoury, I cut off her little finger."

Tomás' eyes widened. "So *that's* the grisly addition to your chain! I wondered!" He looked impressed.

He still had her necklace. Umberto had cautioned she might strangle herself with it. Or choke on the bones.

He was in a better mood than she expected. Maybe he would indulge her as he had promised. "Can I have it back?"

He leaned into his chair. "In time. Do you think the glamoury will last?"

She shrugged. "I see no reason for it not to." She reflected on breaking the ward. "The only thing that might reverse it is stronger magic."

"Blood work."

"Yes."

"Well, I see no reason to change yourself to what you were. You're much more pleasant to look at."

A knock came at the door. To Tomás' *come,* Umberto entered with the birds. Tomás glanced at her, his demeanor placid, as if they had been sharing anecdotes. "So, you'll scry for me, now?"

He was being so strange! He had never framed a demand as a question before. It was still an order, but the new tattoo had him in high spirits. On the other hand, if she refused, his thin veneer of civility would vanish. He would torture Angél as he had said. There was only one way to answer him. "Yes."

"Excellent." He smiled. "Umberto, give her the birds."

The old man presented her with a gilded cage of white doves. As if sensing their fate, they batted their wings against the bars in a flurry. Gorge rose to her throat. The idea of cutting them...she couldn't stomach it. She had never quailed over blood before. It had to be the pregnancy.

Tomás noticed her reluctance. "What's the matter?" His words bit. He misread her unwillingness.

She was going to vomit. "I...I can't!"

His eyes narrowed. "You know very well what will happen if you don't."

"I tell you, I am going to be sick!" Without warning, her mouth filled with the remains of her supper. She clapped a hand to her lips and ran for the *garderobe* before either Tomás or Umberto could stop her. As she vomited into the chamber pot, Tomás appeared in the doorway.

"What's wrong with you? Are you truly ill?"

She panted over the pot. "I don't know. Maybe it's the glamoury. A brief vision of Tanya, just before she gutted her, filled her mind. Panic doused her in a chilly flood, sweeping the image aside. "I...I can't seem to stomach the idea of blood!"

"Well, you'll have to stomach it. I need you to find Miriam and Joachín de Rivera."

She wiped her mouth, feeling shaky. "I don't know if I can."

He shouted over his shoulder. "Umberto, bring Angél Ferrara to me!"

"No!" She clawed at his legs. "Tomás, I swear, I'm not trying to trick you! Truly, I'm not myself! I'd sacrifice the doves, but I don't think I have the strength!"

He stared down at her as she clung to his knees. She grasped at faint hope when he didn't kick her aside. Finally, he reached down and hauled her to her feet. His hands were vises on her arms. His golden eyes bore into hers. After a moment, his grip relaxed.

"Very well. I believe you. You're pale. I can see you're not all right. Perhaps the glamoury has changed you. Umberto can throttle the birds. I've no talent for reading the bowl. You'll have to control yourself to interpret the blood."

She nodded, praying she would be able to do so. To her surprise and revulsion, he ushered her from the *garderobe* with an arm about her shoulders. He sat her in her seat once more and patted her hands. "There now. Afterwards, we'll drink a little sherry to settle you, and then a good night's sleep." He nodded curtly at Umberto. "Sacrifice the birds."

Umberto gave a start. "Me?"

"Yes, *you*! Who do you think I'm talking to, the walls? It's obvious she can't do it!" He turned back to Rana, still holding her hands.

Sucking in his lips and knowing better than to argue, Umberto reached into the cage. Scowling the whole time, he wrenched each bird by its neck, dropping every one onto the table.

Tomás nodded in approval. "Good. Now the blade."

Umberto removed a knife from a pocket in his sleeve. He presented it to Tomás who took it and pressed it into Rana's shaking hand. "Now," he whispered, nuzzling her ear as if muttering endearments, "we'll carve them together."

She shuddered. Her belly lurched, she gagged on her tongue, but there was nothing more in her stomach to lose. Tomás picked up the first bird. Gripping her hand beneath his, he set the point at its breast. With a sharp thrust, they began.

Her breathing sped, she had a sense of being watched, but Tomás' hand upon hers chased that fear away. As the blood dripped into the bowl, she suffered a second episode of panic. Her sense of smell spiralled out of control; she felt awash in blood, the coppery scent clogged her nose, coated her throat. Through all of it, she kept reminding herself that failure meant Angél's death. The knowledge steadied her, helped her to cope.

As her vision tunnelled, everything disappeared but the blood forming pictures in the water. At first she saw nothing, then realized she was gazing at a scene at night. A ghostly woman stood at the rail of a *nao*, staring out over an endless sea. She was veiled–Miriam shielding herself as she would have done from suspicious eyes. She reported what she saw to Tomás, but her voice was distant as if she straddled two places at once. Here and far away.

"Where?" His question drifted towards her, like a ship appearing out of fog.

There were no discernible landmarks. She concentrated on the *nao's* stern. A name came into focus. The *Phoenix*.

She told him.

"Good. We'll make inquiries. Now, de Rivera. We must make sure he's also on board."

In the lowest deck, she found Zara, Luci, Casi, and the Tribe. Also Ximen. But of Joachin, there was nothing.

"He isn't there."

"Find him."

She wasn't sure the blood would hold, or if she would. Once again, she tasted copper on her tongue and wondered if she had bitten herself. *Show me Joachin de Rivera*, she willed. Greyness swept over her vision. She felt faint. She fought it, knowing she mustn't fail Angél. Tomás kept his hand tightly upon hers.

The vision darkened. There were bodies, rows and rows of them, lying on shelves. Joachin de Rivera lay on one of them, sleeping fitfully, His back was a crosshatch of angry red scars.

"I think he's on a slave ship. I can't be sure," she murmured.

"Get me the name of that ship."

She concentrated on the lettering at the stern. Joachin disappeared. The ship, a carrack, judging from her build, was also at sea. From beneath the bright windows of the stern cabin, the name *La Estrella del Mar* appeared.

She reported it to Tomás.

"Two ships? Why, I wonder? Well, no matter-we'll soon find where they're bound. Focus on de Rivera. See if you can learn why he's a prisoner."

She tried to do as he said, but the water failed to offer more answers. The metallic taste in her mouth faded. Her vision cleared, although she felt weaker than ever. "It's done." She removed her trembling hand from beneath his.

He clapped her on the shoulders. "Too bad. Even so, you did well. It's amazing what a little motivation will do. Umberto, bring the sherry. She can use some."

Looking more put-out than usual, Umberto shuffled off to do his bidding. He soon returned with an amber decanter and two goblets. Tomás waved him away as if he were no more than a troublesome dog. Umberto retreated to stand by the door. Tomás poured a glass for himself, and gave one to Rana. He held up his cup to propose a toast.

"To us," he said expansively, "and a fresh start. You'll find I can be as generous as I can cruel. I think you'll prefer the former. Drink up. It'll soothe you."

Her fingers shook. In Diaphani culture, pregnant women weren't supposed to partake of alcohol. That didn't matter. Tomás must never know. She set the glass to her lips and sipped.

When she finished her cup, he ordered her to bed and joined her. In the darkness, she waited for him to force her legs apart, but thankfully, he left her alone.

Chapter Nine: Boyle

FRANCIS THANKED SUL as Joachin de Rivera opened his eyes. The man had had a restless night, often moaning in his sleep. From the hatch above, a bleak light seeped into the slave deck. The sharp peals of the watch bell cut over the constant creaking and groaning of the ship. To Francis' reckoning, it was dawn of the tenth day since they had set sail from Tenerifa.

He must be parched, Francis thought as Joachin licked his lips. In spite of the change in watch, it was anyone's guess when the crew would arrive with their gruel and water. Over the past few days, Iago had insisted the sailors give a portion of his water ration to Joachin. Barto of Andor had pried open his mouth so they might splash it down his throat. He had been impatient with the process, but his rough ministrations were finally paying off. Joachin de Rivera had finally come to his senses.

"*Buenos días.*"

Joachin met his glance. His gaze slid to the grill above. He reminded Francis of a fox, searching for a way out of its cage. "I'm here, on behalf of your wife," he added.

That caught his attention. "I remember you," Joachin said hoarsely. "You were in Don Lope's cabin."

"Yes. I insisted they treat you. You would have died, otherwise."

He nodded. "My thanks."

As he shifted to accommodate his back, Francis caught another glimpse of his tattoo. It reminded him of snakes crawling out of a box. Iago had said it was rare for Diaphani men to cut themselves, but as to why Joachin had done it, he wouldn't say. One thing was certain: Joachin de Rivera was no ordinary man.

"So tell me," Joachin rasped, breaking his train of thought, "why does a priest concern himself with the Diaphani, and in particular, with my wife?"

Francis hesitated. The deck was too open; there were too many ears. Don Lope knew of his involvement–the gold nuggets had been in his possession, after all–but he didn't know the extent of his connection to Inglais. "I'm not sure we should discuss that here."

"Where then? The vizconde's quarters?" Joachin quirked an eyebrow.

Francis smiled. In spite of everything he had been through, Joachin de Rivera still maintained a sense of humour. He liked that. The only people about them were slaves, kidnapped or sold to slavers from rival groups. It wasn't likely they would understand Esbañish. "Very well," he said. "I'm a Papal Nuncio, but don't hold that against me."

"I'll reserve judgment if Miriam sent you."

"She did."

"There has to be more to it than that. I can't believe you're motivated simply out of concern for my welfare. Or my wife's."

"I may be a priest, but we're not all bad."

"Eagles and doves."

"Excuse me?"

"The Diaphani and the Temple. We both know what happens when the two fly together."

"Ah, yes. But which one is the eagle, and which one, the dove?"

Joachin grimaced. "Isn't it obvious? You won't find many eagles down here."

"I guess I'm not really an eagle, then. I'm more of a...house fly."

"A house fly?" Joachin choked on a laugh.

"Let's say I buzz around a lot. I represent the interests of a certain personage who has nothing to do with the Temple."

"A personage."

"A woman."

"A priest with a woman." Joachin smirked. "Why am I not surprised?"

"It isn't how you think."

"How is it, then?"

Barto let out a snort. He appeared to be sleeping, but perhaps, he wasn't. While Joachin had been delirious, he had directed a lot of his resentment Joachin's way, blaming him for their predicament. Better to explain things when they had a moment above. "Let's discuss it, later."

Joachin's eyes narrowed. He didn't press, but his hand crept towards his tattoo. It was a stealthy move. *What's he up to?* Francis wondered. He was too adept at sleight of hand not to notice it.

And then, something grabbed him about the chest. For an instant, he couldn't breathe. There was an awful squeezing and then the thing was in his head, a foreign presence like disembodied hands tossing his memories to and fro. A vision flew past him–Ilysabeth, red and golden.

"You're involved with her, yet not," Joachin murmured, trapping his gaze. "Whoever she is, she's a beauty. You have excellent taste."

Too stunned to speak, he wasn't sure which upset him more, that Joachin was somehow rifling through his mind, or that there was nothing he could do about it.

A second image burst into his thoughts–Marco at fifteen, with his silky black hair and hooked nose. He was leaning in for a kiss. For a moment, Francis tasted the sweetness of his lips, and then Marco vanished.

"Really? So in spite of that red-haired beauty, you actually prefer men?"

Francis bristled. "You have no right! You're invading my privacy!" Marco had been his first love, nearly as special as Ilysabeth. How was Joachin shuffling through his mind? Did he hone in on emotionally-laden memories, like a hound scenting game?

"You hide beneath the habit, but it's all a cover. You're really an advocate for...for...."

Another probe, painful in its thrust. Ilysabeth burst into his mind again, flying past him like a comet. It was too much. His self-preservation reasserted itself. Joachin de Rivera wasn't the only one proficient at prying or in knowing how to deflect it. He had been a spy for far too long not to have some ability in that arena. He threw him an answer. "The Queen of Franca!"

"That's a lie!" Joachin dropped his hand from his chest as if he had touched filth. The intense scrutiny stopped. "I don't know what story you fed my wife, but I doubt if it's in our best interests." He turned his back on him.

Impossible as it was to believe, there it was. Joachin de Rivera had the ability to know the truth. "You didn't have to force it from me!" Francis sputtered. "I would've told you everything you wanted to know. I just didn't think *now* was the best time!"

"You have nothing I want to hear."

"I think I do. Not everyone around you is trustworthy."

That won him a begrudging look. "What are you talking about? If it's Iago, you're wrong—"

"Not Iago. Your sleeping friend there."

Joachin scowled. "Barto is fine."

"I'm not so sure."

From the look on his face, Joachin didn't want to believe him, but then, he hadn't been present when Barto had grumbled about keeping him alive. In any event, it was time to change the subject, especially while Joachin was willing to talk. "That tattoo on your chest–most men would choose strength over truth-discernment."

He grimaced. "I didn't choose it. It was forced upon me. By your good friend, the Grand Inquisitor."

"He's no friend of mine."

Joachin looked dubious.

"If you don't believe me, touch that tattoo of yours to confirm it." He waited for him to do it. When he didn't, he continued. "It must be hard, knowing the truth all the time."

Joachín shrugged, dismissing it. "It's harder because I can't lie. Tomás forced this tattoo on me so I would divulge the location of my people. Then he hunted them down and butchered them like the monster he is. I'm sure you can guess how I feel about *that*." Coals of anger burned hotly in his dark eyes.

"So you've a death debt you want to collect. I can help with that."

"The question is, why would you want to?"

"I'll get to that. Tomás also bears a tattoo. Do you know what it does?"

"It gives him exceptional speed."

"It can't be that exceptional. He still bears a wound." It dawned on him Joachín might have been responsible for it. "You?"

"If you mean the one on his face, yes."

"What about the one on his ribs?"

"Possibly. I tried to stab him, twice. The first time I failed. The second time, I succeeded because Miriam got in the way."

"Sounds like an interesting story."

"Another time." He turned to face him fully. "So who is this mysterious woman you represent? Your red-haired beauty?"

He hadn't wanted to say much with Barto present, but maybe it didn't make much difference. Even if Barto told Don Lope about him to better his lot, they were still at sea. His situation could hardly be worse. He might also earn Joachín's trust. "She's fairly important as world events go. My hope is she'll be the next Inglaisi queen."

"Inglais already has a queen."

"She would be the next in line, after Maria."

"Maria! She's bloodier than Tomás! Burning anyone not aligned with Roma...except...." Joachín faltered like a clock losing time. "Gods! You're here on behalf of, of...," and then he laughed, a feeble, helpless sound, "the Princess Ilysabeth! They say she's terrified the queen will behead her at any moment for high treason, and you, you...!"

Francis heard the approval in his voice, the endorsement of such a perilous attempt to save a woman he loved. Because he *did* love Ilysabeth despite his usual inclinations.

Joachin shook his head. "Gods, could any quest be more hopeless?"

"It won't be. Not if we have your help. She's the only woman I have ever loved, Joachin. The one true passion of my life."

Joachin touched his tattoo with the tip of his finger. There was a slight nudge, but it wasn't the invasion it had been. "Not so. You love *both* Ilysabeth and Inglais."

"Aren't they are one and the same?"

He had no answer for that, but Francis sensed his opinion of him had shifted. They were of similar mien, brothers in spirit, fueled by the same dangerous dreams.

Francis smiled to himself. He had won Joachin's trust.

Now, to see what things they might do.

Over the next half hour, they considered how they might escape. The slave deck was less than half full. It was likely Don Lope would dock in Dakra to take on more slaves. They stopped discussing it when the crew appeared with their gruel and water. Iago awoke and expressed his thanks to Lys that Joachin was alive and able to take his own food. Barto remained sullen. Twenty more slaves had died during the night. The crew complained they were a nuisance and threw them overboard. After that, everyone was forced onto the waist where they were doused with sea water. They formed a miserable, dripping group, about fifty-five slaves in all.

From the quarterdeck, Don Lope supervised the dousing. Francis couldn't help but sputter as the bosun upended a bucket of water over his head.

"A new kind of baptism for you, Priest?" Don Lope joked. His officers sniggered.

Francis glared at him. Gods, but what he wouldn't give to silence the man. "This isn't the last of it, you scoundrel! Once we make landfall, you'll answer to my contacts in Roma!"

Don Lope waved a negligent hand. "Give him another. He stinks worse than bilge."

Francis braced himself, but the second bucket never fell. A thin shout came from the crow's nest above. "*Capitán!* Northeast by east! Sail!"

The three officers drew their spy glasses to study the horizon. The crew hung motionless in the rigging. The morning sun filled the sky, making the waves as blinding as glass. Lieutenant de Silva, Don Lope's first mate, shouted at the main top. "What's she showing?"

"Red coat of arms! Five blue escutcheons on a white field!" floated down the reply.

De Silva turned to Don Lope. "She's outside the boundary." He shouted up at the crow's nest. "Is she coming toward us?"

"*Sí, Teniente!* Closing steadily!"

Don Lope dropped his glass and looked irritated. It was about time something didn't go his way, Francis thought. "Get those slaves down below!" he shouted.

They were hustled back down the stair, with no thought to the lengths of chain binding them. One man fell, pulling the rest of the line to their knees.

"Sort them!" de Silva yelled.

Portugeli, Francis considered, as he was shoved onto his pallet and re-shackled at the leg. The papal bull of 1493 decreed all lands one hundred leagues west of the Cabo Verdes were Esbañish possessions. Technically, the Portugeli ship was trespassing, but only if her intentions were malign. *Let it be so*, he thought.

Joachin caught his eye. His glance said it all: what were their chances? *Next to none*, Francis thought. At least, not while they were still chained.

Another collective shout came from above decks. Their guard dashed back up the companionway.

Iago poked him in the back, startling him. "What do you think she is?"

He reached for calm. "Portugeli, but maybe not. Even if she is, we can't hope for deliverance. As far as I know, Portugel and Esbaña are on good terms."

"I want these damned things off." Barto pulled at his shackles.

If Barto kept struggling, he would jar Joachin, possibly re-open his welts. "Leave them," Francis said. "You're not thinking about—"

Too late, Barto did it. Joachin gasped in pain.

"Now look what you've done!" Francis glared at Barto. Why did people not think before they acted? The last thing they needed was for Joachin to lapse back into insensibility. "Are you all right?" he asked him.

Joachin shook his head. "No. We're not."

"We?"

"The ship approaching us. I've seen her. I dreamt of her last night—"

"Dreamt of her?"

"What is it, Joachin?" Behind him, Iago trembled with excitement. "Do we escape Don Lope?"

Francis' mind spun. What was going on? Ever since he had set foot on this ship, events were whirling faster than a broken compass needle. Above them, men were running back and forth. Don Lope was shouting orders to reposition sail.

"We're about to be boarded." Joachin stared at the ceiling above. "Captain is over twenty stone, built like a barrel. Calls himself... Boyle."

"That's no Portugeli name!" Iago punched their pallet.

Francis jumped. "Stop that?" he demanded. He hated it when he wasn't in the know, which was almost never. "What are you two *on* about? Who is this Boyle? How do you know him?"

"Joachin's a dreamer! I thought you knew that." Iago sounded nonplussed.

"I don't seem to know anything! What's this about dreams? Doesn't everyone dream?"

"Not like Joachin does."

What was Iago suggesting? Weren't dreams the detritus of one's hopes and concerns? Nightmares borne from fear? Gods! Unless Joachin actually.... Francis stared at him. "Do you mean to say, you dream the *future?*"

Joachin nodded. "I was born with the gift, unlike the other which was foisted upon me."

"And your dreams come true?"

"They wouldn't be much of a gift if they didn't."

The prospect was stunning. Joachín had not one talent, but two. Not only did he speak the truth, but he also dreamed true. Could his truth-saying apply to future events? Or to things he didn't yet know? Gods, what a combination. "Say it! Say, Boyle is Portugeli."

"What's the point? We both know Boyle's an Inglaisi name."

"Humour me. I suspect if you can't say it, it isn't true."

Judging from his astonishment, the idea had never occurred to him. "Boyle is...is Por...Pppor...I can't say it! Sweet Lys!"

"Then he's not Portugeli, and the colours they're flying are false." Francis felt a flush of victory, but it was short-lived. "Which means only one thing. The ship approaching isn't who she claims to be."

The sudden boom of cannon fire confirmed it. When their ears cleared, panicked shouts came from every quarter of the ship.

For three terrifying hours, they listened to the thunder of guns as Don Lope sought to outrun the threat. *La Estrella del Mar* was built for cargo, broad-beamed and not easily manoeuvrable. Having only twelve *medio-culebrinas* amidships, she was pitifully out-armed. They heard the crew's panic as their attackers closed, the curses of the invaders as they drew alongside, the scrape of grappling hooks, the screams, crash, and thump of hand-to-hand combat. One deep baritone out-boomed the rest. By the time they were forced to stand on a blood-soaked deck, it was plain their new masters weren't there to save them. Instead, they taunted the wounded and tossed the dead to the waves. Francis stood with Joachín and Iago, while Barto remained slightly apart. Don Lope and his lieutenants had been propped against the main mast with their hands tied behind their backs. One side of the vizconde's face was bloody. He appeared to be missing an ear.

"By the tits o' yer mother whore, what were y' thinkin', y'stupid Esbañish git?" The captain, a bristling black-haired man, aimed a vicious kick at Don Lope's head. "When yer threatened by Boyle, y' don't run! Y' surrender! Y've made me lose half me crew! Worse, y've ruined m' stole!" He yanked a sticky pelt from about his shoulders and shook it in Don Lope's face. "Do y' know what this is? It's *ermine*, y' snot! I should cut a new one from yer stinkin' hide!" He raised his cutlass to strike him.

His first mate intervened. He was a tall, auburn-haired man, not as ostentatiously dressed as the captain, but well put together and cleaner than the rest. He moved with an easy grace. "Hostages, Captain," he reminded him, his expression tight. Francis wondered if the two had crossed verbal swords before.

Boyle stared him down. "Y' interferin', Mister Dirk?"

"Of course not, sir. But being noble, they're worth more to us alive."

"Which means I got to parley with bloody Esbañish gits, when I hate 'em all!" He pointed his cutlass at Don Lope. "I'd rather string his guts aroun' th' mast."

Some of the crew cheered at that. Others remained watchful. Francis suspected they had seen such barbarity before.

"It's up to you, of course." The mate lifted his hand in a negligent way. "But if you take him, it's for your entertainment alone. I still maintain the men should have their share in the ransom."

An uncomfortable silence fell, broken only by the snap of sail. Everyone awaited the captain's decision.

Boyle kicked Don Lope in the ribs, striking the sneer from his face. The vizconde fell like a sack to the deck. "Stupid boot licker! Where's all th' silver you Esbañish are rumoured t' have? I got no use for slaves!" He stomped back and forth and then spun about on his heel. "Next time, fly a proper flag from your Sul-blasted ship!" He spat on him and turned away. "Sort the salvage, Mister Dirk. Might's as well see what we've got."

"Aye, sir." Dirk directed several crew members to the task. On the quarterdeck, Boyle dropped into a chair Francis recognized from Don Lope's cabin. "Fetch me a drink, Tucker," he said, ordering the weasel-like man behind him. "Surely to Sul, they've sherry on this bloody ship."

A moan drew Francis' attention aside. Beside him, Joachin was swaying. His eyes were glazed, and his lips were tight with pain.

"Sul's Balls!" Iago caught him as he fell. He stared at Francis in horror. Red stained his hands. Several of Joachin's welts were bleeding.

A member of Boyle's crew approached them. He eyed Francis with glee and clapped a hand upon his shoulder. "Oy! Captain! We got us a Solar, here!"

Boyle lurched to his feet. "A god-buggerin' Solar?" His breathing grew hoarse. "Bring th' bastard up here!"

"Can't! He's chained, Captain!"

"Well, unchain him!" Boyle waved at Dirk who held the keys. "See to it!"

Francis' mind whirled. Boyle was eyeing him as if he were a boatload of dung. It had to be personal, but why?

"What's your business on this ship, Solar?" the first mate asked him tersely. Something flickered behind those grey eyes, a reluctance to mishandle a priest perhaps, or something else.

"I was attempting to buy these men's freedom." Francis nodded at Joachin, Iago, and Barto. "The vizconde chained this man..." he indicated Joachin, "to the floor of his cabin and abused him."

"Abused him?" He lifted a ruddy eyebrow.

"Not like that. He used him for a carpet. They have a history—"

"Dirk! What the hell are y' doin? Bring th' bugger up here!"

Dirk faced him. "There's a story, here, Captain!"

"I don' give a rat's arsehole! I only care about givin' back what was got!"

Francis considered the captain. They were both Inglaisi. Maybe he could appeal to him on the basis of their shared heritage. Most Inglaisi hated the Esbañish. "Don Lope double-crossed us! We're the victims, here!"

"So, the Solarium didn't get its tithes like it hoped?" Boyle sneered. "I don't give a shite! Y' know why? 'Cause I hate priests!" He gathered up his crew with a glance. "I'm all for some entertainment! How about you?"

They shook their fists and cheered.

Francis could only imagine what kind of entertainment he might provide. Boyle seemed to detest priests even more than he loathed Esbañiards.

"Surely, we should hear his tale first, Captain!" the first mate said.

Francis regarded him in surprise. Why was he intervening? Was it superstition? Or fear of calling down Sul's wrath? Was he motivated by greed?

"I'll tell yer a tale!" Boyle was so flushed he reminded him of a turnip in velvet. "How about th' time I strung m'self a hand necklace from th' last buggers who crossed me? Feckin' priests are too ready with their hands—"

"Captain, it will stink. Like the last time," the first mate reminded him.

The last time? Whose hands had they been? Francis wondered. Tales that grisly always made the Temple rounds. The Holy Father would have called on every government to put an end to the perpetrators, no matter what the cost. Why hadn't he heard? *And worse, he's talking about me! My hands!* Sweat beaded his upper lip.

"Fine. Cock fight, then." Boyle slumped back into his chair, a king tired of arguing with diplomats. "Solar versus Vizconde." He leaned on one elbow. "Whoever wins can weave us a tale. Make a ring, you lot! Arm 'em with swords! First one to kill th' other, wins the day. Either one steps out o' line, an' y've m' permission t' carve 'em t' mince."

"I hope you know how to defend yourself, Solar," Dirk muttered, unshackling him. He gripped him by the elbow and led him through the throng. Murmuring followed in their wake. Bets were being made. He suspected he wasn't the favourite. The crew shoved the slaves out of the way.

Two more men pulled Don Lope to his feet. As well as missing an ear, fresh blood stained his doublet. *Broken ribs, hopefully,* Francis thought. As for himself, fear was spurring him, but he didn't know how long it would serve. He had killed before, but never when he was this dehydrated or weak.

Dirk pressed a cutlass into his hand and stepped back quickly, leaving him to face Don Lope alone. Another member of the crew armed Don Lope similarly. The pirates gave them a wide berth. The shouting began.

Don Lope stared at his weapon as if he didn't quite believe he held it. Then he barked with laughter. "So, it comes to this." He regarded

Francis. "We're to butcher each other, like cocks in a ring. I finish you, and they grant me life. You kill me, and you hold them a Mass."

The crew howled with laughter.

"Get on with it," Boyle yelled from the quarterdeck, "or I'll come down there an' carve ye, m'self!"

Don Lope straightened as if emboldened by his words.

So much for cracked ribs. Francis revised his earlier estimate. The vizconde began to circle him slowly, searching for weaknesses with a sharp eye. If the loss of an ear pained him, he gave no indication of it. Francis countered each step, making sure he didn't come too close. *Oh, for a pouch of my blue powder*, he thought. Herbs were less messy than swords and blood.

With a sudden lunge, Don Lope leapt at him, the point of his cutlass jabbing for his chest. Francis jumped out of reach. The vizconde's upper lip had twitched before he moved, giving him away. *How like the old commedia days, when I used to play to the crowd*, Francis thought. It was such a relief not to be on the offensive. Looking cowardly was exactly how he wanted to appear. *With luck, he'll get caught up in the excitement and forget I'm not a priest.* Not that Don Lope knew who he was exactly, but he had his suspicions.

Time for a little theatre. "Deliver me from my enemies, O Sul!" he cried. "Protect me from those who would rise up against me!" It was an old psalm about the smiting of enemies. Every pirate, save Dirk, the first mate, roared.

Good audience, Francis thought.

"He's prayin'! Can y' believe it?" From his perch on the quarterdeck, Boyle slapped his thigh.

"Ddd...deliver me from evildoers and bloodthirsty men!" Yes, his voice had just the right tremulo to it. As he ran, his black hem bounced about his knees, making him look even more ridiculous. Don Lope mimicked him, trotting after him like a pony.

"Oh, Lord! Show the wicked no mercy!" He darted for the main mast. If he put it between them, the vizconde would be forced to open his guard. As he expected, the thud of boots increased behind him–Don Lope sprinting to close their distance. From the corner of his eye, he watched as the don lifted his blade to deliver a killing blow.

And...now! He tumbled out of the way. Don Lope's cutlass whizzed over his head. There was a thunk as the sword struck the mast. He rolled to his feet, swinging for the back of the don's knee to hamstring him.

Instead, a boot struck his shin. He fell to the deck with a crash. In horror, he stared into de Silva's sneering face. The lieutenant had his hands behind his back, but he had lashed out, knocking him off balance. Shouts of foul rose from amongst the crew. The back of his neck felt too exposed. He twisted and grabbed the lieutenant by the shoulders, pulling him hard against his chest. Don Lope plunged his sword into de Silva's back. He and Francis rocked from the impact.

De Silva's face contorted, his expression reminding Francis of sexual ecstasy at a most inopportune time. Fortunately, Don Lope also gaped and faltered in shock. As de Silva baptized him in blood, Francis threw him aside and swung his cutlass at Don Lope with every bit of remaining strength he had.

The blade took Don Lope through the neck. Still wearing an expression of horror, his head flew through the air like a badly lobbed cannonball. Men scattered out of its path. Don Lope's body toppled at Francis' feet, spurting blood. From behind them, Carlos, Don Lope's second mate, screamed threats. With his hands still tied behind his back, the boy struggled to his feet and charged.

Francis spun about and stabbed him through the eye. The ferocity of the blow pierced the boy's skull, the point erupting through his head.

The crowd went mad—in outrage, in support, Francis wasn't sure. Carlos fell to the deck beside Don Lope, pulling Francis off balance. Teetering unsteadily, Francis righted himself and set a boot to Carlos' shoulder to pull his sword free. Shouting filled his ears. He had had no choice but to kill the boy. Honour would have dictated Carlos collect the death debts for both his uncle and his brother. Had he lived, he would have found a way to exact his revenge.

Once again, the deck was slippery with blood. Francis regarded the ring of wrathful, calculating faces about him. Many of them weren't happy; they had bet against him and lost. He wished he wasn't shaking so much. His heel slipped on the wood. "Anyone else?" he asked with more bravado than he felt.

Dirk, Boyle's first mate, approached him with caution. He held his own cutlass at the ready. "Drop your sword."

He eyed him, not trusting he could take on another. But if he had to, he would fight.

Dirk seemed to read his mind. "It's over. You've won."

"So, I have my life?"

"It means, we talk." He cast a careful glance at Boyle.

The captain was glaring down at them, his scowl suggesting he was not at all pleased with this turn of events. His hands kept squeezing and releasing the deck rail as if he wished it were Francis' neck. The moment lengthened. Francis read his death sentence in Boyle's eyes. Seconds later, the pirate confirmed it. "Doesn't matter. Kill th' bastard!"

"No!" a few members shouted, although there were also a few 'ayes'.

"That's not fair, sir," Dirk replied. "The lieutenant interfered."

A number of the men added their protests to Dirk's. Perhaps they were the ones who had bet against the odds.

"I am captain!" Boyle bellowed, reminding them. The crew exchanged glances.

"A vote?" Dirk appealed to the company.

This time the ayes were in the majority. "Aye!"

While in Roma, Francis had read about the Brethren. They formed a democracy of sorts. Boyle might not like it, but he was as bound to his men as they were to him. He could hardly dismiss the crew's idea of justice, warped as it was.

Boyle eyed Dirk sourly, as if he were a tick burrowing beneath his skin. "Fine. We'll abide by the rules o' the Fellowship." He took a long moment to survey each mate, as if to coerce him into voting his way. "What fool here, thinks we should let th' Solar live? All in favour, say 'aye'."

"Hold!" Dirk raised a hand. "A word before we vote! We've lost men. We need good fighters. The priest has demonstrated he's more than what he seems. I'm not a religious man. Perhaps Sul is on his side, I don't know. But despite what the captain thinks, it may be bad luck to kill a priest. If the Solar agrees to join us, why not let him? Think on that, before you cast your vote!"

"Are y' done?" Boyle demanded.

Dirk nodded.

"Then who thinks th' Solar should be spared? Say aye if y' think he should live!"

A roar of ayes resounded in Francis' ears. Dirk had made a winning argument. Either his skill or their fear had won the day.

"Against?" Dirk prompted.

A few half-hearted shouts accompanied Boyle's booming "Nay!"

"It's settled then, Captain," Dirk said unnecessarily. "He lives."

Boyle clasped his hands behind his back and scowled down at Francis. "Very well, Mister Dirk. I'll abide by the Comp'ny's wishes. Bring Father Shite up here."

Father Shite. Apparently, he had earned a new nickname. He could live with it if he had to. All of a sudden, he was weak in the knees. Grey shrouded his vision. The stress of the day was taking its toll. He shook his head and fought to stay on his feet.

Dirk sailed into his line of sight, smiling at him. Despite feeling faint, he felt his blood quicken in a way he hadn't experienced for a very long time. Gods, his smile–it was warm, inviting. Could it be? In all likelihood, he wasn't of the persuasion. But even if he were...no, I can't afford the distraction. It has to be the after-effect of killing three men, Francis decided. Dirk set a hand on his forearm and guided him up the stair.

"My friends, also," Francis whispered.

"What friends?" Dirk's ruddy brows drew together.

He pointed at Iago, Barto, and Joachin.

"Don't push your luck."

"I must."

Dirk drew a deep breath. "Very well. I'll do what I can." They climbed the companionway to the quarterdeck together. Boyle loomed before them, as friendly as a rabid bear.

"So, th' vote's been made, and you've won yer place," he said testily, "but no one serves on the Raven who doesn't sign." There was a hopeful glint in his eye. He meant the Articles, of course, the contract signed by all members of a pirate ship, although Francis had never seen one. He wasn't sure he could agree to its conditions. What if

Boyle took an Inglaisi prize? Would Ilysabeth turn a blind eye? On the other hand, if it ever came to it, he could say he signed under duress. "Perhaps, if I knew what I was signing?" he asked.

Boyle settled into his chair. "Advise 'im of 'is rights and requirements, Mister Dirk."

Dirk recited from memory. "Article One: every man shall obey the captain in all respects." Francis nodded. Boyle's nostrils flared as if catching a waft of fart.

"Article Two: when prizes are taken, the captain receives two shares, the first mate…," Dirk flashed him another dazzling smile, "one and a half shares, the helmsman, carpenter, bosun, and gunners, one share, the remainder to be split equally among the crew."

Francis nodded.

"Article Three: any man stealing from the company, keeping a secret, or running away during battle, will be marooned or shot."

Francis kept his face bland. The last thing he wanted was to let on about Joachin's abilities. His duo talents as truth-sayer and dreamer would be seen as either a boon or a liability. He wasn't sure which way the captain would sail. He nodded.

"Article Four: no fighting on board. All quarrels to be ended on shore and decided by cutlass or pistol." Which was rich, considering Boyle had wanted him dead.

"Of course."

"Article Five: no dicing, hiding women or boys on board, or carrying bare flame without a lantern. He who offends, earns forty lashes.

"And finally, Article Six: musicians to rest on Sul's Day, but no other day with favour."

"You needn't have told 'im th' last one," Boyle said irritably. He glared at Francis. "Y' don't sing as well as fight, do ye?"

"No."

"Pity. Thought all priests sang. 'Specially on a fire ship."

He was still testing him. It would be that way for the entire tour, wherever they sailed. One of the sailors had fetched the contract from their ship. With a flourish, Dirk handed him a quill. Without hesitation, Francis signed Father Shite at the bottom of the bond. It was just another alias, known only to Boyle and his crew. "Now, for my friends," he added.

"What friends?" Boyle looked outraged.

"The men who accompanied me." He pointed out Joachin, Iago, and Barto.

Boyle reddened. He looked as if he were about to say something, then snapped his mouth shut like a marlin on a hook.

"Is there a problem, Captain?" Francis had the strangest feeling Dirk was baiting Boyle.

Boyle glared at him. "The giant, maybe, but not them other two. I want them off my ship!"

"Where would we put them? On the Raven?"

"No! Sul's balls!"

"Do they offend you in some way?" Francis asked.

"Do they offend me?" Boyle sputtered. "Do they...you offend me, y' goddamned Solar! Diaphani are bad luck!"

"What do you suggest we do with them?" Dirk asked.

"Toss 'em overboard!"

"We can't do that."

"Why th' hell not? What makes you so damned charitable all of a sudden, Mister Dirk? You love gypsies, now? And priests?"

"It isn't charity. It's appearances, sir. The men will wonder who you'll eliminate next. They look like us, sir. If Shite vouches for them...."

"Bloody hell! I'll get rid o' them m'self!" Boyle shoved Dirk aside and charged for the companionway, brandishing his sword.

Francis stepped in his way, striking Boyle speechless. Boyle's eyes bulged with rage. "There are gold nuggets in Don Lope's quarters!" Francis said before he could recover. "From Xaymaca. The gypsies know where to find them. The older one-he's seen a map." It was the only thing he could think of to save Joachin and Iago.

For a brief second, he thought Boyle might cut him down where he stood. He breathed heavily, but Francis detected a shift in his mood. Perhaps it was the chance he had taken in confronting him, or maybe it was something else. Boyle's eyes lost their wildness and his expression turned cagey. "A map?"

"Yes. Of a gold mine."

He stuck out his chin. "How much gold?"

"It's from a vein as thick as your arm."

His gaze settled on Joachin and Iago. Some emotion Francis couldn't fathom crossed his face–suspicion, fear?–and then it was gone.

"Perhaps a trial period, to see how they work out?" Dirk suggested.

Boyle spun about on his heel. "Learn what they know. An' keep 'em out o' my sight! I don't want t' see or hear 'em. Better they were never on board."

"Aye, sir." Dirk shared a look with Francis and shrugged.

They watched as Boyle lumbered across the deck, intent on reaching the great cabin to search for the nuggets. The crew shoved slaves out of the way to allow him through. As he drew near Joachin and Iago, he made a curious gesture with his right hand. It happened so quickly, Francis couldn't see what it was.

But Joachin did. It had an effect. He seemed to dwindle, almost to disappear, as if wanting to fade into the crowd.

Chapter Ten: Knots

AFTER BEING A week out from the port of *Santa Sul*, Miriam and the Tribe suffered less from sea sickness. The twelve foot waves took some getting used to, in spite of Captain Vrooman advising them the sea was calm. As the *Phoenix* sailed south-west, the days grew warmer and the breezes brisker. The orlop deck turned stifling. Miriam and the Tribe spent much of their time above decks, doing their best to stay out of the crew's way. Luci gained the approval of Henk Ostrander, the second mate, when she and the other women offered to mend damaged sail. Zara helped prepare food. No one got sick from bad food or water. These allowances weren't seen in a good light by Jager de Groot or the starboard crew, but they kept their mutterings to themselves. The women fell into a routine. The larboard crew didn't mind the distraction they provided, and they were a much politer group than their counterparts.

When the work was done, or it demanded less attention, Ignaas regaled them with stories of when he was a young man encountering tribes along the Afrikaan coast, or when he fished for *bacalao* in the north where ice mountains grew as huge as castles.

"They don't get that big, surely," Zara scoffed as she poured a sack of beans into a pail.

"That they do, Missus. I seen 'em with m' own eyes. I'd never mislead ye." His intimation that he was an honest man with honest intentions wasn't lost on Zara, nor anyone else. Despite her unrequited love for Ximen, she found Ignaas a pleasant distraction. Luci and the women mended sail not far off, while Casi and Kip practiced knots.

"I'm not sure I'd like to get that close to one." She pursed her lips.

"Well, it might take some time getting used to, but it would be well worth yer while."

"Why, it'd be freezing cold!"

"Only at first. With a little encouragin' from ye, it'd melt." He winked at her. She blushed. Miriam hid her smile.

"That's *not* how you do it." Kip pointed at Casi's snarl of rope. "You pass the tail through the loop, then wrap it around the end. Then you pass the tail back, to finish it."

Casi frowned. "I did that."

"No, you didn't. You tied the tail around the loop."

She glanced at him in sudden annoyance and threw down her length of twine. "I'm *not* a stupid girl! You've had more practice!"

His mouth fell open. "I never said!"

"Might as well! You thought—" She snapped her mouth shut. Luci glanced up from her mending.

"I never did!" Kip looked both guilty and dumbfounded.

"Of course, you didn't, Kip," Luci said smoothly. She shot a look at Casi. "Casi jumped to that conclusion. Didn't you, *niña?*"

Miriam and Zara exchanged a glance.

"Here, let's all get along," Ignaas said gruffly. "Show me yer knot, Casi."

She picked up her length and gave it to him.

"Ah, there's yer problem. Y' need to slip it back through th' loop to get a proper bowline."

"That's what *I* said!"

The old man regarded Kip. "Sometimes, it's *how* y' tell a lady that makes all th' diff'rence, boy. You gotta talk to 'em polite an' gentle." He smiled sweetly at Zara. "He'll learn."

Kip coloured. Casi blushed too.

She's growing up, Miriam thought. Zara and Ignaas weren't the only ones who were interested in each other.

Casi glanced up at her in astonishment. Miriam bit her lower lip. She couldn't prevent Casi from hearing her thoughts, nor could anyone else, for that matter. Kip must have thought her a stupid girl, but he had done it out of self-defence, not knowing how to manage his attraction.

Casi grew wide-eyed.

It's all right, Casi, she told her silently, holding her gaze. *He's probably a nice boy, deep down. He just feels a little awkward around you.*

"Like this?" Casi turned to Kip to show him the corrected knot.

"That's right!" He seemed genuinely pleased she had asked him instead of Ignaas.

Miriam smiled. Casi was young, but she was already developing a rudimentary understanding of the opposite sex.

"Let me show you how to do a running bowline." Kip beckoned her to follow him, so they might sit slightly apart from the group. He pointed to a rat line. "You tie it to another line or a pole. It's a good knot for hanging things."

"Mind, you take that down as soon as yer done," Ignaas called after them. "Can't have that blowin' loose in th' wind."

"We will," Kip replied. Near the port rail, he and Casi soon had their heads together. Miriam wondered if their talk would remain on knots.

"It's nice they've someone their own age t' talk to," Ignaas told Zara.

"Like us oldsters, I suppose." Zara shifted on her stool.

"I may be old, but not you! When I look at ye, I see a woman in 'er prime!"

"Oh! Flatterer!"

"Not at all!"

Ximen walked past them studying the sea, or perhaps he was savouring the breeze. He ignored Zara, but nodded politely to Luci as he passed by. Zara eyed him surreptitiously and then sniffed, her intent clear. His lack of acknowledgment was of no importance to her.

"You an' him." Ignaas hadn't missed the exchange. "You connected in some way?"

"He's a distant cousin."

"Strikes me, he's not too keen on y' ladies helping us out 'round here."

"It isn't that." Miriam watched Ximen navigate his path. "He has a great deal on his mind." She would check with him later for his daily update on Joachin's condition. She was thankful Joachin was recovering as well as could be expected. Ximen had told her earlier that Iago had been giving Joachin portions of his water and food.

"His eyes. He's got them *catracks*, don't he? How's 'e see?"

She wasn't about to tell him that Ximen was blind, but he saw the immediate past through the Tribe's eyes. She often wondered how he did it. The environment onboard a ship was in constant flux. Perhaps that's why he waited until everyone else was above decks, so he might see the lay of things. "He has some handicap in that regard, but he manages quite well," she said.

"I seen others with that much white. Happens after a life at sea. Th' sun an' water blinds 'em. I'm one o' th' lucky ones, I guess."

"You've never wanted to settle?" Zara stirred the beans. "Find yourself a good woman to cook and keep house for you?"

"Guess I never found th' right one." He grinned at her. "Or maybe, I hankered too much after adventure an' change."

"Oh, I know *all* about change. One doesn't have to go to sea for that. Lots to see and do on land. We Diaphani don't stay in one place for long."

"It's temptin'. Mebbe I should trade m' sea legs fer a wagon. In th' meantime, I got this meal t' do."

"If I had thyme, I could make these beans fit for a king." Zara sighed.

"I got thyme! I been saving it for th' rice an' fish, but if y' think y' can make th' pork better—"

"You just watch me, Master Ignaas! You'll think you've been to heaven and back."

"Heaven? Can't say no to that, Missus."

"Zara."

"Missus Zara."

"Just Zara. I'm a widow, you know."

Miriam rose. Everything seemed to be well in hand. She should return to the orlop deck to see how Alonso was faring, learn if he had anything new to tell. "I can fetch the thyme if you like," she offered.

"No, Missus. Kip'll do it. Kip!" Ignaas hailed him. "Put them ropes away, and go below. I need you to fetch Missus Zara some thyme."

Kip and Casi glanced his way. "Want to come?" Kip asked Casi.

She hesitated, then shook her head. "No. It's better if I stay up here. Maré might need me."

"Okay." He shrugged.

"But you can tell me more when you get back!" she added. "What did you say those things were, when you slide on the canals when they turn to ice?"

"Skates."

"Skates! How do they work?"

"It's easy. You attach 'em t' yer boots an' push off—"

"Kip! You can talk 'er ear off, when y' get back." Ignaas waved him away and turned to Zara. "His *moeder* used t' take 'im skatin' in Amsterden 'fore she died. It's one o' th' things he misses most."

"Skating? I never heard of it."

"Y' glide, like a swan." He demonstrated, holding his arms aloft. "When I was a young man, we'd race...."

Miriam didn't hear the rest of the story. She followed Kip down the companionway. They descended to the main deck, where Jager and his cronies were huddled in the dusky light. Jager scowled as she passed, but she ignored him. At the cooking station, Kip turned off. She continued down the companionway until she reached the orlop deck, thankful for its peace even with the air so close. She soon found Alonso. She stretched out her hand and his rat scampered toward her.

Thank Sul, you've come. He sprang into existence as she tucked the rat into her pocket. *Pirates have taken La Estrella del Mar off the Cabo Verdes.*

Fear punched the air from her lungs. *What? Dear Lys! Are Joachin, Barto, and Iago all right?*

I can't tell. There's been a fight, hand to hand combat. Don Lope and over half of La Estrella's crew are dead. The rest have surrendered. The pirates have forced the slaves below.

What will they do with them, do you think?

Sell them once they reach a port.

Gods help us, which one?

I have no idea.

What of Francis?

Interesting you should ask. He killed Don Lope in a sword fight. Now, he's part of their crew.

She was so stunned she had to lean against a barrel to catch her breath.

It may not be so bad. If Francis can convince the pirates, they might sign Joachin, Iago, and Barto, too.

Sign them?

Under what they call the Articles. It's a type of contract, binding the crew together. Rules about sharing plunder, that sort of thing. Francis also mentioned the gold on Xaymaca.

So they might sail there? I pray they do! On the other hand, if they're caught.... It mattered little which naval power apprehended them. Pirates were hung for their crimes. She hated to ask him to return so soon to *La Estrella del Mar*, but it was necessary. *Can you go back? See what else transpires?*

I'd rather stay here, with you.

But if you go now, we can learn of their plans. I'd feel much better knowing, Alonso.

He sighed. *Very well. If you like.*

She didn't like, but she needed to learn where their future lay. She wished they had the luxury to snuggle in the dark and not worry.

The thought mollified him. He blew her a kiss and faded away. The rat slipped from her pocket. She held still, afraid it might bite her, but Alonso's influence seemed to have bewildered it. It crawled from her lap and disappeared into the dark.

The thyme wasn't where Ignaas said, so Kip took longer to find it, despite the ruddy light arising from cooking pit from the deck below. As he searched the galley, he thought of Casi, the Diaphani girl. She was pretty, she made him feel important. Which was good, because being the lowest ranking member of the *Phoenix*, he was never treated with much respect. It was nice to be thought of as smart. He especially liked it when she asked about his old life. On the other hand, her accusing him of calling her stupid *had* been creepy. He had thought it, but she had responded as if he had insulted her out loud. Did girls read minds? Alarming thought.

Or was she something even more sinister, a witch, like Jager and his cronies said? That couldn't be. She was young and sweet, and a bit shy-not at all like the crones selling bread on the corners of Amsterden. She was also a lot easier to talk to, once she had stopped accusing him of his thoughts. Maybe she had imagined it, like her *moeder* had said.

Girls were whimsical creatures. They imagined stuff all the time. Boys, too.

He blushed deeply. Pray to Sul, she didn't suspect him of *that*.

The thyme finally revealed itself above a barrel of salted herring, one of Captain Vrooman's concessions to the northerly-born crew. Kip didn't like herring, but Ignaas assured him it was good for building muscle and growing a beard. He rubbed his chin and felt soft down there. *I wonder what she thinks of beards*, he thought. A beard would make him look older.

He retrieved the box of thyme, stepped from the galley, and caught his breath. Jager de Groot stood in his way, all pale blonde hair, massive muscles, and peeling skin. He looked like one of the northern ice trolls his granny used to tell him about. "I got a task for you," he growled. "It's a small thing."

The bosun scared him, although he would never admit that to anyone. "I don't take orders from you," he said stiffly. He was Ignaas' assistant. He wasn't required to listen to Jager. He shoved past him.

Jager grabbed him by the arm and slammed him against the galley's bulkhead, knocking the wind from his lungs. He gasped to catch his breath.

"I don't like your cheek, Monkey. You and Gimp-Leg." Jager shook him. "You got some nerve interferin' with me and that veiled *hoer*."

Kip swallowed.

"Furthermore, it's just a matter o' time before those *heksen* do something, so I'm goin' t' help the captain see their evil. This is what yer goin' t' do." He handed him a tiny packet, folded over a number of times. "Yer goin' to add this t' the captain's food. Only a few grains at a time."

"What is it?"

"Never you mind. Only a few grains at each meal. Do that, an' I'll take it from there."

"And if I don't?"

Jager grabbed him by the throat and slammed him a second time against the wall. Pain shot through the back of his skull. His knees melted into seawater. "'Cause if y' don't, you'll pay th' price." Jager released him and he collapsed to the floor. The box of thyme tumbled and split, scattering herb everywhere.

Jager poked the evil packet into Kip's shirt. "Remember what I said. A few grains, is all. Any more, an' yer committin' murder. I'll expect t' see th' results o' yer efforts later t'night. Tell anyone, an' you'll get more o' this." He kicked him in the ribs. Then he slipped from the galley.

For several minutes, Kip lay where he was, unable to move. Then slowly, painfully, he climbed to his knees. He bit his lip to keep from crying and swept up the thyme.

Chapter Eleven: On La Serina del Sol

ANGÉL'S CHARTER, LA *Serina del Sol* was a broad-bellied, twenty-four gun galleon, sturdily built for transporting cannon. Tomás was in high spirits. They had received confirmation both sought-for ships, the *Phoenix* and *La Estrella del Mar*, had several ports of call, the first being Tenerifa in the Canarias. After that, their paths diverged. The *Phoenix* sailed for Nueva Esbaña, to make final port in Xaymaca, while the *La Estrella* bore directly there. Tomás had also learned *La Estrella* was a slave ship, owned by his old friend Don Lope, the Vizconde of Qadis.

"And to think as I guested in his *palacio*, de Rivera lay in the dungeon, right beneath my feet." It was mid-morning. He and Rana stood on the wharf, watching their trunks hoisted aboard *La Serina del Sol*. Rana cast a sidelong glance at Tomás. He was actually smirking, the first time she had seen him do so. To keep up appearances, he had replaced the bandage about his head, but had risen from their chamber at dawn, much improved. The cut across his jaw was nearly gone. The new tattoo was working quickly. He no longer limped.

Capitán de Carazo appeared at the ship's rail near the gangplank. "Welcome aboard, your Radiance! And welcome to your beautiful *hermana*! Everything is in readiness for you. Your quarters are ready. Allow my men to help you cross."

Two sailors were dispatched to assist Tomás along the gangplank. Two more strapped Rana into a harness and hoisted her on board. Her stomach dropped to her knees as they swung her across the gap between ship and dock, but she managed to hold onto her breakfast, refusing to embarrass herself as they manoeuvred her onto the waist. Angél was there, quick to release her and help her embark. His hands were warm and his expression earnest. Her heart fluttered at the sight of him.

Under the premise of untangling her from the ropes, he murmured into her ear. "I'd speak with you, later. In private, if possible." He looked haunted. She could tell there was much he wanted to say. Whatever his confession, it wasn't meant for her. The knowledge stung, but his love had always been what she coveted, even if under a ruse. She doubted they would have a chance to talk. If she wasn't at Tomás' side, he would confine her to quarters.

As it turned out, Capitán de Carazo, believing she was Tomás' sister, had taken Tomás at his word. He had prepared a small cabin for her alone. It contained a tidy bunk, a small writing desk and a wardrobe. Her trunk had been stowed at the end of her bed. No lock would keep Tomás out for long, but the seclusion was an unexpected luxury. Feeling tired from the morning's preparations, she sat down on her bed and sighed.

Tomás appeared at her door, displeased. "I should have expected this. We'll have to be discreet."

He stepped into her cabin but allowed the door to remain ajar. Here, on a ship crowded with officers and crew, and watches changing every four hours, little remained private. He would find a way around it, of course, but it would hinder him. The knowledge bolstered her.

"Tonight, after we dine, I'll come to you when it's convenient. Perhaps, we'll share a bottle of wine. I'm much better this morning. Almost myself."

She forced herself to nod. As much as he might value her for her magic, it was wiser to lull him into believing she preferred their new arrangement, that his lack of cruelty had shown that life might not be so unpleasant. At sea, she would have to endure him for another six weeks, but after that, she could escape with Angél after persuading him their lives were in danger. As for the child she carried, babies arrived sooner than expected, all the time. She need only bed Angél once to convince him he was responsible.

"We're about to leave port. Would you like to watch from the rail? It's quite the sight, sails billowing as the wind catches them, the dock receding, the cries of the officers as they direct the crew. I expect you've never seen it."

She couldn't believe the courtesy he was extending her. It had everything to do with Miriam Medina.

"I'm tired, Tomás." She rubbed her forehead. She had barely slept the night before, fearing he would awaken her. "I'd like to rest."

He frowned slightly and glanced about her quarters, looking for anything with which she might hurt herself. Other than a letter opener, which he tucked into a sleeve, there was nothing. "Should I have someone attend you?" It was plain he was annoyed with her for not wanting to join him on deck. The underlying threat beneath the question was obvious. If necessary, he would have her watched twenty-four hours a day, no matter what gossip it provoked.

"I don't intend on harming myself, if that's what you're afraid of."

"We must remember, there are others on board whose best interests we must serve."

He was always so clever. Anyone hearing him would think despite his position, he was a simple friar. She hated him for it.

"Very well. I'll have Umberto look in on you. We dine with the captain at two bells, an hour before sunset."

She glanced at her trunk. She had no idea what Umberto had packed for her. Her shoulders remained tight as she waited for him to leave. When he finally did, she lay upon her bunk and shut her eyes.

Hours later, she awoke to a harsh knocking. She sprang to her door, only to find Umberto there, peevish as usual.

"I've been sent to see you're properly attired for the evening meal. Apparently, I am now a lady's maid." Scowling, he closed the door behind him.

"You're...to dress me?"

"I'm here to see you choose the proper clothes. Trash like yourself has no idea."

"And an ugly old priest like yourself does?"

He trundled over to her trunk, opened it, and snatched a gown and kirtle she assumed were the height of Esbañish fashion. The *ropa* was a rich black brocade with long splits exposing under-sleeves of creamy silk. The bodice was also black, but adorned with golden bows and a belt of cloth of gold. Tomás had spared no expense. He had even provided a triple rope of pearls. She had never known such opulence.

"Put this on first." Umberto handed her a thin, linen chemise.

"What is it?"

"If you were a lady, you'd know."

It could only be a type of undergarment. She glared down her nose at him. "Am I to strip before you?"

"Don't talk like a whore, even if you are one. Get those on, and then I'll return to correct whatever you've botched." He pointed out the hooks attaching one article to another. "Also, this." He tossed a golden net studded with seed pearls onto her bunk.

"What's that?"

"A caul, you ignorant slut. For your hair. All ladies of quality wear one. You'll find combs in the trunk. Don't waste time. Supper is in half an hour."

"And if I decline?"

"Then I've been ordered to dress you." He smiled nastily.

Her skin crawled. "Get out."

"As you wish, m'lady." He smiled and bowed, only to clutch his back in pain.

For the first time in weeks, she laughed.

She had a problem with some of the hooks and also with her hair, but she was mostly ready when Umberto reappeared. As usual, he looked upon her with disfavour. As he fixed some of her mistakes, he wasted little time and handled her roughly, shoving her this way and that. Finally, he pushed her out the cabin's door.

The passageway was narrow and cramped, but they didn't have far to go. The captain's suite lay below them, in the stern. As Umberto ushered her within, she found Tomás, Angél, Capitán de Carazo, and his officers in attendance. Noxolo, de Carazo's manservant, was also there, ready to serve whatever steamed inside the chafing dishes.

On seeing her, the men rose. Tomás rushed forward to greet her and take her by the arm. "How beautiful you are, *mi hermana*," he murmured. She fought down her revulsion. The other men voiced similar sentiments. Umberto looked as if he meant to join the party, but Tomás dismissed him. If it were possible for him to look even dourer, he did. Swearing beneath his breath, he closed the door.

Tomás seated her between himself and Angél, a silent reminder of what was at stake. Whether it was her pregnancy, the rise and fall of the waves, or her fear for Angél, the scent from the first course made her stomach rebel. She grabbed her napkin and held it to her face.

"Are you all right?" Angél asked. Tomás, who had been regarding his plate of salted beef, glanced up at her sharply.

"A little seasick." Her head spun. She was going to faint.

"Dear girl," Capitán de Carazo said sympathetically. He waved a hand at Noxolo. "Pour her some wine. It will restore her." He glanced back at her as Noxolo topped her goblet. "Don't worry, child. In a few days, this will pass. Some fresh air, Noxolo." The black man nodded and opened one of the stern gallery's windows.

She refused the next two courses as the men chatted and ate. The wine, a rich *rioja*, helped. When dessert finally arrived, a custard she wouldn't see again for the rest of the trip, eggs being a rare commodity, she ate a small amount. It restored her somewhat.

"So, you've been *gobernador* of Puerto Pío for how many years?" Tomás dabbed his lips as Noxolo refilled their wine.

"I'm in my eighth year." Capitán de Carazo lifted a finger for Noxolo to desist. "I also served a decade ago, a short time only. My successors didn't have the experience to run the island, so I was reinstated."

"The Crown must view you with much favour. As I understand it, Puerto Pío is not only an island of substantial wealth, but of much mystery. Was it not Ponce, the great explorer, who thought it might contain the Fountain of Youth?"

Capitán de Carazo smiled. "The very one. Unfortunately, the Fountain isn't to be found on Puerto Pío. Men better than I have searched for it thoroughly." He shrugged. "Still, there are many islands."

"But an intriguing idea, is it not?" Mateo, de Carazo's nephew spoke up. Rana considered him. He was young, not much older than she, about sixteen, with black wavy hair and a ruddy complexion. "To think one might actually find it! I don't know whether I'd keep it a secret, or make a fortune selling its marvelous waters!"

"You'd claim it for the Crown, Mateo," his uncle remonstrated.

"I suppose I would have to." He looked downcast.

Tomás' eyes grew distant. "From the writings of Herodotus to Prester John, there are many stories about the fabled fountain. I think it highly likely it exists in the New World."

Mateo nodded. "How can we doubt? Prester John's kingdom is one of the Three Indias. What is Nueva Esbaña and all the islands of the Esbañish Main, if not one of these? The Fountain must be here! We just haven't found it yet!"

De Carazo smiled. "Forgive his enthusiasm, Fra Tomás. He's young. Life has yet to disappoint him."

"Not so. The boy displays unusual faith."

Mateo glowed beneath Tomás' praise.

"What do you think, my dear?" de Carazo regarded Rana. "Do you think the Fountain of Youth exists?"

The Diaphani had such a legend, but she wasn't about to share it. She studied her fingers. "I know nothing of such things."

"Oh, forgive me! I've caused you embarrassment. It's only right you know nothing, being the lady of quality you are." He glanced at Tomás. "So you, Radiance. Am I to understand you'd finance such an expedition, if you had a hint as to the Fountain's whereabouts?"

Tomás pursed his lips. "I'd have to be convinced of such intelligence."

"There are rumours. I've not given them much credence for they are based on the myths of the Tain."

"The Tain?"

"The original inhabitants of the islands. Many of the slaves are *cimarrónes*, descendants of natives and imported blacks. It may be superstition, but their stories endure. If you're interested, my steward can tell you."

Noxolo stepped forth. Rana shivered. The air about him was chilly. "In the Blue Mountains of Xaymaca," he began, his voice gravelly and low, "there are three tall peaks. On the highest, *Los Buitres*, it is said there is a small cave from which flows a stream of gold. This stream comes from a magical fountain said to cure all ills. Only those of the purest heart may partake of its waters and remain unscathed."

Tomás sniffed. "And for those who aren't so pure?"

"Tales vary. Some say a man-eating demon guards the cave, others, vultures. They strike out the eyes of the unworthy, flay the flesh from the impure."

For a moment, no one spoke. Finally, Capitán de Carazo cleared his throat. "I suspect the fountain is only rumour. At best, the stream may hold a large vein of gold."

"Either one would be worth finding."

"Indeed. But it's unlikely. Xaymaca has been well searched."

Tomás tapped the table cloth. "Perhaps another search is warranted. One of the men I seek is bound for Xaymaca. I see no reason why I can't pursue both ends, to find the gold and bring him to justice."

"It may be easier to find the one than the other. Vultures aside, there are landslides and floods, toxic toads, and snakes. Also pockets of *cimarrónes* who hide deep within the hills. Any Esbañiard who enters their territory, soon finds himself dead."

"*Their* territory? Xaymaca is an Esbañish possession. Surely you have the means to deal with them."

"I would, if Xaymaca were my charge. The island is run by an inept descendant of the great Christophe Colon. Instead of rooting out the runaway settlements, he devotes his men to more pressing matters."

Tomás raised an eyebrow. "Such as?"

"Protecting the town and fortress from pirates. Xaymaca has become something of a haven. Not only is she small and mismanaged, but she also has many inlets in which they hide."

"I see. So floods, pirates, and renegade slaves. Hardly a place for a marvel."

"Not so, Fra Tomás." Noxolo spoke up. Tomás frowned. "Sometimes, the best things are to be found in the places most protected."

Rana waited for Capitán de Carazo to discipline him for speaking out of turn, but he did nothing. Their relationship was strange.

Noxolo glanced at her as if she had spoken aloud. Was he a mind reader, or was it simple coincidence that made him look her way? Something cold brushed past her. It left a shimmer trail, an almost imperceptible bending of light that ran from the man to her. It also left a faint odour, like spoiled meat. As one who had experimented and suffered, she recognized the presence of dark magic immediately. Her skin pimpled into gooseflesh. Power. Noxolo reeked of it.

He gave her a wide, deliberate smile. Dizziness overtook her. She grabbed for the table's edge.

"Dear Sul, we've tired her with our talk!" Capitán de Carazo said. Angél, who had been silent throughout the conversation, reached out to steady her. Tomás eyed him. He withdrew his hand.

"You should retire," Tomás told her tightly. He turned to Capitán de Carazo. "I best accompany her to her cabin, although the talk has been engaging."

"I'll take her," Angél offered.

Rana glanced at him in surprise. Surely, he knew what he risked annoying Tomás further.

For a moment, Tomás said nothing, but she knew he was deciding, calculating how he might best use Angél to his advantage. "Yes," he said finally. "If you don't mind, *Ser* Ferrara. Take her onto the spar deck for some fresh air before escorting her to her room." His glance settled on her once again, as bland as a snake's before striking. "I'll check up on you in an hour or so, dear one. Until then." He returned his attention to Capitán de Carazo. Noxolo watched without comment as they took their leave.

"Let me help you." Angél set an arm about her shoulders as the door closed behind them. "You're pale."

She nodded, relieved to have him help her to the waist. They ignored the crew as he steered her to the starboard rail. Night had fallen, the breeze was brisk and cool. Above them, dim sail bellied, capturing the wind. Half way up the main mast, the fighting top swayed, cutting across the stars.

Her stomach rebelled at the sight of it.

"Steady," Angél murmured as she sagged against him. "Breathe deeply. It'll pass. I'm glad we have this moment alone. I want to explain my actions to you. About what happened on the quay in Qadis."

He meant turning her over to Tomás to save himself. As much as she had despaired of it, it had also given her comfort. He had sacrificed Miriam, which meant he didn't love her as much as she thought. Angél had been a coward, but that bothered her less. She said nothing and concentrated on her breathing.

"You think I betrayed you. I regret how that appeared. That isn't why I did it, Miriam."

He still believed she was his precious Miriam. Why wouldn't he? Tomás was maintaining the hoax. She drew in a deep breath. "Why, then?"

"When you wrote to tell me you didn't want to go to the New World, that you wanted to stay with me, I knew then that Tomás valued you more alive. Otherwise, you would have perished in the fires in Elysir. The fact that you were with him meant he had no intention of killing you. I knew that somehow, you had escaped him when you wrote to me. I also knew that after he recaptured you in Qadis, you'd still be safe."

Safe. He had no idea what Tomás' interpretation of *safe* meant. Rape, torture, enslavement. Placing vulnerable loved ones–him–under threat.

"I thought if I released you to him, I could negotiate your freedom." He looked crestfallen. "I tried, Miriam." He squeezed the rail. "You've no idea how horrified I was to fail. If only Rana hadn't interfered–"

"This has nothing to do with her."

"This has *everything* to do with her. She told him where you were. Otherwise, how would he have known where to find us?"

He was wrong on so many fronts. But he wasn't a coward. He had tried to buy Miriam's release. It didn't matter. She was Miriam now.

"You should have listened to me. You should have stayed at the inn like I told you. If you hadn't run off to say goodbye to the Tribe, things would be different."

He blamed her for their predicament? She hadn't gone to say goodbye, but to find him! There was much to his side of the story she didn't know. There was more he didn't know about hers. "I'm sorry, Angél."

He had been staring over the star-touched waves. He studied her closely now, his expression turning anxious. "Did he—?"

"Did he *what*?" He had no right to question her virtue, especially after all the terrible things she had had to endure.

"Did he take advantage of you? Force himself upon you?"

She bit down on a laugh. "He's the Grand Inquisitor, Angél. The head of Holy Father Church in Esbaña. He's supposed to be celibate."

"He's still a man."

"No. He hasn't taken advantage of me."

"Then why—?"

"Why does he want me? Why do you think, Angél? As you said, I'm an asset, a valuable tool. He uses me to scry, which is why he'll never let me go. The only way to be shed of him is to escape." She had been tempted to say *kill him*, but Miriam never would have said that. "I want to be free of him, Angél. *We* need to be free of him."

"Then we must find a way to leave, as soon as we make landfall."

"Yes."

"It'll be difficult."

"Yes."

"I may have to take you through jungle, but I promise, I'll find a way for us, Miriam."

"I pray you do, Angél."

For one blessed moment, her nausea was gone. They hadn't drawn attention to themselves, the crew no longer paid them any mind. She met his dark eyes and murmured, "I love you, Angél. I always have. I always will."

He leaned in to kiss her when a strident voice broke their spell. "She's had enough of the sea air, I think!" Tomás strode towards them, his hands tucked into his sleeves. Terror rooted her to the spot. Had he seen them? Did he guess what they planned? Angél looked as if he had been hung from a yard. "I'll escort her from here," Tomás said coldly. "Thank you, *Ser* Ferrara. You may go."

She could see Angél didn't know what to do. He nodded and left.

Tomás slipped an arm about her shoulders. "Having a nice little tête á tête with an old lover?" he whispered. "It certainly looked that way."

"We were talking. That's all."

"Oh, I'm sure. It best remain so. I wouldn't want that young man placed under suspicion for corruption, would you?"

"I hate you."

"Do you?" He shoved her across the waist. "Well, you know what they say about love and hate, *querida*. They're *primos*, first cousins." He ushered her into her room and announced loudly for anyone within hearing distance, "A little sherry to settle you, my dear. And then, your beauty sleep. I'm sure you'll feel better in the morning." He pulled the door shut behind him to hide them from prying eyes. He leaned against it and watched her.

"Such a fascinating discussion we had about the Fountain, don't you think? Tomorrow, you'll try your hand at finding it with a little blood and water." His colour was high. There was no sign of the cut he had taken on the jaw or the gash at the back of his head.

"And how do you propose I do that? The ship has a limited supply of chickens."

He removed his cape and tossed it to the chair. "I don't think the cook cares how the hens meet their ends. Umberto can suggest it's better not to ask." He removed his surplice.

She stiffened. "What are you doing?"

"What does it look like I'm doing? I'm getting undressed. I feel much better compared to last night. Because of the new tattoo, I'm completely healed."

"What will the crew think? If you touch me, I'll scream."

"You won't. Because if you do, your beefy love will be clapped in chains. Once we make landfall, Xaymaca will hold its first *auto de fé*. No one opposes the Grand Inquisitor and gets away with it. If they do, they'll be burned. Undress. You're wasting time."

"No."

"Fine. I'll go have a chat with the captain." He reached for his surplice.

"No, wait! All right. I'll...do what you want."

"Good. And it'll be good for you, too. I haven't bothered to pleasure you before, but I'm capable of it. I know about these things."

She bit her tongue to keep from gagging. As she struggled with her bodice he removed his robe.

"Oh, for the gods' sake. You're taking forever."

She wished she had a knife to slide between his ribs. He fought with the wooden rings of her *verdugado*, and then in a pique, yanked off the entire framework. Then he pushed her flat to the cot and hoisted her knees about his waist. She clutched at the blankets to brace herself.

A strange expression came over his face. His scrotum wobbled against her maidenhead, but he remained limp. He reached down to stroke himself to erection. Nothing. He couldn't perform.

She sniggered. He drew away from her, outraged. "What have you done?"

Her mirth vanished. "Nothing! I've done nothing!"

"Did you cut a tattoo to stop coitus like *she* did?"

She had no idea what he was talking about.

"Where *is* it? I'll hack it off!"

"I don't have any new tattoos, Tomás! You've seen every one of them!"

"Then how...?" He looked down. His pubic hair, normally a dark brown, was sparser and greying. He sputtered in horror. "What have you done?"

"Nothing! It must be your new tattoo, the one you carved on yourself! It may speed healing, but it's also making you age!"

He looked as if he wanted to strangle her.

"When you don't pledge yourself to Lys, there are complications! That's why the first tattoo must always be a dedication to her! Even the grimoire warns of it!" If she didn't convince him now, she would never leave this room alive. He stood there, panting and listening. Good. He believed her. She was worth more to him as an advisor, than as a sex toy or blood worker. He might even bow to her wishes about Angél.

"Sometimes, the aging process can be stopped, but it's a matter of finding the right glyph! I don't believe I've seen such a one in your grimoire." The book had belonged to a member of the Tribe, a healer.

Not for the first time she wondered how he had come by it. "The most successful tattoos come from experimentation and desire. The one who cuts the tattoo must want its efficacy for the bearer!"

"Meaning, I shouldn't have cut myself. Someone else should have done it."

"Yes!"

"And you think you can give me the right tattoo." He reached for his robe and threw it over his head.

"I don't know." If she told too many lies, he would suspect.

"You'd like that, wouldn't you? An experimental tattoo, carved by you, and I'm no longer breathing. Let me warn you, *bonita*. If I age too fast, other deaths will follow. Starting with that handsome lover of yours. You'd best think on that, before you try to cross me."

He left without waiting for her to reply.

Chapter Twelve: Bad Dreams

JOACHÍN'S BACK THROBBED. After Iago had caught him, it had been sheer determination to remain upright, even with his help. At any other time, he would have found it ironic, but the pain also focused his will, kept him from oblivion. Every heartbeat cut like a lash, washing him in agony. To fall was death, and not because of his failing body. If not for Iago, the pirates would have tossed him to the waves. And then this pirate captain, this Boyle, had thrust two fingers in his direction, warning him in the Diaphani way to keep his distance. If not, he would kill him where he stood. He was in no condition to defend himself. The only thing to do was to look away, to bow to his superiority. Iago had seen the warning too and had drawn back in concession. Their submissiveness had been enough to appease the man—for now.

"Evaluate the stock, Mister Dirk," Boyle grumbled as he lumbered past. And then he was gone, leaving a stench behind him like a rotten wind.

As the crew culled them, Joachin held onto Iago, grateful for his support. His blood was no longer running in lines down his back, the welts were beginning to clot. For a moment, they were left to themselves. The other slaves who were able-bodied were herded to the starboard side of the ship. Those who were sickly and suffering were pushed to port, their fate soon apparent from the splashes. The terrified women and children were left clinging to each other by the main mast. A grizzled member of Boyle's crew sailed into his line of sight. He grabbed him by the arm. "No!" Iago shouted, pushing the man away. The world spun. His spine felt as if it were being pulled from his flesh. The deck rushed up to meet him and he fell to one knee. Immediately, Iago's arms were about him again. "Joachin!"

"Get up, ya sorry mess!" the pirate ordered.

"Leave him alone!" Iago snapped.

He closed his eyes and concentrated. This time, will alone might not win out.

"Let them be, Tucker," a new voice said. It sounded like Boyle's first mate. "I'll take it from here."

"But Cap'n says he wants 'em separated—"

"He also wants these two interrogated. Deal with the women over there."

If only he had poppy to numb him; he needed oblivion, he needed sleep. That was the way to healing, to Miriam. If Alonso came back—

"What's he saying? Who is Alonso?"

He must have spoken aloud.

"He needs help," Iago explained. "Look here. Two of his wounds have split open. I'm worried about blood poisoning. I want to lie him down. We can set him over there."

He didn't care where over there was. Right here was good, too.

"No, best to get him out of the captain's sight. Iago, is it? Take him back 'tween decks. Don't worry. I'll see you aren't shackled. I'll also get you something for his trouble."

"Thank you." That sounded like Francis. And then they lifted him, and it felt like he was being flayed alive. His stomach rebelled, he wanted to puke. He wasn't sure he didn't. The sensation lasted for all of a second before darkness blotted out the pain.

When he came to, he was lying on his stomach. Someone was dabbing his back with vinegar. The scent was sharp. Their ministrations stung. He winced and sucked in a breath. For a moment, he thought it was Miriam until he realized the hands were too big.

"Welcome back." Francis leaned over him, rag in hand. Iago was beside him. They were on the slave deck.

"Don't stop." His voice came out as a rasp. The vinegar hurt but it brought relief. He needed to get better as soon as possible.

The rag daubed at him again. After a moment, Francis paused. "I think we're done. I need to bandage you. Dirk gave us an old piece of sail. It'll have to do. Here, let me help you sit."

He gritted his teeth as Francis wrapped him. "A man of many talents. A priest, a swordsman, and a medic."

"A poor one, but I know a bit." Francis handed him a cup. "Drink this."

"What is it?"

"Watered wine with a bit of mint, poppy, and yarrow tossed in."

"A wish come true. My thanks."

"I'm glad you're feeling better. We still have a problem, though. Boyle doesn't like you or Iago. He doesn't like me, either, but with you two I think it goes deeper."

"He made a sign of warding as he passed us," Iago said. "We've never met him. Why would he do that?"

"I was wondering the same thing." Francis turned to Joachin. "He isn't Diaphani, is he?"

"Doesn't look it." Already he could feel the warm fingers of the wine teasing him into sleep. If he were lucky, his dreams would take him to Miriam. Dreams weren't enough, though. He needed to be with her in the flesh.

"Something's happened to make him think all Diaphani are a threat," Iago concluded. "If we knew what, we might use it to our advantage, but until we do, it's probably best to keep out of his way."

"Meaning we stay cooped up, down here." Joachin handed Francis the cup. "I hate this. I need to get off this ship. If Boyle hates me so much, why did he give you herbs?"

"He didn't. You can thank Dirk for that. I've a feeling he doesn't get on well with the captain. I think there's a division within the crew. Boyle has his followers, but so does Dirk."

"I'd follow him, any day."

Joachin regarded Iago with surprise. "You'd turn pirate?" That was the last thing he expected to hear from his cousin.

"Well, no. Actually, yes, if he offered me the Articles. But I'd never sign with Boyle."

"You may not have a choice," Francis said. "There are two ships, now. And sure to be a discussion over whom sails which. If Dirk captains *La Estrella*, hopefully, he'll keep us on board."

"*La Estrella* isn't much for gun power. I bet Boyle gives her to Dirk 'cause she's less able to defend herself. He won't want to be taken by other pirates or worse. But *La Estrella's* the richer ship. Don Lope spared no expense on her, in spite of her being a slaver."

Iago hasn't wasted time checking things out, Joachin thought.

"I'll see what I can do to convince Dirk," Francis replied. "He might be able to sway the captain. We know the *Phoenix*'s second port of call is Xaymaca. If Boyle gets it into his head to use the slaves to mine the gold—"

"No. I've had enough of slavery." Joachin shook his head. "I'd never wish it on anyone." He glanced at the despondent men lying beyond them, shackled at the ankles and wrists. One giant in particular, eyed them with a hard, steady gaze. He reminded him of a caged lion.

"Does he know what we're saying?" Iago asked. The man's stare was unsettling.

"Doubtful," Francis replied. "I suspect he hates all whites, even those who have had nothing to do with his captivity."

"I wouldn't want to meet him in his own land."

"Nor I."

"Where is Barto?" Joachin glanced around. Without realizing it, his absence had been tugging at his attention, like a piece of furniture missing from a room.

"Above." Francis looked unimpressed. "He's signed with Boyle."

It shouldn't have come as a shock, but it did. Joachin closed his mouth abruptly.

"He's been uncommunicative ever since we were caught by Don Lope," Iago said.

He should have seen it coming, but he had been preoccupied with his own pain. While his sufferings had been physical, Barto's had been emotional. Barto would have stayed with Tomás, if not for Tomás' treachery with Maia. "I guess I'm not surprised," Joachín admitted. "Barto's happier under a tyrant." It was hard not to feel bitter, though.

"I thought he was Tribe." Iago was also put out.

"I thought so, too, Iago, but don't let it bother you. Barto is only looking out for himself."

"Tribe doesn't turn its back on Tribe."

"No. But some people are less troubled by loyalty than others." It was important to guide his young cousin. "If you know what a man wants, you know where his motivations lie."

Iago sneered. "What about honour?"

"Honour's a curious thing. People define it according to their expectations. But also to their circumstances."

Francis stood. "Considering ours, I should get above. We need to know which ship they'll put us on and what their plans are. I'll come back when I learn anything, or when your bandages need changing, whichever comes first."

The large slave watched Francis go. Then he resumed his study of Joachín and Iago.

Iago eyed him uneasily. "What now?"

"Now, we sleep." Joachín turned his back on the giant and thought of Miriam. If Alonso returned, he could take her a message, reassure her he was all right, that they were heading for Xaymaca most likely. In a matter of weeks, they would be together, again. He eased himself gingerly onto his side.

"Let me help you," Iago offered.

Now that's loyalty, Joachín thought. *One cousin seeing to another, no matter how bad things get.* "Thanks, *primo*," he told him.

His dreams were a series of fleeting images. He didn't see Miriam as he wanted, nor did Alonso invade his mind. Instead, his thoughts floated like gannets over an open sea. At one point, he thought he spotted another ship on the horizon, but her ensigns were unfamiliar. She was neither *La Estrella*, the *Raven*, or the *Phoenix*. He had a vague feeling he should investigate her further, but by then, the dream had shifted and he was floating away. He found himself in a shantytown, drifting behind a sailor rambling down a boardwalk. A fleet lay at anchor in a bay. The scene had a yellowish cast, as if steeped in honey. He had never had such a dream before, but his mother had. Golden dreams revealed the past.

The sailor stopped, confronted by a crone. With a start, he recognized Boyle, but a much younger version of him. He looked lean, about twenty. The broken blood vessels on his nose were gone. He wore the uniform of an Inglaisi able-bodied seaman. He was also quite drunk.

"Tell your fortune, fine sir?" The crone reached for his hand. She had high cheekbones and a hooked nose. Her eyes were a piercing blue. "Before you head to your ship? Old Annie tells your future and your past."

"H...how much, ol' hag?" Boyle lost his balance and righted himself. Judging from the bag on his belt, he hadn't wasted everything on drink. Joachin suspected the old woman had been quick to see that. "Only a copper, sir."

"Tell me everythin' fer a copper?"

"Give me two, and I'll tell you as much as you could ever want to know."

"Done." He fumbled for his bag.

"Oh, not here, sir. Watch don't like old Annie plying her trade in the street."

"Ol' whore, like you?" He snorted as if he had made a fine joke. Then he followed her through a low doorway into a dank room which held little more than a table and a mattress of straw. Beside a cold hearth, a scrawny girl of about fourteen watched them pensively. A little boy clung to her skirts.

Boyle eyed the girl. "How much f' her?"

Anger flickered across the crone's face, but only for a moment. She smoothed her features with a smile. The girl said nothing, but eyed him balefully. "She's with child, sir. She ain't fer sale."

"Too bad. Be p'pretty if she weren't so drab. Dress'r up—"

"Your coppers, sir. Then your hand."

"Oh, aye." He fumbled with the purse's drawstrings and dumped the entire contents onto the table. The crone plucked out the coppers, then returned the rest of the coin to his bag.

"Here, now!" He swatted her as she tied the pouch to his waist.

"There, sir. You're all set. Now, let's begin." She caught his hand. Joachin had the impression she wanted to be done with him as soon as possible. Was she Diaphani? The high cheekbones and hooked nose were indicative, but the blue eyes, not so much. Maybe like him, she was a mix.

"Ah, there you see, sir?" She followed a crease in his palm. "You've a fine future. You'll be captain of your own ship, one day!"

"Aye? Tha's sssplendid!"

"Oh, yes. But not on these shores. Far, far away. Many leagues from here."

"Ppp...Portugel?"

"No." She frowned at his hand. "Farther than that." She pointed. "This line, here. See how it's chained? It tells me yer fleein' a painful past."

He frowned. "Wh...what?"

Her brows knit together. "...things that were done to you as a child." She sucked in a breath. "Oh, now, *that's* bad!"

"What're y' seein' ol' hag?" He curled his hand into a fist. She glanced at him in alarm. "I ask'd, what did y' see?"

She cringed. "Just the lines in your hand, sir. I was mistaken."

"No! Y' said...tell me what y' saw!"

For a second, neither of them spoke. Then her words came out in a rush. "We hate them, too! Solars! They pretend they're Sul's own voice, but they lie, and hurt, and kill! The takin' of a child's soul is the worst thing anyone can do. He should have been flogged for what he did to you! Drawn and quartered!"

"Y' saw a fuckin' priest?"

"I—"

"Y' know *nothin'*!" He clouted her across the head, sending her reeling. She fell and struck her head on the hearth. The girl cried out and sprang to her side. The little boy stood where he was and began to wail.

He shook his fist at them. "A word o' this, an' I'll fuckin' kill all o' ya! No one knows 'bout that! An' *no one ever will!*"

"She won't!" The girl cradled the crone in her arms.

"Damn right!" He reached for the spindly table and heaved it. It struck the wall and shattered into pieces.

"Get out!" The old woman struggled to her feet. Blood streamed down her face from where she had struck her temple against the hearth stone. She thrust two fingers at him. "Get out of this house!"

"Sul-blasted gypsies!" He snagged her by her wrist and fumbled for where she had stowed his two coppers. "I'm takin' back what's mine!"

"No! We need it for food!" She clawed at his face and drew blood.

Her attack threw him into a fury. He thrust her to the floor and brought his heel down on her head. The girl shrieked and pulled at his arm. He knocked her aside and stomped on the old woman again, as if she were a rat. Finally, the howls of the little boy broke through his rage. As his madness cleared, the crone lay at his feet, her face a bloody mash. A pool of blood spread out from beneath her skull. The girl and boy clung to each other in a corner and whimpered in terror.

Without a word, Boyle turned and left.

The girl chased after him. Clutching the doorway to keep from falling, she lifted her arm and pointed, crossing her forefinger over her thumb. "Kill a Diaphani, *die by one!*"

Boyle regarded her with dull, flat eyes. He moved towards her, and then hesitated as if deciding she wasn't worth his time. Turning away, he made his way back down the boardwalk, on his way to the docks.

Joachin woke with his heart pounding. He had known his share of violence, had done some terrible things, but this murder had been so brutal and mindless, it rattled him to the core. She had been a helpless old woman; she hadn't deserved to die like a cockroach underfoot. Obviously, Boyle had picked up some Diaphani lore since then. The warding gesture confirmed he believed in the girl's curse, that a Diaphani would bring about his death. The dream also explained why he hated priests so much. One had abused him as a child.

If I were Boyle, Joachin thought, *I'd get rid of any threats to my life, as soon as possible.*

He and Iago would have to watch their backs.

Several hours later, Francis returned with news. "They've been arguing over who takes which ship," he said. "Boyle isn't keen to stay on *La Estrella*, I suspect because of you two, but he's not willing to leave her to Dirk, either. He doesn't trust him."

"What do you think they'll do?" Iago glanced between the two of them.

Francis was grave. "Boyle plans to strip *La Estrella* of everything she has. Dirk pointed out if he scuttles her, there's little room on the *Raven* for the slaves, which sent Boyle into a rage. I stayed out of it. Dirk reminded him they would need slaves to mine the gold. Those nuggets made a big impression. His greed outweighs his paranoia."

"You've changed clothes," Joachin noted. Francis had shed the black and red habit. Now, he sported a pair of loose pantaloons and a raggedy shirt. He had kept his boots.

"Courtesy of Dirk. We thought it might be better if I wasn't a constant reminder to Boyle about how much he hates priests."

"Good thinking. We're still sailing for Xaymaca?" The sooner they were off this ship, the better.

"Yes, for the gold. Unless Boyle changes his mind."

"Why would he?"

"Apparently, they haven't made land in nearly a year. Many of the crew are sick. They want to spend some of their hard-earned money on women and ale. Boyle keeps changing his mind, promising them landfall, and then chases whatever prize sails within his sights. As I understand it, they've been living off their exploits."

That was interesting. He had always assumed pirates took prizes to enjoy the plunder, although the thrill of the chase had a lot to do with it, too. So, the crew were disenchanted? How many? He put the question to Francis.

"I'm guessing more than half, although if Boyle keeps his word, it's a moot point."

"I suppose. What's the main port on Xaymaca?"

"Puerto Real, a shantytown. I doubt Boyle will anchor there. Too many officials coming and going from Esbaña. The governor maintains a fortress at Villa de la Vía, but it's further inland. If Boyle makes for Xaymaca, he'll find a smaller, hidden cove."

"How long until we arrive?"

"Four weeks. Less, if the wind is good."

Which meant at least a month before he was reunited with Miriam. The *Phoenix* would dock first on Esbañiola. Since the pirates were heading straight for Xaymaca, they would arrive sooner than she did. Pray to Lys Francis was right about Boyle, that he wouldn't dock at Puerto Real. The last thing he needed was a shipload of pirates encountering his wife and the Tribe. He sighed deeply, only to have his back remind him of the rashness of it.

"I should change those bandages." Francis had seen him wince.

"Yes." He spread his arms carefully. "And you?"

"What about me?"

"Once we land in Xaymaca, what are your plans? Still hoping to convince us to go to Inglais?"

"That would be nice, but I suspect your answer would still be no. It'll take enough perseverance for us to reach Xaymaca. Let's see what happens. There are many ways I can serve my princess. Which leads me to ask–are there any tattoos that can strike an enemy from a distance?"

When Miriam had warded the Tribe to prevent Rana Isadore and Tomás from spying, she had protected them from remote interference, a defensive move. Before that, Rana had attacked her with the *hymenoptera*. Maybe some tattoos could be used offensively. "There may be, but I don't know how to cut them. If Ximen were here, we could ask him, but he isn't. So we can't."

"Something to think about, the next time we meet. In the meantime, we'll stay the course."

"Meaning, Iago and I endure these louse-ridden conditions and stay out of Boyle's way."

"No!" Iago protested.

Francis looked apologetic. "Unfortunately yes, my young friend."

"What if Boyle changes his mind? Decides *not* to sail to Xaymaca?" Joachin asked.

"We must see that doesn't happen. It helps he wants your map."

Did Francis search my body as I lay unconscious? he wondered. If he had, he would have been very careful about it, for Iago never said. "I don't have it. I only saw it once."

"As I thought. I'll tell him you remember it only partially, but the landmarks will trigger your memory. What do you recall of it?"

"It's located in the centre of the island, on the largest of three peaks."

"*Los Buitres*," Iago said.

"The Vultures."

"Yes," Joachin confirmed. "It's my understanding the local Indians know of it."

"Assuming they're still alive to guide us. I understand much of the native population has been decimated." Francis paused to study his back. "Those welts are looking better." He reached for the extra strips of sail he had brought. Above, Tucker called for the change of watch.

"Damn! Iago will have to take care of you. I have to go." He squeezed him carefully on the shoulder. "I expect Boyle will give me the worst jobs he can, but I'll come down as soon as possible."

They needed to defend themselves when he wasn't present. Boyle might not come down to the slave deck himself, but he could send a henchman. "Do you have a knife?" Joachin asked.

"Yes. Take this." Francis withdrew a blade from his waistband.

"Give it to Iago."

"Shite!"

They turned to see who approached. It turned out to be Dirk, not swearing at all, but hailing Francis. "Captain wants you. You're assigned to the heads."

"Say it isn't so! I'll reek to high heaven!" Francis made a face.

"Sorry. I said you're not a real priest, but he doesn't believe it."

"I'll try not to be too revolting when I return," Francis told Joachin and Iago.

Joachin waved him off. "As if we're in any state to complain."

When they were gone, Iago turned to him. "I like him, that Dirk."

Joachin shrugged. "He seems a decent sort. But I wouldn't put my trust in him yet, Iago."

Iago looked thoughtful. "Of the three of us, you and I are the luckier. I wouldn't want to be in Francis' boots, right now."

"No."

"Father Shite. I see why the captain calls him that. You know–shite, heads." He grinned.

"I get it, Iago."

Above them, one of the mates gave a shout. This was followed by a wild cheering. The crew had discovered Don Lope's sherry.

"Oy! You, boy!" Tucker, Boyle's bosun, pointed at Iago. "Yer wanted on th' spar deck."

"Me?" Iago squeaked. "Why?"

"Cap'n's feelin' merry. Shite claims y' can sing."

"Shite...? I *can't* sing!"

"Then y' best learn. Cap'n' fancies a dance."

"I'm not a dancer!" He pointed at Joachin. "Joachin is!"

Tucker glared at Joachin. "Cap'n don't want him. Just you."

"Joachin?" Iago looked at him anxiously.

"It's probably all right." Maybe Francis said it to make Iago seem useful, a way to save his skin. "Sing whatever you can."

"What about you?"

Tucker loomed threateningly. "He ain't goin' nowhere."

"I'll be here when you return," Joachin replied.

"Best put yer mind to that map," Tucker told him, as he drew Iago away.

Tucker had forgotten the pail of beans and pork beside Iago's pallet. It was a thin, watery concoction. He hadn't bothered to serve the other slaves. Across the deck, the giant slave watched Joachin intently. A desire for vengeance lay deep within those dark eyes. Given the chance, he would kill him and every other white on board. Joachin had encountered that look a few times–a hatred so intense its bearer impaled his enemies on it. There could be no other outcome.

He stood, then scooped a small handful of mash into his mouth, knowing the giant hungered. He swallowed it down, aware of the effect it would have. "Want some?" he asked, lifting the ladle in the man's direction. The giant didn't understand the language, but he might, his intent. Tucker hadn't given them any fresh water, either.

Francis' stiletto lay where Iago had forgotten it, partially hidden by his pallet's straw. Joachin stowed it in his pants, wishing he had a shirt to cover it. It felt good to carry it, like being accompanied by an old friend.

He approached the man cautiously, as he might a vicious dog. He stood just out of reach.

"I can feed you." He held out the pail of mash. "It's better than what we usually get."

The man eyed him. Loathing lay behind his glance, but also something else—the will to survive.

"It's not right, chaining men." He pointed at the manacles about the giant's wrists and mimed breaking them. The man gave no indication he understood.

"You want this?" He indicated the pail.

When the giant said nothing, he took another careful step towards him. "They feed us like beasts." Don Lope's men had been in the habit of dumping the slop at the slaves' heads. They had to eat it as best they could. Joachin lifted the ladle. Despite the chains on his hands and feet, the slave managed to sit. All the while, he still eyed him as if he'd as soon slit his throat, but for now, survival meant putting aside all thoughts of revenge. He opened his mouth to receive a spoonful. Given the chance, he would still kill him, Joachin knew, but the body's needs came first. He gave him a second helping and then a third. And then carefully, gingerly, for his back still bothered him, he served the rest of the slaves.

Some were too sickly to accept his offering, having missed the culling by Boyle's crew. Others watched as if in a dream. When his pail was empty, Joachin made his way back to his pallet and lay on his side.

The giant continued to watch him.

He reminds me of Barto, angry, obstinate, and a force of nature when it comes to a fight, Joachin thought. It was a pity things had turned so sour. He and Barto had had much in common. And in a strange way, so did he and this slave. Joachin set a hand to his chest. "Joachin," he said.

The giant narrowed his eyes. Then he glanced away.

Joachin drew a deep breath. It had been a foolish hope to think he might win the man's trust. He and Iago needed allies; the big man was an obvious choice. Don Lope had been their common foe and now, Boyle was. They both wanted their liberty-he, so he might find Miriam again, and the giant so he might, what? Return to Afrik? If only they could win their freedom in the New World....

"We're not enemies," he told him.

The giant gave no indication he heard.

They're fine, for now.

Miriam and Alonso were back in their corner, separated from the Tribe by a wall of water casks. She had been waiting anxiously for him to report on Joachin and the men. She breathed a sigh of relief. "Thank Lys."

As far as I can tell, the captain of the Raven plans to sail for Xaymaca, so all seems well. He seemed glad to be able to bring her good news.

Have Joachin and Iago signed with him?

No, but Barto has.

Really? I must tell Maia. Why haven't Joachin and Iago signed?

They haven't been asked. Maybe the pirates are unsure of them. Joachin is healing, but he remains weak.

I suppose Barto would be seen as an asset. Hopefully, he and Francis will watch out for Joachin and Iago. Oh, Alonso! For the first time in weeks, I'm hopeful! We might actually survive this journey!

Indeed. Iago's been asked to sing.

What!?

For the captain. As I understand it, Francis said he could. Something to make him worth keeping, I expect.

Oh dear. I hope he can.

Even if he can't, they might still find him amusing. He does have some ability, especially with the drum.

Thanks, Alonso. I'll sleep better, now.

I thought you might.

She settled onto her side, content to feel him at her back. She didn't see the need to return to the Tribe, in spite of Zara's earlier admonishments. Alonso, her angel, would alert her if anyone approached.

Susan MacGregor

Chapter Thirteen: Keelhauled

ONE OF THE worst jobs in the world was mucking out the heads. Within minutes, Francis was stained to the elbows with the brown and crusted remnants from too many men and no attention to hygiene. His eyes watered in a constant stream. When the buckets of sea water did little to remove the excrement, he used the edge of the pail to scrape it down the holes. After half an hour, he could stand it no more. He poked his head out the door to clear his head.

To his surprise, a celebration was taking place on the spar deck. The crew were well into their cups. They sagged against each other and sang snatches of drunken song. Others skylarked from the shrouds like monkeys, tossing bottles to cohorts or to the sky. In the midst of it all, Boyle roared with laughter and shouted encouragements to his court. In one hand, he clasped a jug. In the other, a dull eyed girl. Francis wasn't sure whether she was numb or terrified.

Two familiar figures appeared from out the hatch. The crew hushed slightly as Iago, prodded by Tucker, was forced to stand before Boyle.

Dirk was nowhere to be seen. Perhaps he had been assigned to some task aboard the *Raven*.

"I un'erstan' y' can sing." Boyle's voice rose over that of his watchful crew. He eyed Iago as if he were a roach creeping up from the hold. "So, sing! Somethin' tuneful an' lively. The maid, here..." he squeezed her as if she were a rag doll, "tells me she fancies a song." She closed her eyes, refusing to look at anyone.

"Who says I can sing?" Iago shifted uncomfortably as the crew regarded him.

"Don' matter who said."

"I'm no singer—"

"Did I ask if y' were?"

"No—"

"Then *sing*!" Boyle jerked the girl roughly. Her eyes flew open, showing their whites.

Iago cleared his throat. "My...my heart is lost, my soul, it weeps—"

"Not that gypsy shite!" He stood abruptly, yanking the girl up with him. "Somethin' cheerful! Like this!" He set the rhythm with a boot. The girl's toes dangled dangerously close to his heels. 'When I first laid eyes, on m' sweet Molly....'"

The crew clapped their hands and joined in. "A maid so fair, she were m' folly...."

"She danced a jig in dear old Glasgooow...." Boyle dipped and bowed, his heels scraping the wood.

"The like o' which, we never seen-oh!"

"She took me up, I flung 'er down...." The girl let out a shriek.

"Stop it!" Iago sputtered.

"Our couplin' was the talk o' the town! Sing, *Parrot*!" Boyle shouted at him.

The girl screamed in earnest.

Gods, this is a trap! Francis thought. *Iago is walking right into it!*

Crying and flailing, the girl managed to free one hand. She raked at Boyle's ear, gouging it with her fingernails.

He stared at her in disbelief and exploded with anger. "Ye think so, y' bloody little bitch? Nobody gets th' best o' Boyle!" He backhanded her viciously. She stumbled into Iago who caught her as she fell. Boyle bore down upon the two of them.

Iago barred his way. "Leave her alone!"

Boyle drew up short. "Leave 'er alone? Who th' hell are you t' tell me anythin', Parrot Shite?" He cuffed him, knocking him to his knees.

"Iago, no!" Francis shouted.

Too late, Iago recovered and launched himself at Boyle, grabbing him by the neck. He was about as effective as a bee on a bull. Boyle shook him off.

"Ye dare, ye dare?" Boyle gasped, as the crew swarmed Iago. "Nobody touches me! I'll keelhaul y' for it! Take him!" he shouted at his men. Iago fought, but was dragged, fighting and cursing, to the rail. With dismay, Francis saw a rope was already in place. Boyle had planned this all along. "Hoist 'im up!" Boyle shouted.

He darted forward. "You can't! You have no right!" He had to buy Iago time. Where on earth was Dirk? If he had been on board, this never would have happened. No time to ponder it now.

His outburst made the crew pause. Every man stared. Stained in feces from hand to shoulder, he was a sight.

"Ah, Father *Shite*." Boyle smiled tightly. "Like all stinkin' turds, y' show up where yer not wanted. Say a prayer for yer parrot. He broke a rule. Never lay hands on th' captain. He has to pay th' price."

It was hard to maintain an authoritative stance when one was covered in shit. Difficult, but not impossible. "You know very well the Articles don't apply to him—Captain," he added acerbically. Might as well call Boyle by his title, so he couldn't be accused of insubordination.

Boyle glowered. "Who said anythin' about th' Articles? I'm Sul on this goddamned ship!"

So much for reminding him of the rules. His obligations, then. "Sul or not, you still need a vote. The boy's property. You only hold a partial share."

Boyle reddened. The crew were listening with interest—more than Boyle liked. "Fine," he said, gaining control of his temper. He curled his hands about the lapels of his great coat. "I'm a fair man. All in favour of th' keelhaulin'—"

Francis held up a finger. "Not *all* the crew are here. We must wait for Dirk."

"We don't need to wait fer 'im! We got...cue...quor...we got enough men, here!"

"Iago intervened on the girl's behalf. She's also property. Which you were abusing."

"That slut?" Boyle cast a careless glance at the girl. Tucker had her trapped in his arms. "She screams too much for my liking, though others don't seem t' mind." Tucker ground his chin into her jaw. She squirmed and pulled away. He grinned and squeezed her harder.

"You instigated it so Iago would strike you. You knew he would." He had to keep him talking. The longer they spoke, the more likely Dirk might show up and stop this.

"I'm a mind-reader, am I? You talk like you reek. I can't stand th' smell o' you. Everyone here agrees with me." He turned to the men at the rail. "Hoist that parrot up and throw 'im overboard. See what the sharks think o' him."

"Permission to come aboard, Captain!" Dirk's clear voice rose from the starboard side. An accompanying bump on the hull indicated the *Raven's* cockboat, carrying Dirk and his band, had arrived.

Boyle purpled, but said nothing. Every man aboard awaited his answer. Clearly, he was caught. There was no reason to deny Dirk permission to board, unless it was to have his way in keelhauling Iago. For a moment, Francis worried Boyle's fury might win out. It wasn't beyond the realm of possibility he might refuse Dirk. They didn't get along.

"Is there some reason we're being detained?" Dirk's question floated on the air. He had asked one of his men.

"Oy! Cap'n!" came a new voice from below. Gibbs, it sounded like.

Still glowering, Boyle waved at the starboard rail. "Granted," he grumbled. "Let 'em come." The ladder was lowered. Dirk was the first to appear. He swept a lithe leg over the starboard rail. A dozen members followed him aboard. "Why the delay? What's going on here?" He swept a glance over the company. Six men had Iago in arms. Tucker held the girl.

"Boy attacked th' captain," Tucker said.

"Attacked? What fool brought him up from below?" Dirk stared at Tucker, then at Boyle. "Why isn't he with the rest of the slaves?"

Boyle hooked his thumbs into his belt. "I don't like yer tone, Mister Dirk. It's borderin' on the insub'...insubord...insultin'."

"I'm entitled to ask questions—sir."

"Then here's yer answer." He nodded at Iago. "Little shite tried to kill me—"

"To protect her!" Francis pointed at the girl. Dirk regarded him with distaste. "Yes, I know, I'm a sight," he added, "but Iago was provoked. The captain struck the girl—"

"There are port-o-calls, as you well know, Mister Dirk," Boyle reminded him.

"Protocols."

If it were possible to turn even darker in the face, Boyle did. "However y' say it! I'll have me due!"

Dirk cocked his head as if considering the situation. "It strikes me the man who should be disciplined is the one who brought him into your midst, Captain," he replied evenly. "The danger should have been obvious. Like placing a scorpion in your soup. Whoever did it should be whipped." He glanced at Tucker who paled but said nothing.

"However it happen'd, ain't th' point. Th' gypsy grabbed me."

"Then birch him. A fitting discipline, for one so young."

"It ain't no birchin' offence."

A silence fell upon the crowd as they stared each other down. Dirk was the first to break it. "I find it interesting such a thing should happen while I'm away." There was no mistaking the inference beneath his comment. "Why does a man, such as yourself, Captain, find a whelp so...disturbing? I'm sure the crew wonders this, too."

Francis was almost certain Dirk had been about to say *threatening*. If the crew hadn't questioned Boyle's fear before, they did now.

"Enough o' this!" Boyle glared. "I'll have 'im keelhauled for assault. Continue to thwart me, Mister Dirk, an' I'll have you clapped in chains for insubord'nation! I think I got it right that time, didn't I, Tucker?"

"Aye, sir," Tucker affirmed.

All about the waist and in the shrouds, the crew shifted uneasily. It had never been clearer there were two factions aboard the *Raven*. The tension was palpable. If Dirk and his supporters planned to mutiny, was that about to happen? Francis wondered.

Dirk sucked in a breath. "If I can't persuade you against it, you must drop him low."

Gods, how was *low* any concession? Iago would be dragged from port to starboard along the keel. They would bring him back, dead.

"I'll drop 'im any damn way I please." Boyle was surly, like a child not getting his way.

"Then you must tell us why you're going to such lengths to kill a slave. The men already wonder a great deal."

Francis marvelled. Dirk was using words, not swords, to do battle. His inference was clear. Once again, Boyle was behaving irrationally. He had been that way for some time, sailing hither and yon over the Great Ocean Sea. The *Raven* had seized prize after prize, but to what end? The crew had been denied landfall, to indulge in their success for reasons they didn't understand. Scurvy assailed them. An unstable captain wasn't fit to lead.

Boyle sputtered in outrage. "Fine! He drops low! Devil take 'im!" He waved the crew into motion. Iago was hustled, struggling, to the rail. Francis stepped forward to intervene. Dirk barred his path.

"We *must* allow it," he whispered tersely. "Pray to Sul, he holds his breath long enough!"

"It'll kill him!"

"Chances are he'll be half-drowned, but he won't be sliced to shreds by barnacles or worse. I've seen men decapitated after being drawn short. We must let the captain have his way. If he tries to kill him again, the crew *will* revolt, all except his most devoted followers."

Iago let out a wail, and then there was a splash. Dirk ran to the port side and stared down. Boyle had returned to his barrel to sit. He stared off into the distance as if he had lost interest.

"Long! Longer!" Dirk shouted, gazing into the green depths. Francis counted a full minute and prayed that Iago had taken a lungful of air. "All right! Deep enough!" Dirk yelled. "Pull him up. Start hauling now!"

The starboard team strained at the ropes. Francis ran to assist, but they told him to leave off. He watched anxiously as Iago was pulled to starboard, dragged up the hull, and grabbed by an arm. As the crew pulled him over the rails, he dropped to the deck like a landed tuna, falling with a wet smack. His skin had been sliced in several places, but none of the wounds were severe. Blood streamed from his face and his limbs. He wasn't breathing.

"Pump his chest!" Dirk shouted. Then, as if feeling responsible, he bent to the task. As he pressed down on Iago, his efforts were finally rewarded with a stream of water spouting from Iago's mouth. After another thrust, Iago gasped for breath.

Thank you, Lys, Francis thought.

A shadow loomed over them in the dying light. Boyle gazed down upon them. "It's change o' crew, Mister Dirk. Get that gypsy out o' my sight and down below. Same goes for you, Shite. Y' stink. Do somethin' with yerself."

He lumbered off for the captain's quarters, grabbing the slave girl and his jug of sherry on the way. The door beneath the quarterdeck closed with a slam.

"You heard him," Dirk told the crew. Two men hauled Iago by the arms and legs to the hatch. Dirk cast a rueful glance at Francis.

"You *do* need a dousing," he said.

He did. But he made light of it. "Not a keelhauling?"

"No. Just a drop in the drink, long enough to rinse that muck from your hide. Don't worry, I'll see your head remains above water."

Obviously, Dirk saw something in him of value. Francis wondered what it was. Considering Iago had just come close to death, it wasn't appropriate to feel his loins quicken in Dirk's presence. What was it about Dirk that drew him? "No sharks, I hope," he joked.

"The only ones you'll find are those above decks." Dirk flashed him a grin.

As they slipped him into a harness and lowered him over the side, he thought he knew what attracted him to Dirk. The pirate was smart, ruthless, and he knew how to wait.

Just like me, Francis thought.

Chapter Fourteen: Dream Warfare

JOACHÍN SAT UP as two of the port watch brought Iago onto the slave deck. He had fallen asleep after feeding the slaves, hoping to dream of Miriam. His body had rebelled, sending him into a dreamless slumber. He needed the rest, healing.

He sucked in a breath. His back was itchy, but also wet and painful in spots. He was bleeding again. He must have lain on it while sleeping. That wasn't important. Judging from Iago's appearance, his *primo* was in worse shape than he was.

"What happened?" He stared down at Iago as the two men lay him on an adjacent pallet. His clothes were dripping. His arms, legs, and face were smeared in blood. In several places, his flesh was badly abraded.

"Cap'n keelhauled 'im," one of the bearers said.

"He got off lucky," added the other.

Sweet Lys, he should have been there instead of sleeping. "Why?" He was shocked and angry with himself as well as with Boyle.

The bigger one shrugged. "Set hands on th' captain."

"Didn't like how th' cap'n was treatin' th' girl," the other said.

"What girl?"

"Cap'n's new bed mate."

As they departed, he barely noticed. Guilt stabbed him while fear plucked at his heart. Iago lay shivering. None of his cuts looked deep, but who knew how an attack like this might affect him? Sometimes, such assaults hurt the mind even more than the body. He draped the blanket Francis had left over Iago. There were no bandages or salve to treat him; he hoped it would be enough.

His cousin had always shared his desire to protect women and children. Had Boyle guessed this, also? Boyle believed the gypsy girl's curse, that a Diaphani would bring about his end. Like any predator, he attacked the youngest and weakest first. Had he ordered Iago above decks to finish him? If so, he had failed. And what of Francis? Had he been there to intervene?

He wasn't sure what he thought of the Papal Nuncio. For a priest and a spy, the man seemed sincere, but he was also dedicated to turning his Inglaisi princess into an Inglaisi queen. *Which might interfere with the Tribe's future plans*, Joachin thought. As for Dirk, he may have impressed Francis, but he was still a thief. He knew his type. He wasn't fooled.

Boyle would find another way to get rid of them, he knew. The pirate's maneuverings made no sense. *Why not thrust a knife through our hearts and be done with it?* He was captain, after all. Wasn't a direct approach the simplest?

For a moment, the answer eluded him–and then he had it.

Boyle couldn't kill them directly because they were property. Every man aboard had a say in how they were handled, every member, a share in their worth. If Boyle wanted them dead, it had to be done secretly, through a ploy. His ruse to frame Iago had failed. It was Boyle or them. But how to defeat him?

The answer came as a half formed idea. He went quite still as he considered it. An indirect approach was called for.

What if–he grew excited by it–what if he didn't intervene directly? What if he infiltrated instead, through Boyle's dreams? It was a subtler approach, one that might have its drawbacks. Most likely, it meant experiencing everything Boyle did in the dream state. It had never occurred to him to do this before; the idea of slipping into another's slumbering body was abhorrent.

But sometimes, a little unpleasantness was necessary. There was no way of knowing how disagreeable it was until he tried it. Besides, why would he think of this now, unless the goddess had set the idea in his mind?

He glanced at the wan light seeping down from the grilled hatch above. Lanterns were being lit. Night had come. It was likely Boyle would be in his quarters at his evening meal or drinking whatever sherry remained.

After he was done with the girl, he would sleep.

Joachín cast a glance at Iago, and then to be sure, set a hand on his shoulder. He no longer shivered, thank the gods.

Sleep well, cousin, he thought. *One of us should have sweet dreams tonight.*

Two hours later, Francis arrived, his watch with the port crew done. He smelled a little better, as if he had been dunked into the sea. Joachín was glad he was back, but he didn't acknowledge him, preferring instead to feign sleep. He needed to get on with his plans.

Lys, guide me, he prayed, believing she would. He was about to attempt the impossible-to actively participate in a dream. Whenever he had tried it in the past, the visions had shattered. He remembered one of the first times he had dreamt of Miriam. Two guards had come upon her in the woods near Granad. She had been holding a shovel to defend herself. Now, he meant to influence Boyle, to weaken him, make him think he was losing his mind.

I'd much rather dream of you, mi cielo, but I must see to our safety first, he thought. He expected to be soiled, mentally and emotionally. It couldn't be helped.

He reached for sleep. His mind kept drifting on dark currents. It wasn't easy, his back ached, but he relaxed as much as he could. Across from him, Iago was fitful. Francis stared at the empty pallet above him, lost in his own thoughts. Finally, the two disappeared and he slipped into dream. There was no way of knowing whether it was his imagination supplying the details or if the vision were true.

He dismissed all doubts. He had to trust his ability, believe Lys was helping him.

He pictured Boyle snoring in the captain's bunk in the great cabin, a flat-bottomed decanter by the bed, goblets rolling alongside it. The girl had slipped from his clutches and was huddled against the cabin's door. There was no way to escape unless she fled through the quarter gallery which overlooked the sea. Perhaps she had already tried.

The pirate was naked and tangled in damp sheets. His flabby chest rose and fell with each jerky breath. He imagined himself floating above him, settling into his skin. The vision was crude, revolting, so he tried not to picture it as much as feel it. There was a percolation, a sense of growing bigger...coarser...then an ugly feeling of being drunk. He was reeling, drowning in putrid flesh.... Gasping, he retreated.

The sensations were worse than he had expected, but the dream had remained intact.

He tried again, floating, falling, entering. Again, that revolting sense of illness, that same sick spin from too much alcohol. Boyle's liver wasn't functioning as it should. His heart pumped too hard. *Gods!* Joachin thought. *I can't!*

Gasping for breath, he found himself out-of-body, again.

You have to bear it, he told himself. *Go for his head, ignore everything else.* He stiffened his resolve, then hovered and dropped, a falcon after prey. There was a sudden squeeze, then a sense of being buffeted by a foul wind–Boyle coming to. The pirate sucked in a sharp breath. Joachin veered away, afraid he had pushed too hard. *Slower, easier*, he told himself.

He had to take his time, not be in a hurry. Time passed in the tiniest of increments, disgusting but necessary. He filled Boyle's every pore, travelled every capillary. His nose grew fleshy, his sinuses thick. Beneath the lids, the pirate's eyes darted to and fro as if he sensed, even in his drunken, dreaming state, that something was amiss. The man tasted of sour sherry and blood. Had he bitten the girl? Joachin sincerely hoped not. Finally, the barriers of flesh thinned. A light flickered beyond them, as through a thin skin.

And then, astonishingly, he was in Boyle's mind, or rather, a construct of it. The dream had cast him as a military portrait upon a wall. Boyle no longer resided in the captain's quarters. He wasn't even on the ship. Instead, he snored in a chamber rivalling a royal suite.

The bed was massive, elephantine, and heaped with silken pillows. Four oaken posts rose from each quilted corner to a velvet canopy. Beyond it, a high ceiling rose, depicting blushing maidens and rosy cupids at play. Numerous paintings of ships, seascapes, and naval battles hung upon the walls. On enamelled tables, ornate clocks ticked beside delicate porcelains of shepherdesses who stared with doe-like eyes.

A gilded door opened on a far wall. A man-servant entered, bearing a silver tray of pastries, boiled eggs, and sausages. "Good morning, yer Grace." He set the tray on a bedside table.

Boyle roused with some difficulty, as if he had had too busy a night. "Gods, Tucker, what time is it?"

Joachin blinked in surprise. It *was* Tucker, although a much cleaner version of him.

"Ten o'clock in th' morning, m' Lord."

"Already? Great Sul, I've overslept. Hand me my robe."

Tucker helped him into it. It was a creamy silk with a violet trim.

"What shall we do about th' vermin on board, Tucker?"

Tucker slipped purple slippers onto Boyle's fat, knobby feet. "Not sure, m' Lord. Best way t' get rid o' rats is with poison."

Boyle pursed his lips. "True. But t'is a coward's path. Taintin' th' food might kill th' men."

Joachin snorted. He was almost sure Boyle never used 't'is' as an affectation. Both Boyle and Tucker glanced about. He froze inside the portrait, his hand tucked into his doublet. Fortunately, they didn't look closely at the picture on the wall.

"Did you snort?" Boyle glared at Tucker.

"No, m' Lord."

"I'm sure I heard you snort."

"You heard somethin', but it wasn't me."

They continued to glance about, Boyle frowning and Tucker peering. Joachin held his breath and didn't move. When no further sound was forthcoming, Tucker changed the subject. "Regardin' the rats, m' Lord, p'rhaps a secret assassination? Under th' cloak o' night, with no one the wiser, save ourselves?" He tapped the side of his nose.

Boyle nodded. "Has merit. We'll have t' keep Dirk out of it, though."

The rats were him and Iago, possibly Francis as well. It was time to act, to wield some influence and fight back. He stared at Boyle's breakfast. *Eat your sausages, Captain,* he said.

To his delight, Boyle surveyed his food. The dream seemed to enhance his own experience; he felt Boyle's anticipation, his appetite whetting–and then, his sudden disappointment. Boyle pouted. "Where's my cutlery, Tucker? You've forgotten it."

"Have I?"

"See for yourself!"

Joachin focused on Tucker. It was difficult. He felt as if he were being pulled from the picture frame, about to materialize in Tucker's place, which wasn't what he wanted to occur. If that happened, Boyle would see him. He strained, built an image in his mind–a shadow-man, tall, red-haired, elegant.

"Allow me, Captain." Dirk materialized in Tucker's place, looking casual and composed. He had come with one piece of cutlery–his sword.

"You'll refer t' me as yer Grace." Boyle glanced up in annoyance, expecting Tucker. His jaw dropped at the sight of Dirk. "Sul Almighty!" He looked about wildly. "Tucker! Help!"

Dirk plunged the blade through his creamy robe. Death through clairvoyant manipulation was too much to hope for, but for one terrifying moment Boyle thought his heart was exploding. Joachin congratulated himself. He had attacked Boyle psychically, his aim to bring the division between Boyle and Dirk to a head. Who knew what would happen, now? With luck, Boyle would challenge Dirk to a duel. Being younger and stronger, Dirk would win out. He withdrew from the nightmare and let out a laugh.

"Good dream?"

Francis was eyeing him like a cat on a sparrow. Gods! How long had he been there? Should he tell him what he had done? Probably best not to. He still didn't trust him entirely.

"Something like that," he replied, forcing his heart to return to normal.

He awoke the next morning to find Francis gone, called to duty with the port crew. Iago was feverish and coughing. He listened carefully, afraid he might hear a dangerous rattle in his cousin's lungs. He wasn't sure how resilient Iago was. If his breathing cleared, it would still take a few days for him to recover. Getting over the shock of being keelhauled might take longer. He doubted the boy had ever faced such treachery before. He winced in sympathy at the sight of his scratched face and arms. "How are you?" he asked as Iago opened his eyes. How he answered would tell him a great deal.

"Alive," Iago rasped.

"Thank the goddess for that." Montoya blood was robust.

"I'm going to kill him," Iago said without preamble.

He meant Boyle, of course. Montoya blood was also vengeful. "I wouldn't advise it. Forget him for now."

"He hit that girl. He was going to hurt her again, except…I got in the way. She looked so scared, Joachin. I had to do something. She's been taken from her family, her land. She's like us. Like *me*."

"You need to get better. After that, we'll settle her account."

"I hate him. He's going to hurt her in *other* ways."

He wasn't about to tell him Boyle already had. "If she's like you, she'll survive."

"She shouldn't be a slave."

"That's true. Slavery is an abomina—"

"*None* of them should be slaves. If we can't go back to our old life, we need to make a new one in the New World. Where everyone is equal, where everyone has a say."

He was passionate about it, which was a bit of a surprise. Robust, vengeful, and idealistic, Joachin thought. Much like he was at sixteen. "That's a lofty goal, Iago."

"It's how things *should* be."

"Then we'll do our best to create that world. Although some of these here," he glanced at the giant, "may not want to join us."

"I'll marry her, if I can."

"*Marry?*" Now the boy wanted the impossible. "Iago, you don't even know her. She doesn't speak our language, she isn't—" he was going to say, *our race*, but Iago took his meaning.

"I don't care!" He began to cough again. "It doesn't matter!" he sputtered. "You should have seen her, Joachin! She was so afraid! And when she looked at me, I saw it in her eyes. She *wanted* me to save her! I had no choice."

Gods above, one vulnerable girl and the boy's in love. He shook his head. At fourteen, his first love had been a twelve-year old prostitute with small breasts and a pinched face. He had been as protective of her as Iago was of this girl. One night, she simply vanished. The other girls had been tight-lipped about it. After six months of searching, he had to accept the possibility she might be dead.

The arrival of the port watch with the food buckets prevented them from finishing their conversation. Francis wasn't among them. Either Boyle had given him additional tasks, or Dirk had removed him to the *Raven* to keep him out of Boyle's way. He hoped the latter. Once again, the morning's offerings were rice and beans.

"Can he manage?" One of the men eyed Iago.

"I'm not helpless," Iago replied.

"Lucky little snot. It ain't much, but I guess yer glad y' can eat."

Instead of dumping the gruel on their pallets, Dirk's team were more mindful. Perhaps Dirk had advised them to take more care, or maybe he thought well-fed merchandise brought higher profits. It didn't matter. They were still their keepers, he and Iago still slaves.

"Hoy! Gibbs!" One of the mates gave a shout from the women's side of the bulkhead. "They's all dead back here! Every last one o' them! The young ones, too!"

"How, by hell?"

The man appeared in the doorway. "They got chain marks roun' their necks! Even the little uns! Looks like they been strangled. There's an old one hangin' from a rafter!"

Gibbs swore. "Well, jus' don' stand there! Get 'em out." He turned to another mate. "Johnstone, go help 'im."

"What if they's sick?"

"They ain't sick. They killed themselves, y' fool."

"Why'd they do that?"

"They got some weird belief their souls go back to Afrik when they die. Now get in there b'fore I wring your neck, too."

As the watch removed the dead women and children from their side of the bulkhead, Joachin felt numb. What would push a mother to murder her own children, unless it was the belief their future held a worse fate? It seemed a sad thing to seek salvation through death. When it was quiet once more and the port watch gone, he sensed a dark regard. He sought the source. Once again, he locked eyes with the giant.

A deep despair that would never be eased, no matter how many years passed, filled the man's heavy gaze. His rage hadn't diminished one iota, but Joachin suspected it had shifted slightly. He and Iago were no longer the focus of his hate.

"*Lo siento.*" I'm sorry, Joachin told him.

"Who are you talking to, Joachin?" Iago had been quiet for some time. The deaths had affected him, also.

"Him." Joachin nodded at the giant.

"Those dead women and children. His kin do you think?"

"Who can say?"

"He reminds me of her. That girl." Iago sighed. "Maybe he's her older brother or something. I guess I should be glad Boyle took her. Otherwise, she'd have killed herself, too." He risked another glance at the giant. "He hates us, doesn't he?"

"We aren't his problem."

"Maybe we can be his solution. If we freed him, removed his chains, he could join us, fight with us." Iago grew excited. "We could take this ship!"

"If we were to break his chains, he'd go on a rampage, Iago. He's lost loved ones who were dear to him. He's like a caged lion. Lions don't care which side they're on."

"Maybe. It's still worth a chance." He coughed again.

"Just get better. I'm working on a plan. Hopefully, it'll force a bigger wedge between the crew. Have some water." He propped him up by the shoulders and helped him drink from the pail.

Iago wiped his mouth as Joachin set him back down. "So, what's the plan?"

"I don't want to say, yet. No point in building false hope."

"Does it have to do with your dreaming?"

Iago's perceptions had become so acute of late. "Like I said, if it works, I'll tell you."

"Fine. Don't say anything. But I still think that's exactly what you're up to."

"Think what you like." Joachin bent to his rice and beans, scooping the mash into his mouth. He wasn't hungry, especially not after the tragedy they had just witnessed, but he had to eat. Across the way, the giant did the same but with more difficulty due to the cuffs on his wrists.

🐍

After eating and relieving themselves, there wasn't much else to do. Joachin told Iago to rest, saying he meant to do the same. Now was the time to press his advantage. He wasn't sure if he was strong enough to overwhelm Boyle with more dreams, especially if the captain was awake. Hopefully, Boyle would be weaker now.

He lulled himself into a doze, that trance-like state where he was able to rouse himself should he and Iago be threatened, but relaxed enough to allow the visions to form. His control kept slipping from his grasp. He needed to sleep. His body was still healing.

He pictured the pirate in his mind. Where was Boyle at this time of day? In his quarters or on deck? And which ship? *La Estrella* or the *Raven*?

Peace, he told himself. He would find him. Lys had helped him before; she would help him, again. As if his faith had been answered, the images began to unfold.

Unexpectedly, he found himself travelling the black road again, the same one with the inky boulders framing either side. That alarmed him at first, but he accepted the vision, trusting it would show him what he needed to know. Beyond the dark hills, the unchanging sunrise tinted the sky, shining on the Summerland of his Ancestors, perhaps. One day he would go there, but not just yet.

A disturbing thought struck him. *I'm not dying, am I?* He decided against it; he wasn't muddle-headed or struggling to reach that land as before.

On a far hill, a beacon sent shimmering rays across the sky.

That was new. The place had to be a landmark of some sort. As he pondered it, he felt exposed. His back prickled unpleasantly. He turned abruptly, wondering what new threat lay behind him.

Alonso de Santangél floated there, shining like a disapproving angel. His pale face bore its usual look of irritation. *I see you've come back here.*

Relief swept through him. Miriam must have sent him. *No. This is the first time I've returned to–whatever this place is.* He considered the shadows about them.

Miriam wants to know how you are. This seems to be the only thing I'm good for–flying back and forth between the Phoenix and here.

Alonso looked as if he had been sucking limes. Was that even possible? *I appreciate what you're doing, Alonso. I'm trying my best to return to her.*

You won't have much luck if you stay on this road.

Was that a hopeful remark? There was little point in being rankled by it. He understood Alonso's frustration. *Perhaps I've returned here because I'm still under threat. The pirate who took this ship believes a Diaphani will be the end of him. He keelhauled Iago, yesterday.*

For the first time in his experience, Alonso seemed genuinely concerned. *What? Is Iago–?*

He survived it. Don't tell Luci or Miriam about it.

The concern vanished. *Why would I? You've upset them enough. Far be it from me to add to their troubles.*

How is Miriam?

She's fine.

Tell her I miss her, that I love her.

It was the wrong thing to say. Alonso's eyes shuttered into slits and his mouth snapped shut. He might have been a shop closing up for the night. *I need to get back*, he replied shortly.

Wait! I could use your expertise! There was so much more he could do, if only he had help–the kind Alonso might provide.

Alonso paused.

At least he was listening—that was something. *I'm trying to attack Boyle. I want to unhinge him, make him do irrational things so the crew vote him out, maybe remove him altogether. Last night, I sent him a nightmare. I want to strike him again, but in a waking dream.*

Alonso frowned. *So what's stopping you?*

There was no other way to earn his help, than to admit his ignorance. *I'm not sure how.*

What do you expect me to do?

When he's up and around, I need to know where he is exactly, what he's doing. I'm not a seer, but you showed Miriam things in the past. If you could do that for me...for Iago...we'd have a stronger chance of surviving. If it works, you can return to Miriam and tell her what we did. Or what you did for Iago's sake. She'll appreciate the effort. Luci will, too.

He watched him struggle with it. Alonso frowned at the sunrise and shook his head. *Gods! To think I might help my worst rival! The one man she might love even more than she loves me.* He glanced back at him with burning eyes. *If our places were switched, would you do this for me?*

It was a fair question, one that deserved an honest answer. Not that he could reply in any other way. *I wouldn't want to, but I would. Miriam's happiness means more to me than my own.*

Alonso didn't say anything for a time. Finally, he nodded. *All right. For her, I'll do it.*

Yes! Thank you! He wanted to punch the sky. Alonso glowered. Best not to dwell on it. *How do I see what you see? I'm not sure of the process.* Better to ask before he changed his mind.

You need to rouse, a bit. When I show Miriam things, she's awake. I might even be able to help you send the hallucinations. I can grab the images you intend from your mind.

Really? Let's try.

We need to leave this place, first. Without warning, he faded. So did the black road and its distant sunrise. The world tipped, and they spun in circles as if spiralling down a long, dark funnel.

When he came to, he was still drowsy, but the world had re-established itself. The place still stank. There was rotting straw and his hard pallet beneath him. He couldn't see Alonso, but his skin prickled as if he were near. Across from him, Iago snored. Francis still hadn't returned. He let his mind go blank and focused on his breathing.

The first image came as a bit of a shock. One moment, there was nothing. In the next, it was as if he stood on the spar deck with Boyle in full view. He turned abruptly, not wanting Boyle to see him or to be a part of the hallucination as it began. He headed to the port rail and stood in shadow. Boyle looked ill-tempered, his face haggard from too disruptive a night. "I want ev'ry piece scraped from ev'ry post n' pillar y' find on this goddamned ship! Every last bit!" he shouted at starboard. He winced as if his own voice were too loud. Half of the crew were busy with knives, scraping away the gilt Don Lope had so lovingly bestowed on *La Estrella*, dropping their shavings into pails. Joachin wasn't sure where the rest were. Dirk was nowhere to be seen, nor Francis. Maybe they had been assigned to the *Raven*.

"No offence, Cap'n, but why this?" Tucker stood near the great cabin, not far from where Joachin watched. "The gold'll hardly be worth th' effort. There's more on Xaymaca, if we find that mine."

Boyle settled himself onto a barrel. "If I say it's worth th' effort, it's worth th' effort."

"All right, keep yer cod on." Tucker went back to his scraping.

Boyle waved and pointed. "Carter, keep an eye on th' wench!" His bed slave was easing herself towards the starboard rail, likely thinking to jump over, Joachin thought. Perhaps she had heard about the other women and children. It was no surprise she might choose suicide over rape.

"Get back there, you!" Carter pointed at the mizzenmast. The girl didn't move. He grabbed her and carried her unresisting back to it. "Cap'n, I can't keep watchin' 'er. Every time I look away, she moves. We got to tie 'er."

"Fine. Do it." Boyle pinched his nose.

It was time to influence him, but how? Like the portrait frame he had infiltrated, he suspected he needed to remain within Boyle's notice, but like a ghost among the crew. Was it like this for Miriam? He doubted it. He had never heard of a seer disembodying herself to influence people or events from afar—which was what he was trying to do. Should Boyle detect him, he would know it was impossible for him to be in two places at once. He would see him as part of the curse.

Gods, this juggling was difficult! On deck, he was a vague presence, but he was also in the pirate's mind. His own body below, without his soul to animate it, was also vulnerable.

There was no way of knowing what might happen. If he focused on Boyle too much, would he draw his attention? Or would the visions be overwhelming enough? Maybe it would be better to wait until tonight, when Boyle was asleep and vulnerable. But if he did, he would lose the advantage of time. He had to strike now, while Boyle was still susceptible from the night before.

He held onto the deck rail to anchor himself. Boyle was suffering from a pounding headache. The sooner they did this, the better.

Do what? Who said that? Boyle glanced about like a startled gull. Joachin withdrew immediately, afraid he might notice him at the port rail. The pirate was still twitchy from the night before.

What are you doing? Alonso filled his mind. Suddenly, they were back on the slave deck. He was on his pallet. Alonso stood shining beside him.

I'm having trouble, he admitted. *I have to maintain a presence above decks. I also need to get inside Boyle's head. I'm not sure how to split the focus, to make him see what I want him to see. Right now, he's too aware.*

What do you want him to see?

Joachin showed him.

Alonso smiled grimly. For a moment, Joachin beheld the Knight Templar Alonso might have become—ruthless, efficient, and cruel. Woe to the Infidels. Plague of the East. *I'll hold him, so you can affect his mind,* Alonso replied easily.

How will you hold him?

It's like opening a channel. We go in together. Then I anchor you, while you play with his mind. His smile grew broader. It was unnerving.

You have a strange sense of play, Joachin said.

You're the one with the vivid imagination.

With no warning at all, they were back on the spar deck. With a start, Joachin realized he was already looking at the world through Boyle's eyes. The captain still had a raging headache, but while he and

Alonso had been discussing things, Boyle had found another jug of sherry. All about him, the crew scraped and toiled. The slave girl had been hobbled, her hands tethered to a rope about the mizzen. She still had a small range of motion, but not enough to reach the rail.

As Boyle took a swig, Joachin imagined Don Lope's decapitated head in his hands. Unaware of the change, Boyle gripped it by the hair and hefted it to his mouth. Don Lope's lips met his own in a bloody kiss. Boyle let out a howl and dropped the head. Inside his ribs, his heart pounded like cannon fire.

"Mother o' Sul!" He gaped at the jug rolling at his feet as if he couldn't quite believe what he had seen. Joachin tamped down his delight. It wouldn't do for Boyle to sense their interference. Alonso did his part by keeping him unworthy of notice. The crew stared at Boyle open-mouthed.

Boyle waved his arms at them. "What th' hell are y' lookin' at? Y' never drop anythin'? Get back t' work!" In spite of his bluster, Joachin caught his thoughts. *Ain't good when y' start seein' things.* There'd been that time in Lisbo, when the black dogs had chased him down an alley. They hadn't been real. Maybe he should lay off the drink for a time. A blessin' it was, he didn't have the shakes....

He righted the jug with a firm hand to show the crew he had reverted to normal. Other than his back and head, he was all right. But gods, what a scare.

As he drew in a fresh lungful to clear his head, Joachin struck him again. The wind came up. The sky darkened and turned indigo. Perplexed, because it was far too soon for sunset, Boyle glanced at the sky. On every inch of *La Estrella*'s yards, a grisly crew hung. Bones shone like ivory through gangrened flesh. Hundreds of black pits for eyes stared down at him. And then, to his horror, the corpses with legs climbed down. Those that lacked them dropped to the deck like rotten slabs of meat. Boyle squawked and felt for the cutlass at his hip.

"Care to join us, Captain?"

A ghoulish Dirk confronted him. He grinned wickedly, his lower jaw hanging from a fleshy string. His doublet was rent in the middle, his intestines spilling through the hole. As if disembowelment was of no account, he had drawn his sword with a boney hand.

With a howl, Boyle drew his cutlass, intent on skewering him. Dirk parried and attacked. Boyle fell back. Joachin congratulated himself on the vision going well. Boyle was well into the hallucination. When he came out of it, he would be convinced Dirk was at the heart of it. He would challenge him. Their rivalry would come to a head. The crew would fear his madness. They would vote him out.

Boyle faltered, shook his head.

Damn it, Joachin thought. He had become distracted, again. He couldn't afford to lose the advantage, now. With a will, he imagined Dirk again, but Boyle was in a half-trance, more confused than convinced. His glance fell upon the girl.

Still tied to the mizzen mast, she watched him dully. Boyle's mind shifted like gears striking cogs. She was responsible for this! That black witch was directing this waking nightmare, it had to be! He'd show her, beat her within an inch of her life, then toss her to the waves!

He bore down upon her like a maddened bull. Joachin fought to regain control, when suddenly, the giant flowered into being, barring Boyle's way. How? The big man was no more present than he was. Their bodies lay below, among the slaves. Was the giant a dreamer too? Was this Afrikan magic? They were said to have strange gods.

Boyle lifted his cutlass to cleave the man in half.

"Cap'n, it's me! Tucker! 'E's gone crazy, mates! Help!"

The vision shattered. Joachin floated free, no longer inhabiting Boyle. Instead, he hovered at the port rail. The crew had surrounded the captain. They held him as he raged, but they quickly fell back sensing his return to sanity. Tucker cowered at Boyle's knees, cradling his head. The captain hadn't cut him to pieces, he hadn't even drawn his sword. Instead, he had battered him bare-handed.

"Get off me!" Boyle bellowed.

"What's going on here?" Dirk had returned from the *Raven*. He hadn't bothered to ask permission to board, or if he had, no one had heard. Francis and a few of the other men stood in tow.

Boyle reddened and glared at Dirk.

Tucker rose to the captain's defence. "I tripped...spilled m' bucket. All the gilt went over the side...." He shared a look with Boyle.

"Gilt?" Dirk demanded.

"Aye. Cap'n says th' ship don't need it."

Dirk set his hands on his hips. "Why wasn't I asked my opinion of this? She's a thing of beauty! We won't get near her worth if we remove her ornament!" He glared at Boyle. "You've ruined her!"

"She's recognizable." Boyle rubbed his head. "Last thing we need is t' have some island guv'nor identifyin' 'er. How're th' stores aboard th' *Raven*?"

The change in subject did little to mollify Dirk. "Short. Someone's been pilfering."

Boyle frowned. Dirk would trust his own crew, Joachin knew. The guilty party had to be one of Tucker's band.

"Well, I'm sure *La Estrella* can make up th' shortfall." Boyle dismissed it. "We'll skimp on th' slaves if we got to."

"They need to arrive in good condition, Captain." Dirk eyed the girl, still tied to the mast.

"They'll suffer it. They're built t' survive a rough life."

"That isn't the point. We need to get to the bottom—"

"Any o' you men stealin'?" Blight shouted. The starboard crew voiced their denials, a few louder than the rest.

"There." Blight thrust his chin at Dirk. "None o' 'em done it, so it wasn't them. Had t' be your watch. Anyone caught stealin' knows th' penalty." He eyed each man in turn and then added, "Could be th' slaves."

"How?" Dirk was dumbfounded by this leap in logic. "They have no freedom!"

"Some of 'em do." Boyle glared at Francis. Joachin stiffened.

"Captain, that's unlikely in the extreme."

Boyle waved Dirk off. "I got a headache. If ye need me, I'll be in m' cabin." The crew parted as he pushed his way through them. When he reached the girl, he paused, then swore and left her where she was.

Seen enough? Once again, Alonso had returned them to the slave deck.

I thought we had him, when he attacked Tucker, Joachin said.

Oh, we upset him well enough. He may have bluffed his way out of it, but the crew will talk about what happened today, even those loyal to him. If more things go wrong, they'll blame him, say he's cursed the ship.

He already thinks Iago and I have done that.

I need to get back to Miriam. In the meantime, keep your wits sharp. When your mind is on Boyle, your body is at risk.

As if he didn't know that already. *When you're with me, wouldn't you be aware of any attempts on my life?*

Probably, but I'm as human as you. It's easy to be distracted when your mind is elsewhere.

It was interesting Alonso still thought of himself as human.

Besides, you've had help from an unforeseen quarter. Alonso directed his attention to the giant who lay watching them.

A surge of excitement ran through Joachin. *He was there, Alonso! I saw him! He appeared when Boyle threatened the girl!*

Perhaps you aren't the only one who wields power in dreams.

The possibility of an alliance was exciting. He held the slave's gaze for a moment until the man turned away. Did he also see Alonso? He voiced the thought.

He might, Alonso replied. *I should go.*

Thank you, my friend. He wished he could clasp him by the arm.

Alonso's face remained as bright and impassive as the moon. *Stay safe,* he cautioned. Then he winked out of sight.

He didn't call me a friend, but he did wish for my safety, Joachin thought. That was something. Together, they had unhinged the captain. Who would have thought? Across the slave deck, the giant appeared to be sleeping, but he doubted that was so. The man was waging his own war. Perhaps their shared motivations would pull them together, unite them in a common cause.

I can only hope, he thought.

Chapter Fifteen: The Beating

KIP WAS ABSENT from their company for the day. Miriam only noticed it because Casi was unusually quiet and Luci grew concerned about her. The women had spent the afternoon above decks, enjoying the breeze and falling into their usual routine of mending and preparing meals. At one point, Luci asked Ignaas where Kip was.

"Kind o' ye t' inquire, Missus," Ignaas said. "Told me 'e was feelin' queasy this mornin'. Must've et somethin' what didn't agree with him, but don't worry." He cast a reassuring look at Casi, "He'll be back t' 'is old self in no time."

The ship's bell rang the first dog watch. Larboard took up their posts and replaced starboard. Miriam welcomed the change. She didn't like how Jager's men constantly watched her, as if they might glimpse what lay beneath her veil. Ignaas was an idler, so none of the watches affected him.

Casi kept her attention on the net she was mending.

"Are you feeling poorly?" Luci asked.

Casi shook her head.

"Then what's wrong? You've hardly eaten a thing all day."

"I'm not hungry, Maré." Her voice was so low, Miriam barely heard her.

"Well, hungry or not, you need to eat some supper." Luci pursed her lips as if food would fix everything.

"Tell you what, Missy Casi," Ignaas said. "After you eat, y' can come with me t' check on Kip. That'll cheer him." He noted her lack of enthusiasm. "Or maybe it can wait 'til tomorrow."

Zara straightened to ease her back. "So tell me, Ignaas, how much longer do y' think we'll be on this boat...er, ship?"

He squinted at the horizon. The sun was due to set in a couple of hours. "Cap'n says we're makin' good time. I reckon 'nother few weeks, we'll dock in Nueva Esbaña. After that, it's a short hop to Xaymaca."

"What will you do once we make port?"

"Me? Why I expect I'll stay with th' *Phoenix* as long as she'll have me."

"You could take up farming. We could use a good man like you."

"Farmin'? I know nothin' of it. I'd be a fish out o' water."

"You could learn. No reason why we can't put our hands to all sorts of things. Luci, here's a weaver. She and her man, Lys rest his soul, dealt in indigo."

"Indigo? Now, there's a fair bus'ness." Ignaas looked impressed.

"And somewhere in them islands, lies the secret of the true red dye. If we found it, we could make a fortune."

"Never fancied such a thing! Been an ol' sea dog for too long, I guess."

Zara scoffed. "You're not old! No older than me, and I'm just over... thirty."

Miriam suppressed a grin.

"Well, when I listen t' you, y' make me feel like life could be a bigger adventure."

"Think on it, Ignaas. When we first started out from Esbaña, I was afraid, but I never let on. No one ever knew. Now, with the New World ahead of me, it's exciting! It'll be hard work, but we'll carve us a place."

"Us?"

"My people. You'd be welcome too, of course."

"Oh, no!" Casi set a trembling hand to her lips. The net tumbled to her feet. She gasped and stumbled for the companionway leading to the lower decks.

"Where are you going?" Luci caught her by the wrist and pulled her aside. They spoke in terse whispers. Casi became even more agitated.

"Somethin' upsettin' her?" Ignaas lifted an eyebrow at Miriam.

"I'm not sure." She rose from where she had been sitting and headed for them. "What's going on?" she asked Luci.

"She says Jager de Groot is beating Kip!"

"Maré, let me go! He's going to kill him!" Casi struggled in Luci's grasp.

"Where are they?"

"Near the cook's station! Down below!"

They ran for the companionway. Without another word to Ignaas, Zara set off after them, as Ignaas stared, open-mouthed.

On the main deck, the starboard watch were settling into their hammocks for a short nap before being called back to duty. They glanced up as the women descended the ladder into their domain. Jager wasn't among them.

"Over there," Miriam directed. They headed for the narrow entry separating the cook's station from the rest of the deck. As they were about to enter, Jager appeared in the doorway, blocking their path. "What do you *vrouwen* want?" he demanded. "You got no business in here." Something ruddy stained his knuckles.

"Get out of our way," Miriam demanded.

"No. Go back to yer hole."

"Is Kip in there? We want to see him."

"He ain't in here."

"Yes he is, and you've blood on your hands!" Miriam pointed out. "Now get out of my way, or I'll shout for the captain."

"Keep yer dress on. Had a bloody nose, is all. I was checkin' up on 'im."

He stepped aside, taking his time. Miriam shoved past him. Kip lay in his hammock, unmoving. The dull light cast by the station's lantern revealed what Jager had done. The boy's face was bloody, his nose askew and resembling a mashed plum. One eye had swollen shut.

"Kip!" Casi was at his side in a moment. "Speak to me!" When he didn't, she burst into tears. Luci drew her into her arms.

Miriam turned to Zara. "We'll need clean water for him, arnica if the ship has it, willow for his pain—"

"You needn't order me, I know full well!" Affronted, she bustled off. Zara wasn't the only one to snap when confronted with a distressing situation.

"Dear gods, why would Jager do this?" Luci looked to Miriam for answers.

"I don't know, but we'll get to the bottom of it." His injuries looked painful. Moments later, Zara reappeared with Ignaas in tow. He showed the women where he kept the medical supplies, and they treated Kip as well as they could.

Jager's 'plan' to taint the captain's food came out once Kip was able to speak. Ignaas was excused from serving the captain and officers' their supper, so he might watch over the boy. Miriam wrapped Kip's head, including his nose, but left holes for his nostrils so he might breathe. Ignaas fed him a poppy extract for his pain. When he was as comfortable as he could possibly be, she asked him what had happened. "What did you do with the packet?"

"Threw it overboard," He squinted at her with his good eye. "Didn't want to hurt nobody."

She nodded, but later, once she and the Tribe had retired to their *hole*, as Jager called it, she voiced her regrets. "What do you think it was?" She put the question to Zara, hoping she might soothe ruffled feelings.

Zara shrugged. "Could have been anything, Matriarch. There's lots that can upset a stomach, even do a body in. Arsenic, maybe. It's tasteless and easily hidden, but who can say? They keep it on board for the rats. Lys knows why that poor boy didn't say anything."

Casi spoke up. "He was trying to be brave."

"Well, brave or no, it would've been better if he'd told someone."

"Do you think Captain Vrooman will believe us if we tell him?" Luci asked.

Ximen shook his head. "He doesn't like problems on his ship. It's Kip's word against Jager's."

Zara rounded on him. "What more proof does he need? That boy was bludgeoned half to death, and all because he wouldn't do what that monster wanted!"

"I think we're missing the point."

Everyone turned to Miriam.

"Why does Jager hate us so much?" she asked. "Is it superstition or religious zeal? We know he thinks we're witches. If Kip had gone through with Jager's plan, we would've been accused of poisoning the captain's food. Then what? Would Captain Vrooman have tried and sentenced us?" She turned to Ximen. "Do you know the protocol?"

He shook his head. "I'm afraid I don't."

"Let's assume that was his plan. How do the masters of merchant vessels deal with attempted murder at sea?"

No one said it, but hangings from the yardarms seemed likely.

Zara stabbed the air with a forefinger. "We need to nip this in the bud. Even if Captain Vrooman doesn't believe us, we have to alert him there are ill goings on. If anything else happens—"

"Without proof, he still won't believe us," Ximen insisted.

"What did Jager say to you, Miriam? About knowing an old woman who talked to the dark?" Luci asked.

"He said she was a poisoner. That she burned, I'm guessing, for witchcraft. Her daughter was a witch too, but she escaped. From him, I'm assuming."

"Maybe they were related?"

"We have no way of knowing. If he's biased against us because of a personal history, we'll have a stronger case against him. There's only one way to find out. We need to talk to the captain."

Captain Vrooman and Second Mate, Henk Ostrander, had just finished their meal when Miriam and Zara requested an audience. They were granted admittance. Miriam had the impression Captain Vrooman considered her yet another ship-board inconvenience with which he had to deal. *It doesn't matter,* she thought. It was his duty to listen. She explained what had happened to Kip and why.

"But if that's the case, why hasn't the boy reported the incident to me?" Captain Vrooman blinked rapidly as if uncomfortable with her allegations. Henk Ostrander looked as if he suspected Jager might be capable of such a thing, but he said nothing.

"That boy was beaten within an inch of his life! How was he to—?" Zara blurted.

Miriam held up a hand to silence her. "Ignaas will come to you to corroborate Kip's story, Captain," she said. "Even so, we understand it's our word against the bosun's."

"It's a serious charge, Madam. You're suggesting my bosun meant to poison me. And my officers, too." He shifted uncomfortably.

"It isn't a charge I make lightly."

"You have no proof."

"No. Kip says he threw the packet overboard."

"There still remains that brute's assault on the boy!" Zara said. "He also struck Casi, my great grand-niece, although we never reported it to you. He attacked her while we were still in port at Tenerifa."

Captain Vrooman frowned. "Why would he strike your kinswoman?"

"He didn't like her going for our water ration! If you can imagine!"

Captain Vrooman glanced at his second mate. "Was there any indication of mental incapacity when you signed de Groot on?"

Henk Ostrander shook his head. "No, sir. He's fond of quoting scripture. I thought it beneficial at the time—a moderating influence to keep the men in line, especially with ladies present."

"I see. Well, perhaps you can look into it further. Speak with the starboard watch, and Piet Spoor, in particular." He turned back to Miriam and Zara. "I appreciate you bringing these concerns to me, ladies. Unfortunately, without proof, there's little I can do—"

"There's Kip! Jager assaulted him! And what about Casi?" Zara said.

"I wish you'd have brought my attention to your kinswoman's assault at the time. I might have been able to do something about it, but too much time has passed. As for the boy, I'll speak with him about the incident."

"*Incident?* Does someone have to die for you to take us seriously?"

Captain Vrooman's lips tightened. "As he and my bosun are members of my crew, they are my responsibility and not your concern, Madam. If you ladies feel unsafe, perhaps it's best you confine yourselves to your area, below."

"We'll suffocate down there!"

Miriam set a restraining hand on Zara's arm.

"Of course, Mister Ostrander will have a word with the bosun and the starboard watch about your concerns." Captain Vrooman turned to his second mate. "Advise Mister de Groot he is to avoid the passengers." Henk Ostrander nodded solemnly. He turned back to the women. "I also suggest you ladies remain in your area. Now, if you'll excuse us...." He rose, indicating their audience was over.

As they left the cabin, Zara was not done complaining. "That captain's as useless as a tit on a tree. A fine thing! We're confined to our cell, while Jager de Groot roams free! Men! They do what's best—for them!"

Miriam said nothing.

"Don't you think it's unfair, Matriarch?"

"I do."

"Then what are we going to do about it?"

Miriam drew in a breath to compose her thoughts. "I'm not sure. Jager has a problem with us. He fears and hates us, so much so, he's willing to create a situation where we're blamed. Maybe he hoped we would hang. If he tries anything again, he'll be more direct about it."

"You think he'll attack us outright?"

"Possibly. But he's also been ordered to keep away from us. I'm hoping when the captain gets to the bottom of Kip's assault, he'll confine Jager as punishment. With Jager out of the way, he may restore our freedom."

Zara looked pained. "Well, it isn't a great solution, but I'll do anything if it means I won't be stuck down here for goddess knows how long." She sniffed and made a face. "I can barely stand my own stink."

They said nothing as they descended to the main deck. Jager and his crew watched them without comment. It was hard to ignore Jager's self-satisfied smile. Miriam had the distinct impression he felt he had won something, even if his attempt to have them judged had failed.

His smugness became clearer when Ignaas visited them in their alcove several hours later.

"What do you mean Kip refuses to confess what that swine did to him?" Zara's voice rose shrilly. They had not foreseen this. Beside her, Luci let out a gasp.

"I'm sorry, Missus! I told 'im, 'You got t' tell th' cap'n what happened, boy!' But I think he's scared of what else Jager might do."

"Surely, he said something," Miriam replied.

"He did, but I'm shamed t' say, he lied! When th' cap'n asked 'im what happened, he said he'd run into a bulkhead. Said he didn't know nothin' 'bout a packet. I can hardly believe it!"

"Why would he do that?" Luci asked.

"He's afraid. That's the only reason," Miriam said. Jager's conceit made sense now. He might not have accomplished his plan of having them accused, but he had managed to punish them all the same. They were trapped down here, where they were out of sight and out of mind. "Thank you for telling us, Ignaas." It hardly seemed something to be thankful for.

"I'll keep workin' on 'im, Missus. Boy's got t' tell the truth, no matter what." He tugged his forelock and left.

"Well if this isn't a spoiled pot." Zara glared at Ximen as if it were his fault. "Who's to say that Jager won't find a permanent way to finish us? Maybe the captain's forbidden him from coming down here, but there's others who will do his bidding. I say, we crush the biggest cockroach to take care of the rest."

Ximen grimaced. "Cockroaches don't work that way."

"Turn of phrase, Old Man! You're far too picky on details."

"Zara's right." Miriam jumped in before they could start bickering. "Jager remains a threat. Since he already thinks I'm a witch, let's confirm it for him."

All about her, the eyes of her Tribe widened in surprise. Everyone waited for her to continue.

"We'll have to prepare, carefully. If what I have in mind works, some of us will have to run for the captain before things get out of hand. But once the trap is set, I think the rest will be easy." She paused. "I'm hoping you can help me, Casi."

Casi's chin trembled, but she stood straight. "I'm not scared. I'll do it for Kip, for all of us."

"Good girl. I knew you would."

"What would you have her do?" Luci looked worried.

"What she does so well, already," Miriam replied. "What I want her to do is *listen*."

Chapter Sixteen: Battle Stations

"**WHAT THE HELL** happened, Gibbs?" On the waist near the port rail, Dirk stood in hushed conversation with Francis and the third mate. The man had taken off his scarf and was twisting it in his hands.

"We was takin' the gilt from th' ship, like he wanted, when suddenly he jumps up and drops his jug like it bit 'im. Then he goes crazy and attacks Tucker...aye, *Tucker*! Like 'e was 'is worst enemy!"

"Too much drink?" Francis eyed Tucker who had returned to removing the gilt from the captain's door.

"Never bothered 'im that way, afore."

"Cupid's Disease?" A night in Venus' arms sometimes led to a lifetime with Mercury, or so the saying went.

"Doubtful," Dirk replied. "We haven't made port in nearly a year. The French disease would have shown up long ago. How are the crew?"

"Troubled," Gibbs said.

"Even starboard?"

"Them that was here. Nobody wants Captain Folly draggin' 'em across th' sea." He nodded Tucker's way. "Tucker's still loyal."

"I need to know who stands with us. Get the men talking. Find out what's what."

The door to the officers' quarters burst open. Boyle sagged against the frame, looking like a dilapidated wine sack. "Tucker!" he bawled seeing him there. "Ready th' cockboat, an' bring me that girl!"

"Aye, Cap'n." Tucker set down his pail and set off to do Boyle's bidding.

"Where's MacFee?" Boyle demanded, glancing about.

Francis hadn't had much time to learn who every member of the crew was, but MacFee was the ship's carpenter.

"Up on th' foredeck, sir. Carvin' dead eyes," one of the mates said.

"Get him. You men," Boyle waved at the starboard crew. "Remove them culverins and refit 'em on the *Raven*."

"What?" Dirk crossed the deck to Boyle. "Begging your pardon, sir, but that doesn't make sense. Where do you plan to cut new ports? There's no room!"

"I disagree. An' I think I know m' own ship better than you do. Ah, MacFee," he added, seeing the carpenter approach with his starboard escort. "I need y' to come with me to th' *Raven*."

"Wait a minute!" Dirk stepped between Boyle and MacFee. "You also told me I'd be in charge of *La Estrella* as we make our way to Xaymaca. I'll need protection if we become separated. Or is that what you have in mind? To dump our guns and put us at risk?" His eyes narrowed.

Boyle's expression darkened. "What are ye inferrin', Mister Dirk? That I'd sacrifice all these good men, here?" He waved his arms expansively as if to take in all the crew. "Keep suggestin' such things, an' I'll accuse ye of incitin' mutiny."

There was something about his bluster that didn't ring true, Francis thought. He was up to something. Tucker arrived with the girl. Boyle clapped a hand about her neck and yanked her to his side.

"I never meant to suggest—" Dirk said.

"Y' never do, an' I'm tired o' arguin'. See to them guns, Tucker. I'll be on th' *Raven*."

"But, sir!" Dirk protested.

"Another word, Mister Dirk, an' I'll have y' clapped in irons."

Dirk's expression fell. He was beaten. *Or he wants the captain to think so,* Francis thought.

"Fine!" Dirk called. "Starboard watch is nearly over. Port will see to it!" From his expression, Boyle didn't like the slight change of plan, but he said nothing of it. As the hands lowered the cockboat to the water, the girl was set into a harness. Boyle clambered over the rail. Tucker headed for the companionway leading to the lower decks.

Dirk stopped him. "Where do you think you're going? I said port would oversee the removal of the guns."

"Cap'n also wants me t' take an inventory o' th' stores."

"Oh? He intends to pillage us, too?"

"Don't know."

"You don't know, *sir*."

"Aye...*sir*."

"You're nearly off duty. For the remainder of it, remove the rest of the gilt on the quarterdeck. I'll have someone else see to the stores."

"But th' Cap'n—"

"If he wants it done, he doesn't care who does it, Tucker. Do as I say or I'll have you confined." Dirk waved him off. Tucker left, scowling.

Gibbs drew in close. "We aren't really goin' t' remove them guns, are we, sir?"

Dirk's expression was tight. "Get down to the stores, Gibbs. Take Shite with you."

I need to come up with a better name, Francis thought.

"See what we have for powder and shot," Dirk added, "then report back to me."

He won't give up the only protection we have, Francis reflected. He followed Gibbs down the companionway to the slave deck. It was murky, but he could make out the bodies lying miserably in rows. Did Dirk think Boyle cared about the slaves, even as cargo? He had done nothing but complain about them from the start. It was unlikely he would chase after the gold on Xaymaca, either. Boyle appreciated what was in front of him—and only that. He had taken the girl and MacFee. Only they and the guns had value.

Near the bow, Joachin and Iago lay in the dark. Francis didn't stop to check on them. Time was short, and he and Gibbs had to see what ordnance was available. According to the crew, Boyle had been acting crazily. Had Joachin been involved? Had he attacked Boyle—in a dream? *Maybe all that matters is avoiding being blown to bits*, Francis considered. He clattered after Gibbs into the hold.

An hour later, a shiver of premonition passed through Joachin as a pool of illumination zigzagged toward him and Iago. As his eyes adjusted, he saw it was Francis, with a lantern in hand. "What's happening?" he asked as Iago struggled to rise.

"Boyle's stripping the ship." Francis was out of breath. "Dirk's been ordered to remove the culverins, *culebrinas*, I think you call them."

"Why?"

"He says he wants to refit them on the *Raven*, but everyone knows that's ridiculous. He'll either sell them...or dump them into the sea."

"That makes no sense," Iago said.

"Unless he intends to leave us defenceless." Joachin shared a look with Francis. "He's planning to attack us."

Francis sucked in a breath. "If you say it, it must be true. It's also what Dirk thinks. He doesn't intend to give up the guns without a fight."

Gibbs appeared on the companionway and peered at them in the darkness. "Shite, what're you gassin' on about? Dirk's waitin'! We got t' go!"

Francis looked disgruntled. "Could you not...? Oh, forget it." He glanced back at Joachin and Iago. "I'll report back as soon as I can."

Iago clutched him by the sleeve. "Where's the girl?"

Francis frowned. "What girl?"

"The girl Boyle struck until I got in the way."

"He took her to the *Raven*."

"We have to get her back!"

"Under the circumstances, there's no way we can do that, Iago. I'm sorry."

"*Shite!*" Gibbs shouted.

"On my way!" He hurried off, taking the lantern with him.

As the darkness closed about them once again, Joachin slid back onto his pallet and closed his eyes.

"What are you doing?" Iago sounded as if he were about to climb out of his skin.

"What I can. You need to calm down, Iago."

"I *can't* calm down!"

"You must. If I can't stop this, we'll need every bit of strength we have, come the dawn."

"What are you going to do in the meantime? Dream?"

"Yes."

"Dreams don't do anything!"

"They do more than you think."

"He'll have his way with her!"

"We have bigger things to worry about."

"We have to get her! I have to save her!"

Joachin sighed. "Under the circumstances, that's impossible, Iago. We may not even be able to save ourselves. Don't dwell on it, *primo*. Let me do what I can." He closed his eyes a second time, listening to his cousin fuss with his straw. *Black space,* he told himself. *Forget about Iago, forget about the vermin underfoot and the sores on your back.* He would shape a new fantasy, a dream where he would paint Boyle's death in the most vivid colour. Goddess help him, but the man had to die.

Dirk had taken over the great cabin. Francis, Gibbs, and several members of the port watch sat about the oaken table. Francis was tense with excitement. He and Gibbs had missed much during the planning session, but what they discovered would be taken as good news. They had found a dozen swivel guns stowed in the hold. Why they were there rather than on the rails was anyone's guess.

"Other than our cannon, how are we fixed for ordnance?" Dirk directed the question to Gibbs.

"*Versos*, sir! About ten out o' twelve that're workable."

"Very good. I wondered when I saw the rail sockets."

"A question." Francis held up his hand. "Why were they stored? Wouldn't it make more sense for them to be mounted and ready to meet all threats?"

Dirk shared an amused look with the crew. "Of course it would, Shite. I've never been able to decide whether the Esbañish are overly sure of themselves or just foolish. They tend to store their *versos* until needed. By the time they need them, it's usually too late. We'll refit them tonight under the cover of darkness. Hopefully, Boyle won't notice. Powder and shot?" He returned his attention to Gibbs.

"Enough to take out any comin' at us from th' shrouds or th' spar deck. Hopefully, he ain't preparin' our own guns agin' us."

"Count on it. The good thing is, despite our lesser fire, we have the better gunners."

The crew exchanged looks of pride.

"Anyone remaining from starboard who would rather stand with us?"

"Aye, Cap'n. All those not ordered to th' the *Raven*."

Dirk's new title was not lost on him. A brief smile touched his lips. "What of Tucker?"

"Not willin' t' be convinced. Johnstone's confined him to below."

Johnstone spoke up. "Tied 'im to a beam 'neath the fo'c'sle, sir. Cussed me a blue streak, he did."

"Why not put him in the hold?"

"I don't trust everyone from starboard, sir. Someone might let 'im go. Better he's tied, where we can keep an eye on 'im."

"Good thinking. The last thing we need is for him to alert Boyle."

"Minute th' guns start poundin', he'll change 'is tack," Gibbs said.

"Did Boyle return the cockboat?" Francis glanced around the circle. For some reason, it seemed important.

"He did. Wish he'd sent MacFee back with it, too," Johnstone replied.

Dirk looked pained. "MacFee's a good man. If there's any way we can save our carpenter, we must. Where's the boat, now? Above decks?"

"No, sir. We left it tethered on th' waves in case MacFee or any o' th' others try t' jump for it."

"Boyle may wonder."

"Maybe, but he's prob'ly too busy with that girl t' wonder anythin'." Gibbs smirked.

"Right." Dirk pressed his hands to the table. "It'll be dark soon. I want every lantern above decks snuffed, save for the stern. We'll need to leave that one to look normal. After the *versos* have been attached, I want them tarped. Below deck, ready the culverins. We hit the *Raven* at first light."

"What about the slaves?" *Am I the only one worried about them?* Francis wondered.

"What about them?" Dirk raised a ruddy eyebrow.

"If it doesn't go well, we can't let them go down with the ship."

"Not to worry, Shite. Your friends are slaves no longer. Feel free to bring them up from below." He smiled magnanimously, a king granting a boon.

"Not them." He had already assumed Joachin and Iago were free. "The others. Given the choice, they might fight."

Dirk looked sympathetic. *Or perhaps he wants me to think so,* Francis thought. "Shite, if we go down, they go down, too. You know I can't release them. Those with any strength are as apt to kill us as Boyle."

I don't know any such thing, Francis thought. Dirk was too comfortable, too dismissive in his prejudices. There were fewer fates worse than being chained to panicking men as cannon balls tore into a hull and water poured into the ship. Did Tucker still hold the slaves' keys? Maybe it was time he was relieved of them. "By your leave then, I'll see to my friends. My thanks."

"Don't mention it." Dirk dismissed him.

He had failed to notice he hadn't called him captain. *I signed with Boyle,* Francis reasoned. *If I have to, I'll argue it.* Given the choice between fighting or death, he bet on the slaves, especially the big man below. If he was wrong about that, chances were Boyle would kill them all, anyway.

In the forecastle, Tucker was still hugging the beam and cursing everyone within earshot. The gun deck, which also served as the men's quarters, was a frenzy of activity. The crew scrambled to stow possessions, clear space, and stack shot. The powder was too dangerous to handle; they would move it, later. As he wasn't an experienced hand, Francis kept out of the way.

"Devil take ya, yer've been nothin' but bad luck since y' come aboard!" a scarlet-faced Tucker accused him as he approached. "Should o' skewered ya t' hell! Hope Boyle blows ya outta th' water!"

"If he does, then he blows you out of the water, too. Really Tucker, that should be obvious. Now, if you'd just join us, I'll put in a good word for you with the captain."

"That poncey fop ain't my cap'n!"

"Actually, he is. And he's a good one, too." He patted him on the back and blocked him from the crew's view. "Let me tell you why Dirk's the better choice. First of all, he's of sounder mind and judgement."

"Judgement my arse!"

"Secondly, he's a master of surprise." Without warning, he grabbed Tucker by the throat and throttled him. Tucker's eyes bulged. He struggled to pull away, but the post prevented him from moving. Francis continued to chat pleasantly, as if nothing were awry. After a few moments, Tucker lost consciousness and slumped against the beam. Francis retrieved the keys from his belt and clapped him across the shoulder. "Good man!" he said heartily. "Dirk will be pleased! You rest, now. I'll get his permission to let you go." On his way out of the forecastle, he retrieved a lantern and slipped away.

Within moments, he was down in the murk of the slave deck. As he threaded his way to where Joachin and Iago lay, chained men watched him as he passed. They were fewer in number now, more widely spaced than when he had first come aboard. Unless they died, the pirates never bothered to move them. The giant lay on his side. Francis doubted he slept. The man was a chained lion, biding his time, awaiting his moment. Nothing passed, that those dark eyes didn't see.

Soon, my friend, Francis promised as he passed him by.

When he reached Joachin and Iago's small space, Joachin was dozing on his pallet. Iago was nowhere to be seen.

"Where's Iago?" He lifted the lantern and looked around.

Joachin's eyes flew open. In one smooth motion, he tumbled from his bed and pawed through Iago's straw. "Gods above, I hope he hasn't.... Damn! The knife is gone!" He met Francis' blank stare.

Iago had been anxious about the girl. "You don't think—"

"I do think!" Joachin side-stepped him and headed for the companionway.

Francis followed him. Iago couldn't swim—or could he? On the other hand, maybe that was something the Diaphani did. There was so much about these people he didn't know.

"If he's like me at that age, he's acting on instinct," Joachin told him. "Gods, but his intuition has been sharp of late! If he's gone above decks to look for an opportunity—"

"The cockboat!" He had no idea how he knew Iago had taken it, but he knew it as surely as Arlechinno had been his alias in the Commedia dell'arte. "The crew left it on the water!"

"Maybe no longer," Joachin replied grimly. They emerged onto the waist. Every lantern above decks, save the one hanging from the ship's stern, had been doused.

"Snuff that light!" someone hissed. Francis couldn't see who it was. It sounded like Gibbs. "Y' want th' *Raven* t' see what we're about?" Every hand not called to the culverins was busy securing the *versos* to their mounts. Two of the swivel guns at the end of the poop hadn't yet been attached. Francis doused the lamp.

Upwind and beneath a rising moon, the *Raven* bobbed on a choppy sea. She heeled slightly to starboard, which gave Boyle the advantage if he chose to fire. *La Estrella's* hull was similarly exposed. Still, they had the benefit of surprise unless a lovesick boy destroyed it. Joachin ran to the rail and looked down. There was no sign of the cockboat bumping against the hull or in the span between the ships. Either Iago had already made it to the *Raven*, or the ocean currents had swept him away.

"What's the trouble?" All business, Dirk joined them at the rail.

"We think Iago might have taken the cockboat to attempt a rescue," Francis told him. There was no better compass spin to put on it.

"Iago?"

"His cousin," He indicated Joachin who looked haggard.

"Gods! If Boyle finds him! Wait!" Dirk ordered as Joachin charged for the forecastle. "Where are you going?"

Joachin ignored him. Dirk slammed the forecastle's door shut and thrust him aside. "Are you mad?" He clutched him by the arm. "You can't go down there! You'll expose us!"

Joachin stared hard at the hand on his elbow and then at the man possessing it. Even beneath the faint light of the moon, Francis read murder in Joachin's eyes. Goddess help them if he did anything rash. "He needs to dream!" he told Dirk in a rush.

"Dream?" Dirk dropped his hand, but he and Joachin continued to stare daggers at each other.

"He's a dreamer! He sees things in dreams at will! It's a gypsy thing, a gift from the goddess!"

Dirk's eyes widened. "Truly? You can do this?"

Joachin's jaw tensed. He was grinding his teeth.

"That's why Boyle was acting so crazy, earlier!" Francis continued. "Joachin affected him! Sent him a hallucination! He has other talents too, which I haven't mentioned. He's a truth-teller, for one."

"My cabin. You can dream there." Dirk pointed at the quarterdeck, opposite. "Shite, go with him. Report back once he learns anything."

"Of course. And...do you think you could call me Francis from now on?"

"Francis?"

"My name." It was one of them, anyway.

"If you like."

He hurried after Joachin.

"And Francis?"

He turned and paused. "When we get through this, the three of us will have a nice, long talk."

He nodded. Dirk would want to know more about Joachin's talents, how he might use them to his benefit. Joachin was already stepping through the doorway to the officers' quarters. Francis followed him into the dark, past the dining area, and into the great cabin.

The pale gleam from the quarter moon glimmered through the stern gallery's great horn windows. There wasn't much light, but there was enough to see. The suite was much the same as he remembered it, except instead of Joachín lying in his own filth, he now claimed Don Lope's chair. *Morpheus descending into his kingdom of dreams,* Francis thought, remembering his study of the classics. Morpheus sent dreams through two gates—one of ivory and the other of horn. The windows had to be a sign. But what would their future be? Dream or nightmare?

In any event, he didn't believe in Morpheus. Better to appeal to a power he did.

Lys help us, he prayed. His own pope would be shocked at his heresy. But what *El Papa* didn't know would never hurt him, and besides Roma was far away, another life. He settled into the chair opposite Joachín.

And please keep a celestial eye on Iago, too, he added.

Chapter Seventeen: The Trap is Set

"HE'S COMING! HE'LL be here in a minute!" Casi said breathlessly.

Luci searched her face. "You're sure?" The Tribe stood in a tight circle about her on the orlop deck.

"Yes, Maré! He's wishing he didn't have to come down here to guard the sherry, that someone else would do it." Her eyes widened, and she turned to Miriam. "You were right, Matriarch! He's seen you with Alonso!"

I wondered about that, the last time he was down here. Shimmering softly and unseen by the Tribe, Alonso floated next to Miriam. As usual, his rat host was safely tucked into her pocket. They had considered the possibility that Piet Spoor might have the Sight. Now Casi confirmed it.

"Good. Here we go." Miriam stepped from the Tribe's alcove. "Everyone stay in their places. He'll need a clear path to run. Don't get in his way."

"Who's to say he won't attack you?" Zara asked.

"I don't think that will happen."

"I'd feel better if you had a knife."

"I'll be fine. I have Alonso."

"Hmph. A ghost who's a rat. What can he do?"

"You'd be surprised, Zara."

"Fine. But I'm still springing into action if he attacks."

It was hard to imagine Zara springing into anything. Miriam set that unworthy thought aside. Finally, they were taking matters into their own hands. Perhaps it was wrong to underestimate Piet Spoor, but he struck her more as a runner than a fighter. The greater danger would come afterwards, once he told Jager.

A thump of footfalls fell from the upper stair. "Hush now!" she cautioned the Tribe. She ducked beneath their privacy blanket and hurried to the nook between the water casks. Alonso drifted ahead of her, lighting their way. *I'm not sure we should be doing this.* He glanced at her over his shoulder.

In some ways he was so like Ximen, who had argued the plan. *Don't worry. It'll be all right.*

They tucked into their spot and hunkered down. She kept her hand on the rat and watched as Alonso condensed to a tight ball, taking most of his light with him. As Piet approached with a lantern, she stepped in his way. The pool of light struck her. Piet froze, sucking in a sharp breath.

"I've a message for Jager de Groot," she informed him coldly.

He hesitated and glanced about. He was looking for Alonso, she suspected. "J..Jager?"

"We know what he did to Kip. We know about the poison he meant to feed the captain so we would be blamed. Tell him he's going to pay."

Some of the fear faded from Piet's face. His eyes narrowed and he drew himself up as if to prove she wasn't a threat. "Oh, aye?"

"Aye. There are powers at my disposal your bosun can't begin to comprehend." She lifted her arm and pointed. Piet's eyes widened as the tip of her finger began to glow. Alonso had compressed himself so tightly she felt the heat. Piet stepped back, as if unwilling to believe what he saw.

"Jager will weaken and fade," she said harshly. Her finger was becoming more painful by the minute. She wanted to shake it free. "In a month, he'll be a corpse. Cross me, and the same will happen to you. NOW GO!" Her hand felt like it was on fire. She threw the point of light at Piet. As it sailed through the air, it turned into an orb, rippling and expanding as it flew. From it, Alonso burst into existence with his molten arms thrown wide. As he reached for Piet, he looked every bit the demon, his fiery visage terrible.

Piet gave a strangled cry and ran. He flew up the companionway so fast, he seemed little more than a phantom himself.

Miriam ran back to the Tribe in their alcove. "Get ready, Casi," she said.

⚘

Slow down! I can hardly understand ye! What d' y' mean, she threatened ye?

She did! But it was mostly you she was cursin', Jager!

Casi sat in the midst of them, her eyes distant as she relayed the conversation going on above. It was eerie hearing her speak. Even her voice took on a different quality, depending on which man was speaking. Luci kept an arm tightly about her shoulders, as if hoping her proximity would ground her.

She said you was goin' to pay! That she knew all about the packet an' what y' intended to do with it!

Casi paused momentarily as if Jager were considering Piet's words. Tense and silent, the Tribe awaited her next pronouncement.

She's a witch, no question! Piet continued. *Said she'd make you weaken n' fade, 'til you was nothin' but a corpse! Said she'd do th' same t' me, if I crossed 'er. An' then...an' then!*

The Tribe was still.

Speak up, man!

She threw a ball o' light at me that turned into a devil! Mebbe even ol' Scorch, hisself!

Casi's mouth twisted, as if to express her disdain. *Could o' been a cheap trick.*

It wasn't, Jager! I felt it grab th' back o' m' head as I run up here! That thing's comin' fer yer soul an' mine! Lest we do somethin', but I can't think o' what! Pray, mebbe?

Let me tell you a thing, Piet Spoor. I dealt with witches afore—m' own wife an' her harpy moeder. They hid it for a time, but I suspected somethin' when I kept gettin' sick! I beat it outta them! Wife ran off 'fore I could catch 'er, but I made damn sure th' ol' hag burned! Good Book says never t' suffer a witch t' live, an' I didn't! Sul is on our side!

Cap'n says y' ain't supposed to go down, there.

Not t' th' orlop, but I'm free to go t' th' lower deck. She visits 'er horse, regular. I'll pay 'er a visit next time she goes.

Casi paused, frowned. Then Jager's voice turned low and deliberate. *Heksen don't like steel.*

Miriam's skin puckered into goose flesh.

Cap'n'll see th' blood, Jager. He'll know.

Then I'll use m' hands. Squeeze th' life from her, with none th' wiser. People die at sea all th' time, under strange circumstances.

How will y' know when she goes?

I'll know 'cause you'll tell me, Piet.

I ain't goin' down there! Not wif that demon flyin' about!

Yer goin' down there, an' you'll report th' second she goes for that horse. Ain't no demon stronger than Jager de Groot! I'll get rid o' that bitch, see that I don't!

Casi stopped. She blinked a couple of times and told them Mister Landseer, the first mate, had arrived in their midst. The men had changed topics.

"Good work," Miriam told her. Casi looked pale despite her praise.

In spite of what she had heard, Miriam spent a calm night. Part of it was knowing Jager wouldn't attempt to attack her in their alcove, which meant the Tribe was safe. She and the women discussed strategy, where they might hide as Jager passed by, and how quickly they might run for the captain and his officers. Zara suggested she might sneak to the cooking station to advise Ignaas. "I'll coax a knife out of him."

"We can't do that, Zara." She held up her hands in protest. "If I were to draw on Jager, he could accuse me of attacking him."

"Who's the captain likely to believe? That brute isn't supposed to go anywhere near you."

"I'm taking no chances."

"Seems to me you're taking a terrible chance. He could throttle the life from you before we arrive."

"I'll keep my distance. As long as you run for Captain Vrooman the minute Piet tells Jager I'm visiting the horse, I think we can count on how he'll react. He'll head for the pens immediately. He'll be so intent on killing me, he won't suspect a trap."

"For your sake, I hope you're right."

"I have to be. It's the only way."

The morning arrived all too quickly. Her nerve threatened to abandon her, but she girded herself with determination. They had to deal with Jager de Groot permanently. Maia looked wan; Little Grim had developed a worrisome cough. Both mother and child needed sunshine and fresh air—*we all do*, Miriam thought. Zara was right. Not all of them would survive the crossing if they remained trapped down here on the orlop deck.

The one thing they could count on was Piet's arrival to guard the sherry. He had always been on time before. Casi confirmed he was on his way.

"I have to go." Miriam regarded their solemn faces. "As soon as he charges back up the steps, everyone take their positions and wait for Jager." She didn't pause to hear their assurances.

She managed to climb to the lower deck as Piet descended from the main. He paused midway on the ladder, lantern in hand, eyes widening at the sight of her. She was almost certain he caught his breath. She ignored him as he pressed his lips into a thin, hard line.

She continued to thread her way past the barrels and pens. It didn't reassure her to hear him turn and race back up the stair. She took comfort in the furtive shufflings of her Tribe as they took their places in the dark.

Fidel snorted as she approached, his nostrils flaring and his ears pinned back. Then they pricked forward as he recognized her. He dropped his head as she drew close, shuddering slightly as she stroked his neck.

"Poor boy. It won't be long, now. Another three weeks, and then—"

A board creaked behind her. Her fingers tightened on his mane. Her heart flew into her throat. Beyond the lantern's pool of light, a large shape loomed.

"Y' think y' can threaten me, an' get away with it?" Jager stepped into the glow. "Piet passed on yer little curse. Too bad for you, I'm immune to 'em. Ain't been th' first time I been hexed, an' it won't be the last." He smiled nastily.

She pressed her back against the rails of Fidel's pen. The stallion shifted uneasily. "You stay away from me. You aren't supposed to be near me," she warned.

"An' you ain't supposed t' be on this deck. Yer supposed t' be down there," he pointed, "in hell." He barked a laugh.

"You're the one who's going there."

"Oh, ya? I don't think so." He lunged suddenly and grabbed her by the head. His fingers squeezed, one hand pulling her ear and the other pressing beneath an eye. Her veil slid from her face.

He let her go suddenly. "POCKS!" He stared at her in horror, his lips twisting in revulsion. She took advantage of the moment and kneed him in the groin. He grunted, but other than that, she had little effect on him. He wrapped his hands about her throat again, then snarled something about pacts with the devil. The world went grey. Her pulse hammered in her temples. She clawed at him, not sure if she drew blood. The world sparkled into black; her knees turned to mush....

...and then, there was blessed release. The fingers about her throat eased. She collapsed at his feet and gasped for breath.

"That'll teach you!" someone cried as he fell on top of her.

What little breath she had flew out of her in a rush. She couldn't breathe, she hurt all over. Then the weight upon her lifted. Someone kicked Jager aside. He flopped beside her, moaning and cupping the back of his head. As he tried to rise, terror screamed at her to roll away, to crawl if she had to.

"Stay where you are, or you'll get another!" the same voice shrilled.

For a moment, the threat confused her, and then she realized she wasn't its intended target. She cracked open her eyes. Zara stood over Jager, a skillet in hand.

"MISTER DE GROOT!"

The imperious voice came from behind them. Mister Landseer, the first mate, strode into view with several of the larboard men in his wake. Behind them, Luci, Ximen, and the Tribe crowded anxiously.

"Get up at once, Mister de Groot!" Mister Landseer ordered. "You will accompany me to the Captain's quarters and answer for your conduct!" He neglected to say anything to Zara or about her possession of the skillet. "Are you all right, Madam?" he asked. It was painful to look at him.

"No, she *isn't* all right! That brute—" Zara nodded at Jager de Groot, "tried to strangle her! When we told your captain he was a menace, you didn't believe us!"

"She's a *heks*!" Jager insisted. "She cursed me! Said I'd be nothin' but a corpse in a month! Ask Piet!"

"He's lying!" Luci stepped forward, looking fierce. "Miriam would do nothing of the sort! We don't want any more trouble!"

"LOOK AT HER FACE!" Jager roared. Zara pulled Miriam out of his way. He pointed a thick finger at her. "If that ain't th' pox, I'm a *grootmoeder*! She came by them pocks by magic! We've a witch on board, Landseer! She tried t' kill me, an' SHE'LL SINK THIS SHIP!"

Everyone, save Miriam, started to argue. "The captain will decide!" Landseer yelled over them all. He nodded at his men. "Escort the bosun to the captain's quarters for questioning. You women will also attend to voice your complaints, including the lady there, if she's able." He regarded Miriam with concern.

"Complaints?" Zara cocked an eyebrow.

"Allegations, if you prefer."

"I *don't* prefer! Look what he did to her! She can hardly stand!" She hauled Miriam to her feet and supported her in the crook of her arm.

Miriam set a hand to her throat. Her larynx hurt, but she was thankful Jager hadn't crushed it. In a day or two, she would recover. The discomfort was worth it if they managed to have Jager confined for the rest of the trip. At the onset, Captain Vrooman had made it clear he would tolerate no ill behavior on the part of the crew. He wasn't the most available of men, but he was a stickler for rules. With so many voices raised against him, Jager would be clapped in irons, no longer a menace to anyone, save himself.

🐍

"Is this *true*?" Captain Vrooman looked as if he hoped it wasn't. He stared at Mister Landseer as Miriam relayed what Jager had tried to do to her. When she accused him of attempted murder, Jager drowned her out with harsh denials, only to be silenced by the captain.

"I don't know about attempted murder, sir, but we came upon them near the horse's pen—"

"She's a witch, I tell ye!" Jager insisted.

Captain Vrooman exploded in anger. "One more word from you, and I'll have you confined! I told you to keep quiet! You'll have your chance to defend yourself!"

Scowling, Jager desisted.

"As I was saying, sir," Mister Landseer continued, "he had her by the throat and then the matron there, struck him with a frying pan."

"I see." The captain looked grim. "So he assaulted a passenger."

"Why was he down there to begin with?" Zara demanded. "I doubt he wanted to discuss the price of sheep!"

"Why were *you* down there, Old Cow?" Jager asked.

Captain Vrooman roared. "I TOLD YOU TO BE SILENT!"

But Jager had asked a pertinent question, even though the captain had dismissed it. Attempted murder was a serious affair. *He might actually hang for it*, Miriam thought. It was more likely they would treat it as a lesser charge.

"We'll assume assault at the very least," Captain Vrooman said, confirming her guess. As troublesome as Jager was, she doubted Vrooman wanted to lose his bosun by finding him guilty of the greater crime. Jager was influential among the men. At the moment, he looked as if he were about to combust.

The Captain surveyed him coolly. "You shall have your say now, Mister de Groot. Why were you and the lady down there, amongst the stock?"

His words came out in an angry rush. "She cursed me! Tol' Piet I was goin' t' die! Look at her! Don't tell *me* she didn't come by them marks by misfortune. She got 'em by makin' a pact with th' devil!"

"He's lying." Miriam broke the silence and rubbed her throat. It was her word against his.

"What nonsense!" Zara said. "I've smelled Piet Spoor as he goes past our nook. It's a rare day when he doesn't reek of sherry." Whether she had actually seen him stealing from the stores, or whether it was a lucky guess, her words had an impact. The captain and first mate shared a glance. It appeared Piet Spoor had earned a reputation for helping himself in the past, or perhaps he had a low tolerance for alcohol.

Captain Vrooman dismissed the accusation. "I don't think we need to consider whether or not Spoor's been sucking the monkey. A quick check of the stores will tell. However, it does bring up something I need to understand. We take the health of everyone on board seriously. I need to know, what are those marks you bear, Madam, and how did you come by them?"

Miriam flushed. "They're of no threat to anyone. They're insect bites, from a rare type of wasp—"

"I never seen bites like that!" Jager blurted.

"—which I had the misfortune to encounter as a child. There is no known cure. I was hoping to travel to the New World to find one."

"You see?" Luci touched Miriam on the arm. "Not one of us has these things. I can touch her with no harm to myself, although I think it pains her for me to do so. I'm sorry, Miriam," she added.

Captain Vrooman frowned.

"Don't you think if she were contagious, we'd all look like that?" Zara said.

"I am sorry for your malady, Madam." Captain Vrooman lifted his chin. "I wish you success in finding a cure. I also apologize for one of my men attacking you."

"I was defendin' m'self!" Jager insisted.

"*You* had *her* by the throat when we found you!" Mister Landseer pointed out.

"If y' don't believe me, then dunk 'er! That'll prove she's a witch! If she floats, she is. If she don't, she ain't! We do it all th' time in Amsterden!"

"This isn't Amsterden, this is my ship," Captain Vrooman replied severely. "What I see is a brute who attacked a passenger under my care. You will answer for it, Mister de Groot. Confine him, Mister Landseer."

The first mate nodded to his officers. In moments, Jager was captive in their arms.

"You mistreat me, an' th' crew won't like it!" he warned.

"Are you *threatening* me, Mister de Groot?" Captain Vrooman's expression turned murderous.

"I ain't threatenin', but I'm tellin' you, Cap'n! It don't matter what you do t' me, but she's bad luck! She'll bring down th' ship!"

"The only bad luck is yours," Mister Landseer said as the captain waved them away.

As the door closed behind them, Captain Vrooman regarded Miriam, Luci, and Zara with a steely gaze. Miriam suspected he held them partially responsible for the unpleasantness that had occurred. "I still have questions," he told them severely, "but I didn't want them answered in the presence of my men. You will answer them for me, now, please. For one, why were *you*...," he lifted an eyebrow at Zara, "on hand with a griddle?"

"I didn't trust him, sir. I suppose I was wrong to take it, but we needed something to protect ourselves." Miriam knew she didn't want to implicate Ignaas.

"I see. I know Mister de Groot has extreme beliefs. I don't approve of them, but what he thinks is his own business, as long as it doesn't interfere with the running of my ship. I had hoped we might make this passage without mishap. Unfortunately, that's not been the case. Normally, I wouldn't expect any woman to witness the punishment I'm about to pronounce, but because you tricked him—"

"All right! So we did," Zara admitted, "but if you'd believed us in the first place, we wouldn't have had to take matters into our own hands!"

"Peace, woman. I won't tolerate a tongue lashing from you."

Zara glowered.

"You will not be excused from bearing witness. I assure you, it's a bloody business. Consider it the penalty for your involvement in this affair. I expect to see all of you in attendance on the waist tomorrow at six bells."

He dismissed them curtly. As Miriam followed Zara and Luci out, she pinned her veil back into place. There was no point in fanning the crew's superstition further. If Captain Vrooman thought Jager's punishment would be too much for her to bear, he had misjudged. She had seen the damage inflicted upon Joachin when Tomás had him whipped in Qadis. It hadn't disarmed her; it had spurred her to action. Jager de Groot would get what was coming to him, and it wouldn't trouble her in the least.

The others might not suffer it so well, though. She worried about Luci and Casi in particular.

Chapter Eighteen: Broadsides

JOACHÍN'S INTENTION TO find Iago overwhelmed and frustrated him at the same time. Infiltrating Boyle would take time. If he hurried the process, the dream would shatter. *Lys, help me*, he prayed. He focused on dark waves, not knowing what else to do. Suddenly, he was opposite Iago in the cockboat. Relief swept through him.

Thank you, Lady, he whispered, recognizing the dream for the gift it was. Despite being disembodied, he still felt the rise and fall of the waves. The wind tasted of salt. Overhead, the stars slid beneath scudding clouds in a cobalt sky. Iago had managed to pilot the boat all the way to the *Raven's* stern without being seen. The watches had been scanning for foreign sails, away from the narrow expanse between the two ships. Another piece of luck: Boyle's crew had hung a net close to the stern gallery to supplement their stores of fish. Iago set the oars on the thwarts, tethered the cockboat, and clawed up the net. With a knife between his teeth, he looked every inch the rover, his wish to turn buccaneer come true. *And all for a girl*, Joachin thought. The boy was too romantic for his own good. It was like seeing a version of himself.

As he made it to the first wale, the net swept dangerously close to the rudder. *Gods, watch it!* Joachin warned, holding his breath, but Iago had the sense to keep well enough away.

He reached the second wale. The quarter gallery jutted overhead, encircling the captain's quarters. The ship's lantern swung crazily, revealing Iago briefly in the light. He ignored the exposure and swung a leg to catch the ledge. Across the water, everything was calm aboard *La Estrella*, but her peace was misleading. Iago hauled himself over the rail and melted into the shadows.

If I weren't so worried about him, I'd be proud, Joachin thought.

On the balcony, Iago hazarded a glance through the stern gallery's windows, then dropped, well below the sills. The door was secure, so he set the knife to its lock and forced it. The lock gave way and he slipped inside.

Inside the great cabin, Boyle snored on his bunk with the girl held captive in his arms. He had dressed her in finery, a red dress from some woman, likely dead. As she caught sight of Iago, her dark eyes widened. He set a finger to his lips. Perhaps she understood the universal gesture for silence or maybe she was too frightened to shout. He crossed the floor on cat's feet and set the knife at Boyle's throat.

Joachin waited, holding his breath.

Gods! He's having second thoughts! he realized, when Iago failed to act. Was he struggling with the idea of killing Boyle in cold blood? Or did he worry he might traumatize the girl?

She watched him, as still as death. Her eyes narrowed, as if noting his hesitation. Before he could draw another breath, she grabbed his hand and plunged the blade into Boyle's shoulder. Boyle awoke, bellowing like a gored bull. She danced out of his reach. Iago dashed after her like a startled cat. They bolted for the balcony's door.

Leaving a trail of blood, Boyle stumbled after them. "Stop! All hands t' me!" he shouted hoarsely for the crew.

Out on the quarter gallery, the girl sucked in a breath and stared at the water below. With a look of determination, she slipped a leg over the rail.

Iago grabbed her hard about the waist. "No! I won't let you kill yourself! There's no going back to Afrik!" They struggled, but his interference was enough to shift their trajectory from the open water. As she clawed at him, they toppled over the rail and onto the net. Boyle appeared above them, hopping about like an infuriated troll. He yanked the knife from his shoulder and fell to one knee. "Should o' drowned ya when I had th' chance!" He hurled the blade at Iago. The knife missed, spiralling into the water. Iago kept his hand locked on the girl's wrist. He drew her down the net and into the tethered cockboat below.

Boyle cursed and blundered back into the great cabin. Joachin floated after him, needing to see what he would do. "Man th' guns!" Boyle cried. A dull red stain was spreading across his shoulder. His eyes were wild, filled with madness. As soon as the cockboat was far enough from the *Raven's* hull, he would fire on Iago and the girl. Then he would attack *La Estrella* with everything he had, even if it meant her guns lay forever beyond his reach.

Joachin came to, breathing hard.

"What was it? What did you see?" Francis leaned over him, looking tense.

"Gods! We're out of time!" Joachin thrust him aside and ran for the door. "Dirk!" he cried, charging onto the waist. "They're about to fire on us!"

Dirk appeared overhead on the poop deck. "How do you know?"

"I saw it! Iago has the girl! They escaped, but she stabbed Boyle in the shoulder! Look!"

Across the span, the *Raven's* lanterns revealed the cockboat bobbing off her stern. Two figures struggled in the small craft, threatening to overturn it. Iago had grabbed the girl about the arms, looking as if he were trying to prevent her from jumping into the sea. She freed a hand and struck his face. They wrestled some more, and then fell across the thwarts. She must have struck her head for he hovered over her briefly, then bent to the oars. *He means to reach us*, Joachin thought. Even from this distance, he sensed his cousin's resolve.

"Iago, no!" He waved him away. If he drew further from the *Raven*, they would be within easy range of the ship's *versos*. Iago was safer where he was, unless both ships exchanged fire.

"Everyone to their stations! Man the guns!" Dirk shouted, leaping from the companionway. Across the water, the *Raven's* gun ports blinked to life, opening like malevolent yellow eyes.

Joachín grabbed the rail as the first volley of cannon blasted forth. The noise was deafening as explosions lit both ships. *La Estrella* rocked and shuddered as the *Raven's* balls tore into her hull. One shot clipped her mizzen and cut through the shrouds. Another crashed through the heads.

Dirk shouted, "Fire!"

The culverins roared. Once again, Joachín and Francis were knocked to their knees. Joachín struggled to the rail to see what damage *La Estrella* had wrought. Iago and the cockboat were nowhere to be seen. Dirk had struck the *Raven* high but true. A section of her forecastle was in splinters.

"She's unfurlin' 'er sails!" Gibbs shouted. The wind caught the *Raven's* skirts. She was starting to turn. "Either we run or she's gonna ram us!"

That made no sense at all. Oared galleys rammed when attacking. But the *Raven* was a galleon, she had no oars.

Dirk sprang up from below. "You men! On those *versos*! Fire on my order!"

There was no point standing there and praying for Iago, Joachín thought. As long as he wasn't caught between the two ships, there was a chance he might survive. How long did they have before Boyle closed? Would the crew from the *Raven* try to board *La Estrella*, expecting to engage in hand to hand combat? He had a horrible feeling the *Raven* was better armed. Boyle also outnumbered them unless.... He grabbed Francis, not knowing whether he could still hear him. "The slaves!" he shouted. "We have to free them! We need the keys!"

"I have them!" Francis yelled back. At the rails, the swivel guns swung. Both ships' *versos* began to fire on each other. The *Raven* loomed, belching shot off her bow like a monster out of hell. On what was left of her forecastle, Boyle raved.

The two men ran for the companionway to the slave deck. They squeezed past crew awaiting comrades turned enemy. Tucker was still tied to his post.

"Wallace! For Sul's sake, don't leave me!" Tucker implored, as a hawk-nosed man raced past him. "Ol' Tuck never did y' any wrong! We were mates! Untie me!" Then he caught sight of Francis and Joachin. "You!" he shouted at Francis. "I'll get ya! See if I don't!"

"That's the spirit! Good for you!" Francis told him.

Even now, he still maintained that half-mocking way he had, Joachin thought. Obviously, Francis had done something to Tucker, but there was no time to question it. He grabbed a lantern and followed Francis down the companionway into knee-deep water. The slave deck was in chaos. Sea water poured in through three gaping holes, submerging the slaves to their chests. Unable to rise, they were in a panic, crying out and clawing at their chains.

"Where are the ends?" Francis shouted.

"There and there!" Joachin pointed. "Four sections!"

"I'll take those!" Francis chose the more dangerous side of the deck. "You take these!" Then he frowned at the ring of keys. "Gods, Joachin! Which key for which?"

He had seen them often enough to know. "That one's for my end! I don't know about the others!"

"All right! All we can do is try!"

He thrust two keys at him and didn't wait to see if they were successful. The water was rising quickly. The ship lurched, throwing them off balance. The slaves yelled in terror, their howls creating such a racket it was hard to think. He nearly dropped his lantern, but regained his footing in time. If he and Francis managed to release every slave, it would be a miracle.

He showed his key to the big slave who was straining at his restraints. "I'm going to free you!" he shouted. "Once I release the lock, I need you to run the chain!" He had no idea if the giant understood him. "When everyone's above decks, we'll deal with the *bilboes*!"

If the slave understood him, he gave no indication other than to stare. Joachin set the lantern on a hook and jammed the key into the lock. It opened and the link fell clear. In seconds, the giant was pulling the cable through his fetters to free himself and the other men on his line. Joachin pushed through struggling bodies and reached the opposite bulkhead. His second key failed to release the lock.

"Joachin!" Francis had discovered the same thing. They had exchanged the wrong key. On his side, the slaves were gulping and gasping, fighting to keep their heads above water.

"I'm coming! Hold on!" Sweet Lys, they were wasting time they didn't have.

As they waded towards each other, Francis shouted. "Throw it! Here's mine!"

Gods, don't! But too late, Francis did. Joachin didn't wait to see if he caught his key and slogged his way to the next post, the giant trailing in his wake. As they were freed, the slaves struggled for the companionway. On the starboard side, Francis wasn't able to liberate as many. Of those he did, less than half of them headed for the stair. The rest floated in the water.

The companionway proved difficult. As the slaves clambered up it, one of the rails pulled free from its mooring, knocking them back. "One at a time!" Francis shouted, amid splashes and flailing limbs. The stronger men ignored him and fought their way up. It was every man for himself. Joachin, Francis, and the giant waited for them to go, then helped the weaker ones to freedom. As the last few made it up, a terrible jolt knocked everyone from their feet. Timbers cracked and more water poured into the hold. *Lys save us,* Joachin thought as the sea came rushing in.

He fell beneath the surface of the water amid floundering bodies. Rising and sputtering, he found Francis clutching his head and looking dazed. He had struck his temple. The water was rising quickly, already at their waists. The ship lurched and tilted a second time.

"Up! Up!" he shouted. Fresh panic lent them strength. Those slaves who could, climbed over the others. He and Francis pushed the rest. Above them, they heard shouts and the clash of steel. *La Estrella* had been boarded. Boyle and Dirk were waging a war to the death. Whoever prevailed won the *Raven* and life. As for *La Estrella*, she was a doomed ship, destined to sink to the bottom of the sea.

Francis clasped the ladder's rail. Together they clambered up the hazardous stair, helping each other. As they made it to the gun deck, they paused to catch their breath. Below them, the slave deck was nearly submerged. Turbulent water roiled there, rippling and churning. At their feet, a large hand broke the surface.

It thrashed wildly, the chain from its fetter swinging as it tried to grab anything within its reach. Joachin froze. The giant hadn't ascended with the others. Nor had he followed them onto the deck. Something was preventing him from climbing to safety.

Without stopping to think, he dove into the water. As the water closed over his head, he bumped into the big man. Lack of breath was making him flail. He ducked beneath his pumping arms to see what pinned him. His *bilboe*, the bar that joined his two ankle cuffs together, had caught upon the broken stair.

Goddess help us. The only way to free him was to convince him to stop struggling and to let go, but how to do that with him in a panic and starting to drown? Joachin pushed for the surface and gulped another breath. Above him, Francis shouted, "Give me his arm!" He dove again, finding the giant growing weaker. The man's hands pawed through the water, still joined by the drooping chains, and then they went still.

He had only seconds to force the rail away and save him. His head pounded. He felt his way down the slack body, past thighs, knees, and finally, to his shackled feet. He pushed the *bilboe* down and shoved the stair away. Suddenly, they were free. Now, to pull him onto the deck above.... Even buoyant, the giant outweighed him by nearly five stone.

There was no time to ponder it, only to hope Francis was waiting to assist. He forced the limp body up and grabbed onto what remained of the floating stair. As their heads broke the surface, his wet hair obscured his eyes. The giant's weight fell upon him as he drew a shuddering breath.

"I'm here! Give me his hand!" Francis sounded shaky, but he reached out to help.

Joachin pushed. "The damned bar between his legs! The stair pinned it!"

Together they struggled to lift him up, Francis pulling from above and Joachin pushing from below. Landing the man was about as easy as tipping a swordfish into a rowboat. They finally managed it and slid him onto the deck.

Panting, Joachin hauled himself up as Francis pressed on the giant's chest. "I have to find Iago," he gasped.

"Yes, go. In the meantime, I'll try not to be sick." Francis looked grey, but he pressed on the giant's sternum, forcing his chest up and down like a bellows. A huge lump was forming on his temple where he had taken the blow.

The ship lurched again. Several of the cannon rattled in their carriages looking as if they might roll free. They shared a nervous glance, and then Francis waved him off. "Go! Iago needs you!"

On the waist, chaos reigned. Everywhere Joachin looked, men fought hand to hand, some with fists, many with knives. A sudden flash warned him, accompanied by the smell of burning cord. He ducked as a hot missile flew past his face. Without waiting to see who had fired, he dove for his assailant, taking him by the knees. They fell into a sprawling heap as more musket-fire exploded above their heads. As his vision cleared, he could hardly believe who it was.

"You!" he stammered.

Barto rolled out from beneath him and crouched, his hands spread. "Aye! Me!"

Joachin grabbed the spent musket and held it before him like a club. "Why?"

Barto drew a knife and slashed at him from the left. Joachin jumped out of reach. "Ever since I took up with you, my life's gone from bad to worse!" Barto cried.

He couldn't engage him. The bigger battle was to win his friend back, to convince him they weren't enemies. "Maia isn't lost, Barto! Nor Grim! We'll find them!"

"She's dead! That witch-wife of yours caused it!"

"Miriam isn't to blame! Tomás is!"

"She set a spell on me! She should've died in Granad!" He swung at him again.

His wish for Miriam's death was meant to provoke him into doing something rash. Had he forgotten how Tomás had used Maia for his private entertainment? How he raped her repeatedly while pregnant, knowing all the while Barto kept watch over their heads? Something had broken inside of Barto. He wasn't in his right mind. "That's not how it was! Tomás abused her! Don't you remember?"

If Barto did, he refused to acknowledge it. His face grew redder. He needed someone to blame. With a growl of rage, he charged him as a brilliant flare lit him from behind. As the shot rang out, Barto gasped, arched, and toppled at Joachin's feet. From out of the smoke, Gibbs appeared. He grinned and leapt back into the fray.

"No!" Joachin sank beside Barto. All about him, the battle raged, but strangely, he and Barto were left alone. As he cupped his head, Barto blinked quickly. He murmured something—it sounded like *Maia*, and then his face went slack. He stared past Joachin's shoulder, as if to wonder at the stars. Joachin let out a moan of despair. They had been through so much, their escape from Elysir, their flight through Esbaña. Barto had even named him godfather to his son, Little Grim. How could he ever tell Maia that Barto had turned traitor? He couldn't. Instead, he would say Barto had died a—

Damn it! He couldn't even think the word! It faltered on his tongue for the lie that it was. *Forgive me, my brother*, he whispered at last. He wasn't sure why he needed Barto's forgiveness, but it seemed fitting. He prayed the goddess would take him, that Lys would be kind. It would be several hours before the ship sank, but no longer. Feeling like a grave robber, he took the knife from Barto's hand.

"Come on, damn you!" Francis pushed hard on the giant's chest. More water spurted from the man's mouth, but there was no answering shudder, no desperate gasp for air. Francis could hardly see; his vision kept disappearing like flotsam behind a wave. In another moment, he would have to admit defeat before death's dark hand also drew him down. The water from the slave deck slopped about the giant's ears. One more push, and that would be all. "Come on!" he urged, forcing the broad chest to cave. It was too much. He fell across the big man's chest, panting. He lay there for a second, imagining a heartbeat.

He was about to pull free, when something snagged him by the throat. His hands flew to a thick line of hemp about his neck. Tucker leaned into his ear. "Told ya, I'd get ya! Thought you was pretty smart, winkin' ol' Tucker like that. Say yer prayers, Shite. Yer dead."

He clawed at the rope, fighting to free himself, but he was too weak, too faint. How had Tucker gotten loose? Someone must have released him while they were freeing the slaves. *Gods, why?* And now, the bosun was singing a horrible sea shanty, as if he were in a public house. He couldn't make out the words. *I'm going deaf as my larynx is being crushed.*

Funny what you think, when your life is done.... His pulse hammered in his ears, his head was about to explode. The world went black....

...and then, it didn't! Oh, blessed, glorious release! He slumped to his knees and clutched at his windpipe. Behind him, there was a frantic scrabbling and the clinking of chain. By the time he was able to make sense of it, he realized the giant had come back to life. Tucker wasn't singing now. The giant had pinned him to his chest and had his wrist chains about his neck. Tucker's eyes were bulging. His tongue protruded like a fat, wriggling worm. Behind him, the giant smiled hugely. He was relishing every moment of Tucker's end.

Tucker turned from red to blue. His hands flapped feebly, as if slapping fleas. When he was no more than a limp sack, the big man tugged the chain. There was a snap. Then he tossed Tucker to the deck, a lifeless, sorry lump.

Francis didn't move. The giant's eyes fixed on him. Did the big man know he had tried to save him? Did it matter?

Wordlessly, the giant held out his wrists, his iron fetters dangling. Francis fumbled for the ring of keys that had fallen to the deck. It seemed important the giant was asking to be delivered, and that he, Francis, was in a position to do it. The big man might have managed it himself.

It took him a few tries before he found the right key. When the cuffs loosened, the giant gave him a nod. The *bilboes* were next. He had the sense of being granted approval, as from a king to a courtier. Despite the water washing away his blood, the man's ankles were bleeding profusely. They had suffered the most damage as he had struggled to free himself from the stair. The giant caught him looking and glanced at the deck above.

"We go," he said in a deep gravelly voice.

Francis' mouth fell open. "You can speak!"

The giant glared at him and repeated it more loudly, pointing upwards. "We go, *now!*"

"Or maybe not so much," Francis muttered. Obviously, he had picked up a few words somewhere, perhaps in the slave markets or even onboard this ship. It was surprising. "Yes," he replied unnecessarily, "we must help each other." Gods alive, he wasn't about to be throttled! It was amazing the strength one could command, when one was granted life. To his further amazement, the giant extended his arm, as if he might escort him up the companionway. Francis took it.

"You slave of Adetokunbo," the giant informed him loftily as they made their way up the stair.

Slave? Francis glanced at him in alarm. What kind of association did he think they had? He was no slave, unless Adet...Adetok...whatever his name was, assumed he was one for saving him. What was the alternative—death? Was he even aware he and Joachin had saved him?

"Not really," Francis said, but there was no arguing it now. They had come to the waist. It was time to fight Boyle's men and free the other slaves before *La Estrella* sank, perhaps win a place among Dirk's crew.

Adetokunbo seemed to be of the same mind. He pointed at Francis' keys and directed him to the slaves. Addressing them, he shook his fist. "A *kolu won*!"

Half of them straightened. Clearly, some of them understood what he had said, but not all.

"What did you say to them?" Francis demanded.

The big man frowned as if he didn't think much of Francis addressing him without first being spoken to, but Francis knew his question was understood. Adetokunbo pointed at the slaves *bilboes*, his intention clear.

"Yes, fine, I'll release everyone! Did you tell them to fight?" Francis held up his fists to mime it.

Adetokunbo nodded. "Fight," he repeated, relishing the word as if it were blood on his tongue. "We attack them!"

"But not all of us! Just Boyle's men!" *Oh, how impossible!* How would they know the difference, and would it matter if they did? After the treatment they had received at Don Lope's and Boyle's hands, he wouldn't blame them if they hated every white on board. It reminded him of that Grecia myth, the one Ilysabeth liked so much. He was Pandoria, releasing the ills upon the world.

Surely, Adetokunbo would see his people couldn't sail without Dirk and the *Raven*. Surely, Dirk would see they would need the slaves, not as cargo, but as crew.

He wasn't sure either of them would see it at all.

Chapter Nineteen: The Boyle is Lanced

IAGO WASN'T ANYWHERE on the water. There was no help for it but to jump the breach between the ships and search for him aboard the *Raven*. Perhaps he had returned there, seeing it was too dangerous to row the cockboat within the *versos'* range. *Only one way to find out,* Joachin thought.

He leapt from *La Estrella's* port rail and landed, rolling, onto the deck of the smaller ship. The wind was picking up; the water was growing choppy. All about him, men fought with swords, knives, or fists, ignoring him. He dodged a grappling pair as they slammed into a mast, attempting to throttle the life from each other. Most of the fighting took place on the quarterdeck or the waist. The only crew hanging from the shrouds were either injured or dead. In the dim light, it was hard to tell friend from foe. Behind him, Francis and the slaves who were strong enough, had joined the fight.

A sudden gleam distracted him. He ducked in time as a cutlass swept over his head. Before his attacker could strike again, one of Dirk's men stabbed his assailant in the back. Joachin darted away, begrudging every moment he had to waste watching for would-be assassins. He dodged combatants and leapt over fallen men. The deck was slick with blood. He lost his balance twice but righted himself.

The door to the great room was ajar. Inside the cabin, all was dark, but a moan emanated from a shadow beside the bunk. Dirk lay there, conscious but bleeding. It looked as if he had taken a musket ball to the shoulder. Outside on the quarter gallery, beneath the dull light of the ship's lantern, Boyle leaned over the rail. The wind tossed his hair like a dirty rag. His sword arm hung uselessly at his side. He was shouting at someone below.

"Think yer safe b'neath that gunwale? Think y've outwitted me?" He waved a matchlock in his left hand. "Once yer driftin', I'll blow y' from th' water!"

He could only be threatening Iago and the girl. Iago must have realized their danger in rowing back to *La Estrella*. Boyle hadn't killed them already because he didn't have a clear shot. Instead of battling it out with the *Raven's* crew, he had chosen to return here, to shoot at Iago and the girl like they were fish in a barrel. Or maybe the temptation had been too great after he had taken care of Dirk.

There was nothing for it but to finish him before he ended them. Joachin had no compunction about stabbing him in the back. It would be satisfying in the same way killing a dangerous snake was. The world was better off without the likes of Boyle. Stepping soundlessly, he eased the gallery door open, his blade raised.

A gust of wind caught the quarter gallery's door, announcing him with a bang. Boyle turned and stared at him in astonishment. Joachin swore and leapt at him. Boyle blocked his attack with his good arm, the firearm making a better shield. Joachin stabbed at him a second time, but his foot slipped on a puddle of wet—Boyle's blood. Boyle swung the matchlock at his head. In spite of the Diaphani girl's curse, a strange luck seemed to surround the pirate. Joachin lunged a third time and stabbed him in his bad arm. Boyle didn't seem to notice, or perhaps rage empowered him. His black eyes had narrowed to slits, his nostrils flaring and puffing like an angry bull's. Heedless of the knife, he grabbed Joachin as if intending to crush the life from him. They staggered against the balcony's rail. Their combined weight was too much; it gave away with a loud crack. They plunged over the side.

As they fell, Boyle released his grip on him. The hull flashed by. Joachin saw Iago's horrified expression as the sea closed over his head. The shock of impact punched the air from his lungs. Beside him a black wall floated—the *Raven's* hull. Something stringy brushed his arm, pale and made of knots. He kicked the net away. If he became entangled in it, it would be his death. He thrashed for the surface.

A blunt shape shot at him from out of the depths—stubby fingers followed by a thick arm. Boyle appeared. Even under the water, Boyle looked crazed. Joachin kicked him in the chest, knocking him away.

Then an invisible force struck them, tumbling them head over heels. As he lost sight of Boyle, he lost sight of everything. For a moment, he didn't know which way was up. And then, thank the goddess, he caught a glimpse of lighter water above his head. The ship's lantern still shone from its stern, lighting the way. With his lungs near to bursting, he swam for that distant gleam, knowing it meant air and life.

"Not him! He's one of ours!" Francis was beside himself. He couldn't be in all places at once. Fired by their newfound freedom and thirsting for revenge, the slaves who were able to fight did. Those who couldn't lay where they were and got in the way. Adetokunbo's army was small in number, but they rushed the crew on the *Raven*, heedless of cutlass, matchlock, or knife. They only stopped when they were cut down, or when Adetokunbo ordered them to desist. And Adetokunbo only ordered them to desist, when Francis, waving wildly, shouted they were attacking the wrong men.

As he ran, yelled, and intervened, he knew if something didn't happen to stop the carnage, then both sides, no, all *three* sides, would finish each other. It wasn't about who led the *Raven*. It was about having enough survivors to sail the bloody ship.

Where was Dirk? If he showed his face, everyone would know Boyle was dead. The battle would be over. Unless...a slight but unpleasant possibility, Adetokunbo wrested control.

Behind him, *La Estrella* rolled like a breaching whale. Beneath the *Raven's* bowsprit, her spar tilted skyward, throwing everyone to their knees.

"She's going down!" someone yelled.

It was true. The two ships' bowsprits resembled crossed swords. If the *Raven* didn't disengage from *La Estrella* immediately, the stresses from the sinking ship would damage the *Raven* further, more than what had already been done to her hull. They had to push her away before it was too late, before the doomed ship drew them down.

Seeing the threat, both starboard and port crews stopped battling each other to grab halberds, oars, and whatever else they could find, to push the *Raven's* bow from the sinking ship. Gibbs bawled for axes. Those men who were able, fell to the task. Hacking at her bowsprit, they butchered the ship, sacrificing her beak for freedom. Finally, their efforts were rewarded. With a lurch, the *Raven* slid off, causing *La Estrella* to tilt her nose even higher. Men scrambled up the *Raven's* ratlines and loosened sail.

※

Joachin broke the surface, gasping for breath. As he swam for the cockboat with Iago and the girl, a wave swamped him. It was hard to see, but it looked as if the *Raven* was starting to turn. "Iago!" he sputtered, spitting water. "Get away from there! Something's happening!"

Either Iago didn't see him or he didn't hear, but the same thought must have occurred to him. He and the girl were too close to the rudder. If that great tail swept towards them, it would crush their tiny boat. Iago fumbled with the oars, trying to set them into their locks so they might row out of harm's way. Joachin struggled towards them, finding the distance between them halved. He hadn't swum any faster, so that meant...the *Raven* was turning. He reached the cockboat and flopped over the gunwale. Iago's alarm turned to relief. "Joachin! Thank Lys, you're alive!"

He shook the water from his face. "No time to thank her yet! If we want to stay that way, we have to move! We're about to be crushed!"

The cockboat rocked violently. The girl, conscious now and clinging to the thwarts, screamed. From the side nearest her, a bloody hand appeared on the gunwale, followed by an even bloodier face. Boyle had been scraped against the *Raven's* hull, the same punishment he had inflicted on Iago. "I'll get you!" he rasped. Beneath the red, he was pale to the point of being grey. The loss of blood from his stab wounds was finally having an effect.

Iago didn't hesitate. Down came the oar. Boyle saw it coming and let go of the side. He resurfaced seconds later, sputtering and looking spent. Then, without warning, the *Raven's* anchor rattled up out of the sea, catching him by the leg. He flailed and shouted as the rudder began to swing.

"Up! Up! Out of the boat!" Joachin yelled. Everyone, save for Boyle, scrambled for the net. Survival lay in clambering up the ropes and reaching the stern gallery in time. As they climbed, they heard a high-pitched scream.

Boyle, snared in the chain, had the misfortune to become caught between the cockboat and the rudder. There was no room to accommodate him. As the *Raven* turned, he was trapped. The rudder was slowly crushing him. Joachin followed Iago and the girl onto the stern gallery and glanced down. He watched as Boyle's head cracked like a clamshell, christening the ship in bone and brain.

So, the curse did come true, after all, he thought. The rudder may have squeezed the life from Boyle, but it was Iago who had brought his death to pass.

He followed Iago and the girl into the great cabin. Iago held her protectively in the curve of his arm. She seemed dazed. Beneath a pool of lamp light, several of the crew stood about Dirk as Francis dug a musket ball from his shoulder.

Francis smiled and held up the pellet to show him. Dirk grimaced and cast a pain-ridden glance at Joachin as he came into view. "Boyle?" he rasped.

"Dead."

"Good. Wrap me tightly, Shite. I mean Francis. I've a ship to command." He winced as he tried to stand.

Francis set a restraining hand upon his chest. "With all due respect, I don't think you're going anywhere yet, Captain. You've lost a lot of blood. You need water and rest."

"Bullocks. You're a medic, now?"

"I've patched a few limbs in my time."

A look, heavy with intent, passed between them. Was their interest in each other more than professional, Joachin wondered? Dirk broke the moment in a fit of pique. "What I *need* is a respite from this bloody ocean. We've been pillaging for nearly a year. Ship's lousy with worm. We may as well careen her where we can all enjoy some island hospitality."

The men gave a cheer.

"Where would you have us go, Cap'n?" Gibbs asked.

Dirk's glance slid past Francis to Joachin. "Xaymaca, I'm thinking. Maybe it's time to seek our fortunes there."

He's thinking of the mine, Joachin thought. It was unfortunate Francis had mentioned it, but he had had no choice. It had been a gambit to save them. At least they were finally sailing for Xaymaca. He would find Miriam. For that, he would share a mountain of gold.

"A little sherry for the Captain, I think," Francis told Gibbs, "and then let's be on our way."

As everyone filed from the great cabin, Joachin considered their lot. Both sides had lost many men. Would Gibbs and the crew train the slaves as seamen? If so, would they be included as Brethren, entitled to a vote? He wasn't sure what would happen. Prejudices weren't easy to overcome.

He changed his mind when he saw what was left of the *Raven's* crew. Both starboard and port were down to twenty men, about the same number as the slaves who sat in sullen, clannish groups. None of the dead or dying remained. He wondered if they had been thrown overboard. Even though the slaves had no understanding of how to sail, he knew they would not accept their old status. Tribal divisions and rivalries aside, they would assert themselves. If they were to make it to Xaymaca, everyone had to work together. He felt a heavy gaze fall upon him. From across the deck, Adetokunbo watched him. Perhaps they were thinking the same things.

As the sky pearled to dawn, the crew climbed the shrouds, dangled over yards, and set sail. With so few in number, they had a hard time of it. Joachin joined Adetokunbo at the rail. The giant tolerated him, so perhaps he considered him an ally, if not a friend. The *Raven's* sails caught the wind. They watched silently as behind them *La Estrella* sank, taking the past with her, as if she had never been.

Chapter Twenty: Cat's Tail

THE NEXT MORNING at six bells, the crew and passengers of the *Phoenix* congregated on the spar deck. The Tribe stood to one side of the waist, while the ship's mates took up the other. The officers, including Captain Vrooman, gazed down upon them from the quarterdeck. Usually, it was the bosun who administered corporeal punishment, but as Jager was the one to be disciplined, that task fell to Piet Spoor. He shook visibly as Jager, in chains, appeared at the top of the companionway, escorted by members of the starboard watch.

"I don't mean nothin' by it!" Piet protested as Jager strode by. "You know I don't, Jager!"

Jager sneered at him. "You think that cat'll cut? Sul protects me!"

Miriam doubted Sul would have much to do with him. Twelve lashes was the standard punishment, but what was this talk of cats? As the men secured Jager to a grating with his broad back bared, Captain Vrooman called for the charges to be read.

First Mate Landseer cleared his throat. "For accosting a woman passenger, with possible intent to rape or murder…" Miriam shared a look of surprise with Luci, "…forty-eight lashes."

Cries of dissent rose among the crew. If Jager survived the flogging, it would take him weeks to recover. Conditions on board a ship weren't conducive to healing. Not only had Captain Vrooman ensured Jager would no longer be a threat to her or the Tribe, but he was also giving the crew a severe warning against retaliation.

"Mister Spoor, let the cat out of the bag," Captain Vrooman ordered.

In a heavy silence broken only by the thunder of sail, Piet Spoor reached into a bag of red baize. His hands shook as he retrieved a thick handle from which protruded nine long cords.

Zara nudged her. "What's that on the ends?"

Miriam stared. What appeared to be a small ball on each was actually a barb.

The first twelve lashes turned Jager's back to stripes, marred by the cruel gouges caused by each claw. Other than flinching, he gave no indication the flogging affected him. His silent stoicism said more to Miriam than had he cried out. Her gift as a *sentidora* flared. His hatred came at her in waves, building and rising, with no crest in sight. Each successive strike added to his fury. At the end of a dozen lashes, Piet Spoor relinquished the cat to a different man as the officers and crew waited, the protocol understood by all.

This time, Jager was struck from the left, the seaman being left-handed, which resulted in a crisscross of wicked diamonds across his back. Jager wasn't so strong now. With each lash, he flinched markedly as his back was cut. He fought to keep his legs locked and said not a word. The crew began to mutter. More than one man glared at Miriam as if she, and not Jager, were to blame for his misfortune. They also cast dark glances at the captain and officers but were quick to look away if their stares grew too hot.

By the third set, Casi began to cry. Luci was quick to hug her. With each blow, Jager sucked in a painful breath. By the end of the set, he was sagging against the grate. His legs had crumpled; his knees gave out. His back was a mash of raw and bleeding flesh. The waist of his breeches had turned scarlet. Only the thick cuffs about his wrists kept him upright.

The cat was returned to Piet Spoor for the final twelve. He shook and dropped his arm. The captain's voice cut across the wind.

"Mister Spoor! You will administer the last with all the strength you can muster! If you fail to do so, you'll suffer the same for insubordination!"

Piet paled. With a snarl of frustration, he lifted his arm, drew back the cat, and struck at Jager as if he were responsible for all the ills under heaven. Jager gasped for Sul's mercy and arched against the onslaught. Piet bit his lip and lashed him again and again, the sinewy muscles of his arm bunching and releasing as he struck. With a crack like a rogue wave striking a causeway, Miriam felt Jager's hatred break. The waves of his fury crashed and fell. He spiraled into senselessness.

The men released him. He collapsed to the slippery deck and failed to move, even when Piet doused him with sea water.

The air prickled. Miriam felt it like a cold front before a storm. With growing unease, she realized it came from the crew. Jager de Groot, their leader and bosun, had been wronged.

"Don't you mind them," Ignaas said, as Piet and a few of the others cast her vengeful looks. "They won't try nothin'. You got the captain, officers, an' me to watch out fer yer. Jager got what was comin' t him, an' I'M GLAD OF IT!" His voice rose on the last as he locked eyes with Henk Dag, one of Jager's men.

Ignaas meant well, she knew. What he said made sense; the captain and officers were on their side. But it was always the smaller element of any population that caused trouble. If starboard were dedicated to overthrowing Captain Vrooman's authority, of having their way....

Best not to think on that and believe Captain Vrooman had the ship's discipline well in hand. It was noon. The sun soared higher in the sky than she had ever seen it. They were bearing south, entering the tropics. She rubbed her arms despite the balmy breeze. She would still have to be careful, but Jager's men would avoid her, believing she was a witch. After all, what she had said had come true. Jager *was* little more than a corpse. The thought brought her no comfort. She was a healer, not a destroyer. But the Tribe had to be protected at all costs. If trickery and lying ensured their welfare, then so be it. She was a trickster and a liar.

Where was that girl from Granad who had looked down on others who did such things? Whose morals reflected a strict delineation between right and wrong? Life became complicated when you were responsible for others, when people looked to you for guidance and leadership. *I'm more like Joachin than ever*, she reflected. *Except now, it's impossible for him to lie, and I do it without remorse.* She would do it again, and worse, if she had to. It was time to find Alonso below decks, to see if he had any news.

The rat wasn't in their usual place between the barrels. Knowing she was out of danger, perhaps he had slipped away to check up on Joachin.

Another three weeks at sea, she thought, heading for the Tribe's alcove, *then we'll all be together, again.*

For some reason, it felt like a false hope.

Chapter Twenty-One: Tanya Bird

RANA SAW TOMÁS at breakfast the next morning. He looked pale but otherwise unchanged. He ignored her for the rest of the day. She returned to her room and suffered her nausea, unsure of whether it was caused by her pregnancy or the sea. The next week continued in the same fashion, a regimented schedule of meals and boredom. There were changes in the crew and the constant up and down of the waves. She missed Angél terribly, worried about when they might find time alone. Queasiness and a lack of privacy prevented her from making plans. On the tenth night out, Tomás reappeared at her door. From what she could tell, he hadn't aged any further. His face remained unlined, he moved with the same oiliness he always had. He was still angry, but his fires burned low.

"I've given some thought to what you said about tattoos. I still hold you responsible for not warning me."

She bristled. "Oh, yes? And I recall you telling me to shut my mouth when I asked if you'd dedicated yourself to Lys."

He closed her door. "If you know what's best for a certain someone, you'll tell me how to protect myself."

"Stay out of harm's way."

"Don't be facetious. Why didn't I suffer ill consequences from my first tattoo?"

She shrugged. "I don't know, Tomás. Maybe you offended Lys."

"How does that make any sense?"

"Maybe she's punishing you *and* furthering her plans at the same time."

"Her plans? That Miriam Medina and Joachín de Rivera should attack me twice without reprisal?"

So Miriam and Joachín *had* been responsible for the wounds across his face and ribs. It was too bad they hadn't finished him. "I asked if I could have my necklace back," she said, ignoring his question. Perhaps the bones weren't meant for her, but the string gave her comfort. Even if Miriam's knuckle was on it, so were Anassa's and all of the other tribal matriarchs who had come before her.

"You'll get it back as soon as I'm sure you won't harm yourself."

"I have something to live for, now." She thought of Angél, and strangely enough, the fetus growing within her. She should have aborted it. It was Tomás', but it was also hers. If she and Angél escaped, they could bring the child up as their own.

"Ah, yes. The handsome blacksmith. Well, I make no promises on his account. I came here for my own purpose. I want you to scry again."

She pursed her lips. "You know where they are. That hasn't changed."

"I don't mean Miriam and de Rivera. I need to know if the Fountain is real and if so, where it is. If I drink that water, I could live forever. I'll have no further need of goddesses or tattoos."

His conceit shouldn't have surprised her, but it did. As the Diaphani understood it, the Fountain granted life, but the quality of existence was never assured. Those who partook of its waters received what they wrought—eternal damnation or everlasting grace. Given the chance, she would never test it. She had too much blood on her hands. Even being in close proximity was a risk. "I don't think it exists."

"I don't care what you think. I only care that you find it. I've arranged for Umberto to bring a lamb."

She forced herself to breathe slowly so he wouldn't sense her fear. "Won't the cook have questions?"

"He knows better than to ask."

There were stains on her soul. She had conjured a demon and had committed murder. There was nothing for it, but to fake the experience. She would tell Tomás that the Fountain was on the highest mountain in Xaymaca. While he sought it, she and Angél would escape.

There was a knock at her door. Umberto entered, holding a lumpy sack that moved sluggishly. He looked more disgruntled than ever. Bits of hay protruded from his tonsure and stuck to his habit. He bore a long scratch down one side of his face, turning him into a grizzled parody of his master. "Next time, get her to do it!" He thrust the bag at Tomás.

Tomás backhanded him across the ear, knocking him to his knees. "You ignorant toad! Address me that way again, and it's your neck we bleed! Get up! Remove that beast from its bag. Miriam, get the bowl."

He had called her Miriam, again. Did he no longer see her as Rana? As she filled the bowl with brackish water, Umberto struggled to his feet. Tomás had struck him so hard it had dazed him.

Tomás offered her the blade. "Do you need me to help you hold the knife?"

A test. If she tried to kill herself or him, the result would be the same. Angél would die. She had killed lambs before, but never like this. It was a small, innocent creature, it had hardly lived a life. But if she didn't sacrifice it.... "No. I'll do it."

"Good. I find this whole business unsavory. Besides, red *is* your colour."

She hoped the act wouldn't make her sick, as it had done before. Umberto brought the lamb near, holding it by the head and legs. The animal struggled and let out a despairing bleat. She closed her eyes and drove the blade into its heart, splattering her face and arms. As it jerked, she carved its chest with the appropriate glyph, pressing her tongue to the top of her mouth so she wouldn't vomit. Umberto tipped the lamb upside-down. Its blood spilled into the bowl.

She swayed, sucked in a breath.

"You're wasting the moment!" Tomás hissed.

She focused on the water, knowing he watched her every move.

She didn't concentrate on the blood particularly, only mimicked what he would expect to see. The room stank of copper and foul old men. It had been some time since Umberto had washed. Her stomach churned. Try as she might to focus on the bowl's white rim, the ruddy swirls in the water kept snagging her attention. A dark landscape was forming, only to disappear when she willed it away. Possibly, it was Tomás' desire for the Fountain creating it. She grew light-headed. The world began to spin—the cabin, the bowl with its bloodied water, the men, even the stench evaporated.

She tried to stop it, and then...everything disappeared.

She came to on a cold, dark road. The place felt wrong, malevolent. A beacon of light shone from a distant peak. She headed towards it, afraid to stay where she was. Boulders lined the road, reminding her of graves. She hurried along, ignoring them until one of them moved. Then all of them did.

She froze. Their movements were small, shifting. At closer look, what she thought were stones were actually lumpy creatures feeding. With that realization came gulpings, gobblings, and clackings. The things paid her no heed, but she now knew where she was. Anassa had warned her of this place. This was one of the dark roads that led to the Summerland. These birds devoured different kinds of sin. Those who had led a selfish life had to make amends here. If they didn't, they would never reach the Summerland.

She had led a selfish life. Her most selfish act had been murder.

She regretted killing Tanya. Would remorse be enough of a shield? Anassa had never said, but if she reached that distant light, she would be safe. The carrion birds couldn't touch her there. She ran.

She managed to get about twenty feet, when one of the creatures launched itself into the sky. The thing was immense, a type of vulture. Panicking, she dashed back the way she had come. Wing beats cracked behind her. She darted off the road, terrified it might snatch her at any moment. Underfoot, the land was spongy and wet. Sticks protruded in brittle stems. She stumbled over flesh and bone.

Whimpering a prayer for forgiveness, she bolted back onto the road. The creature landed before her on splayed feet, cutting off her escape. Instead of beady eyes and a sharp beak waiting to eviscerate her, the bird bore a human face.

The frightened and, at times, vacant expression was gone. Tanya hadn't gone to the Summerland. She had abided here, feeding on betrayers and their ilk. Half human and half bird, she was a monster from nightmare. She hopped toward Rana, her expression crazed. Her mouth split into an impossibly long crease. "At last!" she shrieked.

There was no returning Tanya to life. All she could do was apologize, to plead for mercy. She doubted it would be granted. "I'm sorry, Tanya! I don't blame you if you want to kill me, but don't make the same mistake I did!" She pointed at the distant star nestled on the horizon. "There lies your peace! If you devour me, you'll never leave this place!" Pray to the goddess, Tanya believed her.

"Don't care!" Tanya sprang.

"*Puri!*" Rana screamed. Despite being a Speaker for her Ancestors, she had never had much faith in the gods. Instead, she believed in her people. Her grandmother had died a martyr. She had to be a Diaphani saint by now. Anassa would come at her cry for help. She always had.

In that instant, she saw grandmother. Her *puri* appeared with a terrible brightness, but her expression wasn't kind. Rana wasn't sure whether Anassa was angry with her for disturbing her peace, or if she had come to thwart Tanya. There was no time to know, for as suddenly as she had arrived, the landscape exploded into a thousand flying pieces.

Chapter Twenty-Two: Little Bruja

ACCORDING TO TOMÁS, she had fallen head-first into the bowl and had inhaled a lung-full of water before breaking it. As he pulled her upright, she came to, choking and fighting as if attacked by monsters. He clapped her on the back to clear her lungs and demanded, had she found it? The Fountain?

Huge eyed, she goggled at him to reassure herself she was still alive. Her lungs hurt, her heart raced, but, thanks to her *puri*, she had returned. Perhaps Anassa's presence had been enough to thwart Tanya. The girl might be dead, but she wasn't at rest and she didn't forgive. As Tomás came back into focus, Rana knew she must never scry again.

"What was it? What happened?"

"I...." She had left one nightmare for another. She had to convince him she had seen the Fountain. If she could satisfy him, she might manipulate him, take them on a false journey. Along the way, she and Angél could escape....

"Stop wasting my time!"

She drew a ragged breath. "It was like nothing I've ever experienced!" That much was true.

"Is it real?" His expression was pinched, suspicious yet hopeful.

She glanced at him unsteadily and nodded. Her hands shook. Good. All the better to convince him. "It's more real that you know." She glanced away, hoping he might interpret her relief as awe. "I was there, Tomás. I stood right beside it. It was a beautiful thing, shining, as if made from living light. I knew if I drank from it, I'd find my heart's desire, and then...nothing else would matter in this world."

"I thought Angél Ferrara was your heart's desire." He looked skeptical.

"No longer. The Fountain...you must realize. Once you behold it, you know nothing can ever compare to what it can give. *That's* why I fell into the bowl. I wanted to drink the water." She met his glance. He reminded her of a gyrfalcon sighting a dove. "Of course, I wasn't really there. I was here."

"It grants immortality?"

"I believe it does."

He clutched at the air in victory, and then gazed at her intently once more. "Did you happen to notice where it was located, or were you too overcome?"

"That was the first thing I tried to learn. As it drew me, I'm almost certain I flew over an island shaped like a tortoise." She had seen one of Capitán de Carazo's maps. Xaymaca looked turtle-like. "It may very well have been Xaymaca. It seemed to be located at the apex of a large mountain." Time to embellish the rest. "There were three large peaks, with vultures circling the tallest one." She shivered, remembering Tanya. "I believe they're a type of guardian."

"Or maybe they're just birds. We need specific location markers to save us time and effort. You'll have to scry, again."

"Tomás, I can't. Seeing the Fountain takes something out of you. Please." She set a hand on his wrist, glad she was still trembling. His eyes widened in surprise. "I'm exhausted. I think these attempts affect me, too. All I know is I must rest before trying again. If I don't, my soul may never come back. I want to go, but let me rebuild my strength first. Don't abuse your guide, Tomás, for that is what I am."

She squeezed his fingers. Perhaps it was her pleading or using his name in an intimate way, but he cocked his head, as if believing she had finally accepted their relationship. He wanted Miriam on his side, he had always wanted this, she realized—a woman he considered a near equal and who he could raise to the status of a queen. He wanted someone he could trust, his only vulnerability. *The arrogant bastard*, she thought.

"Very well." He patted her hand. "I suppose we can't have too many lambs go missing. We can threaten the cook to silence, but the captain will wonder why we're always eating mutton." He smiled at his joke, his glance warm. "Besides, we still have time, at least another four weeks before we reach Xaymaca. There will be plenty of opportunities."

If he forced her to scry again, she wanted the bones of her grandmother and the Ancestors to protect her. Anassa had appeared to save her, but there was no telling if she would do so again. The necklace was a rosary; it contained the relics of her people. "Thank you. And if you don't mind, could I have my necklace back?"

"I'm not sure it's a good thing for the crew to see you with it."

"I won't wear it in their presence. But if I must scry again, I'm not as likely to be overwhelmed by the Fountain's waters. The necklace will ground me."

"You could strangle yourself with it. I can't let you kill yourself."

"Tomás, I've witnessed a miracle. The Fountain offers eternal life. Do you think I'd risk damnation now that I've seen the gift it offers?" She thought of escaping him, of being with Angél, of ridding herself of Tomás forever. He would have a flock of vultures awaiting him in the nether world. They would tear him to pieces. Her face shone at the thought of it.

His eyes widened. "Very well. I believe you. You shall have that, and more." He turned to Umberto. "Bring her the necklace and remove that lamb. Also, a cloth and more water so she can freshen herself."

Umberto looked as if he had been drinking salt. "Anything else?"

"Wine. We'll share a nightcap, after she's rested."

Scowling, he left with the carcass and the sack. Tomás inclined his head and followed Umberto out. "Until later," he said.

She lay on her bunk. When he returned an hour later, they drank the wine and attempted sex. He had difficulty maintaining an erection, but they managed it. It was better to keep him pacified. She was glad when he left.

She fingered the string of bones about her throat. The knucklebone on the end was Miriam's—Anassa's mistake. It was tempting to remove it, but the bone was what made her look like Miriam. If she detached it, the glamoury might fail. She hoped her *puri* would protect her if Tomás forced her to scry again. Even with Anassa's help, there was no escaping cause and effect.

She would have to propitiate Tanya, somehow.

A few days later, Angél found her in a rare moment alone. Tomás had allowed her to take some air on the spar deck. The morning was sunny and calm. They were entering tropical latitudes. She had grown used to the swells, and thankfully her nausea was at bay. At supper the night before, Capitán de Carazo had informed them they were three weeks from making landfall. He and Tomás were busy consulting maps in his quarters.

"How are you?" Angél set his hand upon the starboard rail, as close to hers as he dared. He stared over the waves.

"Better." Her nausea had vanished overnight.

He dropped his voice. "I've been thinking of how we might escape the Grand Inquisitor once we reach Xaymaca. Tomás has told de Carazo he wants to visit the governor in Villa de la Vía before exploring the island. He'll need men and equipment to search for the gold. When we get to Puerto Real, we can bribe whatever thugs are in charge."

"Thugs?" She glanced up at him.

"Franca or Inglaisi privateers. *Gobernador* Rosales hasn't been able to rid the island of them. As I understand it, he tolerates them, as long as they leave Villa de la Vía alone."

"Can we trust them?"

"Only so long as we have coin. If they think taking us to Esbañiola will bring them more money, we can trust them. It's better than kidnapping, but not much."

She brushed his thumb with her little finger. "You've thought of everything, *mi amor*."

"It's only a plan. We have yet to escape. There are many ways it could go wrong."

"Don't say that. You'll bring bad luck. It'll work."

He shifted uncomfortably. "I should go. Others are watching." He inclined his head slightly. Across the waist, Noxolo stood at the opposite rail, studying the horizon. His bleached cotton robe whipped and snapped about his lanky frame as if with a will of its own. She shivered, remembering the cold thing that had brushed her arm.

"Angél, wait." She snagged him by the sleeve. "I...I want us to be alone. I need us to spend time together." The sooner they made love, the easier it would be to convince him the child was his.

A smile touched his lips. "I want that, too, *querida*, but we must be patient. When we reach Xaymaca, there'll be time. After we escape."

She watched him as he walked away. He was right. There was little in the way of privacy on board; being together would be dangerous. As far as she knew, she was only six weeks along. After they landed on Xaymaca, she wouldn't yet show. But as soon they arrived, she needed to make sure Angél thought the baby was his.

She would keep it, she knew now. It *was* possible the child's soul hadn't yet attached to the fetus, but she couldn't be certain. If it turned out to be a boy, she would raise him to hate Tomás and kill him. There was justice in that.

"As Esbañiards go, he is a handsome man, your lover."

She turned with a start. Noxolo stood where Angél had been. How had he crossed the waist without her seeing, and how had he guessed about Angél? She wanted to flee, but a strange compulsion held her.

"You're mistaken," she said icily. Was this how the rabbit felt before the hawk? She couldn't move.

"He is also the father of the child you are carrying. You are feeling much better this morning, yes? Consider it my gift, although I'm not sure why a woman of your talents would endure it."

"I don't know what you're talking about."

"Oh, come now. You acknowledged me the other day, as I did you." He frowned. "What I'm not sure of, is your relationship with the Grand Inquisitor. Does he know?"

She stared at him.

"Either he condones what you do, or he has no idea. I am inclined to think the latter. Perhaps his little sister has more sway over him than he thinks."

"I am not pregnant! You presume too much!"

"Little *bruja*. As long as we don't get in each other's way, I see no reason why we can't cooperate. There is no need to play games. Your secret is safe with me."

He terrified her. How could he know? "I have no secrets!"

He smirked. "The air around you says different."

Surely, he didn't mean any lingering traces of Tanya or the nether world. On the other hand, there was that strangeness about him. "What do you want?"

He looked surprised. "Why nothing. I was simply paying my respects. From one equal to another."

"We are not equals! You're...you're nothing but a servant!"

"As are you."

"How dare you even address me! Who do you think you are?"

His affability vanished. He flicked at the air. "You've left all kinds of strings floating about. Messy. Careless. Obvious. Do you think to snag me? I wouldn't try it."

"I want nothing to do with you! Go away!"

His eyes narrowed. "You're young, pregnant, and emotional. I'll overlook your rudeness because of it. What was your purpose with that lamb?"

Her jaw dropped.

"I know you used the blood for something, and it wasn't to feed a *djab*. There are conflicting energies around you. What is your relationship with the Grand Inquisitor? Tell me!"

The words spilled from her mouth, but luckily, not the truth. "I...I'm his sister!"

Noxolo laughed. "And I'm the King of Esbaña." He cocked his head as if listening to something. "It may be you're beneath my notice, after all." He waved a long forefinger before her nose. "A warning, little *mambo*. You may have fooled the Grand Inquisitor about what you are, but you don't fool me. Don't cross or undermine me."

She sputtered. "I want nothing to do with you!"

"Good. So I'll decide when *I* want something from *you*."

"How dare you! I'll have you flogged!"

He leaned towards her, his black gaze trapping hers. His scent was acrid, sharp, as if he had recently handled some noxious herb. For a moment, the world stopped. High above them, the sails hung like deflated bladders. "I don't think so," he said.

A sharp pain stabbed her in the gut as he stepped away from the rail. It was so immediate she doubled over in pain. Then her nausea returned, stronger than ever. She grabbed the rail and vomited her breakfast over the side of the ship, mortified that the crew witnessed her do it. Whatever barrier keeping her morning sickness at bay was gone.

Later that evening, Noxolo stood at the sideboard in the captain's quarters, attentive as always, ready to serve their usual three courses for dinner. The main dish was lamb. When he presented her with the platter, he set it before her with more force than necessary. Tomás and the others didn't notice. She waved the plate aside.

"My dear, I would have thought your seasickness should have subsided by now," Capitán de Carazo said sympathetically. "Perhaps Noxolo can prepare a special tea for you. Dill is good for unsettled stomachs. I'm sure we have a small cache on board."

"No thank you. I'll be fine." She smiled faintly.

"Are you sure? It's no trouble. Noxolo has a comprehensive knowledge of medicinal herbs. I, myself, have benefited from them. I'm certain he could make you feel better."

"Herbs, you say?" Tomás quirked an eyebrow. "That's also an interest of mine. The Solarium considers some plants holy—*origanum vulgare*, for example. I wonder, does it have a counterpart in the New World?"

De Carazo turned to Noxolo. "Can you advise him?"

Noxolo clasped his hands. "As far as I have been able to determine, no counterpart for oregano exists on Puerto Pío. We have a bush mint, which is similar to that which grows in my native land."

"I use it regularly," Capitán de Carazo rubbed his hip. "I have an old sword wound that aggravates me in the rainy season. Noxolo prepares a compound that works wonders."

Tomás dabbed at his lips and set down his napkin. "Interesting. I'm sure there are many marvels to be found on these islands." He cleared his throat and cast de Carazo a steady gaze. "I've given much thought to our recent talk of the fabled Fountain, Capitán. If it exists, why then does *Gobernador* Rosales not exercise better control over Xaymaca? Any place boasting such a miracle would show hints of its existence. The people would be happier and healthier, for example. But this isn't the case. If I've understood correctly, the Tain have been wiped out, except for some escapee *cimarrónes*."

"That's so. We maintain much better control on Puerto Pío."

He eyed him steadily. "Yet your island has been thoroughly searched."

Capitán de Carazo frowned slightly. "What are you suggesting?"

"Let me put it simply. How is it you maintain peace on your island? Puerto Pío is as small as Xaymaca, better situated for ships needing victuals before crossing. The Crown has given you this assignment not once, but twice. You're rich. Nothing bad ever happens on Puerto Pío. Revolts occur in other places." His expression became accusatory. "What's your secret to such prosperity, if not the Fountain's presence? The island is peaceful, even when you're not there."

For a moment, no one said anything. Rana knew Tomás well enough to see his logic was a preliminary to more charges.

Capitán de Carazo and his nephew, Mateo, shifted uncomfortably. Noxolo's dark eyes widened, as if a puzzle he had been pondering had been solved. De Carazo spread his hands. "I assure you, Radiance, we're keeping nothing from you. The Fountain is not on Puerto Pío."

Tomás leaned towards him. "No? How am I to trust a man who may have much to lose?"

"Our wealth comes from cassava! The flour lasts much longer than wheat—"

"I'm not talking about cassava! I'm talking about what you may be hiding on Puerto Pío!"

"There is no Fountain!"

"I question that!" Tomás struck the table with his fist.

Mateo stood abruptly. "Do you accuse my uncle of lying? He doesn't lie!"

"Sit down, boy," de Carazo muttered.

Mateo turned to him, his eyes blazing. "He's insulted you without cause, Uncle!" He thrust a finger at Tomás. "You may be a Prince of the Church, Grand Inquisitor, but my uncle has ultimate authority here! You're not in Esbaña, any longer! You are subject to *our* justice, on *our* ship!"

"Mateo!" De Carazo stared at his nephew in horror, then turned stricken eyes to Tomás. "He doesn't mean to threaten you, Radiance! Mateo, apologize at once!"

"He accuses us wrongly, Uncle!"

De Carazo stood. "As is his prerogative! He's the Solarium's representative, Sul's emissary on this great green Earth! Get down on your knees at once, nephew, and beg him for his forgiveness!"

Mateo scowled. De Carazo grabbed him by the collar and thrust him to the floor. Noxolo stood beside the sideboard as always, a thin smile playing upon his lips. Under the table, Angél captured Rana's hand.

"Do it at once, Mateo! Or I'll have you flogged for insubordination!" De Carazo shook him by the shoulder.

Rana guessed the boy had never heard his uncle pressure him so. His voice shook. "Fff...ffforgive me, Radiance! I was wrong to threaten you!"

De Carazo hauled him to his feet. Both uncle and nephew stood before Tomás, awaiting his judgement. Angél dropped her hand. There was no need to pull her out of harm's way. Everyone, save Tomás and Noxolo, held their collective breaths.

Tomás eyed the two of them, his expression unimpressed. "I can be lenient, if you answer my original question. I'll learn what I need to know, one way or the other. As for penance, we'll discuss that, later."

De Carazo looked pale. "You want to know if the Fountain exists on Puerto Pío. It doesn't. That's the truth, Grand Inquisitor, as far as we know it."

"And if it isn't there, why is Puerto Pío as peaceful as it is?"

De Carazo's glance fell upon Noxolo. "We–"

"We?" Tomás pressed.

De Carazo swallowed. "I control the slaves in a manner that might not be sanctioned by the Temple."

Tomás linked his fingers. "Explain."

"I know we're expected to bring them into the arms of Sul, to teach them the tenets of the true faith. The conversions haven't been successful. Forgive me, Radiance, but I'm only telling you what is so."

Tomás waited.

"Noxolo is a true believer." De Carazo met the man's implacable gaze. "I've given him permission to control the difficult ones, the troublemakers. That's why we have no uprisings on Puerto Pío."

"How are they controlled?"

"Uncle," Mateo warned.

De Carazo glanced at his nephew. "No, Mateo. It's too late to avoid anything. We must tell the Grand Inquisitor what we do, and let him chastise us as he sees fit." He looked ashen. "I take full responsibility for what we've done. Mateo is aware of it, but he's never been involved. I have dabbled in unorthodox ways to manage the slaves on Puerto Pío."

"Continue."

"There are powders that, once administered, render a man submissive. It's the lesser evil, to steal a man's will instead of killing him outright. This is what we do to those who disrupt our serenity. After Noxolo tends to them, they are as beasts, compliant and able to work under direction."

For a moment, no one said anything. They awaited Tomás' response. He ran a finger along the table's grain. "If conversion fails one way, there's nothing wrong with trying another. Particularly, if it's successful." He glanced up at Noxolo with renewed interest. "I should like to know more of your methods."

De Carazo and Mateo collapsed with relief.

Noxolo smiled. Rana had the terrible feeling this was exactly what the man had wanted. The question was, why?

And then, like a curtain falling away to reveal every player on the stage, the answer became clear. It shook her. Capitán de Carazo wasn't the true ruler of Puerto Pío.

Noxolo was.

Chapter Twenty-Three: Bad News

HOW IS HE?

Miriam and Alonso sat in their usual spot, the nook formed by the rows of water casks. The Tribe had turned in for the night. Alonso's rat nestled in her lap, but she hardly noticed it. Instead, she saw him as her knight in ghostly raiment. He leaned beside her, shining faintly, his handsome face looking tired and worn. At the knee, his legs disappeared into a barrel. It was a disconcerting image, but she was getting used to it. He glanced at her in annoyance.

Why is it you never ask me how I am?

She stared at him, feeling chastised. He was right. She assumed he was fine, even when he didn't look that way. *I'm so sorry, Alonso. I guess I always think–*

Don't.

Forgive me. I've upset you. Asking *how are you* now, only seemed like a consolation he wouldn't accept.

I have bad news. He threw it at her like a gauntlet.

She stiffened. *Bad news?*

He said nothing for a few moments, which made her want to shake him. How could he start with something like that, and not tell her immediately? He had to mean Joachín, Iago, and the others. What was wrong? She bit down on her tongue, knowing he heard the thought. And then, losing patience, she barged into his mind like a soldier on a search.

His sense of alarm was immediate. There was more, a kind of turmoil, and then—he shoved her out. It was like being pushed roughly through a door and hearing the click of a lock behind her. *Don't do that! Don't pry!*

I wasn't prying! She was, and she shouldn't have been. But he had never treated her as an imposition before.

He ran a shining hand across his brow. She took a deep breath and tried to compose herself. *Will you please tell me what's going on?*

He said nothing for a moment, and then dropped his hand. The sense that she was still barred from his innermost thoughts remained, but she hoped his reticence was temporary. He refused to look at her.

Please, Alonso. She squeezed his arm and felt a prickle. *What is it?*

He pressed his lips into a hard line, and then gave a little nod as if coming to a decision. It seemed an odd reaction. To what could he need to agree?

The reason I'm having difficulty telling you, is because I don't know how to tell you.

Her heart pounded. She caught her breath and set a hand to her chest as if to protect herself from what he was about to divulge. Whatever it was, it had to be bad. Hopefully, not the worst thing—that Joachín was dead. *Tell me.*

It will hurt.

Someone *had* died! *Is...is it Iago?* She couldn't bear it if it were Joachín. Please, not Joachín.

He nodded. *I'm sorry.*

Tears sprang into her eyes and she let out a small cry. How would she ever tell Luci?

He refused to meet her gaze. An unfamiliar emotion drifted about him like jetsam after a wreck. It felt like guilt, but why should he feel that way? Unless he was feeling remorseful for the pain he was about to cause. She braced herself.

There's more, he continued. *It's also about Joachin and the rest of them. They...they ran into pirates who sank their ship. La Estrella del Mar is gone, taking everyone with her to the bottom of the sea.*

He met her gaze then, but with those words, he may as well have stabbed her. She gasped and clutched at her heart, unable to draw breath. An immense weight pressed down on her chest. Nothing could have prepared her for this terrible news. No remorse on Alonso's part, nor any strength on hers.

What had it all been for, this crazy journey across the Great Ocean Sea, if not to start a new life for them all, a new life for her and Joachin? There was no point in going on. She didn't want to, if it meant living without him. *I want to die,* she thought miserably.

The thought alarmed Alonso. *You don't mean that, Miriam!*

She did mean it. She might as well finish what Jager started, find a way to end herself.

His fear rose, spearing her agony. *But...there's the Tribe to think of!*

She dismissed him and the Tribe. If she threw herself into the sea, she would drown. Then she would travel to the Light, to the Summerland and be with Joachin....

Suicide isn't the answer! You can't die in this stricken state! If you do... Great Sul, I never would've told you if I thought....

He was afraid. His fear pattered about her uselessly, like rain on stone. He stared at her as if she were mad. Tears streamed down her cheeks. She didn't care. What did he have to worry about? He was already dead; the only reason he lived his half-life was because of her. Where was a knife? She would stab herself, set them both free.

You can't! I love you! If you do this thing, you won't go into the Light! You won't reach the Summerland! You'll be as I was, burning in a hell of your own making!

I'm already there—

You have no idea what you're saying!

She collapsed to the floor and wept. She wanted to die. Hope had kept her going. How could she go on, without Joachin?

If...if you do this, the Tribe will be leaderless! Do you think Zara is up to the task? Your death will hurt them more than you know! They'll see what you did and they'll question why you did it. Casi will hear your thoughts as you suicide. Can you do that to her? She's sleeping now, but your despair in this final act will hurt her!

I don't care.

You do care! I know this is a...a shock, a tragedy. But Miri, my love, you must carry on! You promised you'd look after them, see them to the New World. They've all lost loved ones. And now, you have, too. I'm sorry Joachin is gone, but I'm still here! Does that mean nothing to you? I won't leave you! I will never leave you!

She had no words to give him. Only pain.

I...I think he's in a good place. The words sounded empty, things to say to comfort the grieving. *But living a good life will ensure that in the end, you and he will be together.*

She didn't want to answer him, but the lack of a response was cruel. It hurt him to think she would choose death and Joachin over him. He didn't deserve that. She mustered a feeble reply, the best she could do. *How can you know?*

Because, despite our differences, Joachin is...was a good man. He loves you. He'll wait for you. I would have. I do.

She started to cry, again. He suffered her grief stoically, or perhaps there was nothing more he could say. The fact she didn't search for a knife mollified him.

By morning, she could no longer stay in their spot. She sat up stiffly, feeling as if she were crumpled velum, broken in many places. Her arms and legs were dead weights. She could barely open her eyes. Her face felt itchy, especially her cheeks where they had been salted with tears.

How will I hide it from Casi? she asked, feeling lost. Alonso had stayed with her through the dark and terrible hours. He shone softly like the promise of a new day.

You must put Joachin's death from your mind. Distract Casi when necessary, and stay out of her presence as much as possible. It will be difficult, but you can do it. Eventually, you'll have to tell them, but not until we've landed.

That made sense. She would carry the burden for them all. The Tribe didn't need this awful news to slay them before they arrived in Xaymaca. She would tell them afterwards, when the moment was right.

She scrubbed at her eyes. *I don't know what I'd do without you, Alonso.*

I love you, Miriam. You'll never have to worry about that.

His rat stirred and scampered away, breaking their connection. He vanished from her sight. She registered it vaguely, but her thoughts were not of him.

She was a shadow, half of who she was. The part that completed her was dead.

Joachín.

She never felt more alone.

Chapter Twenty-Four: The Bargain

WITH TOMÁS AND Noxolo shut away in Tomás' cabin for hours at a time, Rana had been expecting trouble, but she didn't imagine it to occur in the way it did. As dawn painted the sky in bands of gold, a hammering came at her door. She had taken to locking it after retiring, fearful of Noxolo and his powders. She pulled it open to find Tomás standing there, a sack in his hands.

He brushed past her and threw the bag onto her bed, looking as if he hadn't slept in days. His expression was wild. "Look at me! It's happening, again! How do you explain it?" His face was sallow and sagged along the jawline where it had never drooped before. A net of fine lines spread about his eyes. He was aging again.

Her mind grasped for answers. "I don't know!"

With a growl, he seized her by the throat. She clawed at his hands to pull them away. "Stop it!" she choked. "Noxolo must have done it!" She knocked him aside, which surprised her. He was feeble. He landed on the bed beside the sack.

"It isn't him! You have to do something!"

He seemed so sure of it, she didn't question it. "Like what?"

"Scry! Find the Fountain and bring back a drop of holy water! There must be a way! You said it yourself, even its presence changes you!"

"Tomás, my body remains here while my soul travels! I have no way of retrieving the water!"

"I don't care!" He dumped a dazed chicken onto her bed. "You'll sacrifice that bird and bring me back a drop to reverse the aging!" He pulled a knife from his sleeve and waved it in her face. His pupils were huge, dilated. He looked half mad.

If she scryed again, it was possible the nether world would draw her back to where Tanya waited to finish her. "What if it's beyond my skill? What if I can't do it?"

"You've conjured demons and you resemble Miriam Medina! I don't know how you did those things, but with the right motivation, you perform the impossible. If you don't fix me, Ferrara won't see his next sunrise!"

He would do it. He would accuse Angél of heresy and order his death. "I need my necklace," she told him. It lay on her trunk. She reached for it slowly, so as not to alarm him.

She poured her will into finding the Fountain, not knowing whether it existed in spite of what Diaphani lore said. She trusted her need to save Angél's life would show her if it did. As the cabin faded from view, she was rewarded with a brief image of a white, glowing font. It looked to be made of marble, but there was an energy to it that made her think the stone was alive, that it breathed, or perhaps it was the water itself that pulsed. If Lys had granted her this vision, maybe redemption was within her grasp, maybe she wasn't damned forever. Hope and wonder filled her. Then the fountain disappeared. An unassailable force, as bitter as blame, sucked her down at great speed. The world turned to night, and once again, she found herself on death's dark road.

She stood where she was, holding her breath, not daring to move. The last time she had been here, she had triggered the birds by moving. She couldn't make that same mistake. She eyed the boulders. They remained solid rock.

Her vision greyed. Sooner or later, she would have to breathe. Would it awaken the birds? She expected it might.

So be it, then. She sucked in a deep breath and sprinted for the distant light. All about her, the grave markers shivered and unfolded into life. Ahead of her, one of them sprouted wings and shot into the air. She had no doubt who the death bird was. Above her, a shriek shattered the peace like glass.

"*Puri!*" She reached for her necklace and squeezed Anassa's knuckle, hoping her instincts were correct. On the far hill, the beacon flared. Yes! It had to mean her *puri* had heard her! She would come, she would intervene! Suddenly, the ground beneath her feet trembled. The night shattered into shards. Great jagged pieces of black whirled and glittered about her, caught amid a blizzard of white. Tanya was tossed by the tempest. She battered her vulture's wings against the gale. For the moment, the storm kept them apart.

Rana laughed in relief. She had gambled on the necklace and won. Even in death, her *puri* was protecting her! How appropriate Anassa should come as snowstorm! The old woman had always been as harsh as ice!

The wind became a voice, the shards, a face.

Anassa, her dead grandmother, swirled all about her in elemental fury. Her eyes were black holes, her mouth a shifting fracture. "You *dare* call to me for help, when you commit the gravest sin of all? You brought this upon yourself!" Every word slammed into her like a blow. Rana crumpled beneath the onslaught. "I should leave you to her!" Anassa continued. "Tell me, why should I save you? Why have I been pulled from my rest?" Her voice cut like daggers.

She's right. I don't deserve her help, Rana thought. *But who else can you call upon, if you can't call family?* "*Puri!* I'm sorry for it! For everything! For disturbing you, for killing Tanya! I was wrong! You know I am! You wouldn't have come, if there was no hope for me! Please!" She held out her hands to her.

"You've shattered my peace!"

"Were you really at peace, *Puri?* I don't think so! You always protected the Tribe. You're protecting me, even now! That's why we give a knuckle for the necklace!" She clutched it. "Because it links us! Even in death!"

For a moment, Anassa said nothing. Rana watched her expression shift from frustration, to regret, and then finally, she hoped, to forgiveness. Storm that she was, Anassa continued to swirl about her. "The last bone *isn't* mine," she pointed out.

"No, it isn't." There was no denying it.

"You took it from Miriam before her time. You stole Tanya's life. You owe them both."

"What must I do to make it right?"

"You can't make it right! You murdered Tanya! Do you think you can undo that?"

"There must be something! There has to be!"

A sigh, like a winter wind drifting over snow, swirled about her. "Come in out of the cold. We'll figure something out." One of her eyes swelled and turned into a cave. Her other features faded into snow. Rana hesitated. Entering meant a complete surrender to her grandmother's mind. Nothing remained hidden from her *puri*, but then, what other things had she committed that were worse? If Anassa still doubted her, she would know her repentance was sincere. She stepped into the cavern.

"Sit." Anassa's voice echoed weirdly about her.

She sat. Outside, the blizzard still raged. Beyond the mouth of the cave, Tanya shrieked and struck her wings against an invisible wall.

"She wants her life back," Anassa pointed out.

"I can't give her that. You said so, yourself."

"So you'll have to give her something else. Bargain with her. It's the only way. Until you convince her, we remain in limbo."

"We?"

"Of course, *we*. What do you think?"

Alarm ran through her. She had no idea what her body was doing back in the real world. Likely, she had collapsed over the bowl again. Tomás would be in a state. He would have to deal with it. If she wasn't able to persuade Tanya, she would never leave this cave. Her body would fail and she would die. But at least her grandmother would protect her.

"We all must make amends for the sins we commit, child. If your body dies, then the debt to Tanya is paid because she's trapped you here. In any event, some kind of a sacrifice is warranted."

Rana nodded. She would have to talk her way past Tanya. She approached the cave's mouth as close as she dared.

Tanya saw her. "You killed me, and so now, I'll finish you! You think that ward can save you? You murdered me to break one!" Pellets of ice struck her with every wing beat, stinging wherever they fell. Rana held up her hands to bar her face from the onslaught. Anassa wasn't strong enough entirely to protect her from Tanya's wrath.

"I was your friend!" Tanya shrieked. "You stabbed me as if I were no more than a beast to be slaughtered! So now, I'm going to kill you! I'll devour you piece by piece while you watch! I'll eat your head last! You'll feel every inch of my gullet as I swallow you down!"

She was a gruesome creature painting a grisly fate. "Tanya, I was wrong! I want to make it up to you!"

"There's no way you can make it up to me! Except by dying a worse death than mine!" Tanya smiled hugely.

"Do you want to stay here, Tanya? To dine on vengeance, and never leave?" Tanya had to think about her future, too. "If you let me go, I might be able to destroy Tomás. He hurt you...I know he did, like he hurt me."

"I don't care about him! I only care about hurting you!"

"For just a moment, think—"

"Don't tell me what to do! That's all you ever did! Ordered me around, as if I couldn't think for myself!"

Rana took a deep breath. She couldn't afford to lose her patience. They had to barter. "If there is anything you could have, other than killing me, what would it be?

"Nothing!"

"There must be something! When you were alive, what did you want? Was it a husband? Or a...." Her hand strayed to her belly. She had been about to say *baby*. Tanya had been a simple, uncomplicated girl. "A family?"

"You can't give me that." Tanya's dark eyes widened. "Wait! You're pregnant!"

Rana held onto that hope. "I am. If you kill me, you'll kill the child."

"I don't care! Killing you both will make it sweeter. I take something from you, worth more than your lousy life! Whose is it?"

She hesitated, not wanting to confirm paternity.

Tanya screeched. "Tomás'? Even better! I kill you *and* a part of him!"

"The baby is an innocent! Like you were, Tanya! You wouldn't do that to yourself, would you?" Hopefully, there was still a shred of humanity left in her.

Tanya settled onto a perch. Perhaps Anassa had provided it, sensing a potential for her listening to reason. As she folded her wings, she peered this way and that, as if checking for weaknesses in Anassa's front.

"The child stems from rape," Rana said. "Tomás raped me, like he raped you, Tanya."

"And that makes it worth saving?"

"No. Yes!" Tanya was starting to confuse her. "If you kill me, you kill it."

Tanya cocked her head from side to side, a crow inspecting a nest.

"I don't know if it's possible. You want your life back." Rana took a deep breath. There was only one thing she could offer. "Very well, I can give you a life. I don't know if the baby's soul has attached, yet. I don't know much about that. But if it hasn't—"

"You would give me the chance to live again, as *your* child?" Tanya sneered. "You're a bigger monster than I am."

"Perhaps. As I said, if the child's spirit hasn't yet—"

"It has. You're carrying a boy."

Rana swallowed down her panic. "All right. My next baby, then. After this one. I'll have a daughter if it can be done." Did Lys honour such vows when a balance needed to be restored? She hoped so.

"That would make you my mother."

"Yes!"

"You'll make an awful one. You're a terrible person."

"I am. But if you agree to this, I'll make the next life up to you!" Anassa had remained silent through this entire exchange, but Rana sensed her approval. Perhaps Lys would consent to it, also.

"How do I know you'll keep your end of the bargain?" Tanya peered at her with one eye.

"I'll do my utmost to keep it. If I can't, eventually we'll meet here again. And then you can do whatever you want."

Tanya smiled. "I'll be a bad daughter. I'm going to like that."

"I can accept that. I was a bad daughter, once."

"On the other hand, maybe I won't remember any of this. If we have past lives, we don't seem to remember them."

"You may not remember, but *I* will. If there's any redemption to be had, I'll try to be a good mother to you."

"And to my half-brother, Tomás' bastard."

"Yes."

"You're not going to tell him, are you?"

"No."

"It's better you don't. I'll like having an older brother. I never had one before. Maybe he and I can destroy Tomás, together."

Dear Lys, she had convinced her. "So, you agree? You'll let me go?"

Tanya folded her wings. "For now. If it doesn't work, then we'll meet in the future. One thing, before you go. You must name me Tanya."

Angél will never agree to it. "That isn't a Diaphani name."

Tanya spread her wings and looked as if she was about to shriek in frustration.

"Fine! Tanya it is!"

She settled again and studied her. Rana wasn't sure what more there was to say. "What is your word for *mother?*" Tanya asked.

"Maré."

"Then farewell for now, *Maré*. Until I make my re-entry into the world, I'll be closer to you than breath." She leapt from her perch and disappeared into the storm.

Rana sat for a moment, savouring the silence. It had been so long since she'd had a moment to herself.

"That was a smart thing you did." Anassa's voice echoed all around her.

She studied the tempest beyond the cave. Tanya was out there, somewhere. "I've always been smart, *Puri*."

"True. I'm not sure I would have offered what you did."

"I promised her a life. I suppose it takes a certain bent of mind to suggest it."

"You've changed, Rana. For the better, I think."

That was true. Ever since she had switched appearances with Miriam, she had felt the difference. She didn't even hate Miriam anymore.

"I wonder if her knuckle has something to do with it," Anassa said. "Maybe that's what's causing it."

How like her *puri*, to rob her of any credit. She had negotiated with Tanya. Her future responsibility would be huge. A spark of her old self reignited. "I may have stolen from Miriam, *Puri*, but I'm still capable of doing good. You never saw it." The admission hurt.

"Perhaps not," Anassa conceded.

If the old woman had more to say, she held her tongue. Her *puri* had changed for the better, too. Perhaps that's what paradise did to one. "The Summerland," she began. "Thank you for leaving it to help me. I hoped you would. Before I return, I must know. You taught us the Summerland was a place of perfect peace. It isn't, is it?"

Anassa didn't reply immediately. "Yes," she said eventually, "and no."

"A paradox then."

"It gives us a respite when we need it. But it can't offer perfect peace until everyone learns how to forgive. And to love."

Some people deserved neither. Tomás and others like him.

"Everyone is meant to be Tribe, Rana." Her *puri* sounded tired. "Until that occurs, even the gods do not rest. Take care, child. Of yourself and that baby. I'll be watching over you."

With that, the black cave and driving snow melted into a blur of grey blots. The sense of her grandmother receded. In the sleet, Tanya reappeared briefly, flying in a way that defied logic, her monstrous shape shifting and contracting to the size of a crow. As she landed on Rana's shoulder, the world slipped into darkness.

When Rana came to, she was lying on her bed. It was night. A blackbird sat on her shoulder, its ashen claws pricking her skin.

Sometime later, the door to her cabin opened, flooding the room with light. She squinted against the glare and shielded her eyes. Tomás held a hurricane lamp. Noxolo entered behind him.

"She's awake!" Tomás said unnecessarily.

"I told you she would be." Noxolo's deep voice had a condescending edge to it.

She was parched, shaky, and weak. The bird on her shoulder shifted slightly, as if inconvenienced by the light and colder air. Neither Tomás nor Noxolo seemed to notice it.

"So you did." Tomás regarded him with irritation, as if he didn't like being reminded. Her bunk sagged as he sat beside her. He slid a hand behind her back. "*Mi hermana*," he said, maintaining their ruse. "Let me help you sit. You had us so worried!"

As he pushed her upright, she gaped at him, not believing what she saw. Tomás no longer bore his earlier signs of age. The fine lines about his eyes were gone. The deeper folds along his nose had disappeared. He actually looked younger than she had known him. He smiled ruefully, noticing her astonishment. "When you fainted, I had to find other ways to replenish myself," he whispered.

She glanced up at Noxolo with dislike. The man returned her gaze implacably.

"He knows about my tattoo and its shortcomings. Unfortunately, this," Tomás indicated his face, "is only temporary, so I'll need to rely on him further." He turned to Noxolo, his expression polite. "Would you mind? I want to speak with her in private."

Noxolo inclined his head. "I'm sure I don't need to remind you, Fra Tomás, she's in a delicate state. We mustn't tire her." Rana froze. Had he told Tomás she was pregnant?

Tomás' expression soured. "I know what's best for my sister."

"Of course. I'll have a tray of food sent for her."

He waited for Noxolo to close the door before he spoke. "Did you find it?"

He never gives up. "Tomás, I'm so thirsty—"

"Of course you are. We've been forcing water down your throat for the past three days. The bucket is there." He pointed to a pail and ladle beside her bunk. "I take it you couldn't bring back what I wanted."

"No."

"Well, it doesn't matter. I asked out of panic. We'll find the Fountain, going by your descriptions of Xaymaca."

Thank Lys for small blessings. "Does the captain or Noxolo know for what we search?"

"I haven't told them. I'm not sure I will."

"And you?" The more she knew of what had happened to him, the better.

"When you collapsed, I wasn't sure what to do, so I sought Noxolo. My instincts about him bore out. He practices unusual methods but they work, even if he does forget his place."

She frowned.

"It's best I don't tell you what they entail. Let's just say, they serve me for now, even though they're temporary." He regarded her. "What made you swoon?"

Lying unconscious for three days was hardly a swoon, she thought. The pressure on her shoulder shifted from right to left. She suspected Tanya was finding Tomás' proximity unpleasant. "I told you before, when I get too close to the Fountain, it's like a type of death. I want to leave everything behind. The joy is all consuming."

"You don't look joyful." He eyed her closely.

"I'm half-starved and dehydrated. What do you expect?"

He retrieved a ladle of water for her. "Perhaps we need to focus on the surrounding area. The actual route to its location." He held the ladle to her lips. Her nostrils wrinkled. The water smelled sharp. She looked at him suspiciously. "What's in that?"

"A little lemon and other restorative herbs. Noxolo says they'll help you, especially since you aren't eating."

So, Noxolo hadn't divulged her pregnancy. "I don't want it! Only plain food and water!" He could have put anything in it, including opiates, to make her more easily managed.

"Very well, as you wish." Tomás looked nonplussed. "Why are you so upset?"

"You heard Noxolo say, 'only those of pure heart and body can approach and partake of the waters!'" She hadn't repeated the quote exactly, but she was fairly certain Tomás hadn't paid full attention. "We're hardly that."

A knock came at their door before Tomás could reply. Noxolo had arrived with her food.

After she had been assured the fare was simply that, with nothing added, Tomás left her to eat her meal in peace. Half an hour later, Noxolo arrived to remove her tray.

"Where's Umberto?" she demanded. The irony of preferring Umberto, Tomás' toady over Noxolo wasn't lost upon her. Noxolo ignored the question to voice one of his own. "How is it you now have a *djab* with you?"

That word again, *djab*. Did he mean Tanya? She dismissed it. "I don't know what you're talking about."

"Don't play games with me. You were gone three days. You come back with one, yet you stink of grace. How is that possible? I know where you went."

"I haven't gone anywhere. You're raving."

"You were on the black road. And then, you went somewhere else. You're seeking the Fountain, don't lie!"

"I don't answer to you! If you don't leave, I'll shout for Tomás!"

"You think you can best me? There are powers at my beck and call that are stronger than yours!"

Before she could react, he jabbed a forefinger at her. A vise closed about her chest, forcing the air from her lungs in a rush. She grabbed her throat and choked. Her vision prickled, the world spun, she felt faint....

And then, the weight about her chest broke like a band of snapping iron. She collapsed on her bed, gasping for breath. Something big slammed into Noxolo, knocking him hard against the door. He stared at her in astonishment. Then his expression turned to hatred. He scrambled to his feet and fled.

Tanya had come to the rescue.

For several nights in a row after that, Mateo wasn't at dinner. Rana sat with Capitán de Carazo, Angél, and Tomás. Noxolo served as usual.

"He isn't well," de Carazo informed her, responding to her query. "He sends his apologies."

She frowned. The captain also seemed not to be his usual self. There was something flat about him, bland, as if he were discussing the weather instead of his nephew's health.

Tomás took a bite of his chicken and waved Noxolo over for more wine. Tanya rested on her shoulder, invisible to all, save Noxolo, perhaps. Noxolo filled Tomás' glass, but left hers empty. She wasn't sure if it was because she was pregnant, or whether he was avoiding her and Tanya. Either way, it suited her fine.

"I'm sorry to hear that," she told de Carazo sincerely. She liked Mateo. "Perhaps I can take him a tray of food later. Now that I'm feeling better, I'd like to help." Her nausea had dissipated. She attributed it to Tanya's allegiance. Now that they were linked, it was possible Tanya also suffered from her ailments. It made sense. Tanya didn't want any physical discomfort.

"No need," Tomás informed her, speaking for the captain. He waved his knife before attacking his chicken again. "Noxolo has things well in hand."

She hazarded a glance at the two of them. They both avoided her gaze. She could understand why Noxolo might not want anything more to do with her after Tanya attacked him—such a surprise that had been! Tanya had her interests to protect now too, but the lifeless response was strange, as if the captain were going through the motions of mouthing excuses when his mind was elsewhere. Tomás, on the other hand, devoured his food as if Noxolo couldn't put enough of it in front of him. Normally, he was fussy about meals.

She let the matter drop. There was nothing to be gained in pressing for details. Mateo's cabin was next to hers. She would learn what she needed when she visited him later.

Angél found her on the spar deck after they excused themselves from the evening meal. The wind had come up; the air was humid, threatening rain. The swells were foam-tipped; she worried they might have a storm.

"The pilot tells me this is nothing," Angél reassured her, balancing on sea legs. "Besides, the season for *huracanes* is past."

She shivered, wishing he would put his arms around her. *Soon, we'll be together,* she thought.

He seemed to be of a similar frame of mind. "We're five days out from Xaymaca."

She rubbed her arms. "Did you notice at dinner? Something's not right with the captain."

He nodded. "I thought so, too."

"And Mateo...I think his absence and the captain's state are connected. I don't trust the captain's valet. I think he's behind it."

"How?" He looked puzzled.

"There are things I know about dark magic, Angél. Things I've never told you. But once committed, you recognize those dark stains on others."

He scoffed. "You? Guilty of black magic? I don't believe it. Rana Isadore, maybe, but not you."

That hurt a bit, but she supposed she deserved it. "I...I'm not who you think I am."

He smiled down at her. "Who are you, then?"

She wanted to tell him. She couldn't. "Rana wasn't so bad."

"She was everything the Inquisition accuses us of."

"Every wrong thing she did, she did for you, Angél. She loved you more than life. It's a terrible thing, to love someone who doesn't love you in return."

"And do you love me more than life?"

He was teasing her, now. "Of course. But tell me. Did you ever love her? Even just a little?"

He frowned. "Why are we talking about Rana? She's dead in an alley somewhere."

"Don't say such things!"

"Why not? It's probably true. I thought you were worried about Noxolo."

They had wandered down a perilous path. Why had she been tempted to tell him who she really was? The old Rana never would have. "You're right. I am worried about him. We need to know what's going on. The more we know, the less likely we'll be trapped."

"You think he's capable of wrongdoing?"

"I know he is, Angél."

"Surely the Grand Inquisitor remains a deterrent to him. One act of heresy on his part, and Tomás will have him thrown overboard."

"Noxolo has influence over Tomás." She didn't elaborate. "They're both dangerous."

He considered her seriously. "You really are afraid. What would you have me do?"

"Spy on the captain. Find out why he's acting the way he is. I think he may be drugged." His eyes widened. "In the meantime, I'll visit Mateo."

"I'm not sure that's wise."

"Tomás and Noxolo will spend time together, tonight. They make a habit of it, usually after midnight."

"How do you know this?"

"I hear Tomás leave and return to his room." She neglected to tell him he had also been visiting her. Unlike the old Tomás who had become impotent, sex with the new Tomás was vigorous. Thankfully, the explanation made sense to Angél. He didn't question her further about it.

"So, if Tomás and Noxolo are otherwise disposed, that's the time I should visit the captain. How will that look if he's sleeping?"

"You can always offer some excuse. I worry that he *isn't* sleeping."

They made plans to meet in the morning so they might share what they had learned.

At eight bells, she rose from her bed and listened carefully. Her biggest fear had been Tomás visiting her beforehand and asking why she was still in her dress, but that hadn't occurred. It was hard to distinguish the soft tread on floorboards from the constant grinding of the timbers or the mutterings of the crew, but her ears were sharp. She heard Tomás as he passed. Of Umberto, there was no sign.

She opened her door a crack and glanced out. At the end of the companionway, a lone lantern flickered. The breeze was brisk and threatened to snuff the light. Shadows wavered, making her think of ghosts. She would have preferred checking on Mateo in the dark, but there was no help for it. As she was about to step into the hallway, Umberto appeared. He had been in Mateo's berth.

She closed her door quickly, waiting for him to pass. When she could no longer hear his footsteps, she peered out a second time, only to see his stumpy form lumbering down the stair. He was carrying a covered tray. The ships' lanterns caught him as he made his way to the waist. Perhaps he was heading for the ship's galley. Nothing, not even half-eaten food, was ever wasted on a ship.

She was at Mateo's door in an instant. She knocked gingerly. "Mateo?" she whispered. "May I come in?"

There was no answer.

She had no reason for being there, should anyone question her. It was possible Tomás had not gone to visit Noxolo as she thought. She pushed the door open and stepped quickly within.

A lone candle, set inside a shielding glass, shone from a small table. A lump, covered by a blanket, lay on a low cot. There was also an empty hammock, along with a familiar stink. This was where Umberto had been sleeping.

She lifted the blanket from the boy, fearing he might be dead. What she saw made her wish he was.

Mateo was as pale as a corpse. He still breathed, his chest rose and fell shallowly, but she feared it might stop at any moment. His hands, face, and neck were intact, but strange gashes...bites?...gored his body as if something had fed there. A number of the wounds were scabbing, several day's old. Under ordinary circumstances they wouldn't be seen, hidden by his uniform.

Why? she wondered.

It should be fairly obvious. Tanya preened herself on her shoulder.

It isn't.

Put two and two together, Rana. Tomás is getting younger. This boy is dying. If anyone recognizes impending death, I do.

Those marks on his body?

They're leeching him somehow.

How do you know this?

Tanya paused to scratch at her head. *Let's just say I fed rather well on the dark road.* She made a face. Rana wasn't sure whether it was one of nostalgia or regret.

I see.

On the other hand, they may not want to kill him outright. No point in sacrificing the cow if you still want the milk.

Perhaps they meant to keep Mateo around for a time. It would please Tomás to take Mateo's life in increments, so he might restore himself at the boy's expense. Mateo had threatened him in their first week out. It was so like Tomás to take his vengeance in a cruel way. A frightening thought occurred to her. *Does Noxolo's djab have anything to do with this?*

They're coming! Tanya cried.

Her warning was so shrill, it startled her. She knocked against the small table. The candle rocked in its holder, spilling wax down the sides of the glass. She threw the cover over Mateo and bolted for the door, praying to both Lys and Anassa she might return to her cabin unseen.

Luck or the gods was with her. She closed her door as she heard several people trudge up the companionway.

She quickly removed her bodice and petticoat, going so far as to unfasten and set aside her stays, leaving only her shift. If Tomás had been with the returning party, he would soon be at her door. She lay on her bunk knowing he still might question her burning candle. Sure enough, he knocked on her door once, and then entered without invitation.

"You're still up," he said without preamble. He seemed surprised. Did he think she had waited for him? His skin was flushed. He looked as if he had more muscle beneath his robe. Mateo's life force. It was so evident, now. It wasn't the product of her imagination.

"Yes."

He waited. She hadn't thought of telling him this one thing, but seeing Mateo made her realize she needed more protection than what Tanya offered. Noxolo had become invaluable to Tomás. There was no telling who manipulated whom. She had to take this chance and hope her instincts were correct.

"There's something I must tell you."

"Oh?" He slid beside her and ran a finger along her arm. He wanted sex and assumed she did, too. If he didn't kill her outright for what she was about to say, she might have found a way to prevent him from raping her, as well.

"I know you want to live forever," she whispered. "I want that, too. I can offer you that, and much, much more."

He quirked an eyebrow. "What else *is* there?"

"A ruling dynasty, Tomás. Stemming from us and the children we'll have. I carry your son."

He stared at her as if she had sprouted wings. For one terrifying second, she feared she had erred, that he would strangle her, then and there. Instead, he grabbed her by the shoulders. His face radiated amazement and surprise.

"Truly?"

"Yes. I'm about six weeks gone."

"A son. You're sure?"

She nodded, pretending to be happy. "He won't be immortal, of course, unless you grant it, something you could bestow on him in time. But, Tomás, think of it! We can establish an empire here in the New World. As a ruling family, we would have ultimate power."

He nodded, plainly considering it. "But how do I explain your pregnancy to the outside world?"

"There's no need to explain anything! There's only been one virgin birth since the beginning, but also the promise of the Second Coming! *You* are the Second Coming, Tomás!"

"Not my son?"

"No, because *you* will be immortal."

He frowned, confused by her logic but intrigued by what she painted, even so. "Does anyone else know about this?"

"Of course not! Do I look like a fool?"

"So, this is why you've been so ill, lately. Seasickness had nothing to do with it." He considered her with admiration.

She gave him an encouraging grin.

"*Cariña!*" He pulled her close. She gritted her teeth and endured it. Then he held her at arm's length to regard her with concern. "You're feeling better, now?"

"Yes. The sickness has passed."

"Excellent. Well, we must make sure you have whatever you need." He set a hand on her belly. "You're sure it's a boy?"

"I am."

"Perhaps Noxolo can give you—"

She held up a forefinger. "No. Absolutely not. Only simple food and water."

He slid his hand from her belly to the inside of her thigh. "And can we still...?"

She trapped it. "It's better if we don't. If you want your son to be as healthy as possible, we must sacrifice our passion."

He grimaced and removed his hand from beneath hers. "Well, I suppose I can wait. It's only a week until we make landfall. I'll find a couple of island girls to take care of me while you're indisposed."

What a pig he was. Her face didn't mirror the thought. "We must also think of appearances."

"Yes." He nodded. "The crew thinks we're searching for a rich husband for you. Obviously, I can't be that."

"You could marry me to Angél."

His eyes narrowed.

She set a hand on his arm. "Tomás, I am over him. Now, that I carry your child, I want to be with you, to bring our son up so he might rule by your side. Angél is convenient. We wouldn't have to waste time finding a replacement in Xaymaca."

"So, a marriage...in name only."

"Of course."

He considered it. "Very well. In a way, I like the idea. It's obvious he's in love with you. It entertains me you'd be his wife, but he'd never have you." He smiled. "I'll even perform the ceremony, myself."

Her heart sped. She hadn't expected that.

"But I think it's safe for us to be intimate one last time before the baby is born." Her elation died. "Come." He patted her thigh.

"Let *Padré* say hello to our *niño*. I'll be gentle." Without further preliminaries, he flipped her onto her stomach.

He had promised it wouldn't hurt, but it did. Tomás always broke his promises.

The next morning, Angél approached her as she was taking air on the waist. She still hurt from Tomas' brutalizing. It had pained her to descend the companionway to the spar deck, but loitering on the quarterdeck wasn't done. The captain's and officers' place was there.

"I found de Carazo sitting in his chair, drugged. He was hardly aware of me," he told her. "I doubt very much if he'll remember I was there. I didn't stay long."

"So, Noxolo is manipulating him, too." She told him about Mateo.

"Gods, what a nightmare. The sooner we're off this accursed ship, the better."

"Yes." Her hand strayed to her belly. Rough sex didn't hurt an unborn child, did it? Especially if it was only six weeks old? She hoped not. She suspected Tomás' handling had been a last fling at the way he liked to abuse her; he wanted this child, too. "Have you thought of how we might escape?"

"We'll have to see what transpires. Possibly, we can give Tomás the slip in the shantytown, but maybe not. I don't know the island that well. There are cotton and sugar plantations along the way to Villa de la Vía. The cane would cut us to shreds, so we'd have to make our break through the cotton. Then run through jungle. Probably best not to make our way back to the port as I originally thought, but to find another. "

The invisible weight that was Tanya shifted on her shoulder. *Is he going to be my father?*

Yes, Rana replied. *If we escape from here.*

He's handsome! I'll be gorgeous! Much prettier than I was in my last life!

"It would help if we had some kind of distraction," Angél finished, completely unaware of Tanya.

Look out! Tanya dug her talons into Rana. *Tomás is coming!*

"Ah! Just the two I wanted to see!"

She and Angel stepped quickly apart. Her heart thudded in her chest. They should have been more careful. Even if Tomás had had his way with her last night, it meant little. With enough provocation, he could as easily sign Angél's death warrant.

"A word in your ear, Ser Ferrara," Tomás told him jovially. He drew him aside.

Rana watched as Angél's eyes widened in astonishment. As Tomás spoke, Angél glanced at her quickly. "Of course!" he stammered. "That's what I want! It's what I've always wanted!"

Her heart stopped beating so hard, but it still left her breathless. Tomás was honouring their agreement. Without a doubt, he had suggested to Angél they wed.

Three days later, in the middle of a humid and oppressive afternoon, her marriage to Angél took place. She wore the only finery at her disposal, a bodice and split petticoat of black and gold, with an underpetticoat heavy with embroidery. Dressed in burnished breastplate and armour, Angél looked more handsome than ever. Every member of the crew was present on the waist or watching from the shrouds. Capitán de Carazo, who normally would have presided over the ceremony had Tomás not been present, surveyed the proceedings from the quarterdeck with a wan Mateo at his side. Both uncle and nephew looked somewhat better. Behind them, Noxolo loomed, an unwanted pestilence, as welcome as plague.

She didn't care. She was marrying Angél, and this was her wedding day. Unknown to everyone but herself, she was marrying him again. The first time, he had been forced into it. She had attacked Miriam Medina with the wasp demon, and Ximen had declared them wed. Simple. Final. No ceremony, and no happy celebration afterwards. Instead, Angél had discarded her, only allowing her near him because his parents bowed to tribal law. He hadn't wanted her then, but today was different. She saw it in his eyes.

She threaded through the throng, aware of the admiring glances coming her way. Miriam Medina was a beautiful woman. Angél met her as she approached him on the upper deck. Tomás awaited them, a book of Sul in his hands. Outwardly, his expression was benign, but his eyes were keen. He went on at length about how, despite his position, it pleased him to perform this service because he was a simple friar at heart. All pretense. After the wedding meal, he would deny Angél his rights. That was the only thing Tomás looked forward to. She wasn't fooled.

She smiled at Tomás, the happy bride sharing her joy. Her face gave away nothing of her thoughts. *You may think you've won. Angél's delusions about our marriage may soon shatter, but you haven't bested us. As soon as we land, we'll flee, and your son will be lost to you.*

"Let's begin," Tomás said pleasantly. "Dearly beloved, we are gathered here today, in the sight of Sul, our most heavenly father, to join this man and this woman, in holy matrimony...."

As they murmured their vows, the breeze turned brisk. By the time the ceremony was over, the wind had built to gale force and the waves were rounding into hills. As Angél kissed her to seal their match, Capitán de Carazo descended the quarterdeck on game legs.

"We have to postpone the wedding feast until tomorrow!" he shouted over the shuddering of the masts and clap of the sails. The crew had already jumped to their posts. Mateo and Noxolo had disappeared into their berths. She worried about the boy, hoping that whatever Noxolo had invoked didn't need to feed on him again, so soon. After bawling orders at the pilot, de Carazo lurched for his quarters, confident his crew would see the ship through the storm.

"I'll take my wife to my cabin!" Angél yelled.

Tomás snagged her by the arm. "No. My sister returns to her room, where *I* will keep her protected. Come, Miriam."

Angél was stunned. "But, she isn't your sister! She's my wife!"

"In name, only." Tomás tightened his grip on her elbow and pulled her away. Angél grabbed Tomás by the shoulder.

Tomás turned on him so quickly it made her think of a snake striking a rat. "Touch me again, and you're dead!"

"Tomás, don't!" she pleaded, grabbing him. She turned to Angél. "He'll kill you, I swear!"

"You knew about this?" He looked dumbfounded.

"I did! I'm sorry!"

Tomás hauled her up the companionway. She didn't dare cast Angél a parting glance. Once they were in her cabin and the door shut securely behind them, Tomás confronted her. "So much for your fair words about wanting to rule at my side. I *should* feed him to the sharks! And make you watch!"

She squeezed her hands into fists. "I had to say it! I had to give him something to believe!"

"You're lying. You're still in love with him!"

She closed her eyes. If he refused to believe her, she would have to tell him the truth, but tailored to what he might accept. "All right! I admit it! I do still have feelings for him. He's Tribe, one of my people. But that makes little difference. I carry *your* child."

His glance narrowed. "I wonder."

"It's true! I haven't been with anyone, but you! You've had me under lock and key for months!"

He eyed her balefully.

"If you don't believe me, have Noxolo confirm paternity. I'm sure with everything he's capable of, he can do that."

Her ewer of water slid across the table. Tomás grabbed it as it fell. The storm outside was growing wilder. On its hook at her door, her lantern swayed back and forth, threatening to snuff its flame. Tomás set the ewer on the floor. "No. Noxolo doesn't need to know about that."

His desire to keep some things from Noxolo relieved her. Apparently, he was wary of the power Noxolo exerted. With her and the baby at risk, Noxolo would have more control than Tomás wished. She didn't think it useful to point out Noxolo already knew about her pregnancy, except he believed Angél was the father. As the floor tilted at a drastic angle, their candle went out. Tomás was thrown onto the bed beside her.

The next several hours turned into a nightmare. She expected the sea to rush into their cabin at any moment, drowning them in its black, swirling depths as surely as if they were kittens in a river. Tomás clutched at her as if she were his only link to survival. As frightened as she was, his fear surprised her. In his own distorted way, he loved and needed her.

He also kept muttering, "Sul!" over and over. There were other mumblings she couldn't make out. She didn't think he actually believed in Sul. Unlike Lys, who was said to immerse herself in the affairs of her worshippers, Sul was the creator, his vision turned outward. Tomás would be forgotten or remembered as a bad idea.

The thought sustained her.

Chapter Twenty-Five: Gale

THE NEXT COUPLE of weeks weren't without their challenges. The shifted roles on board the *Raven* were clear: Dirk commanded from his bedside, but on deck Adetokunbo was chief; the slaves took direction from him. It annoyed Dirk to have his orders relayed, but there was little he could do until he healed and the borders of language relaxed. They were all learning, developing their own *patois* unique to the ship. Everyone did his best to teach or learn the imperatives of sailing and navigation. The crew were told they needed to treat the ex-slaves with respect. The freemen saw they needed to overcome their desire for vengeance if they were to survive. To the north, the shores of Esbañiola were a hazy blue smudge on the horizon. They had been skirting its southern coast, anxious to reach Xaymaca, when the sails drooped. Dirk summoned Francis and Joachín to the captain's cabin. He hailed them from his bunk and bid them to pull up chairs.

"So let me understand this," he said, eyeing Joachín. "You dream dreams that foretell the future. You also have a magical tattoo that forces you to tell the truth."

"Yes." Joachin wished he didn't have to admit it. He missed lying. It had been a way to fool an enemy, if that enemy were fool enough.

"So, if there was someone on board I didn't wholly trust," Dirk cast a glance at Francis, "you could tell me if they were lying?"

Francis' mouth fell open and then he snapped it shut. He and Dirk had been spending their nights together. That usually implied a certain amount of trust. "You don't trust me?" he asked, sounding hurt.

"I do. Mostly. But you still have ties to Inglais."

"I've never misled you about that."

"No. But if you had to pick, which would you choose? A life serving *her* purposes, or one sharing mine?"

"I don't see why I can't have both."

This is beginning to sound more and more like a lover's spat, Joachin thought.

"She might forgive you, but she'd never forgive me. I'm one of the Brethren. She'd as likely hang me from a gibbet."

"Ilysabeth is an enterprising woman, Dirk. You might be surprised at what she forgives when it suits her needs. Why do you think I've been chasing the Diaphani all this time? If she's willing to use magic and witchcraft to gain the Inglaisi throne, she'll certainly approve of privateering once she's queen. Secretly, of course. Appearances must be maintained."

"Perhaps." He eyed Joachin. "So what you've told me about the gold mine on Xaymaca is true."

Joachin nodded. "It is. If the map I saw was accurate."

"On the other hand, it might be something you told Boyle to spare yourself."

"I didn't tell him about it. He did." He nodded at Francis.

"Dirk, he isn't lying to you. He can't." Francis ran a hand over his brow. "I had a feeling it would come to this. Look, if you don't believe me, tell him something only you know. Let him decide if it's true or false. That should prove it."

"Very well." Dirk leaned into his pillows. "I'm a child of scandal, the bastard son of an English noblewoman and her groom. My mother gave me up." He smiled tightly. "I was cared for by the village wet-nurse. My grandfather saw to it I received a decent education. But all for nought."

"That's partly true, and partly false," Joachin replied.

"Which part is false?"

"The part about the noblewoman and the groom. You're the bastard son of a nobleman. The wet-nurse *was* your mother."

"Ha!" Dirk sat upright and winced. He had moved too quickly. He settled back into his pillows. "I take back what I said about your claims to be a truth-sayer. So you can discern falsehoods. But that still doesn't prove you can't lie."

"Believe you me, I would if I could."

"Ask him to tell you something he doesn't know." Francis steepled his fingers.

This is where he planned the conversation to go all along, Joachin realized. *Why?*

"It's an idea I've been toying with, Joachin." Francis smiled broadly, as if reading his mind. "I know you can't speak anything but the truth because lies snag in your throat. That still proves nothing. You could be an amazing actor. I was one once, you know," he added, glancing at Dirk.

Joachin frowned. "What are you getting at?"

"It's this. Tell the captain something about his life. Make it up. If you say it, it has to be true. If you can't, it isn't."

It had never occurred to him to try such a thing. But then, there had been the necessity of staying alive. "I...I'm not sure how—"

"Let your mind go blank. Start with what the captain has already told us. Close your eyes, if it helps. You're a dreamer, Joachin. Let your imagination guide you."

His manipulation of Boyle in a dream-state had been a surprise, and now Francis was suggesting he stretch his talent further. He imagined Dirk as a boy, invited on a rare occasion to his grandfather's manor. While his mother shared gossip with the cook and assistants in the kitchen, he had been left to wander. He watched as Dirk entered a grand bedroom. The boy went straight to a chest, opened it, and pulled out a...sword?

The word snagged. Not a sword, then, but a woman's gown? That wasn't it, either. He kept his eyes tightly closed.

"What's he doing?" Dirk whispered.

"Wait for it," Francis replied.

What *was* the thing? He concentrated harder...and saw eight-year old Dirk retrieve a pair of fine leather boots. The boy raced off with them through the halls, down the stairs, and stowed them beneath a bale of hay in the stables.

He opened his eyes. He felt off-kilter, as if his soul had gone somewhere else and then returned to his body but had overshot his form. "When you were eight, you stole your grandfather's boots. He never had any idea what happened to them. You sold them later, to..." a man in a blood-stained tunic crossed his mind, "the local butcher." He gasped. He'd been able to say it. It was true.

Dirk stared at him as if he had grown a tail and horns. Francis burst into laughter and clapped a hand on his thigh. "Well?" he demanded, looking at Dirk in triumph. "That's right, isn't it?"

"How could you know that?" Dirk gaped at Joachin.

His own astonishment mirrored Dirk's. "I didn't know it. Until now."

"So we know what this means." Francis looked as if he were about to burst with glee.

"What?" They asked at the same time.

"We can conjecture all we like—where the gold is, where the ships are, what cargo they're carrying. Joachin can confirm or deny all of it. He's both a dreamer and a truth-teller. Those two talents combined make him even more valuable than each single gift alone. He'll be one hundred percent accurate about *everything*."

The ship lurched. Masts groaned and the sails cracked. Dirk waved them off. "You best go on deck and see what's happening. It sounds like the winds have come up."

Gibbs appeared in the doorway. "It's blowin' from th' west, Cap'n! Comin' in hard."

"Damn! I should be onboard!" Dirk fumbled with his covers.

"Stay where you are," Francis said. "You're not yet fit. We'll deal with this." He and Joachin followed Gibbs from the great cabin.

As they stepped onto the waist, the breeze tore at their clothes and hair. The waves had grown bigger. The *Raven* pitched from side to side.

"Reef them sails!" Gibbs bawled, although the old crew had already jumped to the rigging and were hugging the yards to do that very thing. Most of the freedmen looked bewildered or terrified, but Adetokunbo was quick to repeat the order in their language. They sprang to help.

Joachin remained where he was, balancing on steady feet. The winds, usually from the east, had shifted, which could only mean one thing. A storm was upon them, possibly a big one.

The *Raven* had lost her bowsprit in the battle against Boyle. She still carried too much water despite the repairs they had done and the constant manning of the pumps. Even surrendering some of the guns to the sea hadn't proved enough. They had been lucky with good weather...until now.

Francis suggested he might be able to determine the future. Was the future set? His dreams suggested it might be. On the other hand, those times had also offered choices. Was Miriam caught in this tempest somewhere, beyond his reach, on the Great Ocean Sea?

"Miriam is alive!" he shouted into the wind, testing Francis' theory. He could say it. It had to be.

"Joachin, get up here! We need you!" Francis appeared on the quarterdeck only to disappear again into the helmsman's hutch. He ran to help him and Gibbs with the whipstaff. Three men would be needed to hold the ship steady. If Miriam was safe, he had to remain safe for her, also.

Chapter Twenty-Six: Jager's Revenge

LIFE ON BOARD the ship was difficult because she had to hide her grief. Time passed in a tedium of duty and schedules. Miriam avoided Casi as much as possible and kept the terrible news of Joachín, Iago, and Barto's deaths to herself. When the *Phoenix* was two days out from Nueva Esbaña, the afternoon turned sweltering. A stiff wind came up, and the southern sky turned dark. All hands were piped to stations. As the waves grew bigger, the ship began to roll. A wall of indigo raced towards them. In a stridency she had never heard him use, Mister Landseer bawled at the Tribe to get below.

With the wind whipping her veil about her face, she waited to be the last down the companionway, to make sure the Tribe was safe. As Zara lurched by, she gave a parting glance to the spar deck, only to notice a forlorn figure making his way down the forecastle steps. Crew members dodged past Ximen, shoving him off balance. He held on to the rail, then continued to descend.

Dear Lys! Her heart stopped for one awful moment. He must have been in the heads. At the bottom stair, he tried to determine a path.

Technically, he was blind, but he saw the immediate past through the Tribe's eyes. Through her, he would see the spar deck as it was seconds before, but the deck was in chaos. Things were changing too quickly. The crew dodged everywhere, running to secure line and reef sail. He wouldn't be able to cross the waist without a guide. Two members darted in front of him. Another knocked him aside to charge up the forecastle steps. She gasped as he fell, landing on his hands and knees.

"Ximen! Stay where you are! I'll come to you!" She wasn't sure he heard, but she thought she saw him nod. Over the past weeks, she had become used to the ship's roll, but now, it dropped and bucked, throwing her off balance. A lance of lightening cut across the sky. Thunder cracked above the ship, the energy of the storm, palpable.

"Get out of here, you stupid *vrouw*!" A mate ran by her as she grabbed the main mast. "You'll get y'self killed!" He scrambled up a rat line.

"I'm not leaving him!" She pointed at Ximen who had clambered to his feet. She didn't want to think what would happen if she failed him. Beyond, the waves were white-capped and growing. A large one struck the hull, sending water flying onto the deck. *The sea means to crush us*, she thought, clinging to the mast. Ximen had sensed the wave in time and grabbed the rail. She needed to tamp down her panic. The storm wasn't sentient. It was just a thing, unruly, uncaring. Thunder crashed a second time. *Which doesn't mean it can't kill us*, she reconsidered, with her teeth chattering. She ran, slipping over wet wood.

As she caught Ximen by the shoulders, the sky opened with a roar and the rain came down. In seconds, they were drenched. The ship pitched and rocked as they stumbled back across the waist. More water surged over the gunwales, causing them to lose their footing and fall. Dripping and scrambling for purchase, she hauled Ximen to his feet. It was hard going, even harder to see their way with the veil plastered against her face. A blurry figure waved at them from atop the companionway. As they reached it, it turned out to be Zara.

"If you'd just use the chamber pot like the rest of us!" she scolded, shrill enough to outshout the storm. "I don't know why you're so modest, Old Man! It isn't as if we haven't seen you before!" She drew him into a fierce embrace. He sank into her bosom, protesting and exhausted.

Miriam clutched the wall, giddy with relief. The tension of the past few minutes fell away. She fought a crazy desire to laugh. They might still drown, but trust Zara to ignore the greater issue and nag Ximen on his choice of toilet! On the other hand, maybe it was Zara's way of banishing fear, of mocking it. It had been a terrifying passage, crossing the waist.

"Come along, now! Let's get you in some blankets," Zara insisted.

"You needn't fuss, woman—"

"Apparently, I *do* need!" She continued to natter at him as she led him below.

Thunder rumbled again, but it wasn't as loud. *Or perhaps I hope it isn't,* Miriam thought. With the storm out of view, it was easier to convince herself they might survive. Captain Vrooman was as steady as they came. She would have to trust he would see the ship through the storm and that Lys meant to get them to Xaymaca. The goddess wasn't easily foiled.

As she stepped onto the first tread of the companionway, someone clapped a broad, wet hand over her mouth and grabbed her from behind. Alarm arced through her as she recognized her abductor. Jager de Groot ground his chin into her neck. "*Hallo, heks!*" he crooned as he pulled her back onto the deck.

How had he escaped the lockup? Piet Spoor or one of the starboard crew must have released him. His sodden shirt slid against her back, the flab and muscle reminding her of the rolls on a walrus. She freed one of her arms and knocked his hand away. "Let go of me!"

He laughed and pinned her again. She feared for her ribs, but broken bones were the least of her worries. "You want me t' let you go?" She kicked and fought as he dragged her across the waist. "Aye! That's the plan!"

Dear Lys, He's going to throw me overboard! Where were Captain Vrooman and the officers? She shrieked as Jager lifted her over the starboard rail.

"Good Book says, 'Never suffer a witch to live!' So rot in a watery hell, ye *domme hoer!*"

He tossed her over the side. The wind snatched her breath. The hull flashed by in a blur of rain, wood, and froth, and then the sea struck her—a cold, cruel wall. Water closed over her head and coursed up her nose. She clawed for the surface. It was impossible to see where anything was. The world was topsy-turvy, bubble and foam. The sea sucked her down, spun her in circles.

Alonso! She reached for him with both heart and mind. He had to be with her! He would never leave her...but how could he help without a host? The answer was terrifying as it was obvious. He couldn't. No one could save her, but herself.

By some miracle or an oversight of the gods, she stopped spinning and came to an unsteady bob. The surge cleared, revealing a black wall—the *Phoenix's* hull. Fear crawled up her spine and wrapped bony fingers about her throat. It would tear her to pieces if she got too close. She flailed and kicked, fighting to put some distance between herself and the ship. A dark flange moved—the ship's rudder bidding her farewell. The hull hadn't snagged her, the rudder was moving away. Then its shock wave struck, knocking her end over end.

Her lungs shrivelled to sacks. Blood no longer coursed through her veins, she was filled with brine. The need to inhale became merciless in its demand. Her vision prickled, dwindling to a hole. Within it, her hands floated, feeble little flippers, pawing through the churn. The last things she saw were her fingers, wavering like seaweed until they stilled.

Chapter Twenty-Seven: Rescues of a Different Sort

BREATHE!

A punch to the chest brought her back around, causing her to sputter and choke. Somehow, her head was above the surface, but the world remained drenched and grey, of wave and storm. She felt dizzy and sick. Her lungs were lined with salt. Her throat was raw from choking and her sternum hurt. The *Phoenix* was nowhere to be seen, blotted out by the driving rain. She was too dazed to care.

Something long and firm swam beneath her, holding her up. It kept moving and shifting, as if adjusting to the waves. She thought of sharks, but the thing wasn't interested in eating her. Sharks' skins were rough and coarse, but this creature was smooth and leathery. Better to endure it, than to sink to the boundless depths.

It jerked suddenly. A blunt edge—a dorsal fin?—poked her in the gut. She moaned and let go.

Mi-ri-am! Hold-on!

Alonso! He had come! Relief revived her, as welcome as fresh air. She hugged him, wondering about his host. He sounded so strange.

His voice had a clipped, staccato quality to it. The syllables were fragmented and came fast.

Take-deep-breath! We-have-to-dive!

A wall of grey loomed before them. They rose with the wave. She closed her eyes and sucked in a lungful, anticipating his plunge. As they dove, every inch of her body felt compressed. Her lungs hurt so much. The pressure made her want to expel her air immediately.

She-sick?

Why-help?

The unexpectedness of the voices made her open her eyes. Her hair swirled about her in a black, silken cloud. All about her, a fleeting blur of bodies swam, long and sleek, butt-nosed and cannon-shaped. *Dolphins!* she realized. Alonso had infiltrated a young female, which bore her up. Others surrounded them—a pod. As the wave caught them, the creatures swam with it until it curled past. Her vision began to prickle. Her lungs were about to burst. She could hold her breath no longer. She had to have air.

She released the animal, realizing too late she had miscalculated how deep it had plunged. As the last of her air bubbled past her face, panic ran through her, as strong as an eel's bite. Another dolphin intercepted her and lifted her up. As they resurfaced, she gasped, tasting air and rain. *We-play-tanpét!* the creature said.

Help-be-cause-fun! another added, its voice clicking with mirth.

They seemed unaffected by her distress, but then, why would they be? It struck her they considered her part of a game, like tossing a ball between mates. Why was she hearing them, and not just Alonso? Their voices floated through her mind like bubbles bursting. Did the sea augment their communication, or were they like Casi, able to hear each other's thoughts? They chattered and joked, mostly about the storm as if it were something to outwit. She wished she felt the same. The older ones sang—lullabies it sounded like, to reassure the calves and keep them close.

Mi-ri-am! Alonso shouted. *We-need-to-dive, a-gain!*

She sucked in another breath and held on. This time, she was ready for the drag and managed it. The lack of air didn't help, but there was something reassuring in the feel of a powerful, sleek body beneath her. Perhaps she was drawing from the creature's strength. Or perhaps it was given freely.

She had always wanted to see dolphins, and now Alonso swam with a pod of them. They seemed benevolent animals. They had accepted him, and her, by association. A *Tribe*, she thought with sudden insight. *Their sense of self is less about the individual and more about community.* If only the world worked that way. One thing was certain, she was tiring quickly. She couldn't keep surfacing and diving for much longer.

Tan-pét-no-trou-ble!

We-swim-out!

What was a *tan-pét*? Did they mean the storm? She had no idea. She was traded amongst the pod again. Another female took her. There was a sense of authority with this one; she bore several scars near her blow hole. A calf swam at her side. *What-she?* the calf asked, cocking an eye at Miriam.

I-men. Of-peo-ple. Long-time, a-way. The cow sounded old and wise.

As a child, she had heard the myths—sailors' tales of how dolphins and whales had once walked upon the earth. Then tiring of human wickedness, they retreated to the sea.

This-one-Manman, the dolphin beneath her said. It seemed an introduction.

Mo-ther, Alonso interpreted. *She-is-lead-er. Ma-tri-arch.*

Miriam considered the creature beneath her. She was being carried by a queen of the sea. Lys was also a Queen of the Seas, but there were times when she questioned if Lys had her best interests at heart. She might lose consciousness again, but she had no doubt Alonso and the pod would do whatever they could to save her, moving her from one animal to next.

The dolphins were doing their part. She had to do hers.

Thank you, she told Manman.

The next few hours tested her determination to stay alive in a way she had never thought possible. As if sensing her weakness, the dolphins dove shallowly and rose to the surface more often. She was a land creature, fragile. They brought her through the worst of the tempest and into the aftermath of what it had wrought. As dawn broke, ruddy waves rose and fell in swells, littered with flotsam. Her escort nudged her onto a broken spar from a lost ship. She clambered onto it, grateful to cling to something more solid.

You-are-half-league-from-shore, Alonso told her. He prodded her with his beak. The pod was tired. It no longer chattered.

Thank them for me, she said.

No-need. They-know. Tide-will-car-ry-you. Pod's-leaving. Must-go.

When will I see you, again?

Don't-know. Will-find-you.

How would he appear next? As a parrot? A turtle? She should expect anything. *Where are we?*

No-i-de-a. And then, he was gone. The pod dove, leaving her to drift shoreward.

༄

She was able to make out a beach. Palms curved seaward, their fronds waving in the breeze. Further east there was a coastal tangle of trees and shrubs. The tide wasn't taking her that way which was fortunate; the area looked difficult should she be caught there. As she drifted shoreward, the spar began to bob. Beneath her, branches of pink and yellow appeared, coral reaching for the surface. Closer to the shore, waves caught and crashed.

If that break was what she thought it was, the reef would tear her to pieces. Other flotsam had been trapped there. She watched as a log made a sudden appearance, spearing the sky, only to crash beneath the surf. She might clamber atop her raft like a rat, but the spar had a tendency to roll.

Alonso! she cried. The surge of panic she was feeling was becoming all too familiar. Dear Lys, why had he chosen to leave, now? There was a gap between the froth, perhaps a place through which she might squeeze. She would have to time her passage just right, hope there was a place to slip through the treacherous coral.

She kicked, trying to maneuver her float. It looked as if the waves leapt and then settled after ten feet or so. It was hard to tell. As she drew closer to the place, her raft began to spin. She hung on, knowing the log might knock her against the reef. She would have to let go, and soon. The spar would no longer be a refuge but a threat; she had seen how rocks treated loose wood. She fought to maintain her hold, and then, at the last moment, she jumped.

She landed with a smack amid churning water and surge. The spar's butt end swirled past her. As she flailed out of its way, her arm struck a branch of coral. It burned like acid and stained the water pink—her blood. Ahead, the surf seemed less turbulent. She kicked for the gap, fearing she might also tear her legs. The choice was to swim or die. She swam.

A yellow and lumpy wall suddenly barred her path.

And then, something hard and claw-like snagged her, pulling her by her hair to the surface. Her scalp felt as if it were being torn from her skull. As she gasped, someone dragged her across a gunwale and shoved her into the bottom of a boat. Her saviour turned out to be an adolescent girl, as brown as kelp. Her cheeks were dotted with blue, her torso carved with tattoos consisting of triangles and curlicues. On her right shoulder, she bore a brand: a crude letter G. Miriam struggled to sit.

Before she could speak, the girl lifted a machete from the bottom of the boat. "*No se mueva!*" she screamed in Esbañish. Miriam stopped struggling, obeying the girl's order for her to be still. The girl's black eyes sparked with hatred. "*Eres una espía!*" You are a spy. The girl thought Miriam was a spy?

Miriam hardly dared to breathe. The girl glared at her, and then slowly, set the machete behind her in the dugout. She lifted a paddle and threatened her with it, showing she would strike her, if necessary.

"*No voy a mover,*" Miriam murmured. I won't move. She didn't dare.

How did this wild girl know Esbañish? Was she a runaway slave? The girl sat upon the boat's single thwart and dipped her paddle into the surge. As she propelled them towards the shore, her dark gaze never left her for a moment.

When they reached a point where the dugout could no longer float without scraping the sandy bottom, the girl ordered her out and made her drag the craft up the beach. It was hard going, but she had no choice. Her captor watched with her machete ready and her paddle in hand.

"Shove it under there." The girl indicated an overhang of dense bush. There was a shallow basin in the sand. She watched until she was satisfied the dugout was hidden, and then pointed out a narrow trail leading from the beach into the jungle. "Move. We have a way to go."

"Where are we going? Is this the island of Esbañiola?" That had been the *Phoenix's* original port of call, but it was possible the ship had been blown off course. She considered the trees on either side of them. They rose to dizzying heights, their leaves as big as cart wheels. Lianas twisted up from the forest floor.

"No, you stupid *blanca*. Stop talking."

"Xaymaca?"

The paddle punched her in the back.

"Ow!" She spun about to confront her abductor. The blow hurt, as she suspected it was meant.

"*We* ask the questions, not you." The girl gestured menacingly.

Miriam rubbed her backside. So, not Esbañiola. She was being taken somewhere where there were others like this wild girl. She considered the jungle about them. It wasn't completely dense. She might run and evade her, but the girl would likely cut her down. There was no missing the hatred in those dark eyes. Besides, she had no idea if there was help nearby, or where they were going. It was best to wait for Alonso to show up.

They walked for another quarter of an hour before she attempted conversation, again. The girl bore tattoos on her face. She didn't recognize any of the glyphs, but if her people were like the Diaphani, they might cut them to enhance magical talent. If she established a common ground, she might be seen as having special knowledge. "I see you have tattoos. So do I. I can show you if you like. Beneath my—"

Her captor jabbed her, again.

"Ow! Is that necessary?" She turned about. "I'm not going to run. I don't even know where I am!"

The girl sneered. "I'll stop when I want." She pointed. "What are those marks?"

Miriam frowned. "What marks?"

"On your flesh."

Oh. The *hymenoptera* bites. "Wasp stings."

"You're so stupid, you ran into a wasp's nest?" The girl curled her lip in contempt.

"No. These were set upon me. By magic." She waited for a reaction and didn't get one. "From a type of demon. I survived its attack." Let her think on that.

"Your magic's nothing." The paddle hit her again, as if out of pique.

"Stop striking me!" She curled her hands into fists.

"Or what? You'll set your wasp demon on me?" The girl raised her machete. "I'll hit you when and how I like." She pointed at her chest. "As for my tattoos, I'll tell you about this *vévé*, because it makes you powerless against me. This is for Ogou. He rules my head."

"Ogou is your chief?"

"No! You *blancos* are *so* stupid. Ogou chose me. He saved me from the *blancos*, so now, I fight for him!" She shook her machete. "Which means you're no match for me, *Blanca*. With him, I wreak vengeance!" She regarded Miriam as if she were a bug she might crush beneath her heel. "I could strike your head from your neck, right where you stand."

"Why not do it, then?"

They stared each other down. She thought she detected a tiny flicker of respect.

"Get going. I'm only sparing you because dead *blancos* don't talk. We'll learn what you know and then, if Ogou wills, I *will* kill you."

They continued down the trail. "Perhaps I can offer Ogou something for my life?" It was worth a try. "I was thrown from a ship. My people plan to disembark at the port on Xaymaca. At Puerto Real. They can give Ogou money, whatever he wants."

The laughter behind her was sharp and mocking. "You've nothing Ogou wants. Except blood."

"Surely, there's something—"

"You can't give him anything he doesn't already own. Ogou is Lwa."

"Is that your word for *chief*?"

"No, you stupid *blanca*. Lwa are the gods."

Of course, this girl's people would have their own gods as the Diaphani did. Sometimes, they were similar. "Is Ogou like Sul? We also worship—"

"Shut up. Your squawking tires me. Another word, and your head leaves your shoulders. I don't care what Papa Kodjó says."

She swallowed and held her tongue. The back of her neck felt too vulnerable. She took a deep breath to steady herself. Whoever this Papa Kodjó was, he had enough authority to keep this crazy girl from murdering her. Hopefully, he also had enough wisdom to see how both tribes might work to their mutual benefit.

It's too much to think about. I can't, she thought. A tree root trapped her ankle. She sprawled over it and bit her lip against the pain. Exhaustion was making her clumsy. The day's events were taking their toll.

"Quit stalling."

The paddle poked her again as she expected it would. Her eyes sparked with anger. She would not cry, not in front of this girl, not in front of anyone. She had to keep going, had to stay strong. Jager had failed to drown her. She hadn't been decapitated—yet.

Her resolve faded when she thought of Joachin. Her eyes stung. Suddenly, every step became a burden. Over the past few weeks, she had managed to cap her grief, but it ruptured now like an unstoppable leak. Tears streaked down her face. Why not let this girl satisfy her thirst for blood? Joachin was dead. There seemed little point in going on.

Why? she demanded, glancing tearfully up at a patch of sky appearing through the jungle's verdant canopy. *Does being a goddess make you view life differently? Is mortality a passage you take for granted because death isn't the end? That still doesn't make it any less painful for those of us left behind!*

As usual, no reply came from Lys. Joachin had been expendable, a pawn in her larger game. The Tribe was finished in Esbaña. If a few members were lost along the way to the New World, then so be it. A goddess would allow for casualties. Lys' plans didn't coincide with her own.

She swept a dirty hand across her cheeks. There would be no husband, no child in their future. Maybe there wouldn't be a Miriam as Tribal Matriarch, either. She hated Lys, she hated her life. She even hated Alonso for saving her from drowning, and that made no sense at all.

Alonso stiffened, hearing the thought. *She doesn't mean it,* he told himself, but it still stung. Miriam was exhausted, overwrought. It was hard to dismiss her grief. It was even harder to ignore it because he had been the cause.

You lied to her, his conscience accused.

I didn't lie. I told her La Estrella went down, and so it did.

You told her Iago was dead! And then, because you were uncomfortable with the path you were treading, you let her believe Joachin and the others drowned, too! She'll never forgive you when she finds out.

If she finds out. I haven't looked in on Joachin for a while. Maybe he's dead.

Shame on you for hoping it! You're a better man than that. She needs to know the truth.

Why? The truth only hurts. The memory of Miriam in Joachin's arms revisited him again, something never far from his mind. *Is it right he took my place when I loved her first? That he should love her in ways I can't?*

There's more to loving than that! You should be thinking of her, not yourself. Look at the pain you've caused her. It was impossible to forget the tear tracks running down her cheeks. *Is that loving? Is that kind?*

I'm in pain, too.

Whose fault is that? Sul told you if you came back it wouldn't be the same. And it hasn't been. If it's too much for you to handle, you can always—

Stop badgering me! I'll confess I lied, but only when the time is right. Hopefully, she'll understand. Right now, I have to find a new host. Once she and this wild girl get wherever they're going, she'll need me at her side. There isn't a moment to lose.

Without waiting to hear more of what his conscience might say, he flew off to find a suitable host.

Conscience be damned.

Chapter Twenty-Eight: Off Course

JOACHÍN STARED OVER the port rail of the *Raven*. The sun sparkled on aquamarine waves. Not a cloud dotted the deep blue sky. The *Raven's* foresail hung askew, the forecastle had taken some damage and they had lost their bowsprit, but other than that, the ship was still seaworthy. It was hard to believe that only the night before, they had survived the storm. No lives had been lost.

"She's alive," he said, for what had to be the hundredth time. He had lost count of how many times he had muttered it during the storm, but each time, he had been able to say it aloud. Somewhere out there, Miriam walked and breathed. She had survived the tempest, along with the Tribe. After that, things became more difficult. Whenever he tried to say, 'they're still at sea', the words snagged in his throat. Which meant she and the Tribe had landed—but where? They were supposed to dock in Esbañiola before heading to Xaymaca, but his truth-saying kept insisting *no*. Had the *Phoenix* been blown off course? He was about to determine the details, when Francis hailed him, his expression pained.

"Has Dirk decided where we are, exactly?" he asked Francis. "You should get something for that." Francis' nose was peeling.

"Yes, well, we've so much on board for sunburn." He dismissed Joachin's concern with a wave. "I'll be fine. Dirk says coconut is good. We're slightly northeast of Xaymaca. He wants to find a secluded cove to careen for repairs."

"We're not heading for Puerto Real?"

"No. It seems Boyle made some enemies. As well as the Esbañish and Inglaisi, he also preyed on the Brethren."

"The fool! I suppose I shouldn't be surprised. Dirk will have to deal with them, eventually."

"Oh, he'll find a way to appease them, but first, we need something to offer." Francis gave him a knowing look.

Joachin grimaced and dropped his voice. "Look, Francis, I can't go chasing after the gold. I have to find Miriam and the Tribe. I was just trying to determine if she's on Xaymaca—there! I said it! She's on Xaymaca." He squeezed the rail in relief. "Thank Lys."

"I want that, too. But Dirk has other ideas."

They fell silent as Gibbs approached them. Gibbs nodded at Joachin. "Cap'n wants to see you in his cabin. You too, Shite."

Francis grimaced. "It's Francis."

"Whatever. He's waitin'."

They followed him across the waist. Adetokunbo nodded as they passed him by. Iago, who had been chatting with Femi, glanced up and frowned, seeing Joachin's expression. *He knows I'm upset,* Joachin thought. *I need to calm down.* Dirk needed to believe he was willing to search for the gold. *I can't have him suspect I'm about to run off and find my wife.*

But she was on Xaymaca! *I won't fail you, mi cielo,* he promised her silently. If Miriam and the Tribe kept to their original plan, they would dock in Puerto Real, then travel to Villa de la Vía, inland. All immigrants were required to report there.

In the great cabin, Dirk sat on his bunk, his shoulder wrapped in a fresh bandage. "Ah, Francis," he said, smiling broadly. "You've brought Joachin. Good. I want to know more about that gold mine. We need to re-supply the ship."

So much for pleasantries. He had sailed right to the point.

"I understand you also need to deal with other things," Joachin replied. It wasn't what he had intended to say. He had to buy time, find a way to divert the conversation, but how was that possible when one couldn't lie?

Dirk glanced pointedly at Francis, then back at Joachin. "I see you two have been talking."

"Yes, I told him about Boyle and some of our compatriots. I didn't think it a great secret." Francis waved the accusation aside. "So Joachin and I will determine the mine's location as best we can. Grant us leave to go on a search while you careen the *Raven*. We'll bring back samples of the ore. You're still thinking of using the slaves to work the vein, yes?"

I should have suspected this, Joachin thought. So, the slaves were still slaves. What would Adetokunbo have to say about it? *We saved them. How can Francis...?* Wait—he didn't mean it. This was all an act, the diversion he had been hoping for. Francis was still on his side.

"That was my intention, yes." Dirk's eyes narrowed.

"We know the mine is on the highest of three peaks mid-island, yes?" Francis turned to Joachin for confirmation. He nodded. "Depending on how difficult the terrain is, I'd say we'll be gone a week or two."

"You seem very quick to leave."

"Captain." Francis met Dirk's stare. "I took an oath. I signed the Articles. I swore to serve you."

"That's true. You have. You *do*." Dirk smiled wryly, as if reliving fond memories from the night before. "Oh, very well. You can go. But as soon as we land, Iago stays." He glanced at Joachin keenly.

He thinks he's won this round by keeping Iago hostage, Joachin thought. Iago wouldn't come, anyway. Not without Femi. He and Francis didn't need a couple of love sick teenagers traipsing after them. There was nothing for it but to find Miriam, then come back to collect Iago, and Femi too, if necessary. "We don't need him. I suspect he would rather remain."

"Good. Then it's settled." Dirk waved them off. "I'm tired. We'll make landfall today. I'd prefer you didn't leave until tomorrow morning." He winked at Francis. "Come see me, later."

"Of course." Francis smiled. "Happy to."

They left the great cabin with Francis whistling.
Each to his own, Joachin thought.

Chapter Twenty-Nine: Trial by Snake

NOT LONG INTO their trek through the jungle, Miriam caught a whiff of smoke. The journey had been difficult and mostly uphill; her feet were a mass of cuts. She had also walked through a patch of long grass only to be stricken by tiny insects attacking her shins. As she brushed and scratched, the girl smirked. "Chiggers," she informed her loftily. "You should watch where you're going."

Miriam clawed at her legs. "You forced me through that! Why aren't they biting you?"

She shrugged. "They don't bother me."

How nice...for her. A rash was appearing over her old bites. "Are there aloes on this island? A stream where I can wash my feet?"

"Stop complaining. Your legs are the least of your concerns."

"I'm bleeding. I can't go any further!"

That won her another paddle thrust. "You'll go if I drag you. Get moving. We're almost there."

As she finished speaking, two amber-skinned sentries stepped from the jungle to bar their way. Their black hair was twisted into plaits. They wore loincloths and carried spears, the tips of which shone greasily, making Miriam think of poison. Recognizing her abductor, they stepped aside to allow them to pass. Soon, she was taken to a clearing where women in loose dresses hoed earth about plantings. They stopped their toil to stare. Beyond the garden, a cluster of huts stood, low and conical, with roofs of thatch.

A small boy came running towards them. "Ekua!" he screamed, seeing Miriam's captor. The girl dropped her paddle and caught him in her arms.

If her feet didn't hurt so badly, she would have grabbed the paddle and bolted. But there were too many people about. She wouldn't have gotten far.

"What did I tell you about that?" Her captor squeezed the boy so hard he squeaked. "No names in front of enemies!" With huge eyes, he considered Miriam and then glanced back at the girl.

"It's all right. Don't do it, again. Go tell Papa K I've brought a prisoner." She patted him on his backside and sent him running, then picked up her paddle and waved it. "Move," she ordered.

They made their way through the garden and headed for the huts. A tree, as tall as a temple, rose from the village's compound. Fruit, bread, and other items had been set about its buttress-like roots. They arrived at a small wooden shack. Ekua pulled the door open and shoved her inside.

Miriam confronted her. "What's going to happen to me?"

"Nothing, for now. With luck, Papa K will let me kill you." She smiled nastily.

"There are people searching for me!"

"The same ones who left you in the ocean? If they come here, I'll kill them, too." She slammed the door in her face. Miriam stepped back and winced. The floor was strewn with dirty straw. It smelled faintly of urine and rot. Perhaps a previous captive had died there. She glanced about nervously. "Alonso?" she whispered, hoping he might appear.

No answer. Nothing stirred in the thatch, not even a beetle. She sucked in a breath. For the second time this day, tears pricked at her eyes. Why was everything so hard?

"I hate this!" She stared at the roof. "And I hate you! Do you hear me, Lys? I *hate* you!"

Her legs gave out from beneath her. She fell to the straw, her hands breaking her fall. A shadow chuckled from beyond the cracks of the door frame. Ekua most likely, savouring her distress. Then it passed and was gone.

So let them kill me. What does it matter? Joachín is.... Tears dribbled down her face. Joachín was dead. Alonso waited for her, but to what purpose? He could never live a real life—not as he was.

"You have what you wanted, Lys!" She glared at the rafters. "I brought the Tribe here! They'll survive! Now, leave me alone!" As usual, the goddess was silent. Miriam had no idea if Zara and the rest were still aboard the *Phoenix*, or even if they were safe. Had they disembarked in Puerto Real? Were they searching for her? They probably thought she was dead.

She lay on her side, not caring about the filthy floor or what might have expired there. Lys was a selfish goddess and a liar. She had promised her a family and a future, and those things hadn't occurred. She was a matriarch of nothing. A tattooed queen of grief. She closed her eyes. The losses were too bitter. Nothing mattered anymore.

She awoke sometime later, still despondent, but feeling a bit better. Judging from the light outside her hut, the afternoon had passed. She glanced about her jail, hoping to find Alonso, but he was nowhere about. *Maybe he's hoping to find a bigger host, something to break me from this prison.* That was both a comforting and disturbing thought. She was sure the villagers would kill any animal large enough to attack them. It would also be a quandary for Alonso, not knowing what was about to happen to her. She clawed at her throat. It was so dry in here. No one brought her any food or drink. Her chigger bites itched unmercifully. She was about to scratch them when the door to her cell finally opened.

Ekua stood there, outlined by the light of multiple fires flickering in the compound. "You're to come with me," she said gruffly, grabbing her by the elbow. The joy of conquest ran through her and worse, an anticipation for blood. The contact made Miriam gasp.

She thinks she's going to kill me, she thought, her talent as a *sentidora* flaring into life. Her gift suggested more; anger was Ekua's usual standard, but there was also curiosity. She wanted to know more about her before killing her. That way, the killing would be sweeter.

Miriam jerked her arm away. "Don't touch me!"

Ignoring her, Ekua snagged her again, and hauled her through the doorway. She dragged her to the middle of the compound.

A crowd of about forty people stared at her from every quarter. As well as the loose dresses and pants she had previously seen, they also bore brands on their shoulders: the letter G and the Esbañish royal coat of arms. Everyone eyed her without comment, their animosity palpable. She was taken to a square hut larger than the rest. The wall facing the compound lay open to the night air. On either side of a brazier, two figures sat.

One was a tall man in his prime. He wore a woven skirt and sat on a low stool. A golden pendant lay upon his chest. His dark eyes glinted like obsidian, reminding her of the sentries' tipped spears. The other was a strange figure: an old man, frail and hunched, with white streaks painted across his face and arms. His hair was a tight, grey cap. Unlike the giant who glared, the old man's expression was neither malignant nor threatening. He regarded her as if she were an enigma needing explanation. On a small mat beside him, lay an assortment of shells and bone.

"Sit, *Madame*," he invited, waving his hand.

Madame? He spoke both Esbañish and Frankish? How had that come to be? Before she could comply, Ekua shoved her to her knees. She landed on a chigger bite and winced in pain.

"That wasn't necessary, Ekua." The old man pursed his lips in disapproval. "Oh, my," he said, noting Miriam's sores. "Those don't look good. Do not fret, *Madame*, we'll get you something for them once we've put you to the test, so let's waste no more time."

Put to the test sounded uncomfortably like *put to the question*—what the Inquisition meant by obtaining confessions through torture. He poked at his collection of shells and bones.

"We've been discussing you at length, *Madame*. These tell me you're here by divine will. That you've come to help us, not to harm. You understand our confusion, *oui*?"

She blinked, not knowing what to say.

"This pattern, *ici*." He pointed. "A goddess is involved. But which one?" He glanced at her expectantly, as if she might cast some light on the question. The bigger man shifted on his stool. The old man smiled. "Our *cacique* doubts, but that is what I'm for. To restore faith." He picked up his cowries and tossed them like dice. They fell, forming a wave-like pattern.

"Ha!" He slapped his thighs. "You see, Yoquibo?" He grinned at the brooding chief. "It's La Sirene. As I thought. But we don't yet know all. So you must tell us, *Madame*." He regarded her with what she thought was new respect. "How did you come to us, and how is it that the Queen of the Seas takes such an interest in you?"

She had no idea who he meant by Queen of the Seas, unless he meant Lys, her own duplicitous goddess. "I was a passenger on a ship," she said. She thought of Jager and wondered how much she should tell. "One of the crew disliked me. So he threw me overboard."

"When was this?"

"A day ago."

The old man glanced at the chief, Yoquibo. "A day ago, we were struck by the tempest." His gaze settled back on her. "Your ship was also caught in this storm?"

"If it was the same one, yes."

"Why were you thrown overboard?"

"I was travelling with a group of my people. The sailor attacked me because he thought I was bad luck. When I told the captain, the man was punished, flogged. Later, one of his friends released him because he feared we would be lost at sea. Instead of helping the crew, he sought vengeance against me."

"And yet, here you are, safe and sound."

"There was a spar from a damaged ship. I held onto it until your kinswoman pulled me into her boat."

"We saw no ship on the horizon, damaged or otherwise. To all intents and purposes, it looks as if you've been saved by divine intervention. But there is also something that hasn't been told." His gaze slid to Ekua.

Ekua clenched her hands. "I said all I know!"

He pursed his lips as if he didn't quite believe her, then tossed another cowrie. It landed with its teeth exposed. "No, Ekua. You haven't."

She pressed her lips into a hard line.

"What else did you see? You must tell us."

Yoquibo shifted uncomfortably on his seat.

"All right!" Ekua blurted. "I was harvesting mussels in the mangrove when I noticed a pod of dolphins. That's when I saw *her*. When I paddled closer, it looked as if one of them swam beneath her, that she rode it. Then the pod moved off."

The chief sucked in a breath. The old man, Papa Kodjó, smiled. "You see, *cherie?*" he told her. "The truth isn't so hard." He glanced back at Miriam. "So, it's as I suspected, *Madame*. While you were in the sea, you were under La Sirene's protection."

The big man grumbled something in a language Miriam didn't understand. But Ekua clearly did.

"No!" she shouted, waving her machete at him. He glowered at what was plainly an impropriety, but she carried on. "Remember what her people did to your *cacica*, Majesty! Remember what they've done to all of us!" She pointed to the letter G on her shoulder. "This reminds me of how many times I was raped, of how my mother died for stealing corn, of how we make our way here, instead of pining for Gineh! The *blancos* cause more misery than we ever thought possible! Do we forgive them? Never!" She turned to the old man. "Even if La Sirene protects her, the rest should have a say in what's to be done!"

The old man considered it.

"Throw the bones, Papa K!" she persisted. "She's on *our* land, in *our* power, not protected by the sea! The ground thirsts for blood! See if it should be shed as Ogou wills!"

The old man scooped up a handful of bones. He held them in the smoke as if to sanctify them. Murmuring a prayer, he shook them again. Miriam's heart stuttered as they fell to the mat. Her fate lay in a spiral.

The old man laughed as Ekua gasped in frustration. Clearly, she had hoped for a different outcome. She turned to Miriam, unwilling to be thwarted. "Even Damballah can be provoked when he's angry enough!"

"Who is Damballah?" She hated that her voice shook, revealing her fear. Ekua jerked her to her feet. Papa Kodjó and Yoquibo did nothing to stop her. The girl's annoyance pricked at her in sharp little cuts.

"Don't worry, *Madame*," Papa Kodjó called from behind. "You couldn't have thrown better! Damballah is wise and kind! He protects the helpless! I'm sure he'll find you worthy, as La Sirene does. You will see!"

It wasn't an answer.

"I'm betting Damballah *will* kill you," Ekua whispered fiercely. "If he doesn't, then Ogou will." She made a slashing motion across her throat, mimicking her machete.

The force of Miriam's hatred made her nauseous. *Alonso, where are you? I need you!* she thought desperately. They had arrived back at the shack. Ekua shoved her inside and barred the door.

She stood in the dark feeling dizzy and sick. Moments later, came the pounding of drums.

An hour later, an old woman arrived with a bundle of clothes. She wore a pale head scarf and a loose cotton gown bunched about the waist with a rope. She indicated Miriam should remove her things. It was useless to argue, so she did as she was told, feeling like a victim being readied for slaughter. With shaking hands, she slipped her dress from her shoulders and dropped her underskirt to the floor. The woman gasped and pointed at her ravaged skin.

Miriam crossed her arms over her chest. "They can't hurt you," she said, thinking the woman pointed at Rana's scabs. "They're wasp bites."

The woman drew her arms away and indicated Rana's breast tattoos. "No! Damballah!" she insisted.

It was embarrassing to be so exposed, but her anxiety made her feel worse. She shielded herself a second time. "Please, who is Damballah?"

Before the woman could answer, the door to her cage opened. Ekua stood framed there, looking impatient. Outside, the drums were beating faster, louder. Beyond, more fires flickered about the camp's periphery. People danced around the tree, while others—Miriam wasn't sure she believed her eyes—writhed on the ground.

The old woman yanked a gown over her head and coiled a head scarf about her hair, tying it snugly into place. Ekua dragged her into the light.

In the middle of the throng, Papa Kodjó danced with a huge banded snake. It was at least six feet long and as thick as his neck, yellow at the head but tapering to black. His wiry frame shook beneath its weight. The serpent was unhappy with being handled. Its diamond head drew back in an s-curve and lashed out, narrowly missing the old man's arm. Papa Kodjó laughed.

She drew back in horror. They meant that thing for her. "Oh, gods, no!"

Ekua hauled her determinedly towards the dancing, celebrating mass. Then they were before Papa Kodjó. He held up his hand to silence the drums. Those who were dancing stopped. Those who writhed on the ground kept squirming, caught in a strange trance. Now that the drums were no longer pounding, Miriam heard the people on the ground hiss.

"My children, we're here to learn of Damballah's will!" Papa Kodjó cried joyfully. The snake struggled angrily. "This *blanca*,"—he indicated Miriam— "has been delivered by La Sirene. We acknowledge the protection of our Lady of the Seas."

Some people murmured a tribute. Others remained silent and glared.

"There's been some debate as to whether this woman is under divine protection, now that she is on land. If Damballah defends her as La Sirene does, we must honour his wishes." He lifted the snake high. People screamed and demanded justice.

She saw what was coming. She tried to bolt but Ekua held her fast. The girl's hatred slashed at her, as sharp and as ruthless as a blade. At Papa Kodjó's nod, Ekua released her and jumped back.

The serpent fell, coiling about her shoulders. She staggered beneath its weight and clawed at the banded body. Its aggravation was immediate, cold, intense. The spade-shaped head drew back to strike her face. Pupils, splintered and alien, stared into her own.

"Alonso!" she shrieked.

Here! came the strained reply. He must have been waiting, watching. He had invaded the snake at the last moment. The creature was in a fury, not a god, but a reptile defending itself. She sensed his presence within it, twisting and fighting. Alonso was hot from the effort of preventing it from striking her. It was a healthy, wilful host. *Miriam! I don't think I can hold it much longer!*

Loops tightened about her neck. The snake hissed as she pulled at its coils. *Lys, help me!* she cried in surrender. Yes, she had called the goddess a thief and a liar. She had been angry, despairing over Joachin's death. *I didn't mean it!* But that was also a lie. She had meant it. And now, she was imploring Lys to intervene, to send help, divine or otherwise.

Suddenly, the boa was no longer about her shoulders. Whether it was Lys' help or Alonso's panic, the snake was in her hands, twisting like an animated bullwhip. All about her, people shouted in amazement. Not chancing to luck, she tossed it at the tree's branches. It sailed clumsily through the air and landed awkwardly where it clung to a lower limb. Then, having had enough of people and abuse, it slithered out of sight.

Ekua let out a shriek of rage.

Papa Kodjó lifted his palms to address the breathless congregation. Those who had been dancing were helping those who had been entranced. "Damballah has answered us," he said calmly, ignoring Ekua's cry. "Perhaps none of you saw it, but I did. Damballah considered whom he was about to bite. He stopped mid-strike. He didn't strangle her. Instead, he allowed her to lift him up, to return him to his tree. His will is clear." He pointed at Miriam. "She is under Damballah's protection. Therefore, she is also under ours."

"No!" Ekua rushed forward and tossed a burlap sack at Miriam's feet. Papa Kodjó frowned at the interruption. Before Miriam could react, a second snake slid from the bag and coiled at her ankles. Unlike the constrictor, this one was amber coloured and had dark triangles on its skin.

"*Terciopelo!*" someone shrieked. People scattered.

It whipped into an S shape and bit her hard on the calf. Then it struck again. The effect from its bite was immediate. Her leg was on fire. She crumpled to her knees as something bright and metallic flashed past her eyes—Yoquibo attacking the snake with his machete. With two strikes, the thing was dead. Bloodied and in pieces, it twitched beside her.

"Get Ekua," Yoquibo ordered tersely. As fast as she had appeared, the girl had fled. Men ran into the forest to find her.

Papa Kodjó knelt by her side. His face was becoming fuzzier by the minute, fading in and out of her vision. "I'm so sorry, *Madame*! I should have anticipated that. I'm afraid you'll be in for a bad time. Even should you survive—" He shook his head.

"A viper?" She couldn't stop her voice from shaking.

He nodded. "Yes. The *Terciopelo*. Its bite is terrible, but its skin is as soft as velvet, why it is so-called." He grimaced. "Perhaps it isn't such a good name. We must get you to a quiet place, do what we can to help. I pray the two who rule your head will save you."

Had she heard that right? "*The two who rule...?*"

"La Sirene and Damballah." He waved some women over to carry her. She was set onto a plank and carried into Yoquibo's hut. Her thigh felt like a sausage about to split its casing. The women set her down by the fire.

They took turns sucking and spitting. She hadn't the strength to tell them the best way to stop the poison was to tie off her leg and set it in warm water. As her delirium set in, she thought of Casi, of how she and Alonso had saved her from a viper's bite, so long ago. Where was Alonso now? Where was her Tribe? Was she really going to die this time? *Joachín*, she thought. The only consolation was they would finally be reunited. Fever overwhelmed her, and she descended, hot and spinning, into a place that was flaming and red.

She was in hell. She had to be. Blood bubbled through her veins, only to break through her flesh where it pooled and dried. In spite of the torment, it also felt as if tiny pellets were striking her body and abrading the scabs. Fear overcame her pain. When she finally found the strength to open her eyes to see what they were, she wished she hadn't. Wasps covered her from head to toe, gorging on her blood. The *hymenoptera* Rana had invoked so long ago had found her again. Demon that it was, it had returned to feed upon her agony.

She bit on a scream, afraid the wasps might crawl into her mouth. At the same time, she realized her pain was lessening. She still burned, but her suffering was no longer the mind-numbing torment it had been. The wasps shifted and crawled, landed and scraped.

They weren't stinging, she realized. *They were eating the scabs.* The understanding sickened her, but she endured them, afraid to move. Her heart pounded. That was something. It was beating, again. The horrid percolation in her veins was also subsiding. She drew a tentative breath.

How was it that a demon that had once attacked her, should now be her antidote? The swarm fed on her dried blood and skin, but also, she suspected, on the *Terciopelo's* poison. Were they replenishing themselves? Possibly. She was feeling was less pain by the second. How strange that Rana's curse should also be her cure.

Through closed eyelids, she continued to see red, but instead of it coming from an outside source, it became more uniform. The wasps landed on her less and less, until finally she felt them lift away. She remained where she was, pain-free and whole, but too exhausted to move. There was a hard surface beneath her back. It didn't feel like the plank upon which she had been set. There were no other sounds except the beating of her heart and the susurration of her breath. She remained in limbo, in an other-worldly realm.

It didn't feel like such a bad place. Why was it red here and not white? It wasn't the pale void where she and Alonso had last seen Inez.

She opened her eyes. She lay upon a road. She sat up, and saw that it climbed into hills. Above, the sky was swollen with scarlet which accounted for the redness she had sensed. Beyond, the horizon was rimmed with gold. On one peak, something dazzled. It was easy to believe the sun was caught there. Behind her, a black road disappeared across a plain littered with rock.

This was a strange place. She stood, feeling drawn to the light.

She took a step, as feeble as a new-born lamb.

Not yet, Miriam.

A woman's voice. The world dissolved into ruby dots. She spun, caught in a ruddy squall. It was disorienting. She felt sick. Then, as quickly as it had begun, the vertigo receded and the whirling stopped. Stability reasserted itself. She lay on a cot. There was heat from a nearby fire and smoke. She opened her eyes. Above her, a roof of thatch stretched in a way that was both lofty and comforting.

"Papa Kodjó! She's awake!"

Female faces appeared above her in a ring. Papa Kodjó pushed two of the women aside and smiled down at her in relief.

"Welcome back, *Madame*." He reached for her hand and patted it like a kindly grandfather. "We were worried about you, but it appears you have strong *ashe*. Not only did La Sirene and Damballah spare you from the *Terciopelo*, but they've healed your hurts. Look!" He lifted her arm gently to show her. The *hymenoptera* bites had faded into scars. Unfortunately, she still wore Rana's body. The women echoed his sentiments.

She was glad to be alive, but she would have welcomed death. Joachin...if she had reached that brilliant light, would he have been waiting for her there? There was something hopeful about that place, as if it offered a new day, a brand new start. Perhaps it marked the entrance to the Summerland.

Not yet, Miriam.

She had startled at the words. The goddess had finally spoken. It seemed Lys had forgiven her for calling her a liar, but she still reminded her of her duty to the Tribe. She had forced her back to life and had withheld Joachin, her reward.

Lys never played fair. What kind of a goddess sent a demon to do her dirty work?

A practical one, came the reply.

The answer was in her mind before she even finished the thought.

Chapter Thirty: Ekua

ACCORDING TO PAPA Kodjó, she had been delirious for three days. Ekua had been captured and was being held in Miriam's old cell. Now that Miriam had survived, a council would determine what Ekua's punishment would be for interfering with the proceedings.

"I don't understand, exactly," Miriam said a few hours later. She had taken a little food and water, but she still felt shaky. "How is one snake any different from another? If you wanted to kill me—"

"Ah, but we didn't want to kill you, *Madame*. We only wanted to make certain of Damballah's will. The shells told me, but I also had to prove it to the tribe. And I did, until Ekua interfered, a blasphemous thing to do. Damballah *never* comes as a viper."

She didn't see what difference it made, except in the mode of dying. Strangulation or poisoning accomplished the same thing. Dead was dead.

Actually, that wasn't quite true. Alonso was a case in point, but there was no time to pursue that now. "I thought you said Damballah was a kindly god."

"Of course he is, *cherie*. He's the universal serpent, the oldest in the pantheon. He created the world from his skin and the stars from his coils."

"Then how is he represented as a living, breathing snake?"

"He's a god. He comes as he chooses. You noticed some of our people in trance."

"Yes."

"They were being ridden by Damballah. After they awaken, they know they've been blessed. Damballah brings clarity to the mind and health to the body. He bestows good fortune. It was his compassion that brought you to us."

She wasn't about to argue. Once she was reunited with her own Tribe, they would need a foothold on the island. "My people also worship two gods," she said. "Sul is the creator, and Lys, the spirit who energizes that creation."

"Ah. Like La Sirene or Ayida Wedo, our goddess of the rainbow. She is Damballah's wife. Together, they represent pure love."

She thought of Joachín and grimaced. Papa Kodjó cocked his head to one side, making her think of one of those exotic birds she had seen as Ekua had driven her through the jungle. "You've lost someone recently, I think."

She nodded, her throat growing thick.

"Everyone here has lost someone. For some of us, many someones. Our grief unites us." He shifted on his mat as if his legs bothered him. "There's something else I must tell you. A goat has been trying to enter this hut. Odeh keeps chasing it out."

"Odeh?"

"One of my wives. The woman who brought you your clothes."

"I see. And the goat?"

"An old beast, Odeh says is ready for the stew pot. I've forbidden her to sacrifice him, because I think he is more than he appears. Perhaps you agree?"

She thought of Alonso. "Perhaps."

Papa Kodjó glanced past her. It was midday. The compound was empty. Likely, most of the women were working in the garden, and the men, hunting. "Untie it, Odeh," Papa Kodjó called.

From the side of the hut, a brown and white goat appeared, trailing a rope. Odeh marched behind it, muttering. "Ain' no place for that smelly beast. No good 'cept for stewin'. I tell 'im, but he don't listen...." She continued to complain as the goat jumped up the stairs and skittered across the hut as if it couldn't escape her fast enough. It slammed into Miriam, knocking her off balance.

Sorry! Alonso righted himself, looking as if he had tripped over his hems. *It's old, but strong!*

She wrapped her arms about the goat's neck. *I'm so glad you're back.* She drew away quickly. He smelled of sweat and dung.

It's the best I could do. Anything wild, and they would have bludgeoned me on sight. I don't relish a death by clubbing. He was out of breath.

"Madame?"

She had forgotten Papa Kodjó. How to explain Alonso to him? Papa K considered them as if they were two guests invited for tea.

"I...." She wasn't sure where to begin.

"Perhaps I can help." Papa Kodjó squinted at Alonso. "*That* isn't really a goat. That is a spirit riding a goat."

Her mouth fell open. "You can see him?"

"I'm not four-eyed, but I recognize the signs. An ancestor?"

Obviously his people revered their ancestors like the Diaphani did. "No. We aren't related."

Papa Kodjó reached for a rattle. "So if not an Ancestor, then what? The Inquisitors warn of a goat-headed demon." He sprang to his feet and shook his rattle fiercely, making Alonso jump. "*Bonjour, Monsieur Lucifer!* Do you think to snare me? I would think twice about it!"

Miriam choked on a laugh. "That isn't Lucifer! His name is Alonso!"

It isn't funny! Alonso snorted.

It is!

Papa K stopped shaking his *asson* to regard them. She caught her breath to explain. "In life, Alonso was a high priest in Esbaña! Hardly a devil! But he was murdered by a demon just the same."

Papa K set down his rattle, as if relieved. "Ah, that explains it, then. He is Ghede."

"Ghede?"

"One of the vengeful dead. Usually, they're from these islands, but I suppose he might be considered one, now that he's here. Tell, me, *Ghede* Alonso," Papa K addressed the goat. "In life, did you wear a high hat and eat apples?"

Miriam suppressed another wild desire to laugh.

Apples? Alonso was baffled. *Do they even have them here? And who is he talking to? Me or the goat? I suppose I did wear a high hat.*

She chuckled at that. Perhaps it was from relief in finding herself alive and reunited with Alonso, or perhaps she was still overwrought. She had never met anyone who exercised such a strong belief in the unseen as Papa Kodjó, except perhaps, Anassa. She missed her old mentor. And Ephraim, her papa, too.

"Did I say something funny?" Papa K asked.

"No. It's just that you were right about the hat." She smiled remembering the Masses over which Alonso had presided.

"I only ask because it's important to confirm what I hear from other sources, but perhaps that's a topic for another time." Papa Kodjó cleared his throat. "It appears you are not here by chance. Therefore, we must ask why."

She found it strange he didn't need further explanation about Alonso—in particular, how he had become connected to her. Perhaps in Papa K's mind, Alonso was just another game piece brought into play by the gods.

"I think I can answer that." Here was an opportunity to share her vision for their future. "I think it was Lys' plan, La Sirene's, if you will, that I ended up here. I believe your tribe and mine are meant to work together."

He nodded as if that made sense. Then he sighed. "Some will work. But others will take advantage."

"That is true. And it's wrong."

"So, you're saying we are equal."

"Of course."

"You won't convince the plantation owners of that."

"Then we must make our place in spite of them. I need to find my Tribe and bring them here. Like your people, we have been persecuted by those in power. We must help each other."

"A lofty goal, *Madame*. Unfortunately, not all of us are so progressive. There are others here, who will need persuading." She wondered if he meant Ekua. "Where was your ship bound, when you were thrown overboard?"

"Its final destination was Xaymaca."

"So your people will arrive at Puerto Real. A dangerous place. Elsewhere on the island can be more so."

"Dangerous how?"

"Pirates. They anchor in many of the coves. There are also our old slave masters who hunt us now and then. In Villa de la Via, you, being a *blanca*, should be all right, although you're also a woman alone. Some might take advantage. Your people may have arrived, but also that sailor who wanted to kill you." He said it as if to remind her.

"I still must find them."

He looked thoughtful. "Then, perhaps you shouldn't go alone. I'm not sure how far we can accompany you." He indicated the brand on his shoulder. The G was there, along with a newer mark. "I originally came from Esbañiola. I escaped from there, and made my way to Xaymaca by boat. Now that Damballah and La Sirene have shown us we must accept you, this will be a discussion to share with Yoquibo and the tribe."

She felt a twinge of guilt. Was it wrong to let him assume it had been his god who had saved her from the constrictor, and not Alonso? That her exposure to Rana's wasp demon helped her survive the *Terciopelo's* bite? Perhaps she would tell him in time, once a greater trust had built.

People were reappearing in the compound. The women were returning from the garden. The men had had a successful hunt, bagging turtles and some birds. Odeh appeared at the bottom of the hut's stairs. She set her hands on her hips and scowled at Alonso as if he were an insult to the Lwa of cleanliness and propriety. "Yoquibo sent me," she informed Papa Kodjó disapprovingly. "Everybody knows th' girl recovered, so the chief says we need to talk 'bout Ekua. There's a council after supper, so you clear out, ol' man. I need t' clean up."

Miriam glanced at the floor, hoping Alonso hadn't dirtied it. Luckily, the goat had maintained control. Papa Kodjó helped her to stand. Alonso pressed against her legs.

"Not Ol' Stinky," Odeh shook a finger at him. "He goes back to th' pen, with th' others."

I'll come find you, as soon as I can, Miriam told him.

Good. And in the meantime, I'll find a new host.

Odeh closed in on him with splayed arms.

Several hours later, after they had eaten their fill of dove, turtle meat, and a mashed white yam called *fufu*, Yoquibo called the tribe to council beneath the Ceiba tree. Alonso hadn't reappeared, but Miriam thought she saw a green flash settle on one of the tree's lower branches.

She was directed to sit beside Papa Kodjó. Ekua stood before them. Her hair was matted, and she had dark rings beneath her eyes. She glared at Miriam as if wishing she had her machete in hand. Papa Kodjó rose to address the gathering.

"Three nights ago, we were graced with a visitation from Damballah. Many of you were ridden. You *chevaux* won't remember it, so it's up to us who received messages to share them. Did any of you receive word about this woman? Over and above what we witnessed with the snakes?"

Miriam stiffened. Had Alonso's interference not been proof enough? Or her surviving the *Terciopelo's* bite?

Papa Kodjó waited. No one spoke. "Well, I'd hoped for more, but it isn't for us to test the Lwa."

"Wait!" A small boy stood. He was the same child who had run up to Ekua in the garden.

"You've something to say, Yoofi?" Papa Kodjó asked.

The boy fidgeted from foot to foot and met Ekua's hard stare. He nodded and swallowed.

"What is it?" Papa Kodjó smiled encouragingly.

"Damballah, he hiss at me. An' he says that girl," he glanced at Miriam and then looked at his feet, "he says, she's goin' t' kill us all. So, we got to do her first."

"Good." Papa Kodjó clapped his hands. "Therefore, you'll be the one to do it." Without a word, Yoquibo handed the stunned boy his hunting knife. Papa Kodjó pulled Miriam to her feet and held her firmly by the arms. She choked and stared at the boy in horror. Surely, they weren't serious.

"Do it!" Ekua screamed, her hands clenching into fists.

Yoofi lifted the knife. Papa Kodjó released one of Miriam's arms and restrained the boy before he could strike. "Before you kill her, I must warn you, Yoofi. If you lie, the gods will smite you. Even Damballah, as sweet-tempered as he is, will throw a lightning bolt that will turn you to dust. So I must ask you again. Did Damballah really tell you to kill this woman?"

Yoofi's chin trembled.

"Kill her, Yoofi! Remember what the *blancos* did to our mother!" Ekua cried.

Papa Kodjó waved a forefinger before his nose. "You mustn't let hate rule you, Yoofi. If Damballah spoke to you truly and told you to kill her, you'll be held blameless for what you do. But if he didn't," he cast a look of rebuke at Ekua, "then you mustn't listen to lies. Vengeance doesn't make a man stronger. Only truth does, coupled with mercy."

"Ogou demands blood!" Ekua shook a fist.

"*Her* blood?" Papa K held Miriam by the arm. "Ogou avenges, *oui*, but always with honour. He doesn't spill the blood of innocents."

Yoofi looked up at Papa Kodjó. "Will Damballah really strike me down with lightning, if I lie?"

For a moment, Papa Kodjó looked uncomfortable. Miriam suspected the boy had caught him in the very thing he had cautioned against. As the silence lengthened, the crowd shifted. "He could," Papa Kodjó said, "but I don't think he will. This is your test, Yoofi. One you'll answer for, if not in this life, then in the next. Decide. Do you act upon lies? Or do you act upon the truth?"

Yoofi's lips trembled. His hand shook, and then he dropped the weapon. "Only the truth, Papa Kodjó. Ekua told me to say it."

"Good!" Papa Kodjó squeezed him on the shoulder. "Yoofi has proven he's a man!" he announced to all. There was a trace of relief in his voice. Yoquibo held his hand out for his knife. Yoofi returned it to him.

"I'm not afraid of lies or lightning!" Ekua shrugged off her guards. "Let *me* put that tale to the test!"

Yoquibo thrust out his chest. "Be quiet! It isn't your place to argue. Twice now, you've offended not only me, but the Lwa."

Ekua pointed at the ground. "The dead cry out for justice! The *blancos* killed your wife, *Cacique*! And my kin!"

"I TOLD YOU TO BE SILENT! I don't answer to you! Nor do the gods! This *blanca*," he indicated Miriam, "isn't one of those who murdered my wife! And try as you might to destroy her, she has survived! She was sent to us for a reason which is becoming clearer to me by the second! She's to be our intermediary. She will better our lot and hers!"

Miriam sagged with relief.

Yoquibo's voice grew harsh and low. He stared at Ekua as if he were disgusted with her. "You have been insubordinate, you've lied, and have interfered with a holy rite. We can't survive if we have dissention in our ranks. What remains is for *me* to decide what I will do with *you*."

A hush fell, broken by the call of a night bird.

She stared back at him. "Kill me, then, if I'm so loathsome. At least, I prove I'm not a—"

"Enough!" Papa Kodjó shouted, before she could utter the one word that would end her life. Yoquibo wouldn't tolerate being called a coward. "There's only one outcome we can achieve from all this. With your permission, *Cacique*."

Yoquibo was too affronted to answer. Miriam suspected he had also known what Ekua was about to say.

Papa Kodjó took his stillness for assent. "In cases such as this, where the gods are involved, we revert to tribal law as we've always done. The offender owes the offended. From this day forward, for the period of a year and a day, Ekua is enslaved to this *blanca*—"

"No!" Ekua shrieked. "I'd rather die!"

"—who has come amongst us. Ekua will cook and hunt for her, draw her water and do her bidding in all manner of things—"

"No!" Miriam held up her hand. No matter how Papa K interpreted it, he was still suggesting slavery. The idea was offensive.

Papa Kodjó regarded her with bright eyes. There was something in his glance that made her think he had gambled and won.

"I don't believe in slaves," she said, striving for calm. It didn't matter if this was another of his tests. "The thought of slavery disgusts me. My people don't maintain slaves, nor will we, ever!"

"Well, that's for you to decide." Papa Kodjó shrugged as if it were of little account. "I've spoken for our *Cacique*. It's out of my hands. Ekua is yours to do with as you will."

"I don't want to do anything with her. Free her! She owes me nothing."

"Except for her life," Papa Kodjó pointed out dryly. He turned to Yoquibo. There was something in his manner that struck Miriam as mummery. "What are we to do, *Cacique*?"

Yoquibo considered, also grave. "She must release Ekua, personally. Then it's final."

She wasn't certain, but it felt as if they were all involved in some kind of charade. So be it, as long as she didn't have Ekua underfoot. The girl was as likely to slit her throat and complain of an accident once the deed was done. "Fine," she said, impatiently. "What must I do?"

"You must tell her so, directly," Papa K said.

Miriam turned to Ekua. "You aren't my property. You don't belong to me. You belong to yourself."

If it were possible for Ekua to regard her with even more loathing, she did.

"You know what this means, Ekua," Papa K said. His statement had a finality to it.

"Yes." Ekua bit off the word.

"Then tell her," Yoquibo ordered, his face a blank.

Ekua turned to Miriam and glared. "You've given me my life." She set a hand to her chest and clenched her fingers, as if wishing she could crush Miriam's heart, there. "So now, I'm dedicated to saving yours."

Miriam stared at her in amazement. Ekua wasn't a slave. She didn't have to wait on her hand and foot. But driven by her own sense of fairness and the last word in tribal law, she had unwittingly turned her into a bodyguard.

Chapter Thirty-One: Fond Farewells

"*YOU'RE ABSOLUTELY CERTAIN* she's alive," Zara demanded. The Tribe stood in a tight knot around Ximen. Hope welled in Casi's chest. She had heard Jager's cruel thoughts as he and Miriam had grappled on deck. They had flown at her through the chaos and terror as the Tribe ran for safety from the storm. She had tried to tell Luci, but fear had propelled her *maré* down the companionway. By the time she was able to stammer the news, Jager had thrown Miriam overboard.

"How is this possible?" Luci stared at Ximen in wonder.

"It was hard for me to understand at first. She was dazed." He frowned. "I think Alonso turned into a dolphin, or a pod of dolphins—but I can tell you this. Miriam is on Xaymaca. She's been captured by natives—"

"What!?"

Casi wanted to giggle. Zara sounded just like a parrot.

Ximen held up his hands to stave off further protests. "She's fine! There's much to tell, but they have accepted her."

"That girl has more luck than a fox in a hen house. How is it you've only learned this now, Old Man?"

"I finally thought of her today, when I felt I could handle it. I didn't think of her before because the loss was too keen."

"The rest of us managed it. You should have done it, sooner."

Luci set a restraining hand on Zara's shoulder.

I know why he does that, Casi thought, regarding Ximen. *He has to shut out the Tribe's memories like I have to shut out everyone's thoughts. If I didn't do that, I'd go crazy.*

"I suppose the first thing is to find her." Zara frowned at the horizon.

"No." Maia stepped forward, with Little Grim asleep in her arms. Casi considered her with surprise. Maia hardly ever spoke. "As immigrants, the first thing we must do is register with the governor. Then we ask after Barto, Iago, and Joachin. Perhaps we can learn of their fates. If they've landed here, maybe someone has bought them. Or maybe they've escaped. Ximen says Miriam is fine, so they must be our first responsibility."

"Yes, of course." Ximen nodded. "And perhaps the governor can advise us of the situation here, if it's safe to venture out on our own. Villa de la Vía, it is then."

"We don't register in Puerto Real?" Luci asked.

"The customs office is there, but the seat of government is further inland, at the governor's fortress. He runs the island from there."

"Well, I thank the goddess we're able to get off this floating tub." Zara sniffed. "I don't think I'll ever get used to boats."

Ximen pinched his nose but didn't bother to correct her.

Casi smiled. As usual, Auntie had the last word.

At mid-day, they stood about the waist, waiting to disembark. The *Phoenix* lay at anchor in Puerto's Real's bay. The town ran along a peninsula. The buildings were a clutter of wooden and stone structures. Some were two-storied and timbered, but the majority were little better than shacks. Two docks, at either end of an esplanade, extended over the water. Palm trees dotted the town haphazardly, as if no one had thought to cut them down yet for firewood. *It doesn't look like much,* Casi thought. There were no stone walls surrounding the town like those in Esbaña, but still, it was exciting to be here. *We made it!* she thought happily. *I sailed all the way across the Great Ocean Sea! I thought it would never end, but it has!* She recalled the treehouse she had planned to build of palm fronds and reeds. *I was such a child then,* she thought.

As the crew lowered the cockboats down the side of the ship. Ximen thanked Captain Vrooman and First Mate Landseer on behalf of the Tribe. They looked embarrassed; they hadn't been able to explain Miriam's loss other than to confess they thought she had fallen overboard during the storm. Casi glanced about, fearful she might catch sight of Jager de Groot, but he was nowhere to be seen. Then everyone was clambering down the ladder to the cockboats below. Zara went first, then *Maré*. She was pleased to see Kip manning the oars, but she felt a little shy around him, too. They hadn't spoken since his beating.

"There y' go." Ignaas held out a hand to steady her. "Sit b'tween yer *moeder* an' *tante*." With the three of them sitting athwart, it was a squeeze. She glanced at Kip, but he didn't meet her eye. The swelling over his temple had receded but his nose was still askew.

I'm going to miss her.

Heat flooded her cheeks.

I never met a girl like her. I hope she'll be okay. I wish–

"Put some muscle into it, lad. We can't be here, all day," Ignaas said.

Oh, why had Ignaas interrupted? Casi twisted her hands in frustration. She stared at Kip as he bent to the task. Behind them, the *Phoenix* slowly receded.

They passed several heavy bellied ships at anchor. Kip concentrated on rowing the cockboat, so she gave up trying to hear his thoughts and studied the port ahead. People were moving along an esplanade. There were sailors and merchants, men with servants at their heels, well-dressed women who strolled in the sun and others who lingered in shadows–a real mix. *Maybe we won't be so strange here, after all,* she thought. The Tribe had always been different. It was both a blessing and a curse.

Kip drew the cockboat up to the far right dock. Waves lapped at its piles. The water was none too clean; seaweed and detritus floated about the pillars. Flies buzzed everywhere. She didn't like them, but flies meant they had finally reached land. She waited while Kip clambered up a short ladder to tie off the cockboat, and then Ignaas helped them ascend. As she climbed to the deck, she wished it had been Kip who had helped her. *Maré* and Zara stood waiting for Ximen who was in the second boat. Zara turned to Ignaas. "You could come with us, you know."

He gave her a grizzled smile. "Aye, I could, Missus. But we both know what would happen in th' end."

"What?"

"I'd long for th' sea, and you'd long for yer blind man." He nodded at the approaching cockboat with Ximen and the others.

"What nonsense. I don't long for him!" Zara looked annoyed.

"No? Then, tell me. What would y' do with an ol' octopus like me?"

She gave him a bold look. "You might be surprised."

Casi flushed with embarrassment.

Ignaas laughed. "Y' can do better, Missus. But I'll tell y' this. If I ever give up th' sea, I'll come lookin' fer ye. If yer still a single woman; y' won't be any longer."

Zara's expression softened. Beneath the sags and wrinkles of her face, she seemed a younger and quite lovely woman. Was that what love did to one, Casi wondered? But then, auntie didn't want Ignaas, she loved Ximen. Maybe it was Ignaas' attention that made her look that way.

"You'll always be welcome, Ignaas," Zara whispered. Ignaas caught her hand and kissed it gallantly, as any knight his lady.

Fingers plucked at her sleeve. Casi turned in surprise. Kip stood next to her.

"Over here," he muttered. "Got somethin' for you." Under his freckles, his face was flushed. She reached for his thoughts, but they were awash in embarrassment and determination. With their backs turned from Zara and her mother, he held out a leather sheath.

"It's a knife. Ignaas gave it t' me after...well, you know." He shrugged it off as if it were of little import. "I can always get another."

He's worried about me! He wants me to be safe! "Are you sure?" she asked. Good knives were hard to come by.

He nodded. "You might need it t' protect yourself. Especially since...I can't be there to do it."

"But what about you?"

"Jager's gone. Captain ain't lettin' him back on board. Says he don't care how good a bosun he is, he's trouble. I'm sorry I lied. I shoulda told th' cap'n th' truth."

"I...thank you, Kip!" She had never received a gift from a boy before. This was her first. She had always thought it would be more romantic—a flower or a necklace—but it didn't matter. He cared! He wanted her to watch out for herself. "I've nothing to give you!"

"Don't matter. Makes me feel good, knowin' y' have it."

She hugged it to her chest. "I'll keep it forever."

As she tucked it into her waist band, she heard his thought. *Do it! Now, when no one's looking!* She blinked up at him in confusion. Then he leaned in and kissed her quickly on the cheek. The thing was done before anyone noticed. Her lips parted in surprise. They stared at each other, both turning a deep red.

"Ready t' go, now, Kip?" Ignaas frowned slightly as if sensing he had missed something.

"Just gave 'er my knife." Kip sauntered toward him without looking back.

He kissed me! He likes me! For a moment, Casi was too stunned to move. Then, realizing she couldn't stay where she was, she followed him. *I like you, too!* she told him as he strode on ahead.

I did it! Kip was pleased with himself. He had finally kissed a girl. And not just any girl, but the prettiest one in the world. The thought popped into Casi's mind like a shining, rainbow bubble.

She ducked her head to hide her smile.

Chapter Thirty-Two: Ambush

MIRIAM SAT INSIDE Ekua's hut. The tribe had dispersed. Yoofi was asleep on a mat. Ekua brooded outside the doorway, staring at the dying flames of the compound's fire. Yoquibo had ordered they share the same abode, so, in silent protest, Ekua refused to enter and rest there.

"You can come down, now." Miriam glanced at a roof beam. "The boy's asleep." A green-feathered parrot swooped from out of the darkness and landed on her shoulder. Alonso sprang into existence at her side.

You found them? She tried not to squirm. His claws pricked.

I did.

Where are they?

On their way to Villa de la Vía, a few leagues distant from the port. They want news of you and the.... They hope someone found you, that you washed up on shore.

He had been about to say *and the men*, but had changed the subject so as not to upset her. The loss of Joachin and Iago was still keen. Maia would want word of Barto, too. Not something she relished telling the Tribe when they finally met—that their men were dead. *They're travelling at night?*

Zara wanted to stay in the shantytown, but Luci was worried about Jager. She wants to put as much distance as possible between him and the Tribe. After he threw you overboard, he sneaked back to his cell and denied any wrongdoing. The crew knows, but they won't say. Now that the Phoenix has docked, his punishment is over. Captain Vrooman released him from duty. He no longer wants him on board.

It's a pity you couldn't get through to Casi.

Isn't it? Zara kept waving me off with her shawl. I ask you, how does one mistake a parrot for a bat?

I don't know. Maybe she doesn't like parrots either. Let's try Casi, again.

They concentrated, silently calling her name over and over. Finally, Alonso desisted. *I don't think it's working. She told me she blocks the noise if it becomes too much.* The parrot lifted a claw to scratch itself on the neck. *I think this bird has fleas.*

"Gods!" She knocked him from her shoulder. He squawked and fluttered to the ground. Yoofi stirred in his sleep, but didn't awaken.

Sorry! She reached out for him. *Are you hurt?* He landed at her knee and pecked at a wing in annoyance. Suddenly she felt itchy all over. It wasn't as bad as the chigger bites, but unnerving even so. What she wouldn't do for a bath. She set a cautious hand on the parrot's back, hoping it wouldn't nip her with that vicious beak. Alonso reappeared at her side.

Try not to do that, will you? Clearly, he was irritated. *The bugs are bad enough, without being bashed about the head.*

Forgive me. It won't happen, again. If you can't contact Casi, we have no choice but to find the Tribe. How far is it from here to them?

About ten leagues, as the parrot flies. I've no idea how long that is on foot.

I need to talk to Yoquibo and Papa K. I want to leave at first light.

Do you think they'll send some of their people with you?

They might, but I doubt they'll go as far as Puerto Real. It's too dangerous. They might be recognized. She thought of Ekua. The girl would be expected to lead her, despite the risks.

That's true, but they also know every valley and mountain on this island. They'll be cautious near the plantations.

She stood. It was time to seek the advice of both *cacique* and *houngan*. Alonso flew before her and out the door. As she stepped from the hut, Ekua curled her lip in contempt. Miriam ignored her and made her way across the compound. Above the Ceiba tree, the stars burned against a vault of black. They were so close and thick, she thought she might pluck them. A soft padding thudded behind her.

She turned. Ekua paused, machete in hand.

You don't have to do this, Miriam told her silently. Even had she voiced it, her dismissal would make no difference. Ekua was bound by duty and honour.

Several people were still awake in Yoquibo's hut. The brazier backlit their shadows as they sat and talked. She paused at the bottom of the steps, with Ekua not far behind. Odeh, Papa Kodjó's wife who had disliked Alonso as a goat, confronted her at the top. The other women looked on. "What you want?" she asked.

"I'd like to speak with the *cacique*."

"He ain' here."

"Papa K?"

Odeh waved a hand at the compound. "Look aroun' you. You see any of the men? They's gone to find *your* people. An' I pray they don' get killed on your account." In the hut, the other wives grumbled their assent.

"I would've gone with them, if not for *her*," Ekua said.

Miriam ignored her. "But where would they know to go?"

"Where you think, woman? They'll poke 'round Shanty Town. Or mebbe Vil' de la Vía. Best time to go's at night, when no *blancos* can see you."

Alonso settled on her shoulder. She tried not to think about fleas.

"What's with you an' them animals?" Odeh demanded. "I know that goat wasn't no ol' goat! An' now, he's a feathered devil! You think we don' see? You keep that *djab* away from us! Don't you bring him up here!" She snatched up Papa K's *asson* and rattled it to keep her at bay. The other women looked alarmed.

Clearly, a *djab* was a type of demon. She set a hand on Alonso's wing to show he wasn't a threat. "This is Alonso! He isn't evil." The explanation felt sorely inadequate.

Odeh shook the rattle harder. "You stay away! I'll tell Papa K 'bout him, soon's he gets back!"

Miriam retreated, nonplussed. Perhaps it was best to wait until Papa Kodjó returned with Yoquibo and the men. They would be better at dealing with the tribe's superstitions. They might also have word of Luci and the rest, perhaps even bring them back to camp. If only she had known they were going! She could have written Zara a note, or sent Luci something to show that Yoquibo and Papa K were allies.

She marched back to the hut with Alonso on her shoulder. Ekua glared and gave them a wide berth.

As it happened, the disembarking from the *Phoenix* took longer than expected. The Tribe had to wait for Fidel, Joachin's horse, to be docked, in spite of Zara's objections. The stallion, skinny and unhappy from his long confinement, still proved to be a handful. Casi watched nervously, afraid Jager de Groot might be among the men unloading him, but Jager didn't appear. By the time the Tribe finally collected Fidel, it was nearing the supper hour.

"Y' best avoid Dock Street, if y' can," Ignaas told Zara. "Rough area. Most of th' public houses are there. Take Fishmonger's Alley, then turn onto High Street. Soon's yer past th' graveyard, yer nearly out o' town. Couple o' leagues through plantations, and you'll see th' walls o' th' fortress appear. Takes a few hours, on foot. Gods' speed!"

"And to you, dear Ignaas!" Zara gushed. Casi watched as Ximen grimaced. Was he jealous? She then cast a parting glance at Kip. Leaving now felt anti-climactic. An hour before, he had kissed her. She hadn't imagined it.

She grabbed him by the arm. "I won't forget," she said in a rush. "Not the knots, not you!" She bussed him clumsily on the lips and then, face aflame, ran after Luci.

"Neither will I!" he shouted after her, coming back to sudden life.

"What was that?" Luci hadn't seen the exchange. Fidel had barred her way.

"Nothing," Casi replied quickly. She didn't look back, but Kip's thoughts followed her like a sweet strain of music. When he was older, he would come back to the island and woo her, see if he didn't!

She shied away from that thought, not wanting to consider the ramifications of *woo*. It was enough he was happy, whistling. As the Tribe passed the cemetery, she forgot about him and thought of phantoms rising from the headstones, floating after them with fingers reaching. She glanced nervously over her shoulder. There was nothing, save long shadows thrown by the graves. The sky was a burnished gold.

"What are you doing?" Luci held Fidel by the cheek strap. The horse was restive. She frowned as if it were Casi's fault.

"I just wanted to see if anyone was following us."

"There's only the town, Casi. We mustn't lag. The sooner we reach the gates of Villa de la Vía, the better."

"You don't think Jager is following us?"

"No, I *don't*. And I don't want you saying such things. You'll only scare yourself."

She wasn't the only one who was frightened.

They trundled to the town's end. The cobbles petered out and the road turned to ruts. Beyond, fields of sugar cane waved in the evening breeze. She was surprised by how tall the cane was, but her awe was short-lived. Despite what *Maré* had said, she considered listening for Jager and his cronies, but the idea of hearing him made her sick. *I just can't*, she thought.

It was better to distract herself. Sugar was sweet. She wanted to try it. Now that they were on the island, maybe she would have a chance. As they drew closer to the field, the walls of green closed in to tower over their heads. Strange rustlings stirred in the undergrowth. She clutched Luci's hand.

Luci caught her breath. "What is it?"

"I'm hearing things."

"What things? Thoughts?"

"No. Noises. In the field."

"It's just rats foraging, Casi."

"There are rats on the island?"

"Of course. There are rats everywhere."

She didn't like rats, but there were worse things. She thought of Jager, again. "What if it isn't rats, Maré? What if something bigger is following us?"

"I told you not to worry about Jager. We'd hear him and his men if they followed us. Cane leaves are sharp. They won't pass through this field. They're likely drowning their woes in a tavern somewhere."

It reassured her a little. The day faded. The cane crop receded behind them. The road continued through fields of cotton. It was good to see what was around one. Beyond, the jungle loomed, mysterious and dark. The breeze carried a scent of spice, flowers, and damp earth. As pleasant as it was, it didn't make her feel any better. *It's all right*, she told herself. *There's nothing. If there were, I would've heard.* Except—she had barred Jager from her thoughts. If she wanted to know for certain if he followed, she would have to listen. *All right, then. I'll do this—for the Tribe.* She drew in a deep breath to steady herself.

His thoughts struck her like the blows from a cudgel. *Any second now! 'You must set your face against them and cut them off from all people!' Allow a witch to live and be defiled!*

Fidel snorted and reared. "Maré!" Casi cried. "He's here!"

Shadowy figures rose from where they had been hiding in the cotton and launched themselves at the Tribe. Zara screamed, echoing the terror of all the women. Someone big grabbed Casi; she recognized Jager's sour smell. *An' th' youngest o' these must be destroyed, lest th' sins o' th' moeder be stronger in her. Spill not the tainted blood, lest it defile the land!* He clapped a meaty hand over her mouth. She bit down and tasted thumb. He roared in pain and released his hold.

Beside her, Luci had disabled the man who had attacked her. He was doubled over and cupping his crotch. Then, leaping like a tigress, she jumped onto Jager's back. Cursing, he tried to shake her free, reaching behind to grab her by the hair. The other man, the one she had kicked, stumbled to his aid.

Fear for her mother burned Casi's terror away. "You leave my *maré* alone!" she shrieked.

She found herself pressed up against Jager. Somehow, Kip's knife was in her hand. Jager might not be willing to spill a witch's blood, but she was under no such compunction to spill his. She squeezed the hilt, and then the blade was in his eye. Blood spurted over her knuckles, messy, black, and hot. His other eye stared. Blood bubbled from his lips. That was good because the knife was killing him. *I don't care*, Casi thought. *He'll never hurt, or think hateful thoughts about me, or my maré, again.*

All about her, the Tribe screamed. Fidel reared. She barely heard it. The noise seemed to come from a long way off. There was an element of surprise to it, as if something more was happening. Jager toppled at her feet. She fell with him, unwilling to release the knife. There was a dull gurgle, and then...nothing. There were no more thoughts. He was gone.

So was she. The world faded. She found herself in a tight, quiet place, where darkness was her friend. It was nice here. She would stay a while. Part of her knew she straddled two realms—the real world where her hand was glued to the hilt, and this hidey hole, where she was safe. If she took her hand away, her sanctuary might shatter. She would have to face the light, acknowledge things she had done.

I don't want to, she thought.

"*Mademoiselle*, do you hear me!" The voice drifted in from the outside, invading her haven. Then came the thought: *to do what she has, and one so young!* "The bad man is dead," the voice continued. "You and your *mama* are safe. Can you remove your hand from the blade, *cherie*?"

She supposed she could. But if she did, she would have to leave her den, and she didn't want to. The disembodied voice spoke again, but not to her, it seemed. "She's in shock, *Madame*. It's understandable. This was her first killing, no?"

"Lys preserve us, let it be the only one! I can't believe she did this!"

"She saved you, *Madame*. It is amazing what even a child can do for love."

Someone was shaking her. *Maré*, she supposed. "Casi! Wake up!"

No. She hugged her knees.

"Ah, there. She's done it. She's let go of the knife."

She had released it without meaning to, but thankfully, it didn't affect her den. It wasn't the grass hut she had imagined, but it was cozy enough. The dark was less distracting, here. *I want to sleep*, she thought.

"Do not fret, *Madame*. We'll set her on the horse, and you'll hold her against your heart. I'm sure, given a day or so, she'll be fine. You must let us know if you tire on the way. It takes a few hours to get where we're going, but you'll see your kinswoman by dawn."

"Miriam! I can't believe she sent you!"

"Thank Damballah and La Sirene. Or that goddess of yours, Lys, if you like. It is their will."

Such a strange dream, I'm having, Casi thought. *I wish Maré and the rest would stop talking so I can go to sleep.* There was a sense of nestling into a warm blanket. It smelled like *Maré*, which was good.

The chatter subsided.

She tucked her chin under oblivion.

Chapter Thirty-Three: Escape

BY DAWN, THE storm had passed. Rana and Tomás stepped onto the waist to see what damage their floating refuge had suffered. The foremast was gone, snapped in half as if by Lys' vengeful hand. The shrouds were in a tangle. It would take a week to set them aright. The pilot had informed Capitán de Carazo the storm had swept them past the southern coast of Esbañiola. They would arrive at Puerto Real, sooner than expected. The island was visible to the southwest, a hazy blue gem on an aqua sea. The sky was bright and clear, the promise of ease to come.

"Where we wanted to go, all along!" Tomás murmured as if his prayers had been answered.

"Was that a hurricane?" Angél directed his question to de Carazo. Rana was glad to see him. She had worried he had been swept overboard. The sea was afloat with debris, wood, and rigging presumably from other ships, as well as the limbs from trees.

"Not an actual *huracan*, no. We wouldn't have survived that, but certainly, a tropical storm. We must thank Sul we did."

Tomás turned to him. "Indeed, yes. I can't wait for us to disembark. And then we must make haste to Villa de la Vía. You'll accompany us?" He was in such a good mood, he had framed the demand as a request. *A rare event*, Rana thought.

"Of course. I must pay my respects to *Gobernador* Rosales, even if I don't respect him." De Carazo laughed, also in high spirits. "Mateo and I will join you. Noxolo as well. We can provide an escort of six men."

"That will be enough to guarantee our safety?"

"More than enough. Villa de la Vía is only a few leagues inland. No bandit will accost a company of twelve."

The captain could have included Umberto in his count, but the old man was nowhere to be seen. *Not that I care*, Rana thought, but it was strange. Why hadn't he come on deck with everyone else? Tomás expected it. She hadn't seen him since the night she discovered what Noxolo had been doing to Mateo. And Umberto had not attended her wedding.

"I'm looking forward to getting there," Capitán de Carazo added, interrupting her train of thought. "Villa de la Vía isn't as pleasant as my fortress at San Sul, but it has its comforts." He clapped an arm about his nephew's shoulder. Mateo didn't look well. Was the boy even aware of what was being done to him?

"I suggest you ready yourselves to disembark. We should arrive at Puerto Real within the hour," he said.

Back in her cabin, she questioned Tomás as to Umberto's whereabouts.

He eyed himself in her hand mirror. "Don't let it concern you." He hadn't aged any further. Hopefully, Mateo hadn't suffered more on his behalf.

"I was just curious."

He studied the line of his jaw. "There's a fashion amongst the nobility to keep lap dogs as pets. I've never understood it. They do nothing but yap, lick, and shit all over the carpet. Dogs should serve us, not be filthy, annoying companions. Once they've served their purpose, they should be discarded." He tossed her mirror into her trunk. "You've things well in hand here. I need to pack." He left her staring after him, open-mouthed. She didn't know the *how* of it, but it was obvious what had happened to Umberto.

I watched Tomás and Noxolo do it! Tanya cackled with glee. *The old geezer put up a fight as they leeched him, so they garrotted him to finish him off. Afterwards, they tossed him to the fish.*

Rana glanced at the ashen crow sitting on her shoulder. *Why didn't you tell me?*

Tanya shrugged. *You never asked.*

Perhaps Umberto had irritated Tomás once too often, or perhaps he had dried up as a rejuvenation source. If Tomás was willing to kill Umberto, he would sacrifice anyone. The sooner she and Angél were free of him, the better.

And me, Tanya added.

The shantytown of Puerto Real was much as Rana expected, the types of people milling along the esplanade the same as anywhere except for a stronger dichotomy between rich and poor. Those who owned the plantations wore fine cotton and sported clock-watch pendants, the latest fad, Tomás informed her. Their servants, many of whom were amber-fleshed like herself, ran after them, ragged and barefoot. She didn't understand it. Why was brown skin not seen as a thing of beauty? Before the *hymenoptera* had attacked her, hers had been perfect and creamy, the envy of all of her friends. *Such a long time ago,* she thought. She missed her old self.

By the time they set out, it was past the supper hour. Street torches flickered along the way, their meagre illumination swallowed by the velvety night. There weren't many people about. The wealthier members of the populace had long since departed for their plantations; the local folk had gone home or frequented the inns. At a stable, Capitán de Carazo arranged for horses and servants to handle their baggage. Tomás directed her to ride with Angél. *Of course,* she thought. In the eyes of both public and crew, she and Angél were married. Appearances had to be maintained.

"I can't believe he's allowing this," she murmured, clasping Angél about the waist as they trotted through the town. The moon had risen, silvering the fields. No one else travelled the road. She wondered about brigands.

"Just be ready," he whispered, squeezing her hand. "I'm praying for a distraction."

She wasn't happy with that solution, but then, how likely were they to get away on a single mount? Not with a troop of riders flanking them. There was also Noxolo to worry about. She had assumed he would carry baggage like the other servants, but that wasn't the case. He rode beside Mateo as if entitled to be there. Perhaps he was.

Ahead, the road entered a field of sugarcane. She had hoped they might ride in darkness, making it easier for her and Angél to escape, but the crew lit torches to light the way. Shadow snakes, created by the brands, writhed across stalks as they passed. She was thankful when the road finally opened into a cotton field.

They trotted along for another ten minutes, when suddenly, Capitán de Carazo signalled a halt. Tomás remained mounted, while de Carazo shouted orders at his men. An obstacle of some sort barred their way.

Angél allowed the rest of the troop to pass, then slipped from the saddle and lifted her down. "Come on." He pulled her into the cotton field. She wondered why they were leaving their horse, but it soon became obvious. They had a better chance of escaping on foot. She held his hand tightly as they bent low and ran.

"What was in the road?" she whispered at his back. She hadn't been able to see.

"Bodies. About six of them, from what I could tell. They must have been caught unawares."

She shuddered, hoping they weren't heading to a similar fate.

It was awful! Tanya flew over her head. *Some of them looked as if they'd been hacked to pieces by machetes. Others, as if their eyes had been stabbed out. Or pierced with arrows, and then the arrows removed.*

She had to be careful. Angél wouldn't understand Tanya at all. She mouthed the words. *Did you see who did it?*

How could I? I'm not a seer, like you.

Let me know if you sense anything.

Of course. I can't have my future maré not living up to her promises.

They were half way across the cotton field, when a shout rose from behind them. They had been missed. Angél didn't stop to look, but she imagined riders milling about and Tomás cursing beneath his breath.

Oh, he's angry! Tanya confirmed.

Which way is he—?

Look out! They're coming!

Blind luck or some dark instinct was prompting Tomás to follow their path.

It's that Noxolo! He's directing him! Tanya shouted.

Can you do something? Distract him?

I don't know! I'll try!

Her absence wasn't so much a lessening of pressure as a sudden loss. Rana hadn't realized how accustomed she had become to having Tanya on her shoulder or flying above her head. It made her anxious.

Behind them, a horse reared and screamed. There was a crash and more shouts.

"Come on!" Angél urged. They had come to the end of the cotton field. Before them, the jungle loomed, but it wasn't as impenetrable as she thought. They darted into it, able to run with care. The way underfoot was strewn with vines and roots.

"Careful!" Angél warned.

"Where are we going?"

"We'll head deeper into the jungle. Circle around and make our way back to Puerto Real. Keep our heads down. From there, we'll hire a ship."

Unless they were caught by Tomás or worse. Weren't there snakes and poisonous frogs in the jungle? She had heard there were crocodiles....

I did it!

Tanya's sudden appearance made her jump.

I spooked Noxolo's horse, and it threw him! I hope it broke his lousy neck! We'll get away from him, now!

Rana wasn't so sure about that. There was still Noxolo's *djab* to contend with, but if Tanya wasn't concerned, then neither was she. Besides, her *puri* was watching over them from the borders of the Summerland. Between Anassa's protection and Tanya's self-interest, she and Angél would escape. Maybe Lys would even forgive her for past sins. She could hope.

After stumbling non-stop for a time, they entered a moonlit clearing to catch their breath. It looked familiar, or perhaps it was just one of many they had crossed. Angél swore.

She clutched at a stitch in her side. "What is it?" Her dress was torn, she was dizzy.

"We've been through here, before. The moon plays tricks. It's a miracle they haven't caught us, yet." He clawed at his hair.

"Maybe they're going around in circles, too." *Or maybe Tanya did something more to confound Noxolo*, she thought. Tanya had disappeared again to spy on the troop's movements. The air smelled of peppery sap. She leaned against a felled tree. "I don't hear anything."

They listened to the night. There was the call of a night bird, but other than that, nothing disturbed the peace.

"Maybe we lost them. I can hope." Angél drew in a deep breath and sat down beside her. "You look beautiful in the moonlight."

She stared up at him. His eyes were dark and probing, his lashes thick enough to be a girl's. He was as handsome as ever, but his compliment didn't thrill her as it might have once done. It was Miriam he praised. As much as she wanted his love, she wanted him to love her for herself. She glanced away.

"It doesn't please you to hear how lovely you are?"

She shrugged. There was no way to fix this. "It isn't that."

"What is it, then?"

She would tell him. She couldn't. He would never understand. He would hate her all over again, the worst thing of all. She stared down at her hands. "You...you don't really know me."

He looked bemused. "Of course, I know you."

"No, you don't. You only see the surface. You don't see who I really am."

"You're the love of my life."

"But *why* do you love me, Angél? You love what you see. Whereas, I love you for who you are."

"I love you for who you are, too."

She faced him. "Then, tell me. Who am I?"

He smiled faintly. "I'll tell you *what* you are, instead. You're beautiful, yes. But you're also strong and tenacious and gifted. You fight for what you want, Miriam. You're passionate, so much so, I think you would die for me."

"Would you die for *me*?"

"Of course! But let's not talk about dying." He tapped her playfully on the nose. "I think instead, we should talk about going. Even if we're lost, we need to be—" His eyes bulged and his hands flew to his throat.

"Angél!"

He clawed at his neck and choked.

"What is it?" She couldn't see what was attacking him.

Tanya! Help! She held onto him to stop him from falling. A force slammed into her, knocking her breathless.

I'm here! Tanya shouted. Then the world lurched. A man-sized shadow had Angél by the throat and was squeezing the life from him. It was amorphous, constantly expanding and diminishing as if his struggles gave it strength.

It's killing him! Get it off him, Tanya! Rana shouted.

You don't have to tell me! Tanya appeared behind the thing and clawed at its head.

The shadow gibbered angrily and squeezed Angél even harder. Then it sank its teeth into his neck. Angél cried out. He glowed briefly, a torch flaring, and then his light began to ebb.

We're not saving him! Rana screamed.

The thing was a life-sucker, a type of psychic leech. She had heard of such things. They were associated with dark Afrikan magic. Noxolo's power.

Tanya wavered and metamorphosed into her vulture form. The shadow turned to bite her. She sliced at it with her claws, severing a part of its essence. It dropped Angél like a discarded pod and enveloped her in a man-shaped balloon. She fought it for all she was worth, but she couldn't break its hold.

Terror ran through Rana on tiny rat's feet, making her want to surrender to panic. At the same time, its bite spurred her to think. Tanya couldn't die a second time, nor could she leave Angél to face this thing alone. How did one fight such an evil?

She had been a Speaker in her old life, which no one, including herself, considered much of a talent. She had been a tool, a vessel though which the Ancestors spoke. Was it possible she had never seen the true value behind her gift? Some abilities involved the marshalling of forces, of knowing whom to call when one needed help. Evil couldn't stand before a community of grace.

Puri! she cried, clutching her necklace. And then, in fervent hope, she beseeched as many of the Tribe's matriarchs as she could remember, all the great grandmothers who had come before Anassa. She remembered only six names. As a last resort, she implored the goddess. *Lys, help us! Forgive me! Don't let Angél die!*

The world flared white in a terrific flash. A shock, as sweet as love, as determined as passion, swept through her to Angél, and then into Tanya and the leech. She caught a brief glimpse of Anassa, followed by the mirror images of the other matriarchs she had named, every one of them a knuckle on her string. They had come. And then, a presence so immense and immediate, as warm and as nourishing as milk, enveloped her and everything she knew. The shadow engulfing Tanya disintegrated into bits and melted away.

The wash of white faded and the night returned. Tears streamed down Rana's face. Diaphani saints were said to shed milky tears, or those who had been touched by divine grace. She wondered if hers were.

A weight settled upon her shoulder. *Was that–?* Even Tanya seemed cowed.

I don't know. Maybe. Her last entreaty had been to Lys.

Angél groaned. She knelt beside him and helped him to sit. He looked at her goggle-eyed. She wondered if he had experienced the same marvel she had.

"You," he said in amazement, "saved me from that...."

Djab, Tanya supplied.

So, that was what a *djab* looked like. It had to be Noxolo's. It was good to know they could defeat it. "I had some help," she replied.

"For a moment, I thought you were...,"

He had seen past the glamoury. He had seen her as Rana. She held her breath, hoping he would admit it. "Who?"

"I must have been mistaken." He swiped at his neck and grimaced at finding blood there.

That thing fed on him. Tanya sounded disgusted, which was ironic, considering what she used to eat as a death bird.

All right! Don't remind me! She ruffled her wings.

Sorry. Rana was so tired, she wasn't being considerate. *It doesn't matter what you did. All that's changed. I've changed, too. We need to take care of Angél.* "Can you stand?" she asked him, wrapping an arm about his waist. Tanya settled on her shoulder, opposite.

"Even if I can't, I have you to defend me." He smiled wanly.

She squeezed him. It was good he found some worth in her, over and above who she looked like.

They limped along a trail, remaining watchful. Who knew if Noxolo's *djab* could resurrect itself? Or if Noxolo might invoke a new one? Tanya dozed on her shoulder, recovering from the fight. Even in spirit form, she needed replenishment. *There's so much I don't know*, Rana thought. If she ever had the chance, she would ask Anassa about it. She glanced at Angél. He looked pale. She was about to suggest they stop, when Tanya awoke with a start. *Look out!* she screeched, flapping about her head.

A ring of barely clad men stepped from the trees, encircling them with machetes and spears. She might fend off spiritual powers, but physical forces were harder, especially when she and Angél were only two. She was even more startled when a familiar voice hailed her, "Rana Isadore! What are *you* doing here?"

Zara stepped out from the ring of native men. Rana stared at her, open-mouthed.

"Oh, I know who you are!" Zara thrust an accusatory finger at her. "Don't you deny it! Ximen confirms it!" Ximen and other members of the Tribe appeared beside her.

Rana swallowed. "I don't deny it. Angél and I are running from Torch Bearers."

"Dear Lys!" someone gasped. Luci, Rana saw.

"They're on the island?" Zara's voice rose in alarm.

One of the men wore a gleaming medallion on his chest. He was tall and grim. *He must be the chief,* Rana thought. How had the Tribe come to be associated with these *cimarrónes* as Tomás had called them?

Angél spoke up. "How is it *you* come to be here, Zara?"

"Seems we took a ship, same as you,"

The big man lifted his spear for quiet. "We must go. We can talk later."

She and Angél were nudged into place along with the rest of the Tribe. It was a night of strangeness and marvels, unexpected meetings and terror. It seemed to bother Angél more than it did her. This had been fated. She believed in destiny now, more than ever.

It seemed the bodies Capitán de Carazo's troop found, were those of rough sailors who had accosted the Tribe. As they travelled, Luci filled Rana and Angél in on what had happened. The native troop, indeed runaway slaves with whom they travelled, had found and rescued Miriam. Incredibly, she had convinced them she wasn't a threat, that both tribes might benefit from shared purposes—or so, the old man called Papa Kodjó had said. These men had come to collect the Tribe and had dispatched the ruffians. They had heard Rana and Angél in the forest and decided to investigate. Such a strange coincidence, was it not? Luci asked.

I don't think so, Rana thought. From the way Luci's eyes shone, she didn't think so, either. Luci had always been religious. Always thinking Lys was hard at work, arranging events to the benefit of her people. *Which might not be so far from the truth,* Rana reflected.

She hazarded a glance at Angél. He had been quiet throughout much of Luci's account. *He's either furious with me for letting him think I was Miriam, or he doesn't believe it.* He was also weak from the *djab's* attack, she knew.

They travelled all night. By dawn, she was faint with exhaustion. Angél could barely walk, but they came at last to a cluster of huts and a community of *cimarrónes*. There was one other, whom she recognized the moment she saw her.

Wearing her own ravaged body, Miriam Medina rose from where she had been sitting by a fire, to greet her long lost Tribe.

Chapter Thirty-Four: Wrongs Made Right

THEY WERE BILLETED in various huts. She and Angél were left to sleep the morning away, but he kept his back turned to her, which was upsetting. By noon, she had collected enough of her courage to emerge from their hut. Miriam and the rest of the Tribe were sitting around a camp fire. When everyone noticed her, all talk stopped. She hesitated, but forced herself to keep going.

"We should have left *you* behind for the Grand Inquisitor," Zara said, by way of greeting.

"Don't be unkind, Zara." Luci cradled Casi in her lap. Casi's eyes were wide and staring. "We must believe everything happens for the best."

Rana frowned. Luci had said it as if she had doubts. Something had happened to Casi. Whatever it was, wasn't good.

"I've lived long enough to know *that* isn't true," Zara countered.

Miriam eyed her dully, looking as if most of the life had been drained from her. It was strange seeing Miriam as herself. She would look like that again, *hymenoptera* bites and all, once the magic was reversed. It didn't matter. Feeling the goddess' presence rush through her the night before had changed her in ways she hadn't expected. It was time to make things right.

"I know you all hate me," she began. She tried not to flinch under their baleful stares. "I don't blame you. I've done much that *is* hateful." *The worst of which, you don't even know.* "I've suffered for of it, but I've learned from it, too. I want to make amends."

"How can you make amends, when you look like her?" Zara nodded at Miriam. "You stole her body. Lys knows how you did it, Rana Isadore, but it must have been a wicked thing. Murder, I'm thinking!"

Ximen regarded her with his queer white eyes. He would have seen what she had done, second-hand. Ximen knew everything.

"I hope to make amends for that, too." On her shoulder, Tanya shifted from foot to foot. She wondered if Ximen was aware of her.

"I'm no diviner, but I believe she will," Ximen said.

It meant a journey back to the sea and standing opposite Miriam in the waist deep water. Both tribes, Diaphani and *cimarróne*, watched from the beach. She wasn't sure why Papa Kodjó and his people attended, unless it was to witness foreign magic. Angél had come too, but he made no move to speak with her. She tried not to think about him. The afternoon was mild, the breeze soft and warm. Again, she was taken with how depleted Miriam looked. Many of the *hymenoptera* bites had healed, but the scars remained. *I'll bear those again*, Rana thought. For a moment, she was tempted to flee, but she held on to her resolve.

Her ancestors had saved Angél from Noxolo's *djab*, because she had asked them to do it. The goddess had come to her aid, too. None of that had been her imagination. Such experiences changed a person. They brought insight, taught you things you never knew.

She removed the necklace and offered it to Miriam. "Anassa named you Matriarch. This is yours." The knowledge stung, but her *puri* had chosen well. She knew that now. From the very beginning, Miriam had been devoted to the Tribe while she had only been devoted to Angél. "The knuckle on the end is yours. I never should have taken it, or placed it on the chain. The bones are meant to be added only after you die." She swallowed. "I'm sorry."

Miriam nodded. The moment lengthened, turning awkward.

Rana pressed on. "A Matriarch bequeaths the necklace to whomever she sees fit. It's usually a daughter or granddaughter, but whoever exhibits the strongest talent is the best choice. You'll have to do the same and name an heir."

"I will never bear a daughter or a son."

She stared at Miriam in surprise. Had something happened to Joachín? Was he dead? If so, that might explain her lethargy. "Well, you'll have to pick someone, eventually," she replied. "Before I give it back, you have to throw your knuckle into the sea. That part of you is dead, so it must be surrendered to Lys."

"If I cast it aside, how will it end up on the necklace?"

"You have *another* knuckle." Miriam really was grief-struck if she couldn't see it. "After you die, the Tribe will—"

A tiny frown appeared on Miriam's brow. "All right, I understand."

"Good. Take it." She slipped the knuckle from the string and closed Miriam's fingers around it. Suddenly it was easier to breathe, as if a burden had been lifted from her shoulders.

Miriam gazed down at the knuckle that had once been part of her right hand. Then she threw it into the waves.

They waited. Nothing happened. Miriam glanced at her questioningly.

"That's only the first part. Now, I ask for Lys' blessing on you, and... and I place the necklace around your throat." It was hard to keep her voice from shaking.

"A blessing. From Lys."

"I know, it seems strange coming from me, but don't question it. Bow your head."

Angél was watching them from the shore. She was about to lose him, forever. *I could stay as I am*, she thought, feeling the first tuggings of panic. *Talk my way out of this. He might still believe me.* But without fixing Miriam, the Tribe would despise her more than ever. If Angel left her now, she would need their support, So would the baby—

What do we do about that? Tanya burst into head unannounced. *He's supposed to be my father! But if you change, he won't touch you! You promised—!*

I don't know, Tanya! She couldn't cope with Tanya right now; she was about to fall to pieces. *All I know is I have to do this! I'll find you another father!* Her heart stuttered in her chest. It was now or never. She had to finish this or walk away from it. She forced the words out in a rush. "May the goddess b..bless you!" she told Miriam. "May you serve Lys with a pure heart, dedicated to love and care for the rest of your days! In return, may she protect you and grant you her b...bounty!"

Her voice gave out. Once again, she would be ugly, unloved—a pariah. The knowledge destroyed her, but she had brought this upon herself. Feeling as if the necklace were as heavy as stone, she dropped it over Miriam's head.

A wave slammed into them, knocking them off their feet. As she fell, water closed over her head and funnelled up her nose. She clawed at the sandy bottom, only to churn up more grit. Finally, she found her feet and rose, dripping and spitting, to glare at the sky. The fear of fainting was gone, chased by a sense of being ill-used.

"That wasn't *nice!*" she sputtered. She flinged a stream of water heavenward. The dunking had the goddess' sense of humour all over it. Another wave rolled by, threatening to sweep her from her feet a second time. As it passed, it gurgled like laughter.

Miriam had also resurfaced, staggering and gasping for air. She clawed aside a wall of black hair from her face. The necklace swung about her throat. She had returned to herself, beautiful once again, if a little wild eyed. As she caught sight of her hands, she stared at them wonderingly. They were long and smooth. The little finger on her right hand was still missing, but everything else was as before. No *hymenoptera* scars marred her flesh. "It worked!" she said in amazement. "And you, Rana!" she cried, looking at her, "You've changed, too!"

Of course she had changed. Miriam was lovely again, and she was her awful old self.

A tiny line creased Miriam's brow. "No. I don't think you understand. I mean, you've really changed!"

Between you and Angél, I'm going to be sooooo pretty! Tanya cried.

Her hands flew to her face. Her cheeks were wet but smooth and firm. The puckers from the *hymenoptera* bites were gone—her fingers didn't lie. She gazed down at her dripping arms. Her flesh was perfect, if a little tanned. "Dear Lys, I'm back. I'm *me*!" She started to laugh. Giddiness held her in its grip. She grabbed Miriam by the shoulders and danced her up and down in the surf. "I did it! For both of us!"

Miriam mouthed a protest at being bounced about, but Rana was too happy to care. Even losing Angél couldn't diminish this moment of joy and relief. On the shore, the Tribe let out a cheer. En masse, they charged into the waves, heedless of their skirts and shoes.

Soon, she and Miriam were surrounded by a splashing, chattering, feminine mob. Zara and Luci caught her in a fierce embrace. She endured more hugs and kisses than she ever remembered receiving. On the shore, Angél waited with Ximen and Papa K's people.

She caught his glance, surprised to find him watching her. As everyone waded back to shore, she expected him to follow Miriam's every move.

Angél kept his gaze locked on her.

An hour later, they were back in the *cimarrónes'* camp. While Miriam and the Tribe dried off by the communal fire, Angél led her between two huts. A tall bush with orange, bell-shaped flowers bloomed over their heads. He seemed ill at ease.

"So, you've been Rana, all this time." It wasn't quite an accusation, but it wasn't a casual observation, either.

"Yes." She knew what was coming.

"Why mislead me?"

"You know why, Angél. You've always preferred Miriam to me. If you'd known, you wouldn't have forgiven what I did. You even might have killed me, thinking it could reverse the spell."

He didn't confirm or deny it, but stared moodily across the compound. Some of Papa Kodjó's people had joined Miriam and the Tribe by the fire. She touched him tentatively on the arm. "After we transformed, you kept watching me. Why?"

"I'm entitled to look where I want." His gaze strayed to the *cimarrónes*. "I don't trust these people. Miriam wants to join them, but they aren't for us."

"Us?" Her heart beat a little faster.

He glanced down at her and frowned. "Of course. What did you think?"

"I don't know. You didn't answer my question." In the past, he had never liked being pestered for answers, but that was then and this was now. "I have to know, Angél. I need to know why you watched me and not her." She gave Miriam a cursory glance. "She's the one you've always wanted."

"She isn't who I thought she was."

"And I *am*?" She choked on a laugh.

"You're something of a...surprise." A smile touched his lips. "Do I have to spell it out for you?"

"I think you do."

"It's simple. I'm an ambitious man. Because of that, you're better suited to be my wife."

Meaning she would serve his objectives in a way Miriam never would. Angél valued wealth and power. He would expect her to help him attain them. But she was ambitious, too. Not for worldly things, but for him.

"You're the stronger talent. It's no secret I've always wanted a talented wife." He made a face. "You saved me from that *thing*."

"Djab."

"Whatever it was. That deserves some consideration."

He was still so arrogant. "So you're willing to grant me the privilege of staying married to you." She wasn't sure that was enough. She wanted more. He was beginning to lose his shine.

"Now, don't go all huffy on me." He caught her and held her close. "I know I'll be happier married to you. With the *hymenoptera* bites gone, you're as beautiful as Miriam is. In fact, you're more so. Besides, you have something she lacks."

Her breathing sped. Despite still being damp from the sea, she was beginning to feel overly warm. It was annoying to react to him in such a way, especially when he was being so charming. "And that is?"

"A certain ruthlessness I find arousing."

It was the same thing she found exciting about him.

He released her as if it were all decided. "So you will grace my side," he held up a forefinger, "with one stipulation. You must never lie or mislead me, again."

She eyed him steadily. He still planned on heading for Esbañiola. She could go with him or remain with Miriam and the Tribe. She had always wanted him, but things were different now. She was pregnant with Tomás' child. If Tomás ever tracked her down, he would imprison her, perhaps kill her if she became inconvenient. Worst of all, he would turn their child into a monster like himself. For all his faults, Angél would make a good father. For her son and for Tanya, too.

I am ruthless, she thought. *More than you'll ever know, Angél.* She set her hands in his, the meek, little wife. It was clear who manipulated whom. But she loved him and would always have his best interests at heart. "I promise I will never lie or mislead you, again."

"Good." He squeezed her fingers. "Then we should be on our way. If we're careful, Tomás won't find us if we lie low in Puerto Real. Once there, I'll make inquiries. We'll find a ship."

She kept her arms about his waist. "It's late. Perhaps we should set out tomorrow at first light? Then we'll have the whole day. Why hurry now, when the afternoon has so much to offer?" He frowned which made her laugh. He was so obtuse at times, which, all things considered, was a good thing. "We owe the Tribe something. They should know of our plans before we go. And besides..." she glanced at the empty hut they had vacated earlier, "after all we've been through, shouldn't we consummate our marriage properly, find joy in each other for once?"

He actually blushed. It pleased her to see she had unsettled him. Or perhaps her breast tattoos were having their effect. It didn't matter. In seven and a half months' time, Angél would be a father. If he questioned it, she would insist that sometimes babies came early. Their son's birth would be a miracle.

Yes! crowed Tanya. *And then, it's my turn!*

Find something to do for an hour, Tanya. And no peeking, Rana told her.

Angél didn't protest as she drew him away.

In the shade of the Ceiba tree, both tribes sat amicably together and chatted in small groups. Zara and Odeh had their heads together, discussing the properties of some bumpy yellow fruit. Luci rested beside Maia, with Casi in her lap. Above them, Alonso perched on a branch, a green flash among verdant leaves. Miriam was glad to have her body back, but it seemed a small thing after all that had happened. Papa Kodjó disagreed, insisting strong *ashe* showed divine investment.

"*Ashe?*" she repeated.

"What you might call life force. Personal power. The ability to make things happen."

"I didn't create this change. Rana did."

"That's true. But what happened today was enabled by La Sirene. It's clear to me she has plans for you both. For all of us." He smiled beatifically.

It all came down to Lys or La Sirene, as Papa Kodjó called her. She was Lys' puppet. As long as the goddess' desires came to pass, it didn't matter who became collateral damage. Lys could have saved Joachín from drowning, but she let him go down with the ship. Iago and Barto, too. How could she tell the Tribe they were dead? *Luci will be devastated, and Casi is still in shock.* She couldn't do it. Yet she had to.

Papa Kodjó squeezed her fingers briefly. It felt like a hug. "Something still troubles you." He released her hand. The sensation receded.

"Yes. I have some bad news to share." She glanced at her Tribe.

"Then I'll leave you to do it." He rose awkwardly as if his hip were bothering him. "I'll be with our *cacique*. Send Ekua if you need anything."

As he shuffled away, a number of his tribe also stood and headed off. From outside their hut, Ekua watched from her post.

Miriam called for everyone's attention. "I have something to tell you." No longer having Odeh to talk to, Zara settled beside her. It was hard to dismiss the lines of worry creasing Luci's brow. Maia clutched Little Grim as if sensing ill tidings, while Ximen gazed on. Casi, still unaware of what was happening around her, stared off into the distance.

There was no way to soften it. "It's bad news. I've known for some time, but I haven't had the chance to tell you until now. I'm sorry. It breaks my heart...." She felt dizzy. Her lungs were turning into iron. A steel band clapped itself about her throat.

"Matriarch?" Zara reached out to steady her.

It came out in a rush. "Joachin, Iago, and Barto are dead."

Luci murmured, "No!" Maia sagged over Little Grim. The baby let out a squall.

"How?" Zara was the first to sputter.

She found her voice, somehow. "The ship went down—"

"So they—?" Zara couldn't bring herself to say *drowned*.

Ximen gaped at her. "What do you mean? They aren't dead. Who told you this?"

She stared at him. "What do you mean they aren't dead?" She felt as if he had slapped her.

"I mean I've been aware of them for some time. Ever since they set foot on this island."

"Joachin is *here*? They're all here?" Above her, Alonso shuffled back and forth along his branch.

"Old Man, why didn't you say something? You'll drive me mad!" Zara released Miriam's hand.

Ximen glared at her. "When should I have told you? When you were making fool's eyes at that cook? Or when we were attacked by Jager and his crew?"

"I wasn't making fool's eyes!"

Miriam didn't have time for this. "Tell me again! That Joachin is alive, and on this island!"

"He is. In fact, he and that Inglaisi spy are looking for you right now—"

"Iago?" Luci asked breathlessly.

"With a crew of pirates." Ximen held up a hand before she cried out in dismay. "It's all right, Luci. He's fine. At the moment, he's helping with ship repairs on the opposite side of the island." He avoided Maia's eye.

"And Barto?" Maia asked, unwilling to be ignored. "You haven't mentioned him. Is my husband alive or dead?"

"I don't know," Ximen said slowly. "Barto isn't Tribe, so I can't see him."

She looked down to hide her disappointment.

Miriam glared at the parrot above them. She hadn't been this angry in weeks. "Excuse me a moment. I have things to discuss with Alonso."

He ruffled his wings.

"*Now*, Alonso." She stalked away, not caring what Papa K's people thought of her ordering a parrot.

He flew after her into the garden, beyond the ring of huts and people. She allowed him to settle on her shoulder because it was necessary. As he sprang into existence, he looked grim, even unapologetic. He shone as he always did, but his glow was much diminished.

You lied to me! she accused, confronting him.

Yes. He crossed his arms.

How could you do that? Do you have any idea how much I've suffered, thinking Joachin is dead?

He nodded. *I think I do.*

Then why?

Isn't it obvious? I was jealous! I was tired of being your errand boy, of checking up on him. How would you feel if he asked you to check up on some woman? One that he probably loved more?

Her lips parted. The thought had never occurred to her.

Maybe you might have done the same? Lied to your loved one because you're sick of it? Because all you want is to have her for yourself?

She took a deep breath. *I wouldn't have lied, Alonso. I would have admitted it.*

How principled of you. Which just goes to show, it's him you want and not me. It never was me.

She shook her head. *That isn't true. I do love you.*

Why stress the do? Why not just say, 'I love you, Alonso.' Are you trying to convince yourself?

She gasped. *It isn't like that! You know it's not!*

Choose, Miriam. Him or me.

You aren't being fair! You're both a part of my life!

I was there first.

And then you died! I didn't think you'd come back. When you did—

He was already on the scene. You couldn't have loved me very much.

I can't stop how I feel! We don't decide who we love, Alonso! We just...love!

THAT ISN'T TRUE! *He was so angry he turned molten.* There's a moment when we choose! You may not think you had a choice, but you did! I decided to love you, Miriam, after we found your friend Gaspar burned at the stake, after we fled Granad. You were desolate! And me? I was a man who had lost his faith, so instead of Sul, I chose you! It was as simple as that! Don't tell me we 'just love', Miriam! We don't! Make up your mind. Him or me!

I can't! You know I can't!

He flew off, a green blur vanishing into the tree tops. She stood where she was, too upset to call him back.

Chapter Thirty-Five: In the Wrong Place at the Wrong Time

"*I'VE USED A* compass before," Francis told Dirk.

"Good. I'd hate to think of you wandering around in circles—"

"We'll be fine," Joachin cut in. It was hard to curb his impatience.

The three of them stood beside last night's campfire. The tide was out. In the shallows, the *Raven* lay careened on her side. The crew was rebuilding her mizzen and refurbishing her worm-stricken hull. At the jungle's verge, the rasp from biting saws and the crack of falling timber was heard. Not far away, Adetokunbo sat scowling beneath a palm tree. He wasn't the only one in a bad mood.

Dirk lifted an eyebrow. Joachin avoided his look. It was already mid-morning. He had been anxious to be off, but Dirk had been reluctant to let Francis go, as any lover loath to be parted from their paramour. As far as Dirk knew, they were heading out to find the gold mine. Once he and Francis were out of sight, he would determine Miriam's position. Francis advised Dirk not to worry. With a cheery wave, he bid him farewell and they set off, taking a trail into the jungle.

As the morning waned, they didn't spend much time talking, except to stop every so often to correct their direction. Soon, the ground rose and the air grew mist-laden. They came upon a fern-shrouded stream and followed it along. After another half hour, Joachin took another reading. "Oh, no," he muttered, realizing his mistake. He should have been checking for obstacles. A direct line hadn't been the best way to go. He shared a glance of dismay with Francis. "Listen."

Ahead, the sound was faint, but there was no doubt as to what it was.

Francis confirmed it. "Waterfall. Maybe we can find a way around it?"

"Only one way to find out."

They trudged on. After twenty minutes, the jungle split and they were confronted with a deep blue lagoon, framed on the far side by a cascade plunging down a black cliff. There was no avoiding it.

"I suppose we'll have to scale that thing." Francis squinted at the cliff. "Are you up for it?"

"I'll have to be." He was mostly recovered from Don Lope's flogging, but his back was still weak. He wasn't sure he would ever recover his former strength. But Miriam lay ahead. They had to keep going.

Where the water didn't scour the cliff to rock, its walls were choked with vegetation. Mosses and ferns clung tenaciously, and a number of lianas ran its length. By the time they circled the pool, they were soaked with spray. Francis tested one of the vines. It seemed secure. "I'll climb first. That way, we'll know if it holds."

The offer stung. He was coddling him. This was his quest, not Francis'. "I'll be fine. It's my wife we're searching for."

"I know." Francis set his foot to the wall.

"Hold on!" Joachin grabbed his arm. "Didn't you hear what I said? I should go first."

Francis dropped the line and set his hands on his hips. "Look, Joachin. One of the things I've had to learn over the years is to admit my shortcomings. There's no shame in acknowledging weakness, especially if it keeps you alive. You aren't in the best of shape. I'll go first to make sure it's safe. To tell you the truth, I'm tempted to tie a rope around your waist—"

"Over my dead body!"

"Suit yourself. But I think you're being foolish."

"*I'm* foolish? I'm not the one risking my neck with a vine that might give way half way up."

"Better me than you."

Before he could stop him, Francis was clambering his way up. "He'll make it to the top," Joachín muttered, relieved he could say it. "I'll make it, too," he added, wishing he had thought of confirming it before they had had their disagreement.

The climb wasn't without its struggle, but they both reached the top without incident. He was glad when Francis offered him a hand to help him over the top. His back complained, it would take time to regain his strength, but the effort had rekindled his confidence. *I'm on the mend*, he thought. *All I need is hard work and Miriam.*

After another hour of hiking, they topped a ridge overlooking a coastal plain. Ships rode at anchor in an azure bay. A town huddled on a narrow peninsula as if rethinking the wisdom of squatting there; several roads ran though it, leading to a fortification a few leagues north. Francis squeezed his shoulder. "Puerto Real. You sure she isn't in the town?"

Joachín shook his head. "I'm sure. It doesn't make sense, but she's not." He frowned. "I wonder if she became separated from the Tribe, somehow. There. I said it. It must be true." He pointed. "We need to go that way."

They pressed on. As they descended the lee side of the slope, the vegetation closed in on them but the underbrush wasn't as dense. Unimpeded, they passed through stands of huge trees before entering a clearing with felled timber. *A man with property might do well here*, Joachín thought. This was good, fertile land. There was also the gold mine to think of. Where was *Los Buitres*? He was about to hazard a guess, when Francis stopped and clutched him by the sleeve.

Something was coming their way and making no effort to hide it.

They were too exposed. Without a word, they ran back the way they had come. There wasn't much cover. They ducked behind a fallen log just in time. From out of the trees, a troop of soldiers appeared wearing steel morions and breastplates. They walked in a line, beating the bush with pikes. They were searching for someone. The choice was to fight or run. *Not much of a choice*, Joachin considered.

Francis stood and hailed them. "Oh, thank heaven!"

Joachin stared at him in disbelief. Had he lost his mind? There was nothing for it but to stand alongside him and participate in whatever charade Francis planned. He rose hesitantly.

"Halt!" one of the infantrymen shouted, seeing them, a sergeant or an officer, judging from the ornament on his uniform.

"We're lost!" Francis clasped his hands. "Praise to Sul you've come! We've been going in circles, trying to make our way to Villa de la Via!"

Joachin kept his face carefully bland, but his heart raced. They wouldn't believe that! Francis was many things—a priest, a spy, and an efficient killer when he had to be, but *lost*? With Villa de la Via in easy sight from the peak? What a ridiculous thing to say.

"I'm Fra Francisco! We've been stumbling about for days! You see?" He patted his head. "Even my bald pate is growing in!"

It was a journey too far to belief. What was left of his tonsure suggested he might have been a priest at one point, but the hair over his skull was at least half an inch long. And his habit was long gone.

The sergeant frowned. "Even a village idiot can find Villa de la Via. It's the only road out of Puerto Real—"

"Oh, and don't we know it?" Francis twisted his hands. "This is all my fault. I heard there was this miraculous spring in the mountains, said to cure all ills. Perhaps you've heard of it? So I hired this man—" He indicated Joachin.

Joachin met the sergeant's glare.

"And he led you on a fool's mission to the find the Fountain of Youth?"

"No! He tried to convince me there was no such thing!"

"You aren't dressed like a priest. Where's your starburst of Sul?"

Francis patted his chest. "Now that really upset me! I lost it yesterday, when we were crossing a stream—"

"Spare me your lies. Last night, half a dozen sailors were murdered on their way to Villa de la Via. And now we find you two, stumbling about out here."

"How terrible! We haven't seen anyone suspicious. I'm just a simple priest, really. Guilty of pride, perhaps, but I was searching for a miracle."

"A priest who seems more a pirate or a vagabond. You both look guilty to me. You can tell your story to the governor. He'll decide what to do with you." He directed two of his guards to bind them.

"But...wait! We aren't murderers! Where are you taking us?"

"To Villa de la Via, *Padre*, where you wanted to go all along," one of the guards replied sarcastically. "Maybe you'll find your miracle there."

Three hours later, after marching through Puerto Real and being eyed by the locals, then stumbling along a plantation road between fields of cotton and sugarcane, they finally arrived, dust-choked and worn, at Villa de la Via. *Why does nothing go smoothly?* Joachin wondered. Miriam felt further away than ever. With his double talents of truth telling and dreaming, it should have been an easy task to find her. He eyed the fortress before them. It was a wooden structure with walks along the ramparts and watchtowers at each end. The gates were still open, suggesting things were peaceful this far inland. Inside the walls, a number of buildings lay, including a small chapel and the governor's keep. The sun was setting. They were taken to a jail near the stables.

"When might I have a word with the governor?" Francis asked, as they were shoved into a cell. He had dropped the befuddled priest act.

"Usually drops by to question new prisoners after his supper," the sergeant replied. "Likes to think of himself as a godly man." He shrugged, as if not understanding it.

"Can you unchain us? These are wearing." His wrists were bloody, as were Joachin's.

"No."

"Some water, then? We're out." An empty bucket sat in a corner.

"See what I can do. Anything else? A hot dinner and a fine wine, perhaps?"

"That would be nice."

"Kiss my *culo*." The sergeant closed the door on them.

Two hours passed. From their small, barred window, they watched as torches were lit near the buildings and along the fortress' battlements. Soldiers patrolled the ramparts, but they were a complacent lot, stopping to talk and share skins of water or something more bracing. Joachín tried to ignore his thirst. He lay down in the straw to sleep, only to be awakened by Francis nudging him with his toe.

"Get up. Someone's coming." Francis stared out their small barred window.

He stood to join him. From the keep, a group of five men approached. It was hard to make them out but judging from their dress, the one leading was the governor. He wore so much blue silk satin, he shimmered as he moved. Behind him, a priest and a servant followed. A naval officer and his subordinate brought up the rear.

As they passed beneath a torch, the flame revealed their faces.

Joachín muttered a curse. Francis pressed his back into the wall. Tomás hadn't realized it yet, but he had found them.

The door to the holding room swung open. The sergeant stepped in, lighting the way. The governor, a sturdy little man in teal doublet and breeches, entered, followed by the rest.

This can't be happening, Joachín thought. Beside him, Francis had closed his eyes, as if wishing he could shut out the world.

"You say you found these two near the mahogany?" The governor's voice was high-pitched and breathy.

Before the sergeant could reply, a familiar voice shouted, "Great Sul! It's them!" Tomás shoved his way past the sergeant.

"You know these men, Grand Inquisitor?" the governor asked, apparently surprised.

"Indeed, I do," Tomás pointed at Francis. "That one is an apostate priest. And that one, is a wanted assassin who tried to murder me twice!"

"Truly?" The governor sounded flabbergasted. "Why then, my men are to be commended! Well done, Sergeant!" He turned again to Tomás. "What do you suggest we do with them, Grand Inquisitor?"

Tomás' gaze was on Francis. "I don't suppose you've ever held an *auto de fé* on the island, have you, my Lord?" He smiled tightly. "I expect not, considering you've never had an inquisitor to advise you. Death by fire is appropriate for an Inglaisi spy."

"An Inglaisi spy? I thought you said he was a priest!" He sounded as if he couldn't decide which was worse to offend—Inglais or Roma.

"Oh, yes. A betrayer to Father Church in the worst possible way. Even the Papacy will have to agree with me on that account."

"And this one?" Joachín met the governor's worried glance. His eyes were a limpid blue, as if leeched from years of indecision.

"This one," Tomás said, considering him. "Yes, I've something quite special in mind for Joachín de Rivera. I'm a modern man of a scientific bent. He will undergo...what's the word?" He looked to heaven as if reaching for the term. "Ah, yes. An experiment. Something I've wanted to witness ever since I first heard of it." He turned to the officer. "With your leave, *Capitán*. If I might I borrow Noxolo?"

"Of course, Grand Inquisitor," Capitán de Carazo replied smoothly.

"Do you have what you need?" Tomás directed the question to the servant behind them. The man was tall and loose-limbed. He guffawed. The coldness of his laugh chilled Joachín to the core. "Of course, Grand Inquisitor. A *bokor* is never without his *poudres*."

"*Poudres*." Tomás relished the word. "Good. Let's do it."

"Midnight is best, when the *ashe* is greatest."

"What are you planning to do to him?" The governor looked worried. He shifted from foot to satin foot.

"It's best you don't witness it, my Lord," the captain replied smoothly. "The process is unsavory. Take him," he ordered the sergeant, pointing at Joachín.

"You hurt him, and you'll answer to me!" Francis warned Tomás.

"Oh, yes? I don't see how, when you'll be crisping on a bier." His smile was almost affectionate.

One last chance, Lys, Joachín implored as two men pulled him from the cell. *Let me rid the world of Tomás' pestilence, avenge my maré, finally! I don't care what happens to me.*

He dropped his gaze. Let Tomás think he was beaten. Even so, he caught Tomás' smug expression.

Then before anyone could react, Joachín whipped his chains over Tomás' head and squeezed hard, hoping to snap his neck. Tomás' hands flew to his throat. His eyes bulged and he began to choke. The guards were on Joachín in seconds. He was pulled from Tomás and punched repeatedly in the head. As de Carazo and the sergeant drew their swords to finish him, Tomás waved them aside. "No!" he rasped. "I want him alive!"

"Are you sure?" The governor helped him to his feet. "He tried to murder you, Radiance!"

"And he failed—again!" He waved a feeble hand at Capitán de Carazo. "Take him to wherever Noxolo directs. I'll follow, in a moment!"

"Come back to the keep, Grand Inquisitor. At least let me pour you some wine," the governor said.

As Joachin was dragged from the lockup, Francis shouted after them, "Kill him, Tomás, and I'll destroy you! See if I don't!"

They gagged him and staked him on a low, bare rise, about a quarter league north of the fortress, in a field cleared by fire. The soldiers were dismissed. Noxolo and Capitán de Carazo said nothing to him as they awaited Tomás, nor did they glance his way, but treated him as if he were already dead. His head felt full of lead, heavy and dull. The beating he had received had given him a headache, but it also brought focus. He tested his bonds. The ropes were tight. His wrists and ankles throbbed. The guards had been zealous, affording him no second chances.

Presently he heard Tomás approach.

In the moonlight, he looked like a great black bat. His face, always preternaturally pale, was bone white, save for the dull scar he bore, the wound he had given him for raping and murdering his mother. *If only I had killed him*, Joachin thought. He had been young, too young.

"Are we ready to begin?" Tomás asked.

Noxolo nodded.

Tomás knelt beside him. "I want you to know," he said, his tone light and cheerful as if they were at a picnic, "that this will be the last conversation you and I will ever have. In fact, it'll be your last conversation. Afterwards, you won't understand a thing, save for the most basic commands and the end of a stick. You'll be a beast of burden, and that is all." He smiled coldly.

"The process is quite simple. We make small incisions in your skin. Normally, we'd do it on your palms or the bottoms of your feet, but where's the fun in that?" Noxolo handed him a knife. "I'm going to place the cuts on your chest."

He flinched as Tomás ripped open his shirt.

"Just like old times, eh?" He set the blade's edge against his sternum. "I remember doing this to you in Elysir, when I gave you your truth tattoo. How did that turn out, by the way? I've often wondered."

He gasped as the knife pierced his skin. Beads of blood pooled where the blade nicked.

"There we are. Not too many, yes?" Tomás looked to Noxolo for confirmation.

Noxolo nodded. "That should be enough."

Tomás rocked back on his heels. "Now that we come to it, I feel a bit dizzy. The excitement, I expect. I'll need a tonic once we're done."

"Easily arranged," Capitán de Carazo replied. "There are many here to milk. You could do him, first." He nodded at Joachín.

Milk? What did they mean by that? Whatever it was, he couldn't let it happen.

"I'd rather save him for this."

Which meant what they were about to do was worse. He sent another prayer of intercession to Lys. *I trust you, Goddess! You made me patriarch and Miriam, my wife! Surely, this isn't the end! Show me how to destroy him!* He strained at his stakes. The peg binding his right wrist moved slightly.

A fist punched him so hard in the head he saw flashes of light. "Stop that! I can't have my prize mule getting loose."

Thankfully, a second blow failed to follow the first. Tomás must have thought he looked too stunned to move. As his eyes cleared, he saw Noxolo hand Tomás a pair of thick gloves. Tomás pulled them on and held up a small leather pouch.

"Now this," he said, weighing it in his hand, "is the really amazing part, or so Noxolo tells me. Think of it as a resurrection spell. In three days, I raise you from the dead." He drew open the drawstrings. "Just like our Lord did, for Alazurus."

He didn't have to exercise his talent as a truth-teller to know it was so. He yanked his right arm against its tether with all his might. As the peg flew into the air, he knocked the pouch from Tomás' grasp. It went flying end over end, polluting the air with a powdery, moonlit cloud.

The dust was impossible to avoid. Some of it fell on his cuts. More went up his nose. Wherever it struck, he went numb.

Beside him, Tomás sputtered and waved like a madman. The powder had touched him, too. Noxolo and Capitán de Carazo had jumped well away from the mound.

A coldness ran through his limbs, a dullness that spread everywhere save for his racing heart, but that too, was slowing—the most frightening thing of all. His lungs couldn't pull in enough air, he couldn't breathe....

He was dying, and yet, he wasn't. He was a soul trapped in wood, a puppet-man awaiting the one who pulled the strings.

Too terrible to contemplate, his mind snapped, and his fear fell away. It was winter. Beside him, a girl sat in a bank of snow. She had black hair and perfect lips. She was...he couldn't remember her name, but she was someone he had known, someone he had loved. Tears were freezing on her cheeks, little diamonds of ice. She kept crying his name, over and over. Her name was...she was....

It didn't matter who she was.

It was time to sleep.

Chapter Thirty-Six: Zombi

DIRK WOKE BUT didn't move, his back prickling, warning of an intrusion. Some instinct he couldn't name, but which had saved him many times, had shaken him awake, screaming that someone was there, standing in the room with him. He hadn't risen this high among the Brethren without sensing impending threats. He listened as if his life depended on it. The scrape of a boot or the repressed breathing of an assassin would tell him a great deal about who approached him.

No sound. Which meant his killer was of such proficiency he knew better than to leak such clues. The prickling along his spine grew frantic. His head felt tight, about to burst. He cracked an eye. Someone was nearing his bed, looming like a phantom out of nightmare. He shot his hand beneath his pillows, grabbed his knife, and rolled out of the assassin's reach.

Adetokunbo stood at the end of his bunk, his big hands by his sides.

"What do you want?" Dirk waved the knife at him. It felt inadequate.

Adetokunbo scowled in the semi-dark. "You send my *erú* and his friend off, and now they're in trouble!"

The man was irritated, his usual frame of mind. Dirk dropped his arm. "You don't just waltz in here, free as you please! There are protocols to follow! I'm captain!" He would have words with Gibbs later, see if he didn't. How the hell had Adetokunbo gotten past him? "You scared me half to death!"

The big man grunted noncommittally, making Dirk sorry to admit it. He also regretted taking the giant on. Despite Adetokunbo's opinion, Francis was not his *erú* or slave, but there was little point in arguing it. "How do you know they're in trouble? They only left this morning."

"I'm a Walker. I followed them to make sure they are safe. They are not."

What the hell was a Walker? Did he mean he literally followed them? *Impossible*, Dirk thought. Francis and Joachin would have travelled leagues by now. Some people had unusual gifts—his own sense of impending danger being one of them. Joachin was also a case in point as both a dreamer and truth-teller. "What do you mean, you're a Walker?"

"When I wish to, I send my soul from my body. It's something the kings of my tribe have always done."

Was that even possible? Ever since he had taken up with Francis, the strangest things had happened. And now, Adetokunbo claimed he could travel out of body. "Let's say I believe you. What did you see?"

"They're in a fortress, imprisoned. My *erú* was told he would undergo an *auto*—something to do with fire. They intend to turn the Diaphani into a *zombi*. I couldn't get any closer because of the *bokor* and his *djab*. We must leave at once to rescue them."

An *auto* was an *auto de fé*, the public burning of heretics, what the Esbañiards referred to as an *act of faith*. He doubted Adetokunbo knew the meaning of it. "What do *bokor*, *djab*, and *zombi* mean?"

"Poisoner, demon, soulless man! Why do you waste time asking foolish questions? We must go!"

He must have seen Francis and Joachin at Villa de la Via, the only fortress on the island. Without Joachin, there was no finding the location of the gold mine, which meant no refurbishing the ship or buying off the Brethren. Dirk ran a hand through his hair. "Fine. Awaken the men." Half of them would have to remain with the *Raven*. He would take the rest and follow the coast. Travelling the jungle at night was foolhardy. What kind of numbers were they up against? "Did you, by any chance, notice how the fortress is armed?"

"I only walk when I'm at rest. I can do that once we arrive."

Which was about as helpful as an ant assessing a termite mound. Once they were there, he could see for himself.

Miriam stared up at the rafters, hoping to see Alonso there. It had been an entire day since they had argued and he had flown off. Her heart lay like an anchor in her chest, so heavy it hurt to breathe. She felt sick, lifeless.

Have you really gone? If you have, I don't blame you. She waited, hoping for movement, but no parrot shuffled along the supports. *I love you, Alonso. I've always loved you, from the second I saw you on your death bed in Granad to now. You say loving you was my choice, but I don't know if it was. I'm sorry for your pain, and that's my fault. I never should have resurrected you, never should have brought you back.*

She held her breath, hoping he had somehow heard her apology and would return. No green blur flew through the doorway. She rolled to her side and closed her eyes against the feeling of loss. He wasn't coming back.

But if you hadn't resurrected him, a small voice pointed out, *you wouldn't have escaped Tomás. You would never have become the Matriarch of your mother's people.*

She flipped onto her back and glared up at the roof, unsure if the voice was of her own making or if the goddess was making herself heard. *And where is Alonso in all that?*

He's as much a part of your destiny as Joachin is.

A memory took shape in her mind. She and Ximen were standing near a cliff, just before the Tribe split to travel their separate ways to Qadis. 'Don't worry,' Ximen had said. 'Everything will turn out fine.' He nodded at Joachin, who waited with the horses. 'Under you two, the Tribe will flourish in the New World. Lys chose you because you're the right blend of leadership and drive, and him because of his acumen and responsibility.' Joachin's acumen had been Ximen's polite way of saying Joachín would do whatever was necessary, morals aside. 'You'll keep him in check, and he'll find ways for us to prosper.'

'What about Alonso?'

Ximen looked troubled. 'I don't know. A guide, perhaps.'

She clawed at the mat beneath her fingers. *That's all he is, Lys? A guide? If that's true, then we're all pawns, Joachín, Alonso, and me! I never asked for this!*

But you did. On a distant hilltop in Esbaña, when you and your father were on the run. You wanted to be something special, to have a place. Where your gifts as a sentidora might be appreciated by all. You chose this. And I chose you.

So Alonso was collateral damage? Was my love for him a development you didn't foresee? Or perhaps you did, and it doesn't matter?

Alonso has what he wants. So does Joachín.

At what cost? It seems we're expendable for the greater good!

No one is expendable.

Love shouldn't cost so much! I hate that I love them both!

Love is what it is.

There was a rapid scuffling outside the hut. Three bodies were outlined by the torch light coming from the compound.

"What do you want?" Ekua was barring the other two from entering.

"We have to speak with the Matriarch!" Ximen's voice.

"She's sleeping. As you should be—"

"Wake up, Miriam!" Zara called over Ekua's shoulder. "We have news of Joachín! It isn't good!"

Her heart faltered, then began beating again. She was at the door in an instant.

"He isn't dead," Ximen explained, "but at this point, I'm not sure what can be done."

"It's all right, Ekua. Let them in. Tell me what you saw," she told Ximen.

Fifteen minutes later, they sat with Papa Kodjó and Yoquibo in the chief's square hut. The brazier had burned down to coals, turning their faces ruddy. Her head was pounding, but she held on to the hope that Papa K and Yoquibo would have some answers. "If what you report is true, his condition is very grave," Papa Kodjó said. "I don't work with the left hand, but all *houngan* know how to. Can you describe this *bokor?*"

"I'm not familiar with that word." Ximen frowned.

"Sorcerer."

"You would know him from my description?"

"If he's operating in these islands, possibly. The ingredients of each *coupe poudre* will vary, but every mix reflects its maker. If I know who he is, I can guess what he's used. There lies our antidote."

"He was tall and lanky. With pointed teeth."

Papa Kodjó looked grim. "I know him. He works out of Puerto Pío."

His bleakness didn't fill Miriam with confidence. "How do we reverse what he's done?"

"We must find your man first." He shifted uncomfortably on the mat. "There's a healing plant that reverses much of the process, but it needs to be administered as soon as possible. First, the dartura must be powdered—"

"Dartura?" She had no idea it grew in the New World. Joachín had used it to heal the bite on his cheek; it was also the same herb he had traded Zara's faba beans for, when he had drugged Don Lope in Marabel.

"We know dartura," Zara said. "We call it the goddess herb."

"I'm not surprised. Here, it's also known as the *zombi cucumber*."

"*Zombi?* What is that?"

"A man who has lost his soul." His glance to Miriam was sympathetic. "What her man will become, if we fail to find him in time."

Joachín was, and wasn't, where Alonso expected him to be. He had focused on him, trusting he would find him as he had always done. *Like a fly drawn to a dung heap,* he thought. Not far from the fortress, he discovered him staked to the ground, two ankles and a wrist still bound, but one arm free. There were boot scuffs and disturbed dirt all around him. Whoever had done this had left in a hurry.

He studied Joachín closely. Joachín's torso was scored with small cuts. His chest barely rose and fell, just enough to confirm he was alive. His heartbeat was tentative, a faltering decision each time. The shining cord attaching his soul to his body spiraled off into space. There was also the trace of something unpleasant in the air. It numbed whatever it touched. Alonso drifted out of its reach.

Well, this is unexpected, he thought. What to do? He had planned to return to Miriam but had hoped she might miss him a bit more before going back. If he left Joachin now, she'd find out he had done nothing to help her precious husband. *This is what I get for opening a Pandoria's box,* he thought.

Why does she love you? Why doesn't she love just me? He glared down at Joachin with distaste. There was nothing for it but to find out what had happened and where the thief had gone.

He set a hand upon the shining cord. The world greyed and turned black, a tunnel with only the thin thread to guide him. As he had done before, he rolled and whirled with it. Finally, it brought him to a familiar terrain.

The dark land was still as he remembered it, bleak and bone-littered. Ahead, Joachin cast a long shadow in the ruddy light. He had managed to stagger up the first hill and was bent double as if under a great weight. Behind him, the vulture markers dotted the road, but they remained inert. Whatever strange laws ruling their animation no longer seemed to apply. Perhaps he had put enough distance between them and himself. Above, the sky was a blushing pink, promising hope and joy.

He's dying, Alonso realized with a start. *Whatever has been done to him will finish him off.* Oddly enough, he wasn't sure how he felt about that. It should have made him optimistic, but it didn't. He considered the mount upon which Joachin laboured. Would his cord snap when he rounded that hill? Did the Diaphani's Summerland lie there? The light beyond the crest was so bright it hurt his eyes.

I could let him go. That would solve everything. But then, Miriam would know. Maybe not at first, but she'd find out eventually.

He floated behind Joachin, torn.

"Surely, we can find our way in the dark!" There was nothing worse than being trapped between fear and hope, except perhaps, by the caution of others whose hearts weren't ready to break.

"*Madame*, the shells warn of going prematurely." Papa Kodjó glanced at the thatched wall behind which Yoquibo had retreated. "There are dangers...do you see this combination?" He pointed a gnarled finger at a cluster. "These are opposing forces which have nothing to do with us. If we wait a few hours, those powers will battle it out and smooth our way." He smiled as if offering good news.

"But what if Joachín worsens? Becomes a *zombi*, as you said he would?"

"I don't think a few hours will make much difference."

He's lying to spare me. "Please." She set a hand on his arm.

His gazed softened. "You must trust that Damballah and La Sirene will aid us in this quest. They know best."

She had already argued with Lys. She wasn't about to trust Papa K's gods or her own, no matter what he said. Sleep over the next few hours would be impossible. She fretted at the delay, but there was nothing she could do. If she set out on her own, she would get lost.

When the sun finally broke over the horizon, they made ready to be on their way. As well as Papa Kodjó accompanying them, Yoquibo assigned an escort of ten warriors to the trip, including Ekua.

"We'd come, too," Zara said, "but Ximen's in no shape to travel." Truth be told, Zara wasn't in much shape for another jungle trek either, but Miriam refrained from saying so. It was better Zara stay with the Tribe, even if Ximen was her excuse. Maia and Luci also remained. Casi had not yet come out of her stupor. Rana and Angél had left the day before.

"Of course, you must stay," she said.

"Any sign of Alonso?" Ximen sidled up to her and kept his voice low. She wasn't sure whether it was because he was uncertain Papa Kodjó knew of Alonso, or if he thought by whispering he might spare her feelings. Ximen knew of their fight.

"No." Despite being surrounded by twelve men and one wild girl, she felt alone. Joachín was in terrible danger, and Alonso had abandoned her.

"Maybe he'll come back." Ximen gave her arm a squeeze.

"Maybe." She hoped so, but she couldn't blame him if he didn't.

No bird landed on her shoulder to offer her comfort. Alonso might as well have been a thousand leagues away.

The night passed in a blur of dark jungle and waves crashing on the coast. By the time Dirk and his crew reached the plantations outlying Villa de la Vía, they were dull-eyed from lack of sleep. Their exhaustion would fade once the fighting began, Dirk knew. It had been some time since they had taken a good prize. Francis and Joachín were considerations, but the fort would have riches worth claiming. Nothing in the Articles said they couldn't skewer two guards with one sword.

He surveyed the fortress from the edge of a cotton field, then handed his spyglass to Gibbs. The stronghold was a blocky structure with cannon emplacements along the top. Four watch towers framed each corner, overseeing the road to Puerto Real.

"What d' ye think? Two dozen in th' garr'son?" Gibbs asked. The others awaited his opinion.

"Could be. Probably more." Dirk pursed his lips. The garrison might maintain as many as fifty. His crew was good, but they couldn't win over that number. They had to increase the odds in their favour.

"What you got in mind, Cap'n?"

"A two-fold plan. But first, I'll consult with Adetokunbo." He stalked into the cotton field to find him.

An hour later, shouts of alarm erupted from the south-west watchtower, followed by the frantic clanging of a warning bell. About a half league along the road to Puerto Real, the cotton field was aflame. Adetokunbo and his band had come through. The fortress guards boiled through the gates, followed by a troop manning an unwieldy water cart. Dirk and his party crouched in the field closest to the fort. He didn't expect the whole place to empty itself, but he hoped the fire would draw at least half of the guard. Already, the smoke was forming a thick cloud. As the fire brigade reached the field's periphery, Adetokunbo and his people would rise from behind them and exact their revenge. He had seen the bloodlust in Adetokunbo's eyes. The giant welcomed the chance to fight.

Now, let's hope I can find Francis, thought Dirk.

They waited a full five minutes before rushing the gate. A few more guards ran past them, unaware their security was about to be breached. In their haste to reach the fire, they left the gates wide open.

The slaughter began in the cotton field. There were shouts of alarm and howls of rage. Adetokunbo and his men were striking with all the pent-up fury they had nursed during their imprisonment aboard *La Estrella del Mar*. The fire brigade, realizing they were ambushed, tossed their blankets and pails and struck at them with their swords.

"Now!" Dirk shouted, drawing his musket. He and his men ran for the gates. Below, in the inner courtyard, several more guards milled about on horses. A small man dressed in aqua silk was waving his arms frantically and issuing orders. At the sight of Dirk and the pirates, one of the horsemen yelled a warning.

"Dear Sul! We're under attack!" the silken man cried. He turned and ran on plump legs for the keep. His men reached for their muskets and aimed at Dirk and the troop. The crack of musket fire shattered the air. A missile grazed Dirk's arm. Johnstone cried out and fell. Three of the horsemen also toppled from their saddles, causing their mounts to stamp and mill. Dirk cursed as two remaining guards drew their swords and charged his crew.

He would retrieve Johnstone later, assuming he wasn't dead. He drew his cutlass and ducked as an assailant galloped at him, then punched the horse in its flank, making it rear. "Take him!" he shouted to Gibbs. He didn't have time for this. The governor, for it had to be him, was almost at the steps of his keep. If he made it inside, it would be near to impossible to flush him out. Who knew what kind of fire power he had access to?

"Yah!" Gibbs waved his cutlass to draw the guard's attention. His attacker, having recovered, twisted about to engage him. Another of his men shot the man from behind. An old ploy. He fell from his horse.

Dirk pelted for the stairs. The governor was almost through the open door when he grabbed him by the neck and set his cutlass to his throat.

"Capitán, help!" the governor quavered. A second group of military men, Esbañish naval officers judging from their uniforms, appeared in the passage leading to the great hall. Judging from the goblets still in their hands, they had been adjacent, unconcerned about the fire and the noise. Dirk held the governor tightly against his chest. "One step more, and I'll slit his throat!"

"For Sul's sake, do as he says!" the governor whimpered.

An arrogant looking Esbañiard in a leather brigandine raised his hand to hold off the small group behind him. "You're responsible for the fire?"

"I ask the questions, not you." Dirk pressed the blade against the governor's Adam's apple.

"What do you want?"

"Nothing, providing you let us leave with our mates." Things hadn't gone as well as he had hoped. Looting was out of the question. They would be lucky if they got out with their lives. Behind him, at the gate, poor Johnstone lay unmoving.

"Have I your word on that?" the captain asked.

"For Sul's sake, de Carazo!" the governor cried. "Don't argue with him!"

The captain bowed. "You're right, my Lord. It's a mistake to think one can bargain with such rogues, but I will, to spare your life." He sneered at Dirk. "Release the governor. On my word of honour, you may take your men and go."

"We think as much about Esbañish honour as you think of ours. I'll release him once I know we're safe. I expect free passage for my men, and the two you've imprisoned."

De Carazo quirked an eyebrow. "Is that what this is all about?" He waved at a younger man. "Mateo, find Sergeant Gomez and have him release the prisoner from the lockup, assuming he isn't already dead. As for the other one...." He smiled. "You won't find him here. He's rotting in the field behind."

The governor yelped as Dirk pricked his neck and drew blood. Did de Carazo mean Francis or Joachín? "After you, *Capitán*," he replied tersely. "One false move, and the governor dies."

He followed the Esbañiards, with the governor unresisting as he shoved him along. His own crew had dispatched the remaining guards. Gomez, the sergeant, lay dead beside Johnstone. They left Johnstone where he was. Mateo, the young Esbañish lieutenant, retrieved the keys from the sergeant's dead body. Dirk waited while the Esbañiards released a dour Francis from the lock-up. *Thank Sul*, he thought, relieved he was all right. It was a shame about Joachín and the lost gold, though.

He demanded horses and got them. Then he took up the rear with the governor tied to his back as a shield. Mateo sat, similarly tied to Gibbs. "I have others awaiting me," he warned de Carazo. "Any attempt at a rescue, and the governor and lieutenant die. Hold up your end of the bargain, and I'll release them in the town."

De Carazo gave him a mocking bow. "Gods' speed. May you burn in hell." Some of the fire brigade had managed to escape Adetokunbo's fury. They had fled back to the fort, relaying tales of disembowelment and human torches.

"Sul preserve us!" the governor muttered.

Dirk smiled grimly. It had never occurred to de Carazo that he and Adetokunbo had worked as equals in this enterprise. Such a notion was beyond him. He glanced concernedly at Francis. He wasn't sure what lay behind his grim exterior.

"We have to get Joachín," he said tersely.

"Forget him. He's dead." Dirk kicked his horse in irritation. He had nothing to show for his effort, save Francis, who, even now, seemed less than appreciative. They had had a fine liaison so far, but was it worth it? As for Adetokunbo and the ex-slaves, there was no way of knowing if they survived until everyone rendezvoused at Turtle Bay. To add to his frustration, the governor slumped against his back.

"What the hell?" he muttered.

"He's fainted, Cap'n," said Gibbs.

As they watched events unfold from the jungle's edge, Papa Kodjó's augury proved true: the forces of which it had spoken were the guards from Villa de la Vía and a band of renegade slaves. The men, who Yoquibo had never seen, cut down the fortress guards with such viciousness even Ekua was impressed. The girl offered Miriam details, taking great delight in describing the eviscerations, beheadings, and burnings, even after Miriam told her to stop. Shortly after that, Miriam saw Francis ride out with several men she didn't know—rough types. Francis didn't appear to be a hostage; he wasn't tied as the two others were—a disheveled little man in silks and a disgruntled boy. Joachín wasn't among them.

But then, he wouldn't have been. Ximen had told her where they would find him.

"We can go now," Papa Kodjó said as the last of the soldiers fled for the fort. "They're regrouping. It's unlikely we'll be seen."

Under Yoquibo's direction, the band skirted the verge and made their way some distance behind the fortress. The land had been cleared for planting. In the middle of it, a lone figure lay on a lumpy knoll. She gave a low cry.

She sprang from the wall of trees before Yoquibo could stop her. It didn't matter. No one shouted a warning from the fortress walls.

He was still alive. His chest rose and fell slowly. Wounds dotted his torso, half of them scabbed, but some festering. He stared at the sky, his eyes bloodshot and his pupils huge.

"Joachín," she said softly. He took no note of her. She held her breath and set a hand to his cheek. He winced as if her touch were painful. She might have been a bird pecking his hair, or an ant biting his face. He continued to stare at the sun.

Horror rose inside her like Death approaching on a white horse. *A man without a soul.* What Papa Kodjó had said he would become if they didn't reach him in time.

"Bring him." Yoquibo directed four of his men. They removed his ropes.

She grabbed Papa Kodjó by the arm. "He needs the powder! Now!"

"Once we're away." He was uneasy. They had to retreat before they were seen. Her heart pounded. "Gods! Have we come too late?"

"Don't upset yourself unnecessarily, *Madame*. We will know, once we're in the trees."

As the men hoisted Joachín between them, she followed closely behind. The band didn't pause until they were well within the forest. When they finally stopped, they spread a mat on the ground and set Joachín upon it. Papa Kodjó shook his *asson* rattle and muttered prayers. Yoquibo told her to step back. He and his men arranged themselves about Papa Kodjó and Joachín, their spears at the ready. She was about to demand why, when Ekua warned her not to interfere. Within the ring, Papa Kodjó applied the dartura to Joachín's cuts.

Then he slammed the small pouch over his nose and leapt back. Ekua pinned her by the arms.

Joachín howled and lurched to his side as if struck by lightning. In seconds, he was on his feet and springing at the man closest to him, his fingers curling into claws. Two men leapt on his back, while the others struck him repeatedly with the shafts of their spears.

"Stop!" Miriam cried. Why were they beating him? She struggled to free herself from Ekua. The girl was holding her so tightly she was cutting off her circulation.

"It is *la fureur!*" Papa Kodjó shouted. "The first effect! He will desist in a moment, when he realizes who his masters are!"

"His masters?"

"With luck, he's not so far gone!"

Then as suddenly as his rage began, Joachín cowered and shielded himself. Yoquibo's men withdrew. Papa Kodjó approached him. "*Monsieur,*" he began.

Joachín moaned. He kept his arms about his head.

"You're safe, now. *Comprenez vous?*"

Miriam glanced between them. As Ekua released her, it felt like an admission of failure. She took a tentative step towards Joachín. "*Querido?*" she asked.

He had been trembling, but at the sound of her voice, he stopped shaking. She approached him tentatively. "It's Miriam. I'm here. Don't be afraid. You've been through a terrible ordeal."

She drew his hands from his face. He let her do it, but he stared at his feet.

"Joachín!" she cried, wanting him to look at her.

"I'm sorry, *Madame,*" Papa Kodjó said dejectedly. "Even had we reached him last night, I don't think it would have made any difference. It may be that time will cure him. I will ask Damballah for help."

"He is *zombi,* now," Ekua said unnecessarily. Miriam expected to see a cruel exultation in her eyes, but there was only resignation.

"I apologize once more, *Madame,*" Papa Kodjó said, "but we must tie him to make him follow. Otherwise, he'll wander."

The idea offended her. "You won't! I'll lead him! By the hand!"

"It's better if he's tied. Right now, his mind is like a child's. He understands basic commands, but—"

"He's *my* husband! I won't have it!" She knocked Ekua aside as she bent to tie a noose about Joachin's waist.

Ekua whirled about, her black eyes sparking with challenge. "You're my responsibility, *blanca*. As *zombi*, your husband is my charge now, too. I'll strike you, if I must." She was tense with anticipation. Her fingers twitched. She would do it. She wanted to.

"*S'il vous plaît, Madame.*" Papa Kodjó clasped his hands in supplication.

Her throat grew thick. This was their world; Papa K knew what was possible for Joachin, and what was not. There was no point in arguing with him. Unable to speak, she bowed to their wishes and stepped back.

They returned to the camp with Joachin tied to her waist. She refused to accept this might be his permanent state. Anger sustained her, that hard bulwark against which despair struck at her defenses, seeking to slay her with hopelessness. *Time may heal him*, Papa Kodjó had said, and whatever Lwa he might convince. Surely Lys hadn't brought them all this way, only to have Joachin reach the New World with no more sense than a beast.

Later that night though, her anger abandoned her and she fell victim to her fear. She had been strong in front of Zara, Ximen, and the rest, had endured their dismay at what had been done to Joachin. But now, her eyes filled and she wept into her sleeping mat so as not to upset the others. Tears spilled down her cheeks, leaving tracks that burned. Her chest heaved, her heart was near to breaking. Unless a miracle occurred, Joachin was lost to her, forever.

Alonso had also forsaken her.

What was the point of living, with both of them gone?

Chapter Thirty-Seven: One Body, Two Minds

JOACHÍN NO LONGER struggled, he no longer walked. Rather, he stood where he was, staring at the dawn as if it were glory ascending. His silver cord held him fast, stretching taut behind him down the long dark road.

He might stay this way for years, Alonso thought. *I could finish what Tomás began. It would be the merciful thing to do. But Miriam would never see it that way. On the other hand, if Joachín agreed to it, he could tell her it was his last wish.*

He hovered at his ear. *You're in a bad way, my friend. Tomás did something to your mind. You're in limbo, no longer moving. It might be better if you die, go on to your Summerland. I can snap your tether so you can finish the journey. It's that, or you being a burden to Miriam for the rest of your days. Do you want that?* He waited for him to answer.

Joachín remained as still as a corpse. He wasn't even sure he breathed.

Alonso persisted. *She'll grieve, of course she will. But I can watch her live, and age, and finally, be with her when she passes. Through all of that, I'll never forsake her. And then, she can be with you.*

It was a bit of a question as to where he might end up after Miriam died, but he wouldn't worry about that now. Sul had said when he could no longer take life's pain, he would return to the god. Joachin continued to stare at the sunrise. Had he even heard?

Alonso floated in front of him. *Damn it, man! I should have what you had! A life, a body, the chance to be complete! For a time, you had her and it was good! You loved her as you wanted! And I....* He scoffed as he considered it. *You're worse off than me, now! You're not even living a half-life! If I can't have her, why should you?*

Still no answer from Joachin. He was about to turn away when Joachin blinked. *Is that a yes?* he demanded. *Do want me to help you?*

Again, there was no response. Joachin stared past him at the rising sun. Fury rose up in Alonso in a violent rush. He would awaken him, make him choose! He shook him hard by the shoulder. At the sudden contact, a surge of energy filled him, flushing his anger. It revitalized him, made him feel whole in a way he had forgotten he had ever been. Joachin let out a gasp.

My god! Alonso marvelled. *He felt that! He and I...together! We could both...!*

Joachin didn't have to die or remain as he was. *And neither do I,* thought Alonso.

It meant the joining of forces, of being intimately connected. It wasn't as if they hadn't done it before. Together, they had defeated Boyle. He had actually enjoyed working with Joachin to taint the pirate's mind. If he and Joachin shared a body they might have enough spirit between them to be whole. It would mean personal sacrifices for them both. They would have to work out the logistics of spending time with Miriam, but finally, they would each have what they both wanted. A full life, a shared life—with her.

Alonso clutched him by the shoulder a second time. It took a sustained contact to finally bring Joachin to full awareness. At first, he frowned as if he didn't recognize his surroundings. His gaze kept drifting back to the sunrise.

Snap out of it, Joachín! We need to get back to Miriam! I can help with that. It means we live together...in your body. I did it with her, and I can do it with you.

Alonso? He had recognized him at last. He glanced about. *Why am I here?*

Tomás drugged you. He's tried his best to destroy us, but we can fix that. For Miriam's sake.

Miriam! I have to get back to her.

Yes. We both do. But the only way is if we share your body. If we don't, you'll stay here and eventually make your way around that peak. Once you do that, there's no coming back.

You came back.

That was different. I never made it to the Summerland. I ended up in a strange halfway place, where I pleaded with Sul to let me return. You don't have that option. You only have me.

He took a deep breath. *All right. Let's do it.*

You're sure? You know what you're agreeing to?

Yes. We share my skin. The question is, do you realize what it means?

He meant their love life with Miriam. But he would have those privileges, too. *I do.*

Then let's find our way back to the woman we love. How?

We merge, become like twins in a womb. Then we follow our cord back. I expect life will be confusing at first. We'll work it out.

Joachín opened his arms slowly, as if to reluctantly welcome him. *If that's the way it has to be.*

That's the way it has to be. Alonso stepped into his embrace.

When Miriam awoke in the hut, Joachín was gone.

She sat up with a start, feeling colder than she had in weeks. With him beside her, she had been desolate, but at least she'd been warm. Papa Kodjó had warned her of this. As long as Joachín's spirit remained in limbo, he would search for his soul. *Zombis* wandered. Nearby, Luci and Casi slept. Ximen and Zara snored on the other side of the hut. Had no one heard Joachín leave? Panic spurred her to run for the door.

Ekua wasn't at her post, but as if answering to a summons, she appeared around the side of the hut. Her eyebrows rose, seeing Miriam in the doorway.

So much for being an efficient bodyguard, Miriam thought. She wasn't in the mood to be fair. Joachin must have slipped past Ekua without her seeing. Fear made her sharp. "Where have you been?"

Ekua frowned at her tone. "Seeing to my needs. Why? What's your problem?"

She brushed past her. Joachin couldn't have gone far.

Ekua stared after her, baffled. Then understanding dawned. "I told you to tie him! Why didn't you do what I said?"

Miriam spun about. "Why didn't *you* see him leave?" Another unreasonable expectation, but she didn't care.

"Wait!" Ekua followed her. "You'll never find him on your own."

"I lost him once before. I'm not about to lose him again." She ran across the compound. Maybe in his muddled state, he had taken the least difficult route. That meant following the path to the garden plot.

"I can tell you right now, he didn't go that way."

She turned around. Ekua was studying the ground. It was anyone's guess as to how she was able to make out Joachin's scuff marks from everyone else's with only one torch lighting the compound.

"These are recent." She looked up and pointed. "He went that way."

The trail led them past the bushes the tribe used for a toilet area and came to the small stream's edge. On its opposite side, Ekua found a fresh footprint in the sand. Beyond it, broken blades of grass bent along a nearly invisible game trail.

"Joachin!" Miriam called out.

Ekua grabbed her by the arm. "Don't be stupid!" she hissed. "He won't stop just because you yell! If any *blancos* are nearby, you've given us away!"

"There are no *blancos*. The sentries would have seen."

A branch snapped ahead, followed by a thump. Something big had fallen in the undergrowth.

"Joachin!" Miriam shoved Ekua out of the way.

"Stupid *blanca*! It could be anything! A snake, an iguana, even a croc come up from the mangrove! Go ahead and kill yourself! See if I care!"

In a small clearing, she found him. He had stumbled over a root and had fallen face first to the ground. She rolled him onto his back. His nose was bloddied. She wiped away the red as gently as she could.

Ekua came up behind her. "So, now you have him. You see why I told you to tie him down? Maybe next time, he won't be so lucky. He's a danger, not only to himself, but to us."

She wished she would stop talking, stop ignoring her feelings. Was this how it was to be? Joachin spending the rest of his life with no more sense than the village fool? They would have to bind him, direct him, and see to his most basic needs. Tomás and his *bokor* had robbed him of his life. *My life, too,* she thought. *They've destroyed my happiness.*

Nothing of Joachin remained. He had a body that breathed, a heart that beat, but the soul of her dear, sweet husband was gone.

She crumpled over him, the pain of loss so great it finally slayed her. There was no recovering from this. Her heart was shattering into a thousand tiny pieces, and nothing would ever put it back together. She might as well be dead. Then without warning, a rush of energy surged through her, chasing away the despair. For a moment, she was suspended in space, no longer broken, but whole. Actually, she was *more* than whole—she was one of three. Her heartbreak vanished in the wake of awe. Alonso twirled about her, and Joachin spun about him. They were together, all of them—alive! All her senses flared at once. She heard bird song, smelled orange blossoms and beeswax. She tasted manna, that sweet bread of life, as if Joachin and Alonso had brought it with them from a blessed land. Then Alonso receded, as if stepping back. The world reformed about her and Joachin. She felt cool air on her skin, and the earth beneath her feet. She opened her eyes.

Joachin gazed up at her. "Miriam," he whispered.

He saw her, he knew her! She let out a cry and wrapped him tightly in her arms.

He kept his arm about her waist as if he would never let her go. Alonso jostled for position, so at times it was he she held. The whole experience was unsettling, if not slightly arousing, but she didn't care. She would deal with that later. The two had come to an accommodation. She was bursting with happiness, overflowing with joy.

"Wake up!" she shouted to everyone in the hut. "He's back! Joachin is himself!" Alonso was back, too.

Zara sat up and stared at them in astonishment. "Can it be? What magic...?"

"*Hola*, Zara." Joachin smiled down at her.

"Oh, my dear, dear boy!" She clasped her hands. "You're back to yourself? Is it really true?"

He nodded. Ximen's pale eyes widened, and then he barked with laughter. "The *two* of you! Sworn enemies! I never would have believed it!"

"What are you on about, Old Man?" Zara glared at him. "Miriam and Joachin are no more enemies than you and me!"

Miriam wanted to laugh. It didn't matter what Ximen said, Zara would find fault with it.

"*Not* Joachin and Miriam. Joachin and Alonso!"

"What?" Zara gazed up at the rafters. "I don't see his parrot anywhere."

"Dear Lys, you're well, Joachin?" Luci kept glancing between him and Miriam.

"Yes, and we can thank Alonso for it. If not for him, I wouldn't be here."

Nor me, you, Alonso said.

In her mind's eye, she saw Alonso smiling. She squeezed Joachin, hugging them both. They were being so magnanimous with each other.

"How did it happen? Tell me all about it!" Zara patted the empty spot beside her and Ximen.

Joachin pulled Miriam down with him. "You all know how Alonso used to animate near-dead animals—"

A small voice interrupted him. "Did you have to stop the voices too, Joachin?"

Everyone paused to look at Casi. It was the first thing she had uttered since their attack on the road to Villa de la Vía. "I feel better now you're back. *Hola*, Alonso," she added, waving at Joachín sleepily. She curled back onto her side.

"Sweet heaven! She speaks!" Luci said.

"Why shouldn't she? What happened to her?" Joachín frowned.

There were awkward words and phrases as everyone tried to explain without really explaining. They feared Casi would go back to whatever refuge she had created, Miriam knew. Alonso told him. *She murdered a sailor who meant her harm. Knifed him through the eye when he tried to attack Luci. It sent her into a trance.*

"We didn't know how to reach her," Luci whispered. "She's been through so much."

"We've all been through so much. Why don't we get some sleep?" Miriam suggested. "We can talk about it in the morning." She wanted to hear from Joachín's own lips what had befallen him since they parted. Alonso had told her some of it, but he had misled her, too. Who had poisoned him? Had Tomás been involved? The renegades who attacked the fortress, did Papa Kodjó and Yoquibo know them? They had to plan their future, but for now....

It was still a few hours before dawn. Everyone settled down to sleep. Joachín snuggled against her back. She turned in his arms, not wanting to lose sight of him for a second.

"*Cielo.*" He ran a finger along her cheek. She sucked in a breath. It had been so long since they had been together. She wanted to love him, but they lacked privacy. They would find time for it later. But she could kiss him. The Tribe would expect that. It didn't matter if Zara watched.

His lips were soft, warm, and wonderful, his kiss deep and tender. She relaxed into it, savouring him. She closed her eyes, and....

...found herself kissing Alonso.

Her eyes flew open. Joachín smiled ruefully. He knew. For that one brief moment, she had shut him out. When she closed her eyes, he had had to step aside. And now, Alonso was doing the same, allowing Joachín precedence, making room for him.

"*Sí, mi amor,*" Joachín murmured. "This is how it will be."

He was resigned, but accepting of it. Beneath his forbearance, there was an undercurrent of unhappiness, an unsettledness that was Alonso.

"I love you," she told him.

"I love you, too. More than I ever thought possible."

She closed her eyes. *And I love you too, Alonso.*

I know. I just wish you didn't love him as much.

Joachin was listening. Of course, he was. With her eyes closed, Alonso took the forefront, but Joachin was still there as if he were standing in the same room with his back turned. The situation was difficult, but not impossible. They would endure it, tolerate it for one another.

Alonso kissed her again. She found she wanted him to. They had loved in spirit once, in Elysir, so long ago. The memory of it set him ablaze. His eyes deepened to that of a perfect summer's sky. She was his dove, lost in that boundless blue.

She kissed him passionately and set aside any regrets. She would love them equally. Alonso was her day, and Joachin was her night. One followed the other in quick succession. Neither could exist, without the other. It would have to be. If one failed, then they all did. Life as they knew it would end, their world of three, gone forever.

Chapter Thirty-Eight: A Second Reunion

"SO THAT'S WHO they were!" Papa Kodjó shared a glance with Yoquibo and then regarded Joachin. "Pirates from your ship. I wonder if we shouldn't send a delegation, get a sense of their intentions."

"Would they be welcome, here?" Miriam linked hands with Joachin. She sensed Alonso, as well.

"Only if they're willing to bow to my authority," Yoquibo said. "It's never wise to have too many chiefs in one village. But if this Adetokunbo is reasonable...."

"I don't know that he's not. But I must return there to collect my kinsman," Joachin glanced sidelong at Luci, "and his woman."

"Woman? What do you mean, *woman*?" Luci's eyes widened.

"It's a long story. As I understand it, she's Adetokunbo's niece."

Luci looked more taken aback than ever, but said nothing. Miriam glanced at the diverse group of people about them. Yoquibo was Tain, one of the original inhabitants of the island. Papa Kodjó had come from the western coast of Afrik. The adults were of one ethnic type or another; many of the children were a mix. This would be the island's future, a growing and heterogenic population. It appeared Iago had already embraced that change.

"I also need to rescue my travelling companion," Joachin said. "The Grand Inquisitor threatened him with burning. They're holding him at Villa de la Viá."

"We think he escaped," Yoquibo said. "Before we rescued you, there was an attack on the fort. The governor rode out, accompanied by several rough men. We think they kidnapped him to ensure safe passage."

"If your friend was among that company, will he return to your ship?" Papa Kodjó asked.

"Most likely."

"Then it makes sense for you to reunite with him and your kinsman where they are."

"Can you provide me with a guide?"

"Yes, considering who your wife is, but I must consult the shells."

"Considering?" Joachin glanced at Miriam.

Papa Kodjó smiled. "Your *femme* is a very powerful queen, *Monsieur*. Two Lwa, Damballah and La Sirene, rule her head. Was it not she who broke the *coupe poudre's* hold on you? Even after the dartura failed?"

That wasn't Miriam, that was me, Alonso pointed out.

And we're grateful, Miriam told him.

"Is my husband still alive?" Maia asked. She was anxious for news of Barto. Through Alonso, Miriam caught a flash of Joachin's memory—a blood-soaked deck, the flare of a musket, a hot ball whizzing past his face. Barto had tried to kill him. And then, a man she didn't know, shot Barto in the back. She suppressed her shock as Maia waited.

"He died a hero, defending me," Joachin said woodenly. "I couldn't save him. I'm so sorry, Maia."

Luci set her arms about her. Miriam murmured her sympathies along with everyone else, but secretly, she was stunned. How could Joachin lie?

He didn't. I did. Alonso's need for credit had a prickly edge to it. She suspected he was finding it difficult to share a body and a wife.

"How long will it take us to get to Turtle Bay?" Joachin asked after Luci had drawn Maia aside.

"It isn't far." Yoquibo set his hands on his thighs. "As long as we avoid trouble, we can get there by nightfall."

"Let us consult the shells," Papa Kodjó suggested. He threw them. Whatever the pattern was, it reassured him. "There should be no problems."

Odeh, his wife, spat. "I see nothin' but trouble when a *djab's* shorin' a body." She gave Joachin a dirty look and left.

"*Djab?*" Joachin was taken aback. Papa Kodjó looked embarrassed.

"Odeh is an obiu-woman," Yoquibo explained. "Like your wife, she interprets the wishes of the dead."

So, they know about Alonso, Miriam realized. Again, she was taken with how similar their people were to hers. They both shared a tradition rich in magic and tattoo, a belief in spirits and the gods. Yoquibo and Papa Kodjó had accepted her, and by association, every member of the Tribe. Except Odeh, maybe.

"I'd like to leave as soon as possible," Joachin said.

"Of course. Odeh and the women are seeing to our needs."

That surprised her. As much as Odeh disapproved of them, she still bowed to Yoquibo's wishes.

Half an hour later, they set out. Luci and Casi came along, Luci insisting she couldn't wait to see Iago, and that the hike would do Casi good. Miriam suspected it also had much to do with meeting Iago's new love. Ekua came along as usual, with half a dozen warriors and Yoquibo as well. Papa Kodjó begged off, saying the previous day had tired him. Zara and Ximen remained in the camp.

"Are those two...? Joachin asked, as Zara and Ximen waved goodbye.

I'd lay coin on it, Alonso said. *With us gone, they'll have the whole hut to themselves.*

The idea shocked her. *They can't!* Miriam sputtered. *They're too old!*

Joachin chuckled. *You forget, Zara has a way with potions. They may be getting on in age, but they aren't dead.*

I'm dead! Watch your mouth. Alonso's annoyance flared.

Sorry, Joachin muttered.

Why does everything seem brighter, so much more colourful when one is happy? Miriam wondered. She had given up trying to keep track of the number of greens she saw. There were viridians and emeralds, jades and chartreuses, even a flowering plant with lime and yellow flowers. The jungle was alive with bird call. She felt like singing too, and she never sang. *If I started I might never stop. Everyone would think I've gone mad!* She smiled at the thought and glanced at Joachin who walked alongside her. He was so tanned. His hair was longer and thicker than she remembered. He was still so handsome, in spite of everything he had been through. *Maybe, even more so,* she reflected. There was a graveness about him she had never seen before. He smiled suddenly, banishing that thought.

"What is it?" She felt shy suddenly. Happiness made one transparent.

He squeezed her hand and kissed it. "We're together, here. Me. You. It's a miracle."

"Yes." Her throat grew thick.

He set an arm about her shoulders. "And I'll build us a new home. Just like I promised."

Home. Such a beautiful word when it meant a place to be with the ones you loved. They would never return to Esbaña. They would stay on Xaymaca and amalgamate both tribes. Unless Tomás became a threat.

"It'll take some time." She watched his gaze move over her eyes and lips. She was certain he wasn't speaking of houses now, but of something more immediate and intimate. "It's been too long. We'll start tonight."

She blushed.

Unless I have something to do about it, Alonso countered.

Joachin's face tightened. He glanced away, but kept his arm possessively about her. She was going to have to find a way to segregate them, to establish boundaries. On the other hand, maybe it wasn't up to her, but to them. They would have to work it out. She loved them both so much.

After another few hours, the troop stopped to eat, then pressed on. As the afternoon drew to a close, they heard the crash of surf.

Yoquibo called a halt from beyond the periphery of where they thought sentries might be posted. Joachín was to proceed from there; the crew of the *Raven* knew him.

"I'll go with you," Miriam said. They had been apart for too long. She wouldn't be separated from him.

"If she's going, I'm going, too." Ekua swiped at a liana as if its presence offended her.

"And I want to see Iago." Luci held Casi by the hand.

"We can't *all* go!" Joachín replied, exasperated. "If they see a group, they might shoot first and ask questions later. I have to approach Dirk alone." He gave Miriam a look; she read his plea in it: *don't argue*. She couldn't dissuade Ekua from accompanying her, so she conceded.

"Fine. We'll wait here," she agreed.

They watched anxiously as he made his way through the trees. Ahead, there were shouts of alarm, then cries of surprise and welcome.

He reappeared ten minutes later. "Come on!" he told them, beckoning. "There are people who are wanting to see us." He smiled at Luci and Casi. Luci set a hand to her heart.

Iago wasn't the only one happy to greet them. Francis was overjoyed. "Will miracles never stop?" he demanded. "We thought Tomás had finished you! And now, you're here!" He studied Miriam briefly and then glanced back at Joachín. "You're sure she's your wife and not Rana Isadore?"

"It really *is* me, Francis," Miriam reassured him. "It's wonderful to see you."

"And you! I'm beside myself with joy!" He turned back to Joachín. "How did you manage it? Dirk said you were dead."

"I was. Or nearly so. Tomás drugged me. But Alonso brought me back."

"Alonso?"

"It's a long story."

"And Tomás?"

"We aren't sure," Miriam said. The mention of Tomás was always sobering. "From what our Rememberer relates, we think he may have been stricken by the same drug he used on Joachín."

"Rememberer?"

"One of our gifted. He relives the memories of our people."

"You Diaphani are amazing. Joachín returns from the dead, and you have the ability to change your appearance at will! My god, the things you could accomplish for Inglais! Name your price. Ilysabeth will throw titles at your feet."

"We aren't for Inglais, Francis." Joachín set an arm about her waist. "We've had enough of Temple and State. We want peace and quiet. A farm, or a mill, perhaps. We intend to settle here, on Xaymaca."

"I see. Well, we'll discuss it, later."

She could see he hadn't given up on his hope. Francis turned to Yoquibo. The cimarrón chief had worn his gilded collar and pendant for the occasion. Golden hoops hung from his ears. He had dressed his hair with the red feathers of some exotic bird. "And this distinguished person is?"

Miriam introduced him. "This is Chief Yoquibo. He's come to ask what you intend on his island."

Francis made him a small bow. "Thank you for indulging us, my Lord."

His deference seemed to mollify Yoquibo. "You are *jefe*, here?"

"Ah, no." Francis smiled. "That would be the captain. He's speaking with the men at the moment. He'll be right here."

Adetokunbo had come up while they had been talking and now confronted Francis. "What you do, here, *erú?*" he demanded, as if thinking Francis might be ready to run off. He glared between him and Yoquibo.

"Excuse me." Francis looked a bit rattled. "Allow me to introduce... this is Chief Adetokunbo. He leads the ship's freemen. Ah, thank Lys. Here's Dirk."

The captain approached them with a wide grin splitting his tanned face. He had a refined manner about him, Miriam thought, but there was something calculating in his glance. Behind him, all work on the ship had stopped. Instead of oakum and pitch, the crew held muskets and swords.

"Joachín! Thank Sul you've returned to us! And a party of warriors, too."

"Yes, thank Lys for that. We had to come tell you. And collect Iago, as well."

"Collect him?"

"Yes, his place is with us."

"I see. So you're leaving?"

"That was my intention."

It was an odd exchange. Dirk showed no amazement at Joachin's return to life. Nor did he question how it might have happened. He eyed Yoquibo's men as if determining the odds. "Iago *did* sign my Articles," he reminded him.

"True. But they only apply at sea. Now that you've made landfall, I expect you'll offer new contracts."

Dirk's smile became even broader. Miriam suspected he didn't like being bested.

"Oh, come now, Captain," Francis said, intervening. "We can live without Iago, if we must. Besides, now that we're reunited, we should celebrate! Chief Yoquibo here has asked about our intentions. Let's reassure him and treat him as our honoured guest. Perhaps he can offer us information about the lay of the land." The two of them exchanged a significant look. Joachin shifted uncomfortably.

They haven't forgotten the gold mine, Miriam thought.

"Good point, Francis." Dirk clapped him on the shoulder and then spread his arms as if to embrace them all. Behind them, the crew relaxed. "Come! We have food and sherry aplenty on the ship. Let's enjoy it! We have much to talk about to our mutual benefit."

Despite his joviality, there was something devious about his manner. The Tain chief shifted uncomfortably. *Yoquibo senses it, too*, Miriam thought.

An hour later, they sat around a communal fire, some fourteen of them from Yoquibo's tribe, and twice as many from the *Raven's* crew. Miriam trusted Francis, but she didn't like the thought of Dirk turning against them. Musket fire and swords outmatched spears and machetes. Joachin was tense as well. What had he told Dirk and his men about the *Los Buitres* gold? She expected the conversation would soon turn to it. Joachin must have suspected it, for he forestalled it with a question to Francis.

"How, on earth, did you escape from Villa de la Vía? I thought Tomás was planning your picnic."

Francis smiled grimly. "I have Dirk to thank for that. He and Gibbs sprang me. Wallace, too." He nodded thanks in their direction.

"But that ain't th' best part," Gibbs added. "We ride into Puerto Real, like we's a personal escort to 'is Importantness. Cap'n gets a room for th' guvnor an' th' kid. We tie 'em up real good. Tell th' servin' girl downstairs, th' guv ain't to be disturbed 'till mornin'. We have a few drinks, an' then, we're off for Turtle Bay, ridin' back in style! Cap'n lifted th' guv's purse, too!"

"Stingy bastard. There wasn't much," Dirk said.

"So, you left them tied and gagged?"

Miriam smiled. Joachín had always loved hearing the best parts of a story twice.

"Just as he says." Wallace nodded.

"What about Tomás?" Francis asked.

Dirk took a drink of his sherry. "We don't know. We hoped you might tell us."

"I don't remember much. He staked me to the ground. Set a pouch of a foul smelling powder to my nose. I knocked it away, but it affected me. I think it did something to Tomás as well."

"The *poudre* is dangerous," Papa Kodjó confirmed. "Those who work with the left-hand take precautions."

"Yes. Capitán de Carazo and his servant kept well away," Joachín confirmed.

"What a handsome pendant that is, my friend." Dirk pointed at Yoquibo's golden collar. "Did your people make that?"

"It's been in my family for generations." Yoquibo eyed him coldly. "Handed down from chief to son, for as long as we remember."

"I see. Is it Xaymacan gold?"

"Yes. Once there was gold on Xaymaca. Sadly, no longer."

An uncomfortable silence fell. Dirk gave Yoquibo a measured glance as if he didn't quite believe him. Miriam sensed his frustration. He felt cheated and wanted to blame someone. Despite his courteous demeanor, he was as rapacious as any pirate rumoured to be. *He also considers himself Yoquibo's superior*, Miriam thought.

Francis paled. Only now, had he seen it.

Joachin spoke up. "I was told there is a gold mine at a place known as *Los Buitres*. I've seen a map."

Yoquibo gave a bitter laugh. "Yes. *The Vultures*, your Esbañish name for it. You confuse reality with the myth. There was a mine once, but the gold is gone. Twenty years ago our people were forced to mine that vein. Under whip and torture, we laboured day and night, clawing the gold from the rock until our hands bled. When we fought back, the Esbañiards tied my father to a stake and disemboweled him before my mother's eyes. They left him there, for the vultures to finish. Then they gutted all the men and snatched babies from their mothers' breasts, smashing their heads against the very stones we moved. I was too young to be seen as a threat. They took me and sold me as a slave. Eventually, I escaped and tracked down the man who butchered my father. He had kept this collar as a memento. It reminds me, every day, of who we are up against and what we have lost."

"And the myth?" Dirk hadn't been moved by his story.

Yoquibo smiled. "When a man dies, he walks a path guarded by *los buitres*, or vultures. If he passes them, he arrives at a holy place. A fountain, where the waters of eternal life flow."

Dirk raised an eyebrow. "The Fountain of Youth?"

"You *blancos* call it that, yes."

"Fascinating." He took another sip of his sherry. "There are many such stories. Although the addition of vultures is a new one on me. Seems convenient, don't you think? Monsters to scare away those who would search for the gold?"

"Perhaps there are other sources of gold on the island, Captain," Joachin said.

Dirk considered him coolly. "Perhaps."

"You needn't doubt me. I'm good to my word. I promised you a share of the gold. It may be that this mine is depleted. If I find another vein, I'll honour our pledge."

"Will you." It wasn't a question.

Miriam tensed. Dirk wasn't happy. He had been counting on the gold, perhaps intending to force the ex-slaves and Yoquibo's people to mine it. They weren't evenly matched. If a fight broke out, no one would be spared.

"I didn't mislead you, Dirk," Joachin said. She sensed Joachin feared the same thing. "I believed what I said was true. The only mistake I made was not to confirm it."

"He *can't* lie," Francis reminded him. "Remember, your grandfather's boots? He had no way of knowing you stole them, yet he told you what you'd done."

She had no idea what they were talking about, but apparently, Dirk did. His nostrils flared. He reminded her of a shark, scenting blood. "Say it!" he ordered, glaring at Joachin. "Say, *the mine is dead."*

Joachin swallowed. "The mine is dead."

"Damn!" Dirk swung a fist at the starry sky, then rose and strode about the circle. "Well," he said at last. "I never wanted to be a miner, anyway. Roving is more my style." The tension about the fire eased. "Let's drink to future success, whatever it may be." He sat down.

Miriam clutched Joachin's hand and closed her eyes. Alonso sprang to life, superimposed on him. *Do you believe Dirk?* she asked. *Is he no longer a threat?*

I think Joachin's convinced him—for now. Look at Casi.

Casi had been staring intently at Dirk, but now, she seemed less troubled. Luci rubbed her shoulders, as if the heat from the fire was not enough to keep her warm. Unaware of the passing threat, Iago and Femi snuggled nearby.

Alonso vanished as Joachin took precedence. "I think we can rely on Casi," he whispered. He had heard their exchange. "Later, I can ask myself."

"Ask yourself?" She stared at him.

It seems his ability as a truth-teller has developed of late, Alonso said.

They would discuss it later. *Are we safe for the night?* That seemed the bigger concern.

I believe so. Casi will hear, and Francis remains loyal. Despite what Dirk wants, I don't think Adetokunbo will attack Yoquibo's men. They've both suffered too much at the hands of the Esbañish.

Ekua had crossed the circle and now looked down on them like a disapproving governess. "You should sleep," she said. "We return in the morning. Don't fear for yourselves. I'll keep watch."

Miriam glanced up at her, surprised. "What about you?"

"When it's your turn I'll awaken you."

When it was *her* turn? Didn't she trust Joachin?

She sees you as the powerful mambo, not him, Alonso said.

"Let's make the best of it." Joachin stood.

He led her through the trees. They re-emerged onto a secluded part of the beach. Ekua followed them, but she allowed them their privacy. Beneath a palm tree, they fell into each other's arms, hungry for each other's touch. It had been too long. She closed her eyes. Alonso appeared.

My love, he said, startling her.

She had expected Joachin and feared she had shut him out. Then she worried she might offend Alonso.

It's all right. Alonso held her tightly. *We've worked it out. He's agreed to retreat for now. Just keep your eyes closed, and everything will be fine. You'll be with me.*

Are you sure? Are you both sure?

What else can I be, where you're concerned?

He drew her into a deep kiss. It was the strangest thing. She knew she was kissing Joachin, but with her eyes closed, it was Alonso she felt. His body was larger, his arms longer, his lips not as curved as Joachin's. His kiss was harder and firmer, as well. After a moment, she relaxed, savouring the taste of him. It was easy to be persuaded.

If we had been able to love in life, it would have been like this, she reflected. They had had one night in Elysir. Their joining had been pure energy, a melding of spirits. But this! It was physical, wonderful, rich! She flushed beneath his caresses, grew hot wherever he touched. Her clothing seemed to evaporate. The night should have been cool, but it wasn't.

So long ago she had wanted this, a different path—she, born into a noble house, and he, a lord. The fantasy excited her even more when she imagined him wearing armour, returning home from a crusade. It was as if he tossed his helmet and greaves aside, to love her, erase all those years that had passed.

He was about to climax. She wasn't there yet, but she didn't want to stop him, didn't want to make him wait. She opened her eyes to take him in.

It shut him out.

Tears streamed down Joachin's face. He had witnessed it all, her fantasy, her desire; he had seen her loving Alonso as if they were sharing the same bed. Her heart broke at the hurt in his eyes. He had been through so much. How could she have ever thought this joint loving was possible? She might as well have taken a lance and pierced him with it. She moaned in remorse, but he wouldn't have it. His mouth found hers.

In shock, in shame, she stared into his eyes and sought forgiveness. His gaze held her captive. *It doesn't matter what you've done,* he seemed to say. *We have no choice. I love you. I always will.*

She kissed him hard, needing to reassure him that she loved him as much. His pain vanished and his passion soared. His fingers burned across her back, her hips, her thighs. She clawed at him, wanting him to finish what Alonso had started. Together, they soared, higher, faster. And when he achieved that final peak, she reached it with him. Brilliance flooded her. She pinwheeled into space embracing pure light, only to float gently back to the earth. He had taken her to heaven and back.

Ekua found them some time later, asleep in each other's arms. After the heat of their passion, the night was cold. If Ekua knew what they had been about, she gave no hint of it. "It's your turn to take watch," she said, glancing down at them.

"Fine," Miriam replied. "Give me a moment to straighten myself."

"I'll keep you company," Joachin said.

Chapter Thirty-Nine: The Burden of Mortality

HOW COULD YOU DO THAT TO ME?

Alonso's reappearance not only startled her, but knocked her out of reality. She and Joachin had been sitting against a palm tree keeping watch, their fingers entwined. Now, she was in a place so bright it was hard to see. His edges kept blurring, his expression terrible, an archangel bent on destroying the world. His blue gaze pierced her like lightning.

YOU CHOSE HIM OVER ME! YOU OPENED YOUR EYES, AND THEN....

A small cry escaped her lips. *I...I didn't think. I'm sorry! Forgive me! I didn't mean to hurt you! I wanted to share the moment with you—*

YOU SHARED IT WITH HIM! *It's always with him, always with Joachin!*

I love you both!

NO, YOU DON'T!

He broke into great wracking sobs. She felt as if she were suspended in the middle of a tempest at sea. Everything was thunder and water, blurry and hot. He alternately shimmered and burned, drenching her in his despair.

I can't do this, he stammered. *I thought I could, but I can't. I see that now.* His gaze pierced her. *Sul told me— if mortality ever becomes too great a burden for you, you will return to me. And it will be forever!*

This wasn't happening. She couldn't breathe. Was he actually going to leave her? *Don't*, she pleaded, sensing what was coming.

Can you not see how impossible this is? I can't have you without having him. And in having him, it destroys me!

She reached for him. For a moment, Joachin was in her arms, the physicality of him overwhelming Alonso.

NOT YET, YOU THIEVING BASTARD!

Both men wavered, one appearing over the other in a bizarre battle of back and forth. Joachin appeared to be asleep, unaware of the struggle occurring. Alonso fought and grappled with him, finally shoving him aside.

Don't you see? He heaved for breath. *Every time you choose him, I die a bit more! I thought I could handle it, but I can't. And then, you, you...pushed me away, you were with him....*

She clutched at him. *I won't make the same mistake again!*

You will, because you won't be able to stop yourself! And every time you do, more of me burns away beneath his passion. Eventually, there will be nothing left of me but ash! He'll grow stronger as I weaken. He'll return to what he was, and any afterlife I might have had will be gone. Sul's offer will fade! I'm less now, than I was....

He stared into the distance, as if contemplating the sun. For there *was* a sun, now. With a start, she recognized where they were. This was the void they had come to before, that halfway place where they had last seen Inez, the woman who had claimed to carry Joachin's child. The sun was a portal, but an inexplicable one; space stretched and turned on itself, here. She had thought they had been standing on something solid. She was wrong.

Sul warned me. I refused to accept his offer, because I wanted to be with you. But I can't do that any longer! Not without cost.

We'll work it out, Alonso!

How? Can you promise me you'll never be intimate with him again? He won't accept that. Even if he did, he'd see you choosing me over him. He would come to hate you.

Do you hate me, Alonso?

Never.

For a moment her heart stopped beating. Time, it seemed, had paused. They were caught in this instant until one of them made a choice.

I think I understand now, Miriam. I've denied the natural order for too long. Death is as much a part of the cycle, as life is. I admit, I doubted. But I've finally found my faith. If I leave you, I will re-enter that great march of creation. I think it holds something even more amazing than the love I have for you.

The admission hurt.

I put that badly. That isn't quite right. He regarded the brilliant portal rippling before them, a massive molten doorway to whatever lay beyond. *I think wherever that takes me expands who we are. It will broaden the love I feel for you. If I take these last steps, I'll become more than I ever was. And eventually, you will join me there. Whatever the pains and losses we've suffered will be made right. Or they'll make sense. Maybe it means another chance at life. I have no way of knowing, until I go.*

Alonso, don't! I need you! I can't imagine life without you!

We come into life, parting from it. We leave that way, too. But it's only for a moment, my love. I'll be with you, but in a different way. I believe this now, more than ever.

I don't have your faith, Alonso! What if this is all we have? What if I never see you, again?

I don't think that's possible. Sul is patient and kind. I trust him.

She stabbed a finger at the gigantic sun. *You think that's Sul?*

Part of him. He gestured at the white void around them. *All of this is part of him. Behold, the crucible of creation.*

It isn't all about creation! What about the goddess?

I don't know, Miriam.

But if you go—

Yes, if I go, Joachin will no longer be whole. I'm sorry. He'll return to the same state Tomás left him in. I can't help that. Eventually, he'll come here, too.

The thought of losing them both panicked her. She wanted to clutch at him, to plead, *don't leave me!* He hadn't yet gone, even if the storm of his anger had passed. Now, he waited for her to decide. Even now, she could see he was fading. He would diminish, a torch burning out if she begged him to stay. If he went, Joachin was damned to a useless, shambling state for the rest of his days.

She was dying inside. He expected her to choose. He had sacrificed himself for her once, and he would do it again. But this time, it would cost him everything.

She loved him. She loved Joachin. Joachin would suffer, and so would she, but Alonso was suffering now. It meant letting him go and caring for Joachin for the rest of his days. She couldn't snuff out Alonso, her bright angel, as if he had never been.

She was crying so hard she could barely see. *I will love you, forever.*

And I, you.

Go. Before I think only of myself and beg you to stay.

He beheld her, as if needing to hold on to her memory for all time. Perhaps he wasn't as sure as he claimed. Then he turned and stepped into the light.

The sun flared and then faded to a distant beacon on a far hill. The dark land disappeared. There was no sense of falling through unimaginable space this time, just a coldness that buffeted her like an uncaring wind. Eventually, that faded too, and she felt her body harden, her muscles complaining from immobility. When she found the courage, she opened her eyes to a dark, tropical night. Overhead, a half-moon shone, like a door half closed. Joachin was slumped against her shoulder, as inert as dirt. Soon, she would get up and lead him by the hand. She would have to explain his relapse to the Tribe, that once again, he was beyond help.

She leaned against him, feeling numb.

Alonso and Joachin.

The two men she had loved more than life were gone.

With dawn, came the discovery of what had happened to him. As expected, Luci and Casi were stricken. There was little she could do to comfort them. Iago vowed vengeance on Tomás. Femi failed to soothe his tears. Francis was bleak, and Dirk abashed. There was no more talk of secret gold mines or veiled hints she might know of their whereabouts. Even Ekua was grave.

"You have to tie him, Missus," she said, holding out a length of rope. There was no scorn in her voice, now. "You don't, and he'll get lost on the way back."

Wordlessly, she accepted the rope from Ekua and tied it about Joachin's waist.

The journey back to the camp was not the trip it had been to the bay. Yoquibo and his warriors moved slowly for Joachin's sake. Luci and Casi flanked him, while Iago and Femi followed behind. Francis elected to stay with Dirk; he wanted to return to Inglais, but he promised Miriam he would send her word of his whereabouts. There was an inn in Puerto Real—*El Ancla*—The Anchor, that would hold his mail. He hoped she would write him as well.

Midday, they stopped for a short meal. She despaired when Joachin lacked even the sense to eat. When Ekua forced his mouth open, only then did he chew. When he was done, he stared into the jungle slack-jawed.

At sunset, they arrived back at Yoquibo's camp. Miriam had to endure a second round of questions and Zara being upset.

"There must be something we can do for him!" Zara looked from Ximen to Papa Kodjó.

"I'm sorry, *Madame*. There's very little. In cases as bad as this, sometimes the poor soul dies before his time. It's the best we can hope for."

After supper, she led him to the privy before he soiled himself. At the stream's edge, he stood mutely as she adjusted his clothes. He urinated with no more awareness than a beast in the field. The moon had risen above the trees. He stared at it, as if fascinated.

"Come, Joachin," she coaxed. Would this be their legacy? She leading him through basic bodily functions while he stared at the moon? She took him back to their hut, suffering Zara's continued insistence that there must be something they could do. Luci remained silent while Casi cried. Miriam pushed Joachin down on their mat and lay beside him. His breathing levelled out. She listened as he fell asleep.

A shadow passed by their door. Ekua. As always on the watch.

Joachin stood on the hill, staring at a magnificent, orange sky. If he made it around the summit, he could finally rest, but the road was proving difficult, every step an effort of will. How many times before had he been here? He had lost count, but each time he had come a little closer to his goal.

He lifted his right foot. It felt weighted down by the world.

He strained, gritted his teeth, and tried harder. *Yes! There!* Dust rose from where he had set it.

Now—for the left.

"Missus!"

Miriam woke with a start. Joachin wasn't beside her on their mat. Two shadows filled the hut's doorway. A smaller one, straining to hold back a larger. Ekua and Joachin.

"He was trying to wander! I told you! You have to tie him, even when he's sleeping! Otherwise, they just go!" Ekua sounded strained, exasperated. Unlike the night before, she had managed to stop Joachin from passing her, but he shifted awkwardly from foot to foot. He stared over her shoulder at the fire in the compound.

Miriam was at their side in a moment. She grabbed him about the waist. "I'm sorry! I'll explain it to him." She searched his face, hoping for any sign he might know her, but there was none. He seemed intent on the flames, beyond.

"Joachin?" She shook him gently and stopped herself from gripping him too hard out of grief. He blinked once, then paid her no heed. A line of saliva had dribbled down the side of his mouth. His slackened expression tore at her heart. There was no explaining anything to him. She wasn't even sure he heard her, or if he did, that he understood. She wanted to scream, to let out all the devastation and loss. She could do that. She could fall to pieces in front of Ekua, lie in the dirt, curl up at his feet. She could give up.

Except Joachín would never give up. He would take her collapse as an opportunity to step over her and shamble off to the gods knew where, bent on whatever quest still gripping his dull mind. And instead of remaining a weeping mess, she would rise because that was what her life was now. She was his keeper, his nurse. She swiped at her eyes and clutched at him before he could move. *No complaints,* she reminded herself. *I've lost Alonso, and I'm not about to lose Joachín, too. Whatever is left of him, I'll watch and protect. And if I have to leave for a private moment to scream out my hatred at Tomás for what he's done, I will.* She took a ragged breath to compose herself, conscious Ekua had been watching her the whole time.

They returned him to the hut. Miriam pressed him to the mat, telling him to lie down, and oddly enough, he obliged. Perhaps some moments were better than others. "Joachín," she whispered. "You have to stay with me." She caught him by the chin and forced him to look at her. He considered her briefly. Then his gaze drifted to the thatched roof above them.

She squeezed her eyes shut to keep from crying. It was easier to remember how much she hated Tomás instead falling prey to self-pity. Tomás had burned her father; he had stabbed Anassa; he had slaughtered many members of the Tribe. He had murdered Joachín's mother, Estrella, so long ago. Joachín vowed he would collect her death-debt. Another promise never to be fulfilled. Why did loved ones have to suffer and die? Why did the gods allow such evil to exist? *It seems all we can do is to mop up the blood afterwards*, she thought. She settled at Joachín's back and held him as if she would never let him go.

The next morning, she sought out Papa Kodjó. As she crossed the camp, she sensed a shift in the emotional climate. Her own Tribe seemed forlorn, sad, not only for Joachín, but for the men they had lost. Joachín had reminded them of it. Other than Ekua, Yoquibo's people avoided her eye. She didn't understand it.

"It's because he is *zombi*. Usually, they're malefactors who have offended the community somehow. This isn't your husband's case, but beliefs die hard," Papa Kodjó said.

"Is there nothing we can do for him?"

"I may have spoken too soon, yesterday. There's always hope. Unfortunately, I don't know exactly which *coupe poudre* was used. With some *zombis*, it must be re-administered."

"And if it isn't?"

"The *zombi* grows more aware of whom he is."

"But that's a good thing!" She clutched at that hope.

"Not always. If he realizes what he's lost...." Papa Kodjó looked uncomfortable, then put a bright face on it. "The more you interact with him, the better it will be. It will keep him docile and obedient."

"I don't want him docile and obedient! I want him back!"

"I don't know if that can ever be, *Madame*, but I'll appeal to Gran Bwa for you. He rules the forests and the herbs. He can be wild and unpredictable, but he's also benevolent and loving."

"Thank you."

"You should also pray to Damballah and La Sirene. They rule your head, so trust them! They will hear you."

Damballah and La Sirene—other names for Sul and Lys? If so, they weren't to be trusted. Her involvement with the gods had brought only grief and pain. Their divine vision of the future wasn't hers. If Lys had chosen her to lead the Tribe to the New World, the price had been too dear. Why did *the greater good* always seem to involve personal sacrifice and no reward?

For the remainder of the day, she worked alongside Ekua, Luci, and Casi in the cassava patch. Joachin stood with her, tied to her waist, as brainless as a scarecrow. She tried to engage him by explaining what a hoe was, if only to remind herself not to give up hope. When she set it in his hand, he gripped it for a few moments, then let it slip from his fingers. He was more interested in the birds. At noon, he drank from their water gourd, his mouth swallowing as they held the calabash, but he made no effort to hold it for himself. By mid-afternoon, the day had grown hot. Yoofi, Ekua's little brother, swayed and slumped to the ground. Ekua gathered him in her arms and felt his head. "Oh, no," she muttered.

"What is it?" Miriam ran to help, pulling Joachin after her.

"He's burning with fever. I can't watch you, tonight. I have to take care of Yoofi, keep him separate, until we know what's wrong."

"Too much sun?" The boy's face was flushed.

"Maybe, or some kind of bite. You'll be on your own, watching your man. Don't let him prowl!"

"I won't."

"You'll tie him?" She hefted Yoofi into her arms.

"I'll tie him."

"All right, then. I'm counting on you not to disgrace me."

"I have Luci and Casi to help."

Ekua glowered a final warning and then crossed the compound.

Later, as they readied themselves for sleep, Miriam tied Joachin loosely to her ankle. She couldn't rely on her fury with Tomás as she had done the night before. Her anger had fled; the void replacing it was worse. Alonso was gone. She would never speak with him again, they would never touch. She might hold Joachin, but he was lost, too.

So am I, she thought. *I'm nothing now, but an empty, barren shell.*

The admission triggered a memory. She and Joachin were on horseback, riding to Marabel. He turned to her in the saddle. *Last night, I had a dream,* he said.

A stab of pain gutted her, puncturing the desolation there. Tears filled her eyes. She cradled herself against what was coming.

I dreamt we had a son.

She let out a low cry.

He was beautiful, Miriam, with a mass of black hair....

This was the memory that had carried her when life seemed desolate. Lys had even altered it, making Joachin call her by name, to offer her hope. But the goddess broke promises. Now she would never carry Joachin's child.

She wept at his back, making no sound. If Luci or Casi were aware of it, they made no mention, nor did they try to comfort her.

Chapter Forty: Love Never Forsakes

HE HAD NEVER seen such a wonderful dawn. The sky was opening like a blushing rose. A few more steps, and he would be around the peak to behold the sun.

He started forward. Someone had secured a rope to his foot. He reached down and untied it, thankful it was easy to do. The black road stretched behind him, the boulders no bigger than dots. He was closer to the sunrise than ever. If he reached it, he would find... himself.

Because he wasn't himself. He didn't remember how it happened, but he knew it was so. He wasn't part of that other life he lived, that dream of women and gardens and flitting birds. This place was real. He needed to reclaim himself. His soul waited for him behind that peak. And along with it, a fuller, more completed life.

But it was hard.

He strained to lift his left foot. This time, it didn't budge. The closer he had come to the summit, the more difficult it became. Why? What was holding him back? He couldn't see the barrier, but it was a terrible weight, burdening him, keeping him down. Was it his old life? His mortality? If so, let him be done with it. He couldn't remain as he was. He had to press on.

The woman from his dreams. The woman in the garden, today. She had been so sad. Was she even real?

Insight stabbed him through, as sudden and as sharp as a knife. The blush of a cheek in morning light, lashes closed over eyes that were brown and deep, brimming with compassion or sparking with fire. The competence of cool, steady hands as she worked, and hot, eager ones when they loved. The sway of her hips when she walked, her feet kicking up dust. They had gone so far, this woman and he. She was... who was she?

He ran his tongue over his lips, and tasted nectar. Mmmm. Yes, that was it! Mmmmm. She was like that. Mmmmm. Miriam!

The sudden sweetness turned bitter. Everything that had passed between them came crashing back. Their love, their marriage, their flight from Esbaña. And finally, what Tomás had done to him. Dear Lys. What good was he as a husband to her now? He was little better than an animated corpse shuffling through his days, leaving her to feed and clean him, to see to his most basic needs. This thing that had been done to him—it made him a burden.

I don't want her to care for me like that. I don't want her to have that life.

With that, there was a release, as fresh as freedom, as giddy as flight. He lifted his foot; it was weightless. He took a step, and then another until he was flying around the slope. He would free Miriam, he would free himself, leaving the pain of lost love and a spent life behind. In no time at all, he was around the summit. A huge sun confronted his eyes. It was immense, a door to a new life, perhaps? There was only one way to find out. He took a deep breath and leapt. The sun caught and swallowed him—

—And then it condensed and flattened, shifting from a blinding white to a vivid green. Vertigo assailed him, the scent of myrtle filled his nose. There was dampness on his skin and the sound of water splashing. He landed beside an immense fountain, its brilliance refracting a million shining rainbows through its spray.

The thing seemed made of living light, of glowing alabaster, only slightly denser than the liquid erupting from its crown. As the water gushed, it invigorated the air. A flash of movement caught his attention. On the far side of the fountain, a woman strolled, a white cockatiel upon her wrist. With every splash of the fountain, she changed, presenting a new face, a different body. Sometimes she was young, and sometimes she was old. In every incarnation, she was beautiful.

She smiled, whispered something to the bird, and set it aflight. It swooped over his head. Then she studied him. As their eyes met, there was a sense of enormity about her, as if her body contained a world too great for him to grasp. His legs gave out and he toppled over the fountain's edge. Water closed over his head. Bubbles streamed past his face, ampoules of life. The water was as white as milk.

Drink, Joachin.

He couldn't see her, but he felt her presence all about him, swirling, rejuvenating. She *was* the Fountain as much as she was the woman, the eternal feminine, the mother divine. He could do no less than what she bid. Water rushed into his mouth, coursed down his throat. He had thirsted before, but now he was filled. Life was his in abundance. She carried him along, a leaf in a river in spate.

Love never forsakes.

With those last words, a blinding white overwhelmed him. He lost all consciousness and was washed away.

The dream was a strange one. A white bird filled her mind, its black gaze mesmerizing. Miriam had the oddest sensation it was trying to tell her something. She awoke with a start. The hut was dark—and cold. Joachin's spot was empty. Her heart stopped, then started again. The length of hemp she had tied about his ankle remained on hers, but his end was undone. Luci and Casi still slept. Ximen and Zara snored.

Somehow, he had had the wit to remove the rope, and now he was prowling somewhere in the jungle. How could she have let it happen? Ekua had warned her. She should have tied him to her waist.

She rose quickly, not knowing where to look. The torch lighting the compound had burned down to almost nothing. Beside the hut, there were no scuff marks in the dirt. She clutched at her necklace, hoping it might bring her inspiration but none came. She hoped

Papa Kodjó would forgive her for taking the torch. She set off in the direction he had gone the night before.

The torch helped, but there were no fresh footprints at the stream's edge. She clawed at her hair in frustration. Joachin wouldn't be watching where he was going. A snake might bite him, or a crocodile attack him if he made it as far as the mangrove. She didn't think he could wander that far.

She was about to concede to failure, to get Ekua, when a white flash caught her eye.

It was the small bird from her dream. It sat on a branch of plumeria, one of the few pleasant things she had encountered since coming to the island. Both bird and bush cast blue shadows in the torchlight. The flowers' perfume was spicy, invigorating. It hinted of paradise. *A cruel joke*, she thought.

The bird fluttered to her right. She ignored it and trudged along. The jungle closed around her. She had the distinct impression she was going the wrong way when the bird appeared again, a streak of white. For a brief second, she wondered if it might be Alonso. She lifted a hand to it, but it flew in the opposite direction to where she had intended to go. Not Alonso.

She turned around and trudged on. The bird had lit upon another tree further ahead. Coincidence? Ephraim, her dear father, had accused her of not believing in them. Other than bashing about in the dark, she was out of options. Weren't birds blind at night? This one didn't seem to be bothered by the darkness at all. It flew as if it knew exactly where it was going.

Maybe it does. Very well. She would follow it.

They arrived at another Ceiba tree, this one much smaller than the giant in the compound. The bird flew into its branches. As she rounded the tree, two legs stuck out from behind the trunk.

She gave a low cry. Joachin lay at its base. He was either sleeping, or he had fallen and knocked himself unconscious. She set the torch down carefully and cradled his head. As far as she could tell, he hadn't injured himself, but his hair and shoulders were wet. A small spring welled beneath him, forming a freshet, before trickling into the underbrush. He had stumbled on top of it, falling over the tree's thick roots.

She held him tightly, thankful he was alive. He stirred. She leaned away from him so he might breathe.

He drew in a sharp breath as if coming up for air. Then he opened his eyes.

He focused on her and swallowed.

"Miriam," he whispered, sounding hoarse.

"Joachín?" Her heart thudded in her chest. She wasn't yet willing to believe he had returned to himself, that he had intended to call her by name.

"*Mi cielo*," he murmured. What he had always called her. *His heaven.* "Is this the Summerland?"

He was himself, again. Her paradise.

She caught him in a crushing embrace. "It must be!" she cried.

Chapter Forty-One: The Colour of Eternity

MIRIAM STARED OVER the deep blue water to where ocean and sky met. The morning was calm, the day hot. She and Joachín had left the compound so they might exercise Fidel. They had also wanted some time alone, but that was a contradiction in terms. Ekua had joined them. Fortunately, she had taken Fidel to investigate a sand spit around the point. The tidal offerings were good there. Treasures often washed up from storm-struck ships.

I feel as if I've been washed up, myself, Miriam thought.

"What are you thinking?" Joachín ran a finger along her arm.

"I'm just wondering what we might do, now that we're here." She toed the sand at her feet. "We can't keep relying on Yoquibo and his people, Joachín. We need to do something for everyone's benefit. The trouble is, we have no money. For land, for crops, for anything." They had once talked about setting up a cotton mill or finding the secret to the true red dye. Back then, the future held so many possibilities. Now, not so much.

He stared at the horizon. "That's true. I've been giving it some thought." He clasped his hands about his knees. "So...I asked myself."

She turned to him. "You asked yourself?"

"Yes. We haven't had much chance to talk about my new ability. Alonso must have told you."

She winced. *Alonso.* Even the mention of his name hurt. She glanced up to find Joachin regarding her somberly. "It's all right. Go on."

"You know I can only tell the truth. But there's more to it than that. If I say something aloud, it's also true, even if I don't know for certain if it is."

"I'm not sure I understand. What are you saying?"

"I'm saying, there *is* gold on Xaymaca."

"But you told Dirk the mine was dead."

"It is. But there's still gold to be found here."

She straightened. "Do you know where we might find it?"

"Not yet. But I will. I just have to pinpoint where. And when I do, we can have that plantation we want, or a cotton mill, or invest in a ship for exploration. I can even pay *Ser* Olivares back his investment money."

"What about Dirk? You said you'd pay him his share."

He made a face. "Well, I don't know where he is now, do I? If I don't know how to find him, I can hardly give him his due."

"You could ask." She smiled at him.

"I could. I'd rather not."

They shared a laugh. He *had* changed, but not so much that the old Joachin had disappeared entirely. She had changed, too. She wasn't sure for the better. "What about Tomás?" A cloud occluded the sun.

"He's no longer on the island."

"But he's still alive."

"Yes, but no longer a threat to us. He's on his way back to Esbaña."

"Too bad for Esbaña." She squeezed his hand. It was so good to be with him; she didn't deserve such happiness. He said Lys had saved him, that the goddess had undone the damage caused by the *coupe poudre.* "Tell me again how it happened," she implored. Perhaps there was a hint in what he said about Alonso. Had the gods intervened? Had Sul granted him peace? If so, she might forgive herself.

Joachin's eyes grew distant. "There was a fountain. I fell into it. I lost all sense of direction and limit, other than I swam in it, a tiny jot of life. As I floated, Lys was there with me, all around me. She told me to drink. And then she said, *Love never forsakes.*"

She couldn't speak. She had forsaken Alonso.

Joachin squeezed her by the shoulders. "I know what you're thinking. You didn't sacrifice him, Miri. You freed him, gave him the chance to go on."

They had spoken of this before. He had tried to reassure her then. "Am I so transparent?"

"You are. To me."

"It might have been a selfish thing on my part. Easier for me to tell him to go, so I didn't have to keep choosing between the two of you."

"Do you really believe that?"

For a moment she didn't speak. Did she? Had self-interest prompted her? She had loved Alonso. She hadn't wanted him to suffer, or to cease existing as if he had never been. But there was guilt there, too. She still felt its prick.

"You let him go, knowing you'd have to care for me. In the state I was."

She met his eyes.

"I can't think of anything harder, Miriam. To let someone you love go, and to stay with someone you thought was already gone."

He always knew the right thing to say. The thorns of her self-reproach receded. "But to what did I free him, Joachin?"

"For that, we'll never know until we round that final mount ourselves. We have to believe it's something for which we're meant. *Love never forsakes*, Miriam. I'm a living example of that. I know it's true, with all my heart."

The goddess had saved him for a bigger purpose, or so he believed. Lys had always wanted him to lead the Tribe. They were doing that now, in this New World where the Diaphani had a chance. Others, as well. Yoquibo's people had a new opportunity, too.

She had only seen a small portion of the greater picture. Joachin insisted there was more.

They heard a *whoop*. Ekua appeared with Fidel, dragging something long and wooden behind her on a rope.

"I better go see what she's found," Joachin said.

Miriam remained where she was. Where sea met sky, there was a thin line, a membrane separating ocean and air. *What lies beyond it?* she wondered.

Alonso's eyes had been so blue.

A white gull cut across the sky, it wings beating steadily. Some said gulls were divine couriers, carrying messages between heaven and earth.

Goodbye, Alonso, she whispered as it flew away. *I will love you, forever. Until we meet again, as the gods will.*

The gull disappeared into the distance.

Ekua had found a bracken-strewn and sand-washed figurehead. Its eyes were wide and staring. Its body leaned forward, one arm extending as if to welcome the future, the other behind it, as if linked to the past. Despite the water damage, it seemed the embodiment of hope.

Was that a sign? Ephraim, her father, had once accused her of not believing in signs. She smiled at the memory.

Why not? she thought.

Chapter Forty-Two: The Last Word

A FEW MONTHS later and on an overcast day. Miriam and Papa Kodjó made the journey into Puerto Real. Joachín didn't accompany them. The Tribe, or rather, both tribes, for the Diaphani and Yoquibo's people had amalgamated, seeing it advantageous to both, worried he might be recognized by the soldiers from Villa de la Vía. The *cimarrónes* from Yoquibo's tribe bore local brands, so they couldn't go. Papa Kodjó, having fled from Esbañiola originally, was able to pass as her servant, although they were equals in all things. Miriam had two tasks to attend, the first being a visit to the local assay office. Not far from the original mine, Joachín had found gold. The community had panned it in secret, working the stream. Miriam hoped the nuggets were enough to buy land.

The second task was to see if any mail awaited her at *El Ancla*. She didn't think it likely, but Francis was resourceful. If he had written, it would be good to know how he was.

The assay office lay at the corner between High and Tower Streets, thankfully away from the docks. The last thing she wanted was to draw attention to Papa Kodjó and herself. Luck was with them. The street was nearly empty. No one was in the office, other than a sweaty and rumpled clerk.

His eyes widened at the sight of her cache.

"Where did you get this?" he asked in amazement.

"My business, not yours. I'd like you to melt it down to assess the value."

He shrugged. "As you wish."

"How long will it take?"

"Two days. If you're thinking to trade it for land, I can also act as your agent, make inquiries regarding an *encomienda*."

She wasn't interested in any system requiring slave labour and a tribute to the crown. What they did on their own land was their business, but taxes were unavoidable. The assayer seemed to have both ends of the gold and land market tied up. She had no choice but to trust him. She couldn't resist reminding him though, of what would transpire if he thwarted her. "I may not look a woman of means, but I represent a group who would not take kindly to being swindled. Or reported."

Papa Kodjó glared at him, as if to back up her threat. His scrutiny unsettled the clerk. If he had had any ideas in that direction, she suspected he changed them.

"As I said, *Sera*. I maintain an honest enterprise, here. I only seek your continued business. I will, of course, expect my cut for the service." He was sweating profusely.

"How much of a cut?"

"Seven percent of the estimated value."

Seven seemed a bit high, but if it bought his silence, she could live with it.

"Very well. I'll have your written confirmation of our transaction, here."

"Of course." He weighed the nuggets and scribbled the gross weight on a note. With that in hand, she and Papa Kodjó swept out of the office.

They headed down Tower Street, which ended up near the Mole, made their way along the quay, and came at last to *El Ancla*. The place turned out to be one of the cleaner inns along the waterfront. Francis had chosen well.

She slipped inside and found the innkeeper sweeping a broken jug into a bin. "Can I help you, *Sera?*" he asked.

"Yes. I understand you collect and hold overseas mail? I was wondering if there might be a letter for me."

"Your name?"

"Miriam Medina, or rather, Miriam Medina de Rivera." She wasn't sure which name Francis might use.

The innkeeper grunted and set his broom against the wall. He left her and Papa Kodjó standing in the dark entryway. He returned a few minutes later with a gravy splattered missive. "Just says *Miriam*," he said.

She put out her hand to retrieve the packet, but he kept it, eyeing her. "It'll cost you."

"Since when are we required to pay for the king's mail?"

"Since I say so."

"I don't have coin. But I will in a couple of days."

He quirked an eyebrow.

"Please," she added. Sometimes, mead went further than brine.

"Oh, all right. But next time, I'll expect coin."

"Thank you. Next time, you'll have it."

He handed her the packet.

Out in the sunshine, she broke the wax seal and unfolded Francis' letter.

> *Dear Miriam,*
>
> *I'm penning this from the deck of the Raven. We're in Tenerifa. It reminds me of our time here. You'll never guess who I nearly ran into! The Grand Inquisitor. Tomás isn't himself. He was visiting an herbalist. He can't walk. They carry him about in a sedan chair. What he did to poor Joachín he did to himself. One side of his body is paralysed. The other side twitches. He mumbles and drools. From what I could learn, his mind is whole, but he's trapped inside that ruined body. Evil begets its own! Ha!*

> I'm returning to Ilysabeth. You can send correspondence to Hartfield Palace via any ship making for Inglais. I do wish you'd join me. Perhaps we can find a cure for Joachin. In any event, let me know how you are.
>
> Much love, Francis.

She sighed and tucked the letter into her bodice.

"Good news?" Papa Kodjó asked.

"Mostly," she replied.

Two days later, she returned to the assay office in Puerto Real. Joachin, against all cautions, had come with her. He kept his hat pulled low over his face. They had ridden Fidel in case they needed a quick getaway.

"*Sera* de Rivera!" the assayer said enthusiastically, recognizing her. He dropped his voice, even though no others were about. "I've wonderful news! The gold you brought melted down to two hundred and ninety troy ounces! I've evaluated it at just under three hundred and fifty thousand *soltars*."

Joachin's nostrils flared. She knew he was doing his best to contain his excitement. He hadn't expected so much. They had been quoted a small fortune.

"I've taken my cut, but it still leaves you with a significant amount! Congratulations! I've also been making inquiries into land—"

"Forget about the land," Joachin said. "We'll take the money."

"But it isn't safe! Might I suggest you leave it in our bank?"

"Bank? What's that?" Joachin looked dubious.

"It's a new type of institution where people leave their money protected. You draw funds, whenever you wish. Plus, you gain interest. We have one here, in Puerto Real. It's guarded around the clock by the soldiery. Banks are all the rage now in Amsterden. With all the commerce going on, it's much more convenient to use one. I can open an account for you. In fact, I already have."

Joachin's gaze darkened.

"It might be a good idea," Miriam said, intervening. "He's right. We can't take all that with us. We might be robbed."

"Robbed?" Joachin snorted. "I'd like to see anyone try."

"If you feel better, I can issue a statement," the clerk said helpfully.

In the end, they took only a small amount of coin and a promissory note.

They made their way to *El Ancla* to celebrate. Few people were in attendance, it still being early in the day. Miriam paid the inn keeper double for holding Francis' mail, and he pocketed the coins quickly. Joachin ordered them wine. She watered her glass significantly.

"To us," Joachin said, toasting her.

"To us and the future," she replied.

"You've watered it so much I'm surprised you can even taste the grape." He smirked.

She sucked in her lips, wanting to hide her news. It had been over two months. She couldn't be sure....

He stared at her, suddenly suspicious. "You're not...you can't be...." He couldn't finish the sentence.

She burst out laughing, her joy infectious. They had been through so much, had lost so much, too many family, too many friends. Yet here they were, as they had planned in the New World. The future looked bright.

She squeezed his hand. "I think so," she said softly.

He sputtered, looking amazed. Then he reached across the table to kiss her. "A boy or a girl, do you think?"

Perhaps he had forgotten the dream he had told her so long ago. Perhaps some of his memories were beyond reclaiming. Maybe the gods couldn't fix everything, but she had complete faith his dream would come true.

"You tell me," she said, smiling.

Six and a half months later, Alonso Guillermo Medina de Rivera was born. They named him after the two men they had loved and lost—Alonso, of course, and Guillermo, Joachin's uncle, who had died in the slaughter at Elysir. The birth was straightforward and uneventful, painful as all births are, but ending in joy. That night, because Joachin wanted to celebrate, the Tribe built a fire on the beach. There was food and drink, drumming and song. At one point, and because Miriam was drooping, Joachín took centre stage upon the sand.

"I give thanks to the goddess that Miriam and I have a healthy son," he announced. As people agreed, he smiled at her so warmly her exhaustion fell away. Then he turned to Yoquibo and Papa Kodjó. "Like you, we Diaphani are a passionate people. When we grieve, we sing about it. When we're happy, we sing about that, too. But most of all, we show how we feel when we dance."

On cue, Zara and Luci began to clap. The Tribe joined in. At first, Yoquibo and his tribe looked surprised, but being people of the drum and song, they picked up the rhythm easily. Ximen stood and sang.

> *I will build you a house, a little casita,*
> *We will make it our nest.*
> *And in our casita, with family and friends,*
> *We will see how we have been blessed.*
> *And even though our little house,*
> *Has only four walls and a roof,*
> *Love will shield us through every storm,*
> *Love is our strength and our proof.*

As Joachín danced, his fingers snapping in rapid *pitos*, he laughed at the stars. Tears sprang to Miriam's eyes. He was so carefree. At her breast, little Alonso squirmed, sensing her sweet pain. All about her, people clapped and sang, their happiness floating towards her in waves. The gift of a *sentidora*. She was about to tamp her joy to a more manageable level, when she had a vision.

For one suspended moment, the Tribe had multiplied in number. There were people around her she had never met, and many she had. Anassa sat beside her, glowing. Guillermo leaned against Luci, holding her fingers with a shining hand. Hector, the sherry merchant who had joked about marrying her before he had died at the Womb, toasted her with a ghostly cup. Inez was also there, a pale seraph, watching Joachín dance. And across the circle, burning brighter than any of them, was Alonso, shining like the sun.

I will love you, forever, he said.

Then, as quickly as they had appeared, they were all gone.

She could no longer see them, but they were still there. She felt it.

Maybe that's what being a seer truly is, she thought, marvelling. *Knowing what is real, even if you don't see it, sensing what is there, when there's nothing to behold.*

Finally, you understand.

The voice interrupted her with such immediacy, it made her catch her breath. Like Zara, Lys was having the last word.

Miriam stared up at the full moon. *I have a few things I'd like to say to you!* she retorted. She drew in a deep breath to steady herself. No one seemed to notice her distraction. *I'm grateful,* she began, feeling as if time paused to listen. She had always complained about Lys, about her involvement, her intrusions. She had to make things right. *Thank you for everything that has brought me to this moment. For the magic, for the love, for your vision for us, for my place in it. Thank you for Alonso and for Joachin, and for what awaits us in the future.*

She was tempted to go on, but she suspected Lys knew. Of course, she did. She was a goddess, after all. Miriam listened for a response.

As usual, none came.

Irritation jabbed her, and then she laughed at herself. Lys *was* letting her have the last word. Swallowing against the knot in her throat, she gazed at the moon and imagined the goddess smiling down.

Time reasserted itself. All about her, the *fiesta* sprang into pounding, colourful life.

A happiness bubbled up in her that refuted all logic. Feeling blessed beyond measure, Miriam cradled her small son and watched Joachin dance.

About the Author

AS WELL AS editing two anthologies, *Divine Realms* (Ravenstone Press) and *Tesseracts Fifteen: A Case of Quite Curious Tales* (Edge Books), Susan MacGregor has been an editor with *On Spec* magazine for over twenty years. Her short fiction has appeared in a number of periodicals and anthologies including *Urban Green Man* (Edge Books), *A Method to the Madness* (Five Rivers), *On Spec* magazine, etc. Her non-fiction primer, *The ABC's of How NOT to Write Speculative Fiction* (Copper Pig Writers' Society), has been revised and is featured on her blog, Suzenyms. http://suzenyms.blogspot.ca.

Currently, she is doing research for a new book, the first of a historical fantasy series, possibly set in Devon, England, along the English Riviera. As well, she hasn't completely dismissed another book featuring Miriam and Joachin, where they travel from the Caribbean to England ten years hence, to assist their old friend, Francis, Queen Elizabeth 1st's new spymaster, and to deal with Tomás, Esbaña's Grand Inquisitor, once and for all.

Books by Five Rivers

NON-FICTION

Annotated Henry Butte's Dry Dinner, by Michelle Enzinas
Al Capone: Chicago's King of Crime, by Nate Hendley
Crystal Death: North America's Most Dangerous Drug, by Nate Hendley
Dutch Schultz: Brazen Beer Baron of New York, by Nate Hendley
John Lennon: Music, Myth and Madness, by Nate Hendley
Motivate to Create: a guide for writers, by Nate Hendley
Stephen Truscott, Decades of Injustice by Nate Hendley
King Kwong: Larry Kwong, the China Clipper Who Broke the NHL Colour Barrier, by Paula Johanson
Shakespeare for Slackers: by Aaron Kite, et al
Romeo and Juliet
  Hamlet
  Macbeth
The Organic Home Gardener, by Patrick Lima and John Scanlan
Canadian Police Heroes, by Dorothy Pedersen
Canadian Convoys of World War II, by Dorothy Pedersen
Shakespeare for Readers' Theatre: Hamlet, Romeo & Juliet, Midsummer Night's Dream, by John Poulson
Shakespeare for Reader's Theatre, Book 2: Shakespeare's Greatest Villains, The Merry Wives of Windsor; Othello, the Moor of Venice; Richard III; King Lear, by John Poulson
Beyond Media Literacy: New Paradigms in Media Education, by Colin Scheyen
Stonehouse Cooks, by Lorina Stephens

FICTION

Black Wine, by Candas Jane Dorsey
Eocene Station, by Dave Duncan
88, by M.E. Fletcher

Immunity to Strange Tales, by Susan J. Forest
The Legend of Sarah, by Leslie Gadallah
Cat's Pawn, by Leslie Gadallah
Growing Up Bronx, by H.A. Hargreaves
North by 2000+, a collection of short, speculative fiction, by H.A. Hargreaves
A Subtle Thing, by Alicia Hendley
Sid Rafferty Thrillers, by Matt Hughes
  Downshift
  Old Growth
The Tattooed Witch Trilogy, by Susan MacGregor
  The Tattooed Witch
  The Tattooed Seer
  The Tattooed Queen
The Rune Blades of Celi, by Ann Marston
  Kingmaker's Sword, Book 1
  Western King, Book 2
  Broken Blade, Book 3
  Cloudbearer's Shadow, Book 4
  King of Shadows, Book 5
  Sword and Shadow, Book 6
A Still and Bitter Grave, by Ann Marston
Indigo Time, by Sally McBride
Wasps at the Speed of Sound, by Derryl Murphy
A Quiet Place, by J.W. Schnarr
Things Falling Apart, by J.W. Schnarr
And the Angels Sang: a collection of short speculative fiction, by Lorina Stephens
From Mountains of Ice, by Lorina Stephens
Memories, Mother and a Christmas Addiction, by Lorina Stephens
Shadow Song, by Lorina Stephens
The Mermaid's Tale, by D. G. Valdron

YA FICTION

My Life as a Troll, by Susan Bohnet
Eye of Strife, by Dave Duncan
Ivor of Glenbroch, by Dave Duncan
  The Runner and the Wizard
  The Runner and the Saint

The Runner and the Kelpie
Type, by Alicia Hendley
Type 2, by Alicia Hendley
Tower in the Crooked Wood, by Paula Johanson
A Touch of Poison, by Aaron Kite
The Great Sky, by D.G. Laderoute
Out of Time, by D.G. Laderoute
Hawk, by Marie Powell

YA NON-FICTION

The Prime Ministers of Canada Series:
  Sir John A. Macdonald
  Alexander Mackenzie
  Sir John Abbott
  Sir John Thompson
  Sir Mackenzie Bowell
  Sir Charles Tupper
  Sir Wilfred Laurier
  Sir Robert Borden
  Arthur Meighen
  William Lyon Mackenzie King
  R. B. Bennett
  Louis St. Laurent
  John Diefenbaker
  Lester B. Pearson
  Pierre Trudeau
  Joe Clark
  John Turner
  Brian Mulroney
  Kim Campbell
  Jean Chretien
  Paul Martin

WWW.FIVERIVERSPUBLISHING.COM

The Tattooed Witch
by Susan MacGregor
Trade paperback 6 x 9
324 pages
ISBN 9781927400333
eISBN 9781927400340

Shortlisted for the 2014 Prix Aurora Award, Best Novel.

When Miriam Medina and her father are accused by the Inquisition of murdering a high priest, Miriam knows justice is impossible. Their accuser, the Grand Inquisitor, is in fact, the real murderer. Miriam's only hope is to resort to her long dead mother's magical legacy: the resurrection of the dead through a magical tattoo.

This is a beautifully written novel. The characters are believable and the world well built.

Michael R. Fletcher

If you haven't read the book yet, The Tattooed Witch is a fantastic read.

Goodreads

I loved all the bits of this story woven to hook you. I cannot wait to read the next book.

Amazon Reviewer

This novel is a fast paced, romantic, vividly imaginative story written in historical fiction fashion.

LibraryThing

The Tattooed Seer
by Susan MacGregor
Trade paperback 6 x 9
350 pages
ISBN 9781927400692
eISBN 9781927400708

Book 2 in the exciting The *Tattooed Witch* series

As she flees across Esbaña for a port to the New World, Miriam finds being the matriarch of her people, the magical Diaphani, almost as difficult as being hunted by the Inquisition. Her deepening relationship with Joachín, patriarch and thief, is marred by the sudden return of Alonso, her ghostly lover, whom she thought lost forever. In this alternate historical epic, Miriam's world expands to the larger realms of Esbaña, the Papacy, and Inglais, where one spy in particular seeks tattoo magic to set a new queen upon the throne. Grand Inquisitor Tomás and other old rivals seek their vengeance against Miriam, while new ones fight to usurp her place. As she broadens her understanding of magical power, Miriam learns what it is to lead, to love, to forgive, and to change, for change she must, if she and her Tribe are to reach the New World.

If you are a fan of historical fantasy or romance this book will sit in your sweet spot. But here's the thing. I'm not and yet this book still works for me, largely because Susan MacGregor is a literary craftsman. In my world fine writing trumps genres any time and this is fine writing.

GJC McKitrick (A Walk in the Thai Sun)

Kingmaker's Sword
by Ann Marston
Trade paperback 6 x 9
504 pages
ISBN 9781927400166
eISBN 9781927400173

A re-print of Ann Marston's Book 1 of the much beloved Rune Blades of Celi series.
Triumphing over adversity and evil, Kian dav Leydon brings the fabled Rune Blade Kingmaker back to the Isle of Celi after it was stolen, so the Isle will be ready when and if invasion comes.

This is an exceptionally well-done Celtic fantasy...a multiple-layered prince-in-disguise story...a lively mix of action, romance and cultural details. This one grabbed me from the start.

Locus Magazine

...the plot is wonderfully creative.

Goodreads

A positive joy to read.

Amazon

CPSIA information can be obtained
at www.ICGtesting.com
Printed in the USA
LVOW12s0855281016
510685LV00001BA/3/P